TIMEFIELD

Charlie Nash

FLYING
NUN
PUBLICATIONS

Published in 2021 by Flying Nun Publications, http://flyingnunpublications.com/

ISBN:
978-1-925775-28-0 (ebook)
978-1-925775-27-3 (print)

This project is supported by the Queensland Government through Arts Queensland.

A catalogue record for this book is available from the National Library of Australia

Cover design by nirkri

About the author

Charlie Nash was born near the Viking Way and holds degrees in mechanical and space engineering, medicine, and a PhD in creative writing. Her fiction has been shortlisted multiple times for the Aurealis and Ditmar awards. She breathes technical air by day and wordy vapors by night. *Timefield* is her first full-length science fiction novel.

 charlienash.net
authorcharlienash

Also by Charlie Nash

for the powerhouse in our souls
that holds hope
against reason

I do not think there is any thrill that can go through the human heart like that felt by the inventor as he sees some creation of the brain unfolding to success ... such emotions make a man forget food, sleep, friends, love, everything.

— Nikola Tesla

Waste is worse than loss.

— Thomas A. Edison

Prologue

David had made the journey to past-London more than a dozen times, but there was something different about this one. He knew it as soon as he came to post-transmission consciousness, lying on his side, his cheek pressed into the hard floor of the third-story room. He knew where he was long before he opened his eyes – Victorian London had a smell about it, a bouquet of horse shit and sweat and heavy industry. Even here, inside the Royal Laboratories, that smell was in the air, trekked in on the boots of the workmen. It was probably carcinogenic. But then, this project was nearly over, and he wouldn't have to breathe it again.

At least, he hoped it was over. Hoped it despite the dragging feeling that something was not quite right.

He pushed himself to sitting and rubbed his eyes. The room they used for transmissions was a minimally finished space: raw floorboards, white plaster walls, and a stack of old empty tea chests. The room had all it needed. It was a short distance from the entry to Tesla's laboratory, and it had a door with a lock. David stretched, walking off his unease towards the single window that looked down over the borough. Through the thick Tesla glass, he admired the fruits of what they had done.

Thousands of suspended blinder lights shone beneath the nearly-night sky, lighting every cobble of the streets.

Those wireless orbs were Tesla's work, and had turned the new St Alberts borough into a glittering star field, day and night. On those streets, shopkeepers cried out the end-of-day bargains. Plumes of steam rose from the electrified laundries and the metal works. David had seen the area long before Tesla, long before the poor had been elevated by the free power and light of the Royal's tower. It had been a den of misery then. They had done good things. Great things.

David slid his hands into his pockets, bouncing on his toes, relaxing. He enjoyed the end of a project most, when everything was done. He'd been like this as a newly graduated doctor, when a patient finally went home. Or later, when he'd been on television. The best part was the end of a good interview, when everyone was smiling, and expectations had been more than met.

Except he wasn't quite done here, not yet. He still had to see Tesla.

He checked over his clothes, tugging down the waistcoat, touching the console in his pocket. He blew out a breath, psyching up and testing his voice. "I am Doctor David Blakeney," he told the window, "physician, researcher, and fellow of the Academy of Sciences." *Time traveler*, he didn't add. "Doctor D, Doctor D, Doctor D," he went on, with another little bounce on his toes. Studio audiences used to chant that when he'd been on the morning shows, commentating the latest medical developments to the public. The latest breakthrough in cancer treatment. Or Alzheimer's. Talking it up … even if such a medical promise wouldn't be realized for another fifty years. He'd been younger then. *And more attractive. And not the subject of a lawsuit.*

He stopped the bouncing, and pulled himself into

character. He'd certainly never be explaining any of *this* to the morning shows. Not about being transmitted through The Machine, or about what it was like to breathe the Victorian air and commune with its cholera-filled water. Those things, he could do without. But it had to be done. To make the future right again. It was more important than all the research he'd done in his career. More important than being on television. It was real. And now they'd come this far, only he could finish it.

He strode away from the window, pulling a key from his pocket, only to pause at the threshold with his hand in mid-air.

The door was not locked. The leaf was very slightly ajar, the catch not properly seated. David straightened, that dragging feeling back in his stomach. This had not happened before.

He glanced behind him, looking for more signs, and on the other side of the stacked tea chests, he glimpsed something that was new.

On unsteady legs, he slowly circled until he beheld the whole view. A table sat there now, an ordinary wooden table, on whose surface was spread a device not unlike the inner workings of a large clock. Gears and wheels and long shafts, articulated together in some kind of mechanism. He might have built something like it as a boy, with Meccano. The device was silent, waiting, but in the dim reaches of his mind, David formed a terrible impression of what this was.

He swallowed, his heart an executioner's beat on his sternum. He needed his field notes. Needed them now. Tesla could wait while he went down to his office and read about whatever it was he'd forgotten.

He'd barely formed this thought when a rough hand grabbed his shoulder, and a barker muzzle pushed a dent into his ribs. David caught a whiff of warm wool and harsh soap.

"Verra quietly, now," said a soft Scots voice in his ear. "Verra quiet. Let's keep all those fine innards in yer inners, eh? You're wanted for a word."

Brown. The Queen's private bodyguard.

David's stomach squeezed, shooting gagging bile up his throat. He coughed, unable to reply as the gun pushed him out the now wide-open door of the transmission room. The foyer in front of Tesla's lab went past in a blur, as he was prodded down the stairs, down, down, to the grand entry foyer. There, David was almost sure he saw Forbes, the building's super, standing sentry at the reception desk, but Brown gave him no chance to call out. Down the last half-flight they went, to the building's rear door, and then outside into the crisp night air.

No one looked his way as the barker pressed his kidney, and propelled David up the steps of a dark-windowed carriage. The Scot locked the door behind him, and the leather creaked as David fell into the seat.

David tugged his waistcoat reflexively, mind casting around for how to talk his way out. In as level a voice as he could, he said, "There's no need for roughhousing. Where are we going?"

The Scot just stared out the window. The man had only one allegiance. David would get nowhere with him.

The carriage jerked and swayed into the gathering night. David knew they had left St Alberts borough when the carriage-mounted blinders faded out, and the only light from outside was the intermittent yellow glow of gas lamps. Then, finally, there were no more lights, and darkness crept inside the cabin, making Brown's face into hard lines of moonlit granite. They had left the city behind. David's fears swarmed in his chest. He fingered the console in his pocket, contemplating using precious qubits to send a message to Helen. But what would he say? She could do nothing for him. Until he could return to the transmission room and recall himself to the present, he was on his own.

After what seemed an epoch, the carriage jangled to a halt. Brown gestured with the gun towards the door. David complied, stepping out into an inky expanse of night. A single lantern burned in the black, but David couldn't see much else. He heard the horses snorting the air, which smelled sweet, like the summer hayfields he remembered from his childhood. But there was another sound, underneath the melodic jingling of harness, deeper than the horse snorts. A dull guttural roar.

That roar was unsettling, mechanical, unnatural, and yet he had heard it before.

Finally, he picked out two glinting lines of silver along the ground. Train tracks, those were train tracks, disappearing beneath a matt-black boiler of a massive locomotive. David jerked as a gush of steam hissed and billowed forward, framing the snarling lion in the royal arms. *Jesus*. Victoria's train.

《 〉》

With a shove from Brown, David stumbled towards the saloon. He experienced a momentary relief when he found only Disraeli waiting in a plush lounge chair. Disraeli's dress and expression were, as always, fit for a funeral, but he was intelligent and malleable. David had talked him around more than once. He was infinitely preferable to the monarch of the land.

"Doctor Blakeney," Disraeli said.

David inclined his head. "Prime Minister."

"Good of you to join us," Disraeli went on, in a way that made David jerk into search mode. His gaze ran over the quilted couches, the frilled gold-stalked lamps, and the high-backed upholstered sitting chairs until he found her: a black-veiled figure lurking down the carriage, displaying only her pale hands, one finger ringed with that thick gold wedding band. David's heart stopped. She lifted the veil, revealing the downward drawn cheeks, the wide blue eyes that could lance like an electron beam. Victoria. A face that the whole Empire knew. A person they did not.

David tensed as that dragging dread he'd had in the transmission room returned. Lord, what *had* he done?

"I'll not draw this out," Disraeli continued. "We have become aware of some disturbing developments associated with Mr. Tesla and the Royal Laboratories. Developments that lead the Crown to question its involvement in the whole enterprise."

David dragged his attention back, and found Disraeli frowning at him. "Mr. Tesla c-can be a challenging personality," David said, stumbling to recover his diplomacy. "But all brilliant men are. We've had these issues before. I assure you, whatever the problem, I can resolve it. Mr. Tesla is very reasonable."

The last statement was a terrible lie. David had tried many times to explain to Tesla that his free wireless energy and the entrepreneurial spirit he encouraged in the former lower classes in the borough was unsettling for the industrialists and aristocratic investors alike. To them, the poor were allowed to be industrious, but not to better their station, or become independent of the lords they once bowed down before. Tesla had other ideas, and he was maddeningly apolitical; David suspected any of Tesla's promises to curb the scope of his technology projects were as empty as Victoria's compassion.

Disraeli served David a withering eyebrow. "Your confidence is impressive," he said. "But it far exceeds mine. This goes beyond Tesla. We are talking of a much larger problem. Betrayal. Even high treason."

David recoiled. "Treason?" He hoped he sounded surprised, because he certainly was. "I have no idea what you are talking about."

Disraeli jerked his chin, and a second later, Brown had unfolded a rough wooden table between them and placed a heavy burlap bag on the table, smelling strongly of pigs. No wonder Victoria was keeping her distance.

"What is this?"

Disraeli gestured for him to look. David gingerly lifted the edge of the sack, and found a muzzle pointing back at him. He frowned as he drew the weapon out, the formless dread stirring in his gut. The barrel was gunmetal and rather short, meeting a wide flat body with some kind of short rack to the side. The handgrip was pale, maybe wood or even ivory. Odd-looking, for sure, but recognizably a gun. There was no trigger, but David could see a button in about the right place for an index finger—

Disraeli tutted. "If you value your life, I advise you *not* to press that button. You *do* know what this is?"

David didn't. He sweated, as if a TV anchor had just asked him to explain the second law of thermodynamics, and he couldn't quite remember which the second law was, and what it meant, all while a million viewers waited to judge him a fraud over their Weetabix. It was the kind of moment where it didn't matter how many years he'd been a respected researcher, how many horrendously difficult things he'd done in his life; he'd just look like an idiot if he couldn't answer the basic question. And of course, it wouldn't give him any credit at all to explain that he didn't do *that* kind of science. He was a doctor, for Chrissakes. What the hell did he know about guns?

David retracted his finger, trusting his intellect would catch up if he gave it time. "Where did you acquire this?" he asked.

"From the docks, bound for the American colonies." Disraeli sat forward. "I don't think I need to spell out, for an intelligent man such as yourself, that we did not make this agreement to fund Mr. Tesla's projects only to arm a former colony against us. Any and all weapons are for the exclusive and secret use of the British Empire, and us alone."

David's eyes flicked over the gun again, little pieces of information collapsing under their combined gravity into a single understanding. This was probably a weapon that had leaked from Tesla's lab, a leak that was supposed to have been dealt with. He felt a relief that he had worked out the cause of the dragging dread. Only … it didn't quite make sense. He was missing something, which was part of the uncomfortable reality of the timefield. He didn't always remember the transmissions, and he couldn't take notes back. He swallowed that discomfort often. He wanted his notes.

He forced a small laugh. "Prime Minister, this is surely not Tesla's work. He has not finalized any of the promised military designs yet – you know what a perfectionist he is. This, this … *thing* is some crude imitation made by one of the industrious business men of St Alberts. It is probably a sham, a toy, made to dupe and extract money from desperate men of the colonies."

Disraeli stared at David, and David, encouraged, ploughed on. "It pains me also to remind you, Prime

Minister, that you yourself are a beneficiary of our project. You would not have held your office this long if we had not provided the future knowledge for you to secure your leadership."

David forced himself to stop, the air thick with held breath. He rarely referred directly to the fact that this new London had been brought about through time travel. It was hard enough for David to grasp the idea, and he had actually *seen* The Machine. How much harder must it be for anyone here to understand?

Disraeli now glanced across to Victoria. David didn't like the knowing subtext of that look, that they knew something he didn't.

Victoria was the one who rose, her voice holding a cold edge. "Join us outside, won't you, Doctor?"

David shot a look at Disraeli, searching for signs of what was about to happen. What did he need to say to wrap this up and be on his way back to the city? But Disraeli played with a master poker-face, and soon, David was standing in the damp grass of a field alongside the train. There were no landmarks to recognize, but he'd put money on this being the grounds of a royal estate. Escaping had never really been an option, but now David had to quash even that fancy. He could not outrun royal guards on foot, even when he'd been fit, young Doctor D. And Disraeli probably had commandos hiding in the brush.

Brown was last out of the saloon, bringing the strange gun with him, and moving his hands over it in a practiced way.

"These weapons are not some inferior imitation, Doctor Blakeney," Disraeli said, as if giving a parliamentary speech to the field. "They have been made illegally from Tesla's own plans. Leaked plans, we believe. We have recovered several units. They appear only to fire a few times before their charge is exhausted, but I encourage you to appreciate the effects."

In the distance, under the moonlight, David finally made out a man leading a draught horse out into the paddock.

Brown levelled the gun, testing his aim.

"Wait, what are you doing?" David demanded. He ate steak like anyone, but there was something wrong about killing horses.

Disraeli ignored him, squinting like a general surveying his wargame. Finally, David made out the cart the horse was pulling into view. "In that wagon is the man who was caught with this shipment at the docks. He's guilty of high treason against the Crown with its natural consequences. Do you wish to inspect from a closer vantage?"

David shook his head, frozen with horror. Of all the places this transmission could go, he had not imagined *execution* to be on the list. Brown waited while the horse was unhitched and led away. David's heart pounded. He seemed powerless to do anything. To say anything. He had to stop this. He had to speak. But the night air bit at his cheeks while sweat trickled from his arm pits and he did nothing. Brown took his aim.

The gun's crack split the night in two. David threw up his arms as the sound bounced off the train, and collided physically with his back. *Jesus Christ.* He pulled his hands from his head to find Brown striding off down the paddock, followed by two guards David hadn't seen, bearing torches.

"Better go and see, Doctor," Disraeli said.

David tripped across the field, quite unable to catch his breath, his mind in a near-panic. When he reached the cart, he pulled up, trying to understand what he was seeing. At first, he thought it was empty. Then he appreciated the scattered lumps of flesh, some with visible steam rising. The air smelled strongly of blood and sewers; probably because he was breathing atomized blood and guts. David retched, and clapped a hand over his mouth.

"Heady thang to imagine on the battlefield," Brown said, matter-of-fact. David turned towards him and found the Scot buffing the gun with a pale cloth. Brown paused, peering at the grass before carefully placing his foot, and pointed the muzzle at David's chest. "Imagin' staring down an enemy armed with these things, ya ken?"

David was more frightened in that moment than he'd ever been in his life. It took three long breathless seconds to remember he wasn't of this time. To remember why he was here and recover some indignation. He was saving all these people's sorry futures, for Christ's sake. Some thanks he was getting.

He blocked Brown's aim with his hand. "I'll thank you to point that thing in another direction," he said, and stalked back towards the train, thinking furiously. He couldn't be intimidated. Power responded to power.

Disraeli was waiting. "You appreciate the problem, now, Doctor?"

"What is it you want me to do? If there's leaked plans, that's a security problem." He fell short of pointing out that Disraeli was the one with a newly minted commando force. The Prime Minister did not appreciate direction.

"A security problem," Disraeli said with an arched eyebrow. "In the most secure building in the whole Empire." He paused to squint down the line of the train. "Let me be clear, Doctor. My time as Prime Minister has always been borrowed. You can't threaten me with my position, especially not while I have the favor of the most popular monarch this country has ever seen."

He inclined his head, so that David knew the Queen was still standing there, in a shadow of the train, just out of his view.

"So," Disraeli finished. "Bring Tesla into line. No more leaks. No more missed deadlines. We can't have the whole world benefiting from something the British Empire has paid for."

David inclined his head, relieved that this little power play appeared to be over. They had made their bloody point. Tesla would never agree to being managed, he knew that much, but David never had to come back here again. That was the beauty of living in the future: he could permanently escape.

As soon as he was back at the Royal. He turned for the coach.

"Doctor Blakeney, a moment." Victoria's voice brought the dragging dread back, along with a chill on his neck. Even the crickets stopped.

"Yes, Your Majesty?"

"There is another matter I would bring to your attention before the Prime Minister returns you to the Royal Laboratories."

"How can I be of service?" David enquired, stalling, because somehow he knew she was about to ask him to do something he didn't want to do. He noted Brown, lurking down the end of the saloon carriage.

"Come now, Doctor, we had an agreement, and I have been extremely patient. The time has come for you to honor it."

"Your Majesty, I think the timing would be … imprudent," he said carefully.

"Your demonstration of the device was most convincing. Last time you assured me only small adjustments remained. You cannot maintain it is not ready."

A device. That he'd demonstrated? David felt a fresh qualm. He needed desperately to check his notes, and be absolutely non-committal. "Small adjustments, yes," he said, imagining the Scot's blade at his throat, "but those are most critical. They cannot be rushed."

"It is my experience, Doctor, that anything can be rushed with enough incentive. Brown?" She barely raised her voice. "Tell Disraeli that *we* will convey the Doctor back to the Royal Laboratories."

That was how David found himself back in the carriage, with the Queen of England, pulling towards London. He considered how he could get out of this situation; could he tell Disraeli what Victoria was planning? But his relationship with Disraeli was already tenuous. The best move was probably to appeal to Victoria's vanity.

"Your Majesty, if I may say, you are incredibly perceptive, and I know—"

She cut him off with a lift of her hand, and, no matter what opening he tried, she ignored him, intent on her purpose. David gripped the windowsill as the carriage finally pulled into St Alberts, and the carriage-mounted blinders glowed again. In their harsh blue light, Victoria's face was sallow, pocked with age spots.

"I'm afraid it is long past the hour I had an appointment with Mr. Tesla," David said, leaning on a last hope. "And the building super will be long retired."

"On the contrary," Victoria said. "Forbes is expecting us, and will organize entry with Mr. Tesla." The corners of her mouth lifted. "Doctor, really, your attempts to delay are most tiresome. I have given you land, and funds, and endless patience. I am asking but one small thing in exchange. That's fair, is it not?"

"I am trying to preserve the future of your kingdom," David said, forgetting to be tactful. Lord, was Forbes in on this plan, too?

"And I am preserving its present." Abruptly, she smiled, and his heart petrified. She almost never smiled. "Were I to allow you to continue your protests, I am sure you would ask me to delay, until an agreed time when you make the device finally ready."

"Of course." His words came out high, breathless.

"Brown," said the Queen. The carriage pulled to a halt, and the Scot's shadow fell over the doorway. "Relieve the Doctor of his pockets."

Before David knew what had happened, Brown had swung inside the carriage, pinned David to his seat, and frisked his coat and pants. When the Scot swung out again, Victoria had the console in her hands. David clenched his fists to stop himself leaping up and swiping it back. If he did, he was sure he'd find a dirk in his solar plexus.

"That is not how this night goes, Doctor. You will do this, or I will have your precious Tesla arrested, and grind this whole enterprise of yours into the slum dust it came from."

In shock, David tried to control how the words came out, but his breath was so short and hot he puffed like a steam engine. He imagined having to do what she asked, with all the risks. "This is dangerous, Your Majesty. I need to return to the future to calculate the calibration. Without that ..."

"This you have already done," she said, dismissing him.

Had he? He fell silent, thinking of that machine on the

table in the transmission room. He couldn't imagine a world where he would have done what he suspected he had, but then he didn't remember the last transmissions. All he wanted was to be back in that room, with the console in his hands, so he could recall and never return.

With a rush, he saw a way out.

"Very well," he said heavily, affecting a great reluctance. "But such a first-use calibration should be confirmed. We want precision as to the date and location to ensure correct operation. And to do that, I really do need materials from the future."

She gave him a hard look, turning the console in her hands. "No, Doctor."

David scratched his head, and sighed, as though thinking. "There may be another way," he said. "Inside the Royal is a mechanical calculator. I can program it with the mathematics from that console to calculate the confirmation. If I am to be the test subject for your wishes, I imagine you have as much interest as I do in not dying at the first attempt."

Her look did not soften, but David saw a flicker in her gaze. The carriage pulled to a stop. High above the roof of the Tesla Royal, the tower reached for the London sky, its bulbous top supplying power to all who fell in the radius. The building was dark, but for the light burning in the top floor. The warning sign posted on the gates read:

ELECTRIFIED BUILDING

PERSONS ARE WARNED THAT TRESPASSING

ON ROYAL LABORATORIES' PROPERTY RISKS

SWIFT AND CERTAIN DEATH

The words *swift* and *certain* were capitalized. The sign was hardly needed, for all over the building's brick walls crept lazy arcs of pale blue flame. So it always was when Tesla was here, working late into the night in his fortress. David straightened his waistcoat, waiting on Victoria's decision.

Finally, she held the precious console out to him. "I'm glad we understand each other," she said. "Now, we will go directly to the calculation machine. After you, Doctor Blakeney."

The severe tone of this moniker was much less pleasing than *Doctor D*. David swung down from the carriage under the looming walls of the Royal Laboratories, his leg bones having all the integrity of cooked noodles. Brown kept close pace behind him, fingering a dirk.

As David stepped inside, he had two trains of thought. The first was that as soon as he crossed the threshold into the transmission room, he would recall to the future, hopefully before the Scot's blade could stop him, and then never, ever return here. And secondly, that he must not forget the first point, even if it meant breaking The Machine with his own hands.

《〉》

At the same moment, two floors above, Tesla stared down at the carriage, the vast laboratory cathedral quiet around him. Part of his mind was still composing the letter he had been writing. Another part was standing vigilant, ready to observe changes in the dials and electrical status panels for the building that supported him. The rest was pondering the implications of the carriage.

David Blakeney had missed his appointment, but that in itself was no great matter; Tesla found the visits of the

Time Walkers a distraction from the rivers of thoughts that coursed through his mind. They had given him much, these future-men, he acknowledged that. He had an army of workmen at his disposal, and the ability to bring his visions to life. He worked in a dream he could not have imagined when he was a boy.

But he also knew that David Blakeney had another project in the building, one that drew heavily on the power. Tesla's systems were more than capable of meeting the electrical demand; *that* was not the issue. It was the other kind of power it drew that made Tesla wary. That carriage approaching meant Queen Victoria herself was involved, and where one person in power gathered, so would others. Human power had its own kind of magnetism.

Tesla himself cared nothing for such important people, and he did not question what the Time Walkers did in their spaces in the building, like the ones David Blakeney had asked for. Their future was not his; that was the whole point. He would not have imagined standing in their way.

But Tesla also knew he would have to guard against their discovering his greatest vision, which was not yet ready for scrutiny. Even the future-men were not ready for it. They had come here wanting to save a world from destruction, which was a noble goal. But they did not go far enough. Once a war was ended, one had to plan for how you stopped it starting again. And even these future-men didn't seem to think much about that.

Tesla turned and paced back to his desk, hands clasped beneath his coattails, his gaze taking in the instrument panel, watching the pulse of his building in the dance of the load needles. He could tell from the shifts of those needles, from the noises the system made, where everyone was. Could tell when Forbes opened the rear doors to admit the occupants of that carriage, and when they entered their concealed room downstairs. For now, he would carry on watching, waiting for the right time.

He sat, and took up the pen, pausing before he began to write. Should he use his recipient's well-known moniker? Or his real name? Yes, the latter, for that was more intimate, appropriate for a man he had known in his first life as a close friend.

He pressed the ink to the page. *Dear Mr. Clemens*, he wrote.

PART I

Chapter 1

Leo lay awake in the black London night, listening for sirens. There had been a time when, sleepless with whirling thoughts, he would have stumbled down into his workshop to quiet the neurons with making things on lathes. Or gone out running, his dog-tags cold on his chest. But no one goes out at night anymore, his knee cartilage is mostly shrapnel, and he long ago lost access to a workshop. This tiny flat can't accommodate such things – its only virtue is offering the smallest possible footprint for drone-dropped bombs. Leo himself spent a chunk of his military career making parts for drones like that, ones the Crown sent to make holes in their enemies. So most of what he created is now scrap somewhere deep in hostile territory.

He has a habit of destroying the things he makes.

He stretches out his legs, and his feet hit the wall, a déjà vu to his college-living days where he never fit on the bed. That was back when London had been the place tourists came to gawp at Big Ben and The Tower and buy Union Jack tea towels. The time when Leo had only come to town on odd weekends from Cambridge, and gone out to pubs to drink beer and stare into the distance, thinking about black holes and detonators and whatever else crossed his mind. Now, he pushes a cleaning cart around a lab in Blackfriars. Herds dust bunnies. Unblocks toilets. Ignores the persistent smell of smoke in the air. For a guy who was once on track to run a laboratory, it's quite the step down.

He's turning over when a bell shrills, bouncing off the blacked-out windows. Leo erupts from his bed under the dining table like a bear dragged from hibernation, splintering two chairs and an ugly vase before he realizes it's not a siren but his goddamn phone.

He smacks his head digging for it under the mattress. Dragging the handset out like a denned rabbit, he grunts into the receiver. "What?"

"I need you to come into work," says a woman's voice.

"Ma'am?" he says, brain fully on automatic pilot.

An exasperated sigh. "Leo. Wake up. I need you to come into work."

Leo blinks, his vision full of the chintz cloth that hangs fort-like from the table and the cloud of empty protein stick wrappers around the bin. He doesn't see a weapon or a kit bag anywhere. His cognition finally catches up.

"Helen?" he asks, astonished.

"No, it's the Queen of England," Helen says. "I need you to come into work."

"Say what now?"

Leo isn't normally this dense. He may look like a meat-brained rugby forward, but he's also the son of an Oxford maths professor. He'd read engineering at Cambridge, and scored high enough in military testing to raise some generals' eyebrows. Helen knows all this about him, but she also works in the most secure lab in his building, the one even he can't go into.

"If you've got a backed-up toilet," he says, a little too good now at pretending away his intellect. "Best to find yourself a plunger. I'm off."

"Leo, for the last sodding time, I need you to come in."

There's a tone he's not heard before. He pinches

himself until the skin blanches white, and scrubs a rough forearm across his eyes. "It's one in the bloody morning."

"So there'll be no traffic."

"There's three checkpoints between here and there."

"Then get on the tube. This is more important than whatever you're drinking."

Leo bristles. "I'm not drinking."

"Then do it because I'm your sister."

And she hangs up.

Leo stares at the phone. Through his years in the army, he often wondered what Helen was doing. Helen, his older sister and brilliant physicist, who inherited the family curse for an easy relationship with numbers and difficult relationships with everything else. He'd expected she'd be cloistered in a dusty academic office somewhere upcountry and cheery, like Manchester. Not working in a high security lab he couldn't even ask her about. Then again, war changes most things.

He hadn't learned about where she was until he'd been discharged, not long off crutches and needed work. She had gotten him his job, which he's still not sure he's thankful for. But not once in the last six months has she made contact with him. The only time he sees her is in the foyer, or in the lift, when she has to wait to be alone to swipe her card for the basement floor.

Now she's calling in the middle of the night?

Leo looks up at a blackened window. There hasn't been an attack in a week now, which just puts everyone's blood up, waiting for another. The Warm War combatants make the eighties IRA look like children playing with firecrackers. The London out there is a beaten-down, pockmarked, guerrilla-fragged shadow of former imperial glory. Pubs close early and serve cloudy homebrew from vats in the back. Tesco and Sainsburys sell bags of spotty apples for ten pounds, when they have anything other than shipped-in Eastern Bloc protein sticks. When all this started with the North Korea thing, it seemed containable. Then came the China thing, then the bloody American Second Civil War thing, and the lurking Russians, and now it doesn't seem like it will ever end. The world outside is as grim as the blacked-out window.

He used to feel as though his smarts protected him. Or his weapon did. Or his training. Used to, used to. Always in the past tense. Now in this present, he's just the guy who cleans a quasi-government lab, because he had the right clearance and a nepotistic contact to lean on. He's got no reason to go anywhere.

Except for one thing. Helen is still his sister, and he knows he's done wrong by her before.

"Fucking hell," he says, and goes digging around for his coat.

《〈〉》

The laboratories in Blackfriars don't exactly advertise themselves. The building is faced in a pink-hued stone that in the dim early hours of the morning looks just as grey and nonchalant as the publishing houses and law offices that jostle on either side. Or, former publishing houses and law offices — it's hard to tell. Even in a city under siege, people are still doing business, but no one puts out a shingle anymore.

Leo swipes his card at the door, shivering in the cold air gusting from the Thames, and finds Helen waiting for him by the elevators. She's wearing a faded blue T-shirt and grey trousers, and the sunken eyes of the permanent shift worker. She looks exactly the same as she did ten years ago when she was reading dissertations at two in the morning.

"What do you want?" he asks, because he's tired and sour after being frisked twice on the way here, and also because somewhere in the depths of his soul, he's embarrassed to be what he is before her.

"Nice to see you, too."

Actually, it is nice to see her. Leo is shocked with some undeclarable bond. She's his family, the only family either of them have left. When they were children he looked up to her, desperately wanting her to notice her scrawny, awkward brother. He still feels that, even now, when he probably looks at home wielding a sledgehammer and pounding raw eggs for breakfast. Everything has changed, except her.

She checks her watch. "I need you to fix something."

"If you dragged me out here to change a goddamn lightbulb—"

"It's getting in the workshop and doing some serious machining," she says, which shuts him up. "You can still do that, right? Haven't lost your opposable thumbs?"

She swipes a card at the elevator, and they step inside. Leo hesitates before he follows her. He has to negotiate the lifts here every goddamn day because of the cleaning trolley, but even with his knee, he takes the stairs when he can. He's not good at small spaces. But he imagines her disdain at this weakness. So he sucks in his jitters and steps in the metal squeeze box, trying not to notice how to the floor bounces under his weight, and that he's going somewhere he's not meant to go.

Then the elevator is sinking down into the basement.

"You can't talk about anything you're about to see," she says, as Leo's stomach drops with the elevator. "It's high-level clearance. Or at least, it used to be."

"Yeah, no shit," he says, wondering what could have gone wrong to have her breaching protocol so overtly, all while imagining fantastical things in the basement.

The long hall turns out to hold a disappointing matched deck of plain closed doors. On the left, they have no labels at all. On the right, they pass one with *Workshop* stenciled in cheap black marker, with the addendum *machines and shit* in a round waggish hand underneath. The next sports a brass name plate – *Helen Fawkes, PhD, Particle Acceleration*. The last door, right at the end of the hall, is a fire escape. Leo imagines a nice, wide, comforting stairway all the way up to ground, superbly constructed as the structural hub of the building.

Helen passes her swipe card across a reader. Leo hears bolts *thunk* inside the wall, and the nameplate door opens into a surprisingly spartan space. Now, Leo has been into every laboratory in this building, from the creepy AI medical robots on the first floor, to the nuclear decommissioning people in the penthouse. All the other labs look like junkyards. Tables of instruments, wires and components – and duct tape, always duct tape – cleared in great sweeping arcs to make room for the current apparatus. Which itself is probably swept away for the next thing, the detritus forming an archaeological record of research failures. Not hers.

The lab walls have been covered in carpet, and printouts of graphs are pinned up with thumbtacks behind a computer control station. Some of them are elegant spirals, others jagged see-saws. Two apples rest beside the mousepad, like a present tense comment on the former glory of the four well-cleaned cores in the bin, all in varying degrees of oxidation. She has a single machine, a great hulking thing almost as wide as the room, and nothing else.

Something about The Machine makes his skin crawl. He can actually *feel* it through the floor, an elemental kind of vibration, as if his toenails are shaking apart, atom by atom from the leading edge. There are two fat three-phase electrical sockets plugged into the wall. Leo imagines The Machine converting all that electron-juice into magnetic fields that bend electrons and scatter elementary particles, or whatever it is that particle physicists do for money.

"What exactly is that thing?" he asks.

"Ah, you're back," says a vaguely familiar voice.

Leo's head turns towards a man just emerged from a side room door, dressed in a neat three-piece, jacket removed.

"Doctor D," Leo blurts, recognizing the face he used to see on the morning shows when he was an undergrad. "I mean, Professor Blakeney," he corrects, because this man is also the researcher who works with the creepy android dummies on the first floor. On an upside-down night like this, the old memories matter more than the new ones.

"David, please," says David, clearing his throat. "I haven't been on TV in ten years. So, you're Helen's brother."

"The caretaker," Leo says, feeling he's just stumbled too close to an event horizon where the fabric of space-time is a little warped.

"He has a degree in engineering, David, or at least most of one, and years of distinguished military service, including stints in the drone support team. He'll keep his mouth shut."

Leo shifts his eyes between Helen and David, a strange pairing. David's not the kind of company he ever expected Helen to keep. A showy medical doctor, who used to be on TV until disappearing to re-invent himself in molecular biochemistry? From what Leo knows, David works on artificial brains, which is why his lab is full of droids, the ones that are just torsos and heads, with features squarely in the uncanny valley. Leo had to clear up a spill in David's lab last month, and he dreamed about those torsos chasing him for a solid week, arms outstretched, all the way into an elevator, which just made it nightmare within a nightmare.

Suffice to say, David Blakeney is into the soft, squishy medical end of the sciences. What the hell is he doing here, in particle physics?

It's not the only odd thing. David seems as though he's calling the shots around here, which Helen would never have put up with.

But then David gives him this sad look, and says, "Appreciate you doing this at short notice," as if Leo's just agreed to fill in for a cricket team, not do undisclosed work in a secret government facility. "Getting hard to find good help. I'll let you get on."

And, in that instant, they're on the same side, the one that doesn't quite accept the way the world is now, that can't process a war without clear enemies, without an end in sight. David steps back into the side office.

Helen rubs her face. "I need a thing repaired, okay?"

Leo runs his eyes over The Machine, feeling the secrecy of this place, the questions crammed into the years since he last had a conversation with her. "Helen," he says. "What *are* you doing in here?"

"Particle physics," she says, quickly. "Let me show you this repair."

Chapter 2

The Machine leaves a bare two feet of squeeze space to the three walls of the basement room, and ends a finger below the ceiling beam. Its body is a knobbled mess of boxy modules, retrofitted parts, and snaking cables.

Leo has seen a thousand apparatus like this: it's the true face of R&D, made ugly through accreted growth, pure function over form. An industrial designer's nightmare. It certainly doesn't look much like a weapon; unless it's some kind of nuclear bomb, and he bets it isn't that. He knows enough about these labs to know the research is all high-end. It's a boutique organization of uncertain progeny – though if he had to lay odds, he'd bet on a military-funded tech-tank – the place brilliance comes when it's too edgy for the private sector venture capitalists, but too promising for a government to let run wild. They don't deal in last-century tech here. Although, since this is a secret basement and not the above-board stuff upstairs, Leo really can't be sure.

The Machine's fat power cables are the kind with thick pins and a clip so that they can't just fall out of the wall under their own weight. The chipped, two-level Formica control desk looks like it was recovered from a skip bin, but the four monitors on top are expensive and powerful looking, as is a slimline desktop computer.

"Here," Helen says, and Leo has to stop staring to follow her around the side of The Machine. She shows him one of two hatches fitted into the side, which has a hold-shut clamp on a little hinge along its edge. The hinge is the broken part: the attachment has a popped rivet, its plate deformed. Leo frowns at it. What a weird design. What is this hinge for anyway? It looks like the clamp can be swung around to the inside, and what good is that? Each hatch has a gasket seal. They open into the curve of two pill-shaped chambers, which look uncomfortably like high-tech coffins.

"How did this happen?" he says, fingering the popped rivet.

"Came off in my hand," David says from the side door.

Leo knows this explanation is pure stinky bullshit, because he can see the impression of a three-sixteenths slot-head screwdriver head in the metal under the clamp. He doesn't know which is worse: that some knuckle-head uses a precision-machined tool as a prying bar, or that he lies about it. It's the mechanical engineering equivalent of *I walked into a door*. Leo assumes that David hasn't much experience with mechanical things.

"How fast can you fix it?" Helen says, so Leo lets go all thoughts about the screwdriver.

"Where's your regular guy?" he asks.

"What regular guy?"

"The one you would have called before you called me."

"Indisposed," she says. "How fast?"

"Can I make it simpler?"

"I want it exactly as it was and no questions."

Leo shrugs. "Let's see the workshop."

Two minutes later, he's in the next-door workshop, surveying a cave of creation. The low ceiling makes a squeeze of drill presses, lathes and bandsaws. There's racks of metal stock and a computer to drive a CNC machine, a fancy one that can precision cut metal like a blowtorch through butter. Leo rubs his hands. There's a damp smell, and a constant trickle of running water from the pipes, but he can make serious shit here. There's evidence someone already has, from the piles of drawings on the desk, the offcuts in the bin, and the drifts of swarf collected around the corners.

He can see the whole job for Helen unfolding in his mind, lining up the tools he'll need. Drill, diamond tip. Sheet stock. Calipers. Helen takes one look at his face.

"Do it fast," she says. "I need The Machine operational."

"All right."

"And Leo?" She has a tone that makes him look at her. "Across the hall there's more offices. They're vacant. If you go in there, all you'll find is desks and paperwork. So don't go in there, okay? And don't touch anything else. Anything at all. Got it?"

She isn't joking.

〈〈〉〉

Leo gets to work while David and Helen hang by the little office door, waiting. He can't catch enough of what they're talking about over the whine of his drill, but he can see a little through the doorway, and damn if it doesn't look like there's street maps up on the wall in there, and a row of photographs and old newspaper clippings, as if Helen and David are working on some kind of unsolved murder. Not exactly what you expect in a particle physics lab.

It makes him curious about the other rooms across the hall.

He drills out the rivets and takes the clamp back to the workshop to cut a new baseplate. He does this a couple of times more than necessary. One of those times, he opens one of the doors across the hall. And indeed, it's full of desks. Only there's a coat rack in there, too, holding half a dozen men's jackets. He thinks of all kinds of rationales for them, from the office still storing material from a previous occupant (though that occupant would have to be some kind of community theatre fanatic) to explaining them away as specialized protective garments. All of which is mildly ridiculous.

Something doesn't add together here.

Nothing more so than The Machine itself.

He has plenty of time to study it while making the repair, and he can't figure out what the hell the hatched chambers are for. They can't be gas reservoirs: the hatches aren't sealed tight enough for that. And the thing bristles with cooling vanes like a steampunk hedgepig. So, it must produce massive heat when it runs. He decides it has powerful electromagnets in there, which is consistent with particle manipulation, but then he sneaks a look at the fuse box and thinks, Jesus, this thing is drawing enough to power a city block. That's when he notices the legs of the computer table are bolted to the floor, and all the fine instrument lines running out from those hatched chambers are pinned down with thick ceramic clips. Reminds him of an MRI he had to have once, the one for his knee.

That's it, then; Helen is doing some serious electromagnetism with atomic particles down here.

His thoughts circle back to: what's Doctor D doing with her? Leo doesn't get the vibe they're involved, so ...

These questions are making his brain hurt, so he goes back to finishing what she's asked him to do.

The thing is, Leo's almost sure The Machine is already *running.* Not at full power, but he can feel the energy inside it through its metal skin. Maybe it's just idling, and anything requiring full power has to be done in the early hours to avoid browning out the London power grid. Come to think of it, power seems a point of anxiety in here: there's a huge battery bank in a corner marked UPS – uninterruptible power supply – though Leo would bet even a big battery like that wouldn't suffice if The Machine was powered up, but maybe it could sustain this idling mode for a while. At the very least, someone doesn't want the power to run out.

But what kind of particle accelerator needs a stand-by mode? It's not a fucking television.

The anachronisms make Leo think he's going properly nuts. By the time he's finished, all the romanticism of repairing some secret project machine for his sister and only family has dispersed into the puzzle of what kind of research is going on here.

"Perfect," Helen says, opening and closing the repaired clamp when he tells her he's finished.

"What kind of particle physics gets done in a secret basement?" Leo asks. "You were working on some kind of relativistic shit at Cambridge."

"Light Trajectory Theory."

"Never heard of that one," he says, his brain searching its files of obscure papers and coming up blank. "What's the application?"

"It's called *theoretical* physics for a reason, Leo."

"If you have a machine, it's at least experimental." Leo glances down at her. "You know, when those nuclear guys upstairs had some sensitive material going on, they had MPs on the door. Where's your security?"

He thinks she's about to dodge his question, then she sighs. "They were reallocated after the Westminster bombing, when we were defunded. You're looking at what's left."

Leo digests this. The Westminster bombing was a multi-drone attack more than six months ago. There is still a smoking hole in the ground where St Stephen's Hall used to be. Whatever they dropped there was percussive, and the crater still has a creepy ripple pattern of raised concentric mounds, retreating with progressively less destruction. It was enough for parliament to permanently relocate. Leo remembers the fight slipping out of political rhetoric when that happened. Before Westminster, the talking heads held the party line: we're optimistic of a resolution, there's positive signs for peace with the American separatists, we're working with the Koreans, with the Chinese. After Westminster, Leo could see the fray in all that pretense, showing the fear underneath. He wondered how long it would be until no one wanted to live under these conditions anymore. What they might be willing to give up for peace, to avoid having armed men patrolling the streets. So it's not surprising this program was defunded; they had to staff all the checkpoints somehow. And yet Helen is still here.

"Why are you still working then?" he asks.

"Because it's the most important thing we've ever done. That anyone has ever done."

Which is just about the most bullshit thing anyone could say about experimental particle physics.

❬❬❭❭

Still, Leo can't forget the way she looked when she said that. Like what she's doing in there could be some kind of game-changer. Maybe it really is a weapon.

By the time he makes it back through the checkpoints to the flat in Whitechapel, the early-morning street is populated with huddled coats. People walk closer to the buildings than they used to, except where they have to dodge around piles of rubble. Leo's hands keep reaching for a rifle he no longer carries.

He's just crawled back under the chintz tablecloth when Helen calls.

"I hope you're not going to say come in again," he growls.

"You'd thank me," she says. "If you knew."

"If I knew what?"

Somewhere outside a siren begins wailing. Leo suddenly can't stand how long it's been since he knew anything about her.

"You dating that David geezer, or what?" he asks.

"That's what you've been thinking about the whole night?"

"No, I was thinking about what the hell that machine is for."

The moment he says it, he stops, and he hears the hitch in her breath, too. It's the muscle spasm that reminds him not to talk about anything sensitive on the phones.

"Sorry," he says. At least she hasn't hung up. They sit there, listening to the siren.

"There hasn't been any … incidents recently," Helen says finally, meaning *no one's bombed the shit out of us for a couple of weeks*. "Maybe we should get a drink."

"Maybe," Leo says, remembering the last time they had a drink, when he told her he was leaving Cambridge for the army, and she'd thrown half a pint of warm ale into his face. "Next time I come to work … do I just pretend you don't exist?"

She takes a moment to answer. "I think the regular machinist must be dead. If I need anything, I'll come find you."

When they hang up, Leo has a bolt of déjà vu, as if he's back in the residence at Cambridge, and Helen just called him up to discuss some advanced set theory that he could barely follow. As if none of this new world with its metastatic warfare had ever happened.

And, when he thinks that kind of thing, that's when he worries about what's coming next.

《〉》

As soon as Helen puts down the phone, she turns back to frown at the monitors.

"It must be time to close the timefield down, yes?" David asks. "You said we were across threshold now."

Helen doesn't answer for a full minute, going over the graphs. She's used to David's post-transmission jitters, which sometimes last for days. The pacing. The talking. He always gets this way when he comes back without remembering the trip. She gets it – no one likes amnesia, even if they're expecting it. She's learned just to let him do it.

"Mmm," she says, looking at a little blip in the data. It wasn't there a week ago. But she'd have to go back and compare previous days' records to know when it showed up.

Several more minutes go by before she realizes David isn't talking anymore. She looks up, and finds him staring at the wall over the control desk, at the calibration curves.

"David."

"Mmm?"

"I need to run some comparisons. There's a signal in the data I want to check."

"Really? What is it?"

"Don't know. Could just be an echo from The Machine.

It has that look about it." She turns back to the monitor. Five minutes later, when she looks up again after pulling the data files, David's staring at The Machine this time, his brows knotted down, as if he's trying to remember something important, something just at the edge of grasping.

"David?"

"Yeah, good," he says, pulling down his waistcoat. "Let me know how you get on."

Chapter 3

Now – Leo

In the next week, Leo sees Helen once in the elevator, when he's jammed behind the cleaning cart and trying his best not to hyperventilate. They say nothing to each other, and she pointedly presses no buttons, waiting for him to exit on his floor. But just seeing her insulates Leo against the loneliness of his life, which, despite his evening-consuming strategy of video games and crosswords, has found its way inside him anyway, just like the cold wind coming up the Thames. The next time they meet, it's early morning, just after start of shift, as he's coming in the front door, bound for the industrial bins, in the hope the collectors are actually coming today. Helen steps out of the elevator, presumably leaving from her all-night work. Her hair is lank against her head and her eyes sit in bruised purple sockets. She pauses when she sees him.

"You look terrible," he says, because he's in a good mood. The news this morning was relatively less full of doom and gloom: England had walloped Australia in the off-again, on-again rugby tour. In addition, the Starbucks on the corner actually had coffee to sell, so the world feels as though it might have corrected the tilt on its axis, at least for a moment.

"Always a charmer," she says.

"Long night?"

She nods, fumbling to remove her lanyard and stuff it in her pocket. He offers her his coffee. "I'll make do with my fag on the roof in an hour."

"No thanks," she says. "I won't sleep."

"Suit yourself."

Leo inhales the brew, then chucks the cup into the bins. He rolls them out down the access ramp, and then attends to some unmentionable stain on the floor of the penthouse bathroom. One of the nuclear guys is clearly responsible. Men are fucking animals, he thinks, scrubbing at what could be shit, or dried blood, or Caesium-137 for all he knows. Animals, even if they design advanced prototypes to stick into the heart of a decaying French reactor.

Once that situation is ended, he turns on the Beeb on the ancient set in his caretaker office, which is perhaps the first mistake: they're on a tired track, reporting suspicious activity in the Westminster area. The reporter is interviewing a few passers-by, claiming they've seen coordinated teams of uniforms "securing" buildings. Or, at least, their cousin Gerry said he saw them. The Met and the military deny being involved, so now rumors are setting Twitter on fire, which the Beeb duly tickers across the bottom of the screen.

Leo shuts it off, and goes to sweep up the swarf in the first-level workshop, the non-secret one, which is always a mess: plans askew across multiple tables, machines caked with old lubricant, two precious cylinders of gases unrestrained, one full of acetylene, the other of oxygen.

Well, isn't that just an ironic combination.

Leo walks the cylinders into their wall positions and chains them down like mental patients, like they should be. No quicker way to make a rocket than knock over a high-pressure cylinder and have the valve fracture from the body. And that's before getting to how flammable acetylene is. Not that oxygen is much better. In fact, it might be the most dangerous shit in here. It can make fire-retardant burn like gasoline. Once, on a base, Leo saw a whole liquid oxygen tanker explode when the dude supplying the dewar struck a frozen coupling over the asphalt. One spark was all it took. The mushroom cloud was visible for miles, and there was nothing to find of the delivery guy. Leo might have been high on the stuff when he fractured his leg, but every time he sees oxygen, he thinks oxygen + anything + spark = boom.

Speaking of spark, he fingers the fags in his pocket.

As he returns to the office, the Beeb has moved on to what the UN is doing about all of this (hint: nothing) and whether the last democratically elected US president has any hope of being recognized by the split-away states. Everyone on the TV looks tired and hopeless. It's nothing like an old world-war movie, when there was a clear enemy with a clear objective, and a way to win. There are no trenches anymore, no hills to capture. The front-line is at everyone's front door. Time for a smoke.

He climbs the stairs to the roof. It's a chilly April morning made for sleet up there, the sky steel grey, as dim as evening. Leo busily sucks the guts out of two fags in succession to escape the shame he's not doing anything worthwhile anymore, and the double shame that he doesn't think he could if he wanted to.

He looks out on the Gherkin as his numbed fingers sweep the glowing cigarette tip through the semaphore for 'A'. With a small turn, he can see all the way past The Tower to the tip of the HMS Belfast, and the docks.

And then, suddenly, there's a line of light splitting the sky.

Everything is silent at first, in slow motion, as if he's watching a sunbeam break through the clouds. Next comes an eye-stripping freshness in the air, like inhaling over a bucket of fresh ammonia bleach. Then, there's wall of sound, pressure and time rushing over the gut-sinking feeling that something is very, very wrong.

Later, he learns that the beam first touched earth between Piccadilly Circus and Charing Cross. The streaming high-energy particles vaporized the London Library and all the souls therein, then tracked through the theatre district and a good portion of the standard Monopoly board before it retracted into the clouds.

Now, Leo's first sensation is the concrete tiles rushing up to smash him in the back of the head. There's dirt and blood in his mouth and crud raining down around him, and a hot rush of air roaring through his chin stubble.

He groans, and shakes his ringing head. The air in his nose and lungs is too fresh, or cold, each breath stripping him like razors. He coughs until he's barking. All the time, there's an afterimage on his retinas of a white beam rising up into the heavens, but when he finally scrambles up, all he can see from the rooftop is fire.

He staggers, boots wetly crunching over whatever that shit is falling from the sky, and tries to make sense of what just happened. He can't see much past that afterimage, and the sleet is starting up, making every light into a damn nova.

So he fixes on the fire, and thinks he must be looking right down the curve of the Thames, over Waterloo Bridge. If that's true, the great line of burning red is through Mayfair and Soho. Or maybe it's further south, into Westminster itself.

His thoughts lumber to catch up. The first question is: *what the fuck just happened?* Is this the bombing follow-up he was expecting from the news story earlier? But he knows, somewhere in that deep animal brain he just smacked on the tiles, that this is something else. Something big. He rubs the gritty paste of the skyfall between his fingers. Ash. It's London falling down on him, in tiny little pieces.

His second thought, which should have been his first, is *dear god, my sister just went out into the city.* He has no idea where she even lives.

He stumbles for the roof door. Can't quite walk straight. Leans against the frame. How he doesn't fall to his death down the stairs is a question for the ages, but finally, bruised and after indeterminate time, he staggers out into the lobby and half-falls on the tiles.

Everything that happens next is foggy. He thinks he sees Helen bending over him. She has two pencils stuck behind her ears. They look like antennae. There's a backwards impression of a complex formula in transferred biro across her forehead. But maybe that never happens. Or maybe it's a memory shuffled out of sequence when his mental deck hit the ground.

Her face moves like she's making words, but he can't hear. He tries to stand up anyway, but his balance is offline. She braces her hands on his shoulders, but he's big man and she's tiny, so he just crumples back to the floor.

Then Leo thinks he sees David. In his sluggish brain that isn't quite booting just now, all he can think is that he doesn't need help. He bats David away, until someone says. "Leo. Stop. You're *bleeding.*"

❬❮❯❭

Leo doesn't really pass out, but for a while the world has an unreal quality where time is walled off from him, and his thoughts are mostly a scramble of fragmentary memories, like the reception glitches on a television that's attempting to make a picture. If he'd been fully conscious, he'd have found this comparison ironic, because chunky old-school television sets were themselves simple particle accelerators, painting the picture on screen with a moving beam of electrons.

Some of Leo's fragmentary memories were of vintage science fiction sequences like the heat-ray weapons in *The War of the Worlds*, burned onto his retinas by such vintage TVs. Televisions and heat-rays shared technological DNA, but that was where the comparison ended; declaring that the beam that had just fragged London resembled a TV set was like saying a quaint Graham Bell telephone resembles a Galaxy S9. True, they both took tiny particles and used electromagnets to accelerate them to inconceivable speed. But the heat-ray beam's particles were heavier, and pumped out in bulk. A television beam was like sand falling through an hourglass; the heat-ray was a fire hose of bullets. When those massive speeding particles ran into anything, they unloaded their immense energy in heat. That was why the air glowed around the beam. Why buildings had exploded, material flash vaporizing and expanding into starbursts.

But accelerating a particle with a magnet needs the particle to be charged like a magnet, too. So, the beam's maker machine had to sit up in the atmosphere for a while, stripping down a stock of atoms into charged ones it could fling at the city below. That was the process that had put the fresh smell in the air. The one that Leo will put together soon.

❬❭❭

When Leo finally comes back into sense, he registers he's in Helen's Machine room, laid out on the rough carpet floor. He can hear a television newsreader, and voices: Helen and David.

"God, we're lucky the power came back on," Helen's saying. "That UPS can only sustain The Machine at idle for a few minutes. Imagine if we'd been in transmission?"

"Jesus, *fuck*." This is David, deploying the swears as though he only has theoretical grasp of their use. "All that work, wiped out. Jesus, *fucking fuck*."

Leo's never heard profanity used so inexpertly.

Then David says, "Did we cause this? Did we do something that made whatever just hit us?"

"Impossible," Helen says, indignant. "The timefield is still open. There can't be reconciled changes. We didn't cause it. This is something that was always going to happen."

"But if the power—"

"Yes. The longer we keep it open, the more risk of complete loss. And it's not just power grid failure. You remember the one we shorted from that leak? And if we took a direct hit here …"

"Even more reason to close the timefield, then." This is David again. "After that last transmission, I'm sure we're done. You said the Grid numbers are solid. It should be enough to make the changes."

"That's not a reason to ignore the maths. I've explained this before. We're not past threshold yet," Helen says. "We wait to ensure the changes are stable. We've been at this for months. You want to undo everything for the sake of a day?"

Leo can't work out what the hell they're talking about. He's still muddled about which way is up. His nose is blocked, and he still tastes blood on his molars. He remembers these sensations from before, that time he was on the chopper on a stretcher, tasting blood. He puts a hand to his face.

David catches it, and presses it back to the floor. "You're all still there, don't worry, just scratches and bruises, but your hands are filthy. Wouldn't want an infection, what with penicillin in short supply," he says, then looks across, presumably at Helen. "Concussion, I think, besides the surface abrasions. Be a good idea to monitor his vitals for a while, though. That was a hell of a blast wave. Wouldn't want to miss it if he's blown out a blood vessel in his head. I don't think he was close enough for lung damage. But then, he is a smoker."

Leo blinks. "What the hell happened?"

He twists to look over at The Machine, Helen's words about this being the most important thing ever suddenly loud in his head, along with David's question about whether they've caused this. He puts the two idea cables together in his head and a conclusion falls out.

"Are you working for them?" he asks, trying to sit up, and finding the room uncooperative in remaining still. "Are you?"

"How about lying down again," David says.

"Working for who?" Helen asks.

"The American separatists. The Chinese. The Koreans. Whoever dropped that *thing* just now." Christ, his head is spinning.

"Might be disoriented," David says, very calm and doctorly, and pulling up Leo's eyelids with a thumb. "Can you tell me your name?"

"You're making particle weapons here, right?" Leo goes on, ignoring David. "It has to be something weapons related, or why the big secret? Do the enemy already have them?"

Helen's shaking her head. "Leo, that's not what we do."

Leo is about to go further down an illogical path with his theory, but he stops because there's footage on the TV now. Shaky, hand-recorded footage, but it gets the beam in shot, tracing down from the clouds, and then it becomes so bright the picture oversaturates before it resolves: into a pure white light burning a wide swathe through the London architecture. Finally, it snaps off like a torch, and there's a stunned silence before the footage cuts to the aftermath, the air full of smoke. After that, the male anchor is back, framed with scrolling tickers. He's sallow and missing a tie, like his boss shoved him in the chair without time for wardrobe.

"Experts are speculating this was a new kind of weapon, possibly a particle beam," the anchor says. *"It sounds like science fiction, but sources agree that high-speed particles accelerated from a satellite or atmospheric drone could cause the destruction we witnessed in London today. The high energies involved create ozone in the atmosphere, corroborating eyewitness reports, at least from the ones who survived. There's not many of them, because the weapon incinerated everything it touched, vaporizing buildings and people in this indiscriminate and terrifying act of war."*

Leo sits there dumbly. A particle beam, a fucking James Bond death ray, leaving nothing but grey powder and fire. He presses his head between his hands, asking to be taken away, or at least back to the chintz tablecloth bunker he has at home.

The TV is unrelenting. Next, they cut to a roving reporter out somewhere near Westminster, the ghostly outline of a leaning Big Ben just visible, backlit by helicopter searchlights through the sleet. The air is smudged with suspended dirt. Stunned survivors mill around behind the reporter, who's jammed his microphone in front of a grey-bearded wild-eyed man in a red anorak.

"I'm tellin' you," this man says. "I saw the bloody thing come down! Still got the white line of it in me eyes. It were over in a second, like the bloody hand of god!"

A pack of Russian rebels claim responsibility, but then so do another three groups; who knows, maybe they're working together. It's all guerrilla warfare now, fought in the minds of the citizens as much as on the streets. There's nowhere to send the military when the bastards are everywhere.

Helen mutes the TV, and sits in the control chair. David leans against the wall, the atmosphere black as pitch. Leo's head is still spinning. Finally, Helen looks at David.

"When I was developing The Machine, I had funding interest from the States," she says. "Do you think—"

"What?" he asks.

She shakes her head, as if she doesn't want to imagine whatever thought she just had. She turns back to the monitors. A second later, her body straightens. "Hang on," she says.

"What?" David asks, in a different tone.

The two of them are peering at the screen. Leo slowly stands. Fuck this secrets party. He can't remember what he was thinking two minutes ago. He's going back upstairs.

"You can't leave," David says. "Your vitals need monitoring."

"I'll show you where to stick your monitor," Leo slurs. The door is wobbling, but he can make it.

David is suddenly in the way. "You can't leave." He's not doctorly now. He's got a sergeant's voice on, one that makes Leo wonder if he ever wore a uniform. "You've seen things in this lab you can't disclose."

"I've seen squat," Leo says, trying to remember why he

has the idea to call that hotline number the government has to report suspicious activity. But in order to make this verbal volley, he's had to turn back into the room, and Helen is watching him from the control chair.

"What's he going to do, David?" she says, with a lift of her eyebrow.

"His judgement's impaired. He could blow this all open."

"He knows better than that," she says. "He knows we're on the same side. And after today, that we need to finish what we're doing here. That's the only thing that matters now. If he understands that, he'll stay."

Leo tries to straighten up. After all, he's a head taller than David, has actual pecs and a rectus abdominus under his shirt, but he's still wobbling and David has his hands propped on his hips and a non-concussed brain to rely on. Leo doesn't manage to move.

David finally drops his hands. "Then we agree he stays here. No loose ends."

Leo looks across at Helen, who's watching him with wary evaluation. A week ago, he would have given anything to spend this time with her. Now he thinks, *this is why they say, be careful what you wish for*. And then he looks up at the muted TV, full of shaky footage of London burning, and limp children's bodies. Leo looks at The Machine, idling ugly, the ferrous giant in the room, and says, "I'm not staying till you tell me what the hell this thing does."

Chapter 4

Half an hour later, Leo is sitting in the control station chair, his head in his hands. The woozy spinning has given way to a throbbing headache, and his nose is swelling from the abrasions, adding to the pressure. "You're going to have to say all that again," he says.

"The Machine is a light trajectory device," Helen repeats. "It sends a coded photon beam around a rotating torus, and thereby creates a timefield. Which we can then manipulate."

Leo looks at her blankly. His head feels stuffed with steel wool.

David rolls his eyes. "It's a time machine, Leo."

Leo laughs. Helen doesn't.

"It's *not* a time machine," she says. "That's not what it does. You *can't* travel in time. But you *can* open a field copy of a timeline, and make adjustments. And when the timefield is closed again, those adjustments can be … reconciled."

"But it is, for all practical purposes, a time machine," David argues. "When you go into it, it feels like you travel in time. Start here, end up in 1884. Believe me, I know."

"This is where all the problems start," Helen argues back. "It's not actually 1884. It's just an allegory …"

Leo doesn't follow the rest. He's still stuck on *time machine*. It's not something that he'd have believed, but for two things. First is because this is Helen, who couldn't look more serious if a dentist was drilling her back teeth, and who Leo is pretty sure uses physics instead of hemoglobin to carry the oxygen in her blood. She wouldn't piss around with something like this. And second, he knows a little bit about research like this, between things his father worked on, and the stuff he's not supposed to have seen in the military. The government learned a long time ago that private industry conditions — that is, no red tape — kick along innovation much faster than a bureaucracy can, and all the better if there's a war on. So governments fund research like this and get out of the way. For all he knows, that hand-of-god particle lance that just carved a new canal through London is the product of the same thinking.

There's a happy thought.

"Are you saying," he interrupts them, flinging a hand towards The Machine. "That people get *inside* that thing?"

"You fixed that clamp on one of the chambers," Helen says. "You must have noticed the inside position."

All Leo can think about is how he thought those chambers looked like coffins. His head strikes up the pounding bass note again.

He turns his focus on the computer monitors. The left one shows an interface like any control system — lots of little grey boxes with various numbers and graphs. The right one is split in two, a matrix grid of numbers on the top, and a constantly refreshing track of wiggly lines across the bottom, almost like a heartbeat trace. He doesn't know what any of it means. He glances again through the open office door, where he can now make out plans tacked on the wall, building plans. Not professional blueprints; they look hand-drawn, showing multiple levels. Alongside is a creased map of London, dotted with pins, with old-fashioned threads running to scrawled notes. Next to this are the photographs he spotted before. He frowns at the faces, now he can stare openly. One man looks familiar. Another is definitely Queen Victoria, the dour-faced monarch that was burned into Leo's brain in school, because there was a portrait of her in the library.

The whole thing looks like a two-bit operation, a cacophony of inconsistencies. He can't make sense of anything, and the walls of the room are beginning to shrink. He has an overwhelming need for a cigarette.

"Nice one," he says, getting up. "You almost had me there."

David and Helen exchange a look. "He doesn't believe you," David says.

"No shit," Leo says. "But keep going. Really. The 'we have a time machine' thing must be fun. I get it – physics is dry. You have to entertain yourselves all night."

"You have to understand," David says. "We had a much larger program, more staff before Westminster. This is just what's left."

"Okay, sure," Leo says, digging for the smokes in his pocket. He doesn't really want to climb all those flights to the roof, but he needs to get outside now.

"Where are you going?" David says, clearly indignant the ruse hasn't worked.

"To see a man about a dog," Leo says, as he heads for the stairs.

《〈〉》

Helen watches her brother go with resignation, but not surprise. She's used to this reaction.

Not that many years ago, she'd had the unenviable position of having created the most powerful technology in history, but having no profile in the scientific community. That lack of profile stemmed from the way her technology had been created: she'd gone to Cambridge on a scholarship, where brilliance had an uncanny ability to hide in a theoretical dissertation. Her highly absent supervisor, and deliberate distance from her alcoholic father, did not help with connections. Her work therefore disappeared into the landscape of generally unread physics theses each year.

Light Trajectory Theory had sprung from her early modelling of the light transfer between particles to better understand electromagnetism, a subject that hit the snooze button on anyone but the most devoted physics enthusiast. Helen had been that enthusiast. Eventually, through tunnels in the mountains of algebra, she came to realize what the theory suggested: that it was possible to create a holding space technically outside our own universe, for manipulating particles.

This caught the eye of a start-up investor when nanotech was still a hot word in entrepreneurial circles. He rather misunderstood the theory, but money was money. So rather than publishing her papers, Helen had been lured into the start-up, where any innovation was kept tightly secret to protect patents. She'd had two assistants, a programmer, and a workshop, at least until the money ran out. Around this time, the wobbling American situation created an economic dip, which put any money for the less pragmatic subjects (literature, philosophy and physics) effectively at the center of a black hole – she could go chasing it, but she'd never emerge again to do any actual work. Then the Americans tried to disarm the populace, and a geopolitical meltdown ensued, sucking the last of foreign research money.

And there, Light Trajectory Theory might have died, except for Helen herself, who worked longer and longer hours to make progress. By the time the start-up ran out of capital, she'd moved past particle manipulation and had realized the full and fairly frightening potential. She'd sat for six straight hours thinking that day, knowing if she proceeded, nothing would be the same again. For her, and maybe the world. Two months later, she had her first Machine. And then, she had to use it.

If medicine had Barry Marshall, drinking a flask of cultured *Helicobacter pylori* to prove it caused gastritis, then physics had Helen Fawkes, who put herself through The Machine and into the timefield. By the time the repo men had come to strip the offices of the start-up, Helen had made a dozen transmissions through The Machine, all brief, some frightening – she kept her field notes in a sealed paper notebook – but enough to prove her theory beyond doubt. And, after midnight one night, she used some bemused tow-truck operators to move The Machine safely away from the repo men and to a storage locker near Stansted.

It was a temporary solution. She knew no one in a university would take her on, even in good times – she had no publication record, and her Machine and her theory made her look like a nutcase. The United States had just fractured down the middle, sending shock waves through the entire world order. North Korea and China, who'd already been crying foul over atmospheric weather manipulation, leaped into the power breech. Everyone was busy filling their bathtubs and buying the last stocks of radios and batteries, not advertising jobs or funding research.

In desperation, she went to David Blakeney, whose research she'd used to build The Machine's all-critical component: the microtorus. When his secretary wouldn't give her an appointment, she waited for him after a conference paper he delivered in Edinburgh, and then boarded the same train south to continue the conversation. She knew she couldn't be charming like he was, so she went with relentlessness. By the end of the trip, she had learned he had spent three years re-building his career after being accused of malpractice and disappearing from television back into research. She didn't care about that. She cared that he was about head a new research program he couldn't talk about, working for people he couldn't mention, but in London. Against her better judgement, she offered to show him her Machine.

"Jesus," he said, when she'd demonstrated its capability. "You do realize what we could do with this?"

"World peace?" she'd said, ironically. They were sitting in a local called *The King's Head* at the time, David nursing a second large whiskey. Henry VIII leered down at them from a dusty portrait over the fire.

"Well, yes," David said. "I mean, look at all the wastages of the last century. Imagine preventing the world wars or eradicating small pox before the new world discovery."

Helen had taken a breath, a little uncomfortable at the re-emergence of his on-television persona. "But those are massive changes. The maths doesn't support such changes being stable – the whole timefield could collapse, and then it can never reintegrate. You can make larger changes the further back in time you go, but there's an energy law requirement – the further back you make the timefield, the more juice The Machine needs. There's a point where The Machine can't physically dump that much heat, plus the magnets would rip themselves apart. Maybe in future refinements ..."

But David wasn't really taking any of that in. He was

staring up at Henry, like he was imagining meeting the old philanderer. "Details," he had said. "That's what development is for. Work out how to go around your limitations. Plus, it gives my own research a nice legitimacy. If no one wants medical androids, the molecular assembly won't go to waste."

"I don't want to overpromise—"

David put a hand on her arm. "This isn't just anything, Helen. This is keep-it-from-the-Nazis-at-all-costs kind of research. The world's at war now, and you have a secret weapon. I'm going to make some calls."

A week later, she was working for the same people.

Now, as Helen climbs the last stairs to the roof, she tries to put herself in Leo's place … without the anger of him up and leaving for the army all those years ago catching her off-guard. She'd been all alone without him then; it was hard not to resent that.

She finds him, cigarette in hand, meditatively staring out at the smoke clouds still rising out of the West End. The sky is a heavy mass of charcoal, and the city is all vertical impressionist smudges of grey. The ground out here has a fine layer of ash. The tip of Leo's cigarette is the only spot of color. He's turned up the collar of his gunmetal jacket, covering the yellowing bruises on his jaw from the beam attack. He's always been tall, but he still seemed like her little brother before. He doesn't now.

He's just a man she used to know, with the same doubt on his face that everyone has on learning about The Machine. A man that's lost his drive. That's disappointing somehow.

"What I said down there was true," she says.

"About having a time machine? Or that bollocks about it being the most important thing ever?"

Helen stares at him, thinking about whether she'll need him again before she and David can finish their work. Ah, fuck it, she thinks. Maybe their relationship isn't worth saving. Not when she can save the world.

She's almost back to the stair door when he says, "Suppose I do believe you. Someone actually goes in that Machine, and sends them somewhere else? Or some*time* else?"

She turns around. "It doesn't *send* them anywhere," she says. "It's a superposition state, both here and in the timefield. They're still here … and not. At the same time."

"Fucking modern physics," Leo says, and scrubs out the cigarette under his boot with a scrape of grit. "Nothing is straightforward."

"That why you did engineering? The maths too hard for you?"

"Shall I make the crack about physicists and social skills?"

Helen suddenly laughs. "You could. Then I'd have to say something like, *those social skills must come in handy when you're cleaning toilets for a living.*"

"That's low," he says, wincing. Then, after a pause, "how's Doctor D fit into all this?"

"David got me the position here when the research company I worked for was broke, and The Machine was about to be repossessed."

Leo grunted like a bad-tempered bear. But to Helen, something about laughing a moment ago still feels as renewing as the first daffodils of spring.

"I wouldn't be here without him," she says. "The Machine's internals use his molecular assembly technique, so he was interested from the start. We had a whole big team here, but we couldn't have kept going without him.

He can do the work in the timefield. He can do things I can't."

Because he's good with people, she doesn't say, but Leo nods slowly.

She looks out across the wastes of London. "You think it was really the Russians?"

His brows draw down. "That was high technology," he says finally. "I mean, the Koreans and Chinese have nukes. Hell, everyone's probably got nukes, even if they're untested. But this thing isn't like that. You know yourself what it takes to accelerate particles. And they've put this thing on a mobile device, an upper atmospheric drone or a satellite. They have a command center tracking it, and a long history of infrastructure that developed it. That knocks out a lot of options. If I had to bet, I'd say it's the American separatists, because we supported Canada against them. Or maybe it's the Russians, but stolen from the Americans."

"You don't think it could have been created in a smaller lab, like The Machine?" Helen asks.

For just a second, Leo ghosts a smile. "Only if they had another one of you." Then the smile is gone. "Don't go out into the city alone again, okay?"

Helen stares at him, not knowing what to say at this demonstration of respect and concern. Bonds of siblinghood aside, neither of them are people-people.

He offers her a cigarette, like he used to when they were both at Cambridge, and for just a second, Helen feels that familial comfort he used to be for her. Maybe it isn't too late.

"Those things will kill you," she says, pushing the pack away.

"We dying soon anyway, aren't we?" he says, waving a

hand at the city, and tapping out a fresh cancer stick. She plucks it from his mouth, and turns the white paper over in her hand. The packet must have cost him most of his weekly wage.

"Maybe not," she says, smelling the tobacco, pulling up memories of laughing at some joke on a Friday night. "If we can pull this off."

He gives her a resigned look. "You really aren't kidding around are you?"

"Not even slightly." She breaks the cigarette in half and chucks it on the ground. "Come back downstairs. I'll show you."

All she hears then is Leo bellowing after her, "Why? You going back in time to fix my fucking fag?"

Chapter 5

When he trudges back down the stairs, Leo's head is clearer, and he sees the lab as though it's the first time he's been there. The clean and orderly workstation, with those charts on the wall lined up corner-to-corner, bathed in pale blue LED light. The faint hum of The Machine through the walls and floor and in his own sinuses. The trace smell of oil and industrial cleaner. Compared to the world outside, Helen's lab is order, and calm, and there's something hopeful in that.

"Okay," he says, leaning against the wall near the workstation. "Explain to me what this timefield thing is — you said something about it being just, like, here?"

"It's a copy of our timeline, beginning from a point we choose. A kind of sandbox, where we can change what happens, without affecting our own timeline. A bit like if you make a copy of an image file on your computer, and then you photoshop the copy. It doesn't change the original file. The timefield isn't part of our universe. It's a branch, from a chosen inception point. To be technical, it's an alternative universe which differs from our own in that we made a transmission there — it's tied to us, but not us."

"So going to this timefield doesn't change anything here?"

"Not immediately," she says, holding up a finger.

"So what's the point? You can just, I dunno, kill Hitler in the twenties, and it doesn't mean a thing?"

"Do you think it's that easy?" Helen asks, challenge in

her voice. "You think you could kill Hitler in the twenties?"

Leo straightens. "Everyone knows you use a time machine to kill Hitler," he says, but he glances at The Machine and thinks about it, really thinks about if he was still in the army, and someone put a rifle in his hands and said 'go kill Hitler', what it would take to do it.

"You're thinking about it, aren't you?" Helen says. "Well, can you do it?"

"Are you going to ask me to?" Leo says, nervous, because he doesn't know the first thing about Germany in the 1920s, not the stuff that matters anyway. The stuff that would allow him to plan something like that, to blend in and not call attention to himself, and to get the kind of information that could put him in the right place at the right time. And all of that comes after having the basic fucking courage to put on a uniform again.

"No, that's not what we're doing. Just I want you to appreciate it isn't that easy. I'll come back to that. First, you asked about the point of manipulating the timefield. In actual fact, we don't want changes here straight away. We want to know we have the right changes. We want to measure what we're doing."

Leo nods slowly. "Fair enough. So, what, you send someone there, and they step out of The Machine into some new reality?"

Helen shifts uncomfortably. "The Machine doesn't *go*. It just sends the transmission. You just sort of … just materialize."

"Jesus, you've done it, haven't you?" he asks.

"Quite a few times."

"What's it like? Does it look real?"

"It's exactly like here," she says. "You wouldn't know it's any different. The physics might be theoretical, but the timefield is real."

"Was that a joke?"

She gives him the finger.

Leo re-directs. "And how do you come back?"

Helen pulls out a drawer, and lifts up a small console, the size of a large smartphone. At least, it looks like one until Leo sees it close up. The screen only fills half the surface, and it feels heavier than it should be when she puts it in his hand. "You take this console with you into the timefield, which can communicate with The Machine through entangled qubits."

"Wait ... you're *using* qubits?"

"We have to. There isn't another way to communicate with the timefield."

"But qubits. As in, quantum computing?" Leo groped to catch up. He doesn't really know the first thing about quantum computers, except that they would be revolutionary, and he knew qubits – atoms with a particular state – were important. Entangled qubits were weird behaving things: when separated, if one changed, then so would the other, even if they were on the other side of the universe, what Einstein had called 'spooky action at a distance'.

But Helen shakes her head. "No, of course not. Quantum computing is still decades away. And that's not how qubits work, Leo. Come on. There's no such thing as action at a distance. What we're using is much more primitive. We just assign certain coded message channels to an entangled pair. If either end measures the state of that qubit, then the other collapses, and we have the message."

"These things must be expensive."

Helen sighs. "Very. And scarce. We don't have many qubit banks left, and every time we use one, it's used. Gone.

It's like putting a hammer through a brand-new iPhone every time you send a text message."

"But it lets you communicate."

"Only very basic things, all pre-coded. We confirm each transmission, and have several qubits for other scenarios."

"Like what?"

"A distress signal, like if The Machine has lost power. The time dilation gives someone in the timefield a short window to make an emergency return. The console will always reserve a qubit, and a spare, for calling for a return, and displaying the time you have left. I lost an early machine once from a short-circuit — roof leaked in our previous location. So that's why we have the back-up supply to power a return. You can recall as long as you're within the physical window of where you were sent through. That's why we don't as a rule travel far from the transmission point."

"So, what if you lose the console?"

"Don't lose it," she says, flatly, taking it back.

"All right," he says. "So let's say you've gone to this timefield and killed Hitler—"

"Do we really have to use this example?"

"Say you have. And the world's a better place over in this lovely alternative universe. Then what?"

"Well, three possibilities," Helen says, counting them off on her fingers. "First, we can do a transmission recall, a kind of orderly shutdown of the timefield. That can create an overlaid stable loop, where the timefield sort of … integrates with our universe, and we then experience the altered future here. We actually can't change the past, that's important to realize. The past will always exist. But we can sort of, loop it back to be redone a different way, and thus change the future that hasn't happened yet, as long as it's a stable version of the future, which basically means supported by the events in both our past, and in the loop through the timefield. Like this."

She grabs a sheet of paper and scrawls a line ending in a loop that glances back on the same line before it dives towards the future.

"But—"

She holds up a hand, to stop Leo interjecting with questions. "—but in your Hitler example, that's very unlikely to be a stable loop. The change could be too massive to reconcile with our universe. Basically, the loop would be too tight."

"That ... doesn't sound good."

"Right. That's why we have option two, the destroy-all-traces option. If we destroy The Machine's microtorus – that's the internal part that makes the timefield possible – without closing the loop, then the timefield is simply ended. It's closed off, and separate to us. Anything we did there is lost."

"The get-out-of-jail plan."

"If you like to call it that."

Leo sits thinking about this. He's uncomfortable in the way he used to get in mission briefings, when everything starts to get a little too real. "What's the third option?"

Helen shifts in her seat. "The maths around this is difficult, and hasn't been tested."

"But?"

"In theory, it's possible that a timefield may distort our universe. It might recombine to create a chaotic loop, or something of that nature."

"A chaotic loop?"

"Yes."

"You mean ... a groundhog day, time and space going

over and over in the same path?"

"Something like that. It's highly rare, but possible. The timefield would have to be in some kind of meta-stable state, where it was compatible to recombine with our universe, but only temporarily. The lack of global stability could create quantum aberrations, or it could propagate throughout the universe — the solutions are highly complex."

"This is why I hated theoretical maths," Leo mutters. Helen and their father were the ones who enjoyed this kind of thing. Leo had always been just a little too pragmatic for their tastes. "If the person in there is in some superposition, both here and in the timefield, who comes back? If they, I dunno, cut a finger off in the timefield, is that what comes back?"

Helen ghosts a smile. "I thought you didn't like the maths."

"I thought it was a pretty practical question."

"It's probabilistic," she says. "Sometimes it's the timefield version, sometimes it's the one in The Machine. I don't remember some of the transmissions I made."

Leo swallows, because this is fucking disturbing. He stares at The Machine again, at those coffin-shaped compartments. "In that second scenario, when you destroy the timefield, what happens to anyone who's in there?"

She hesitates. "That hasn't happened."

"But if it did?"

"We wouldn't destroy the microtorus with someone in The Machine."

"Why not?"

She spreads her hands.

"Let me guess," he says. "Because they're in a superposition, both here and *there* and neither, all at once.

If you destroy The Machine, which is describing that state, then the state collapses into only one solution. Jesus, Helen, you mean they could end up *not* being here. That is, lost forever in that closed-off timefield."

"Yes. Don't look at me like that, Leo."

"Just stop talking for a bit."

《〉》

Finally, after thinking a good long while, Leo rubs a hand over his face. "I guess," he concedes finally, "It's not that different from being chucked out of a plane over the Middle East with a sidearm and a stick of gum."

"Well, you don't need a parachute with The Machine," Helen says. "We calibrate the timefield entry very carefully to ensure that. You'd never get me to jump out of a plane."

"Nah, you'll just use an untested time machine to change the universe."

"It's not untested."

"So you said. I mean untested in the ability to bring changes."

At this, Helen goes into the directory on the workstation and opens a file. "Here. Watch. This is a test where the footage came back."

Leo peers at the video on the screen, which shows the same lab they're in now, The Machine clearly visible in the background, and the office door to the left. In the foreground, a table is set up with an old-fashioned retort stand. Attached to the stand is an electronic clamp – evidenced by wires run back to a timer unit on the table – holding a stoppered flask of what looks like bright blue paint. Under the flask is a thick piece of industrial foam. To the side of this apparatus is a cage, containing two piebald mice, both sniffing about like, well, mice. Leo feels a qualm looking at them, and has to drag his gaze to the other parts of the image. In the top right of the picture is a small grid of numbers, and alongside, a graph with no axis labels. A timer runs in the bottom left corner.

"I stayed out of the room for the start of the test. You'll see why in a second," Helen says, as on screen, the timer releases the clamp, and the flask falls gently into the foam. It sits there for three seconds before the office door opens, and Helen herself emerges, replaces the flask in the clamp, moves the foam aside, and then goes back into the office. The mice stretch up, sniffing towards Helen as she does this.

"I don't follow …" Leo begins, then he stops as something happens on the screen, just a tiny glitch. Then everything straightens out. The retort clamp opens a second time, and this time the flask hits the table, smashing glass and blue paint everywhere. The sound of tinkling glass comes from the speakers. The mice scamper away from the noise and chaos, huddling together in the far corner of their cage. But after a few seconds, when nothing further happens, they emerge to sniff at the mess. Leo can see a tiny blue fleck on one mouse coat.

"So … you smashed a bottle of paint. Is that it?"

"Keep watching."

About a minute goes by on the timer with nothing happening, except Leo notices the grid of numbers has changed, and the graph has a step-jump in several lines. When had that happened? He frowns at it, not seeing anything that correlated to a change. Everything looks the same, just an ooze of paint making its way across the table. Leo clears his throat. His eyes keep returning to the pair of mice, to their calm investigations, wondering what's about to happen to them. He knows what happens to lab mice.

He licks his lips, failing to settle his pounding heart. "What are the mice—"

"Biological movement patterns are almost impossible to fake. Interaction between two different animals more so. They're for authenticity at reconciliation."

Leo can't process this right now. "I mean *why* are there mice?"

"Relax," Helen says. "Just watch."

On screen, Helen walks out of the office again, pauses at the computer for a second, then crosses the floor, climbs into The Machine, and pulls the hatch closed.

"We didn't used to have the latches on the chambers," Helen says. "Didn't think of it until later. And the glitches are from the electromagnetic field surges."

Leo hardly hears. He's watching a count-down timer running in garish red above The Machine. And the mice. Numbers, mice, numbers, mice. When the timer hits zero, the lights glow, and there's another micro-glitch in the tape. Suddenly the foam jumps to the side, and the puddle of paint and broken glass is gone. He blinks. The paint flask is now nestled in the foam, intact. The mice are still in their cage.

Leo grunts in surprise. It must be a splice in the footage. There's no other way that the paint could have been cleared up and the foam shift position, except he's sure the mice hadn't jumped position. On the tape, Helen steps out of The Machine. The video ends.

Before Leo can say anything, Helen loads the next tape.

"This is from the bodycam."

The new camera shows the side view of the room in a shaky, body-mounted recording as Helen walks out of the office and towards The Machine, just as she'd done on the other tape. Leo can clearly see the broken flask on the table.

He sees that same paint fleck on the mouse, as it turns to sniff at Helen. She climbs into The Machine, and then there's disruption on the tape, and the image is suddenly looking back on The Machine from across the room. Leo realizes that Helen was now standing just inside the door. He's sure the timer hasn't skipped but somehow, she's travelled across the room without leaving The Machine.

In shot, the flask is back in the clamp, intact, and the camera filming it is also in view. Helen steps towards the table and simply pushes the foam back under the flask.

On screen, Helen says, "This transmission is highly localized. The timefield was created only two minutes before transmission time, and the location is calibrated to be within the lab, to minimize any confounding effects." She steps back from the table.

Then, the clamp opens, the flask drops into the foam. On-screen-Helen pulls out a console and selects a large green icon. She enters a code and several confirmations, and then the video picture disappears into darkness, except for the timer counting on the bottom right. Then, when light returns, Leo realizes the bodycam is showing her stepping out of The Machine. She pauses to show the flask, now back to being smashed across the table, as it was when she got in. The mice sniff around in the left side of the shot.

On-screen-Helen says, "As you can observe, there has been no change yet to the extant timeline."

Then, she goes to The Machine itself, and flips up a cover, under which is a big red button.

"About to destroy microtorus," she says on screen, while swinging the camera view to the table, with its smashed flask. Leo grips his chair's arms. Then there comes another glitch, after which the foam has moved and the flask is suddenly whole, nestled in the foam on the table.

On screen, Leo can hear Helen's breathing is gasping fast, as if she's been running. "Reintegration complete," she says. "And I have full memory of the test, so the footage should be good, too."

Now, real-world Helen stops the videos. "I can load these up to run in parallel and show the concordance of time, and close-ups on the unique serial number we etched in the flask before the test, or the rodent movement tracking," she says.

"Why is that paint fleck still there?"

"Where?"

"There," Leo says, pointing at the mouse, which of course is currently not in a pose where you can see the paint fleck.

Helen ignores him. "Look, the first video was recorded on the original timeline, which is why you can't see me, because I'm in the timefield. You see the electromagnetic glitch when the timefield was created, and you see the new future after the stable loop is reconciled. My bodycam recorded the actions in the timefield, and then the reconciliation. After that, both the bodycam and the static camera are in agreement."

Leo stares at the paused screen a long time. His mind is running in a mobius strip trying to follow all this. Finally he looks at the date stamp. A cold current runs through him.

"The date on this. It's the same as my incident day," he says. The day that left him with the broken leg, and set him on the trajectory out of the army.

"They aren't related," Helen says, quickly.

Leo sucks in a slow breath, thinking he can smell dust and smoke, and his injured leg itching.

"Where are the other tests?" he says finally, his voice sticky.

"What other tests?"

He points to the mice, the screen paused at the point one of them is stretched up high, trustingly displaying a soft pink belly. "You know what other tests. Animal tests. Where you kill the mice and bring them back to life."

Helen pauses for a second. "You don't need to see those."

"I see," Leo says. Then, he calmly walks across the room and throws up into the rubbish bin.

❮❯

Leo finally manages to stop his stomach heaving only because David choses that moment to come back in, and starts talking about needing an MRI head-scan to rule out a bleed, and the last thing Leo needs right now is to be stuffed into a tiny tin can surrounded by powerful electromagnets. He tries for a little while to do the 'this isn't happening' routine, but he knows that it is. Dreams, even the traumatic ones, aren't this real. He goes through the tapes again and again, matching the time stamps, the split-second agreement between those glitch points. This isn't theatrical forgery. So he comes back to the critical question.

"Okay, so I know you aren't using it to kill Hitler. What on earth are you doing?"

Helen gestures towards the hall, to the other offices where Leo snuck a glance inside. "Go take a look."

The office across the hall is larger than Leo assumed from his doorway glimpse. The whole south wall is filled with industrial shelves of archive boxes. The west wall is covered in whiteboards and pin boards, with plans and photographs and clippings above three long tables. The north wall has a rack of clothing. It looks like a move they never got around to unpacking. Except there's still abandoned coffee mugs here, and a layer of dust, like the workers just didn't come in one day.

Leo stares at a floorplan on the wall first. It's a three-level building with a basement. The kind of plans that might be hung up for a fire evacuation route, but rough and hand-traced. Central stairs and a lift shaft are marked on each floor on the long north wall. The basement has a long rectangle marked "boiler", and what looks like a chimney in the short west wall.

A spiral service staircase is tucked into the south-west corner. Hand-scrawled notes mark the large spaces on each floor: "dock" at the east end of the ground floor, "reagents" and "workshop" either side of the first floor. On the second, one small room off a hall is labelled "trans room". The rest of the space is blank, but for a note that says, "Tesla lab". This all looks like a fairly standard building, probably a research facility; though it's obviously not the building they're in now. Maybe it's research in magnetic fields – Tesla is the unit of magnetic flux. A note in the top right of the plans says, *1884 St Alberts Royal*, which Leo assumes is an address.

Leo tracks across to the press clippings. There's a bunch from the increasingly unstable American situation over the last two years, older ones stretching back through the gulf wars, the eighties global warming stories, Vietnam and Korea. More from the last two years about climate change – the wipe-out floods in Bangladesh, the Syrian genocides, the accusations against the Chinese for weather tampering, the American dust bowl that preceded the Second Civil War.

Leo stands back. "I don't get it," he says.

"We spent a long time at the start of this program examining how to prevent the down spiral the world's in now," David says. "Imagine what it would be like if all the wars and bombings and political instability we've had for the last thirty years never happened."

It sounds rehearsed, like a sales pitch. Leo wonders how many times he's given it.

"We had an historical statistician then, a specialist who'd done a huge root cause analysis over the last two centuries. Massive data. Computationally massive. We had time on supercomputing grids to run those numbers. That's how we narrowed in on our target time, and how we were going to do this."

Leo frowns, because any time he's heard the term *root cause analysis* it's been code for *some human fucked up*. Even his own father had done work in his early career on industrial accident data, and had railed against the idea of root causes as an overly simplistic way of looking at anything, overemphasizing what people had done and ignoring equipment design failures and environmental factors. A classic case of people thinking they had more control than they actually did. But the idea of a golden root cause was sexy, and therefore marketable, so business had embraced it and even the army, however misrepresentative an idea it probably was.

"We concluded our best shot was the fossil fuels dependency," David was saying, "and the whole suite of para-climate-change issues. That one idea underlaid so many conflicts and regional power plays, it was a high probability target for altering the timeline. But if we were going to change anything to do with fossil fuels, we knew we had to go back at least into industrialization. By the time we're past the Second World War, the infrastructure for fossil fuels is well established. We couldn't hope to deviate the timeline that late."

"Why not go back further?" Leo says. "Why not the renaissance? Start before anyone starts making machines."

"There's a power law," Helen says from the doorway. "The further back you want to go, the more The Machine has to bend the transmission beam, and the more power it needs. We run into a theoretical limit."

"A theoretical limit?"

"Well, a practical one too. The Machine would just short the grid, or tear the magnets apart. Theoretical in the sense that with different materials, we could go further."

"Okay," Leo says, looking down at the table running the length of the long wall. Along it is a printout from an old-school continuous paper printer, with a timeline marked in month increments. He's standing right in front of 1905, the tickmarks annotated with significant events like *Einstein publishes special relativity*, *Automobile Association founded (UK)*, *HMS Dreadnought laid down*, and another bunch of entries on the Russian revolution and the Russo-Japanese War. Many of the entries are highlighted in different colors, with coded numbers written alongside highlighted strips and large arcs running between events over months and years.

David steps in to his left, and walks earlier in the timeline, pointing. "The maths is complicated, but this is where the opportunity appeared optimal."

Leo follows David's finger to 1873. Here, many of the highlighted lines have converged on *Tesla graduates school, cholera*. "Wait," Leo says. "You're talking about *the* Tesla? Nikola Tesla?"

"None other. Greatest mind of the industrial age. Probably of the last two hundred years. The most underappreciated inventor in history."

Leo looks at the plans of that laboratory again, a hollow feeling in his stomach. "Sure," he says. "And also certifiably insane."

David's eyebrows tweak. "He was *colorful* in his later years, and had a great deal of difficulty maintaining investment, which frustrated him endlessly. But not insane."

"He talked to pigeons," Leo says.

"Quirks are the burden of any brilliant person ahead of their time, you know how it is," David argues, making a gesture at Helen.

"Hey," she says. "Not funny."

Leo takes a breath to say that Tesla also claimed to have invented a *death ray*, but seeing as London has just been fragged with said death ray, his argument rather loses its punch. Leo points a finger at the building plans on the wall. "So what is this place?"

"The Royal Laboratories," Helen says. "In the timefield, they—I mean, *we* brought Tesla to London. In our timeline, he has nearly a decade of lost years before he went to America. We used that time to push him ahead. Set him up with his very own patents, any information we could find from his life, and asked him to realize more than he had in this timeline."

"Push what research ahead?"

"He's the champion of electromagnetic systems. We needed his research to advance enough, and without financial problems, to produce lasting change. It's hard to do. Small changes get washed out in the tide of other social forces. In Tesla's early life, the 1870s and 80s, industrialization already has momentum. There are investors with money tied up in businesses and patents, and that produces a lot of counter-inertia. Coal's already been used for a long time. We needed a critical mass of impact to produce a stable, lasting change away from internal combustion engines and oil-based economies. He was the critical pin, capable of doing the work."

"What about his rivalry with Edison?" Leo asks. "The two of them had a very public brawl about electrical currents in the States. It set the standard for what we're using now. Isn't that important? How can it happen if you've parked him in London?"

"It could happen another way," Helen says. "Or it won't matter at all with what Tesla does here. That rivalry is the old past. It might not figure in the new one."

"The point is, electric power needs to be ahead of the game by the time we're heading into the world wars," David says. "All the analysis showed that. We need a race for solar and fusion in the post-war period, not oil-driven conflicts. And Tesla has exceeded our expectations. He's an amazing scientist. Runs a full laboratory, patrons other development, innovations are incredible. He had wireless power delivery within a year of the laboratory opening."

Leo looks over the building plans on the wall, trying to imagine so much happening in just one place. "And where is this lab?"

"Up near Whitechapel," David says. "Tesla wanted to be located in an impoverished area, so the wireless power delivery would have a true test."

Leo frowns. That's not far from his tiny apartment. He knows the place was one of the worst slums in Victorian times, the scene of Jack the Ripper and myriad Dickensian miseries of impoverished Londoners. But London then was also a city governed by Monopoly-board feelings of geography and class. Changing that one place must have sent shockwaves through the rest of the city, too. This wasn't a small change, it couldn't be. But standing here in a basement, just staring a building plan, he can't imagine what it's like.

Chapter 6

Araminta, Lady Montague, first heard about Tesla in the summer the lights came on in St Alberts borough, which was many miles from her family's very respectable town house. She heard about Tesla because the servants could talk of nothing else. As a lame and generally disagreeable young lady who gave more thought to Darwin's *On the Origin of Species* than she did to the peerage, she found endless fascination in the free conversations to be heard downstairs, and spent many hours eavesdropping behind doors.

There, she learned that a great scientist had opened a laboratory in East London, with a marvelous (her mother would later use a much more derogatory adjective) tower atop, and that all the poor in the new borough now had lights and electricity without cost. The servants were brimming with the scandalous objections of the various noble families, but since the Queen herself was a patron of the endeavor, the objections could not be too vocal. The Queen was adamant about the benefits for the poor, and the new area had been renamed *St Alberts* in memory of her beloved and departed husband, who, she asserted, would have heartily approved of the project, as would god. These two authorities, in that order, quite decided the grace afforded to the whole of Tesla's enterprise.

London quickly acclimatized to the odd borough, which

became fodder for jokes as much as fascination. Tesla himself was rarely joked about. He took on a revered status, at least to the lower classes, and was variously a savant, a savior and a time traveler. Underneath, everyone knew the last descriptor was nonsense. It was merely shorthand to explain his unfathomable brilliance. Only the mystics bought into such ideas. Even Araminta, who hoped beyond all things that Tesla *was* a time traveler, didn't initially give the idea any credit.

That changed three years later, when Araminta accidentally met an old friend.

It happened at an insufferable ball she was forced to attend at her grandmother's house. She'd spent the ball with her back to the velvet curtains, plotting ways to escape not only the party, but the life of marriage and gentle womanly occupations that awaited, while the other young ladies who seemed oblivious to their prison twirled about the floor. It was her most frequent subject of thought at such gatherings.

Finally, after refusing two offers to dance on account of her leg – suitors still asked because her father was rich and in poor health, and she was his only surviving child – she saw her chance. Her mother and grandmother, usually pushing her towards any eligible man, were sufficiently occupied to give her time to slip down the hall, away from the dance and its hundred sweating bodies all overdone in perfume.

This was not so easy to do. The brace on her leg rubbed blisters on her hip, and her walk was slow and heavy, her torso rocking to the side no matter how much she tried to hold straight. She made quite the spectacle, like a wounded animal, and all eyes would turn on her, as if the room were a pack of hunting dogs fixed on their quarry.

On this night, though, there came an indecorous scream from a lady in the company of two inappropriate mashers on the other side of the floor, and so assisted, Araminta made her escape.

She sought out the library, where the air was heavy with the scent of paper and ink. The vaulted ceiling dropped heavy oak cases all the way to the lush carpeted floor, cases stuffed with volumes. These were for status, not to be read, and were mostly on religious or historical topics. At home, Araminta had a secret library, including a copy of Newton's *Principia Mathematica*, not simply any edition but Emilie du Chatelet's French translation. She also had *On the Origin of Species*, a second edition obtained surplus from Mudie's Library, a volume of Leibniz's mathematical writings, and a thick stack of *Philosophical Transactions of the Royal Society* gifted to her, also in secret, from Disraeli many summers ago. She had been so excited at the gift; she hadn't even realized until much later that the ageing Prime Minister might have an interest in making her his much younger wife.

Now, she pulled the desk chair across the ornate carpet and hauled herself up by the first case. She was halfway down inspecting the volumes when she paused, hearing men's voices in the hall.

"I say we take a trip in that revived slum," the first slurred. "What do you say?"

"Into St Alberts?"

"Yes, St Alberts! See the blinders floating in mid-air and the painted Judys, and all the inventions from the future."

Araminta recognized the mashers from the ballroom who'd enabled her escape. She caught a tendril of sticky sweet scent, and pressed herself against the case. Let them not come into the library and find her up on a chair. She knew men like these; they made her nervous, and she couldn't climb down from her perch quickly or easily.

"My cousin went last month and says it's nothing but rank lies. Place is full of swells and netherskens, just done up in better clothes."

Their voices were louder, right by the door.

"Where's your courage, man?" demanded the first. "I wager we'd have a better time than here. We'll hail a cab and be on to a grand evening. Fitzhenry said he got to see the bones in his hands! Better than the sorry cases in this house. And, I hear if you throw a rock at the Tesla Royal, it explodes in a jet of stars!"

Their footsteps were so loud. Araminta braced, her heart all thready in her chest. She heard a guffaw of laughter in the hall, but then nothing more. She breathed a few long breaths, before being sure they'd passed on.

Then came a hot surge in her chest. Well, that was just perfect! Young men could go wherever they pleased; even opium fools like those ones, while she remained a captive to injury and propriety. She wanted nothing more than to see the world that Tesla was making, but her mother had declared that it was a wicked and unsavory place, and had forbidden the carriages to travel past it, let alone through it. The closest Araminta could come was articles in the newspaper, which were sometimes written by Tesla himself. He spoke of free energy for everyone in the world, a new kind of train that could cross continents in hours and that produced neither steam nor smoke. He wanted to raise everyone from poverty and into boundless opportunity. Araminta knew a revolutionary when she heard one; Araminta's mother called him unnatural.

She stood there daydreaming away her anger, her hip aching, for she didn't know how long. Until another footstep close by the library door startled her. She whirled to see a man in black, and promptly overtoppled the chair.

She gave an involuntarily and very unladylike squeal as she fell, landing hard on her hip, and in a tangle of skirts. The footsteps rushed towards her, and she threw her hands up over her face in defense.

"My Lady, are you hurt?" said the man, his hand cupping her shoulder.

Araminta lowered her hands and found before her a greying chin beard, and a long face lit in the glancing light. "Mr. Disraeli!" she exclaimed, at once relieved and deeply mortified. "I mean, Prime Minister."

"Araminta? My, it *is* you," he said, drawing back to look at her. "I'm terribly ashamed to have frightened you. I regret this is entirely my fault. Here, can you rise?"

He fussed about, helping her on to her feet, and then to a padded chaise before he righted the desk chair. Araminta assured him she was fine, which was a lie to conceal how much her leg was paining, and told him he was free to leave.

"Nonsense! I haven't seen you this several years. I was just asking after you this last month, when I had cause to meet your father. Is his health improved?"

Araminta shook her head.

"I'm sorry to hear it. I don't care much for parties. Unless you would prefer to be alone, I would much rather take a few moments here among the books."

"I think we find agreement in not caring for parties," Araminta said, recovering herself. "I also much prefer the company of books."

〈〈 〉〉

They had the most agreeable conversation, about all the books he had read and would recommend. In the company of other powerful men, Araminta could scarce utter two syllables, but Disraeli was always different. Perhaps it was because when they had first met, now some twelve years ago at her father's country estate, Disraeli had encouraged her interests. And if he didn't know much of science himself, he at least had asked after her studies, then treated her as a peer, telling her all about the novel he was writing, and about the political situation of the day. All of this was much to her mother's chagrin, but Disraeli was too important for her to discourage. This first meeting had set the tone for all their infrequent meetings since.

Disraeli's face was now lit with pleasure. "Find anything in that case that you want to read?"

"Sadly, no," Araminta said. "They have nothing on mathematics, or sciences, or anatomy."

"Ah, your tastes are still running to scholarship, then, excellent," Disraeli said. "You must have read all those Royal Society transactions I gave you. Whose work is most exciting your sensibilities right now, then? Do you agree with Darwin, or take exception to his theories?"

"Actually, I am most interested in Mr. Tesla," she said.

This produced an unexpected response from Disraeli. A very slight recoil in his posture, that perhaps another person less attuned to others would have missed, before he slowly nodded.

"But of course. Why wouldn't you be interested in the most public of advancements?"

"Forgive me, Mr. Disraeli. You are not an admirer of Mr. Tesla?"

"Of course I admire him. He is a most inconceivable genius."

"But? I detect some reservation."

Disraeli sighed, and leaned forward, as if her perception

compelled him. "But ... there's a saying in politics, 'two things are best not observed when being made: laws and sausages'."

Araminta laughed, enjoying the rare naturalness of their conversation. "Is Mr. Tesla making sausages?"

Disraeli grinned. "Mr. Tesla is a purist and makes beautiful things. If money and materials were no object, he would spend every hour of the day bringing his inventions to life. It's everyone around him who has to make the sausages."

"He has problems of finance?"

Disraeli hesitated, in a way that Araminta knew he was straying into areas his ordinary scruples would forbid him to talk about. Then he rubbed a hand over his face, so that his wrinkled skin tugged across his skull. He seemed very tired to her in that moment, perhaps tired of not being able to speak freely.

"Finance, yes. What enterprise does not have problems of finance? But also business, and law. Many people have interests in Tesla's work. The Crown has invested money, as has the parliament. And investors want to see returns. They all have competing desires, not least with Mr. Tesla himself."

Araminta sat back in the chair, forgetting the pain of her leg. "I don't understand, Mr. Disraeli. Is Mr. Tesla not doing what they want?"

"Tesla does what *he* wants," Disraeli said, with a trace of bitterness. "He thinks about the far-away future, about improving the plight of the disadvantaged. Honorable, yes. Before he built his tower, the subjects in the surrounding area lived in the most wretched of circumstances. Now, they need no coal, gas, or oil, and yet their homes are lit and heated. Their spirits are lifted, and they embark on business endeavors of their own. I must admit I can't keep up, what with the Eastern question dominating the cabinet. The problem is that Tesla does not want to focus on the things that were promised to his investors."

Araminta, who had leaned right forward through this tract, considered her next question. She had desperate interest to know the details of what Tesla was working on, but she knew Disraeli didn't concern himself with the details of science. He saw the beauty of Tesla's work, but not the beauty in the privileged details. So, she said, "You know they say Mr. Tesla is a time traveler. When you speak of him so, I can almost believe it."

Disraeli paused again, and fixed Araminta with an unexpectedly intense stare. "Would you believe such a thing?" he asked.

"I think it would be the most fascinating ability to have journeyed to the future," she said. "But I know such things are rumors, spread by newspapers and mediums."

"Mr. Tesla has no need of parlor tricks," Disraeli said, still staring. "If I were to request your company for a carriage ride, would you mother object?"

That was how Araminta first saw Tesla's wireless blinder lights, burning in the evening air throughout St Alberts. They were not, as promised, hovering in mid-air, but hung in all manner of places: from slender poles set into the pavement, from lines strung across between the narrow streets, on the horse bridles of waiting handsome cabs: little orbs of bright blue without filament or flame.

Disraeli had the driver take her through all the streets in diminishing loops towards the center. While the houses were certainly impoverished, she saw no beggars, and the air was clean and smelled of something sharp and exotic.

"Smelting," Disraeli said, when she observed it to him.

"The borough is now a hub of small industry. With nearly limitless power, they are producing aluminium in vast quantities. A St Albert's aluminium dinner service is quite the fashionable item, I hear. And there, my dear, is Royal Laboratories."

The cab pulled to a stop outside a great hulk of a building, its walls yellow brick, rising three levels into the evening sky. It was not a handsome building; too blocky and without adornment, its windows strangely flush with the walls, and with a bare stone pavement separating it from the rest of the borough. Light burned in the topmost windows. When Araminta reached for the cab door to get down, Disraeli put a hand on her arm. "I don't advise it," he said. "There are always protestors here. Your mother wouldn't approve of me putting you in such proximity."

Araminta saw then the sad collection of men and women, bearing placards outside the gates. One sign read, *A Woman's Place is in The Home.* Another, *Each in Their Place as God Wills.*

"But what are they protesting?"

"Progress," Disraeli said. "Some believe Tesla is upsetting the natural order of the world through his innovations, which are allowing the underclasses to rise above their birth. And more specifically, because he allows women in his employ."

"He does?" She was nearly breathless with possibility. "Do you believe it's against the natural order, Mr. Disraeli?"

"I believe a woman is the equal of a man in intellect, should she choose to exert it. But my dear, do not believe all you see here is a utopia. There are problems, both that Mr. Tesla and the rest of us have to deal with."

"Problems of what sort?"

Disraeli leaned in, and spread his hands. "Everyone wants what they can get from all this advancement. The Americans have been particularly problematic, trying to buy meetings, make offers to Tesla. Thomas Edison himself sent representatives seeking conferences with him, which we had to rebuff, so instead they are investing in the city, buying up that Underground line for example. But then certain weapons were discovered, a corruption of Mr. Tesla's work, and bound offshore. Fearfully good for the army, that new unit I mentioned before, though we wouldn't want them to fall into foreign hands. Don't trouble yourself, though, my Lady," he said, taking in Araminta's horrified expression and patting her hand. "We have resolved that particular problem. It just all requires constant vigilance."

"Tesla is a man much in demand."

"Yes. Unprecedentally so. Aside from Victoria herself, he is the most visible emblem of the Empire."

Araminta turned back to the shining lights of a world outside. "Mr. Disraeli, back at the party, when I mentioned people say that Tesla is a time traveler, you did not deny it."

Disraeli grunted. "Araminta, if I tell you something, are you able to keep it your sworn secret, and never utter a word of it again to anyone, whether servant or family?"

Araminta's heart was thudding. In the pause before she said, "I am", she had the sense that her life was about to wrench in a new direction, like a moon captured into the orbit of a new planet.

"The rumors are partly true," Disraeli said. "About ten years ago, men from the future – more than a hundred years hence – brought Tesla to London. They set all of his work in motion. Tesla was to be a great scientist anyway, but these men gave him his own future work to build on, and knowledge of the next century. They convinced us it was of grave importance that we sponsor his work."

Araminta's voice carried an edge. She was not at all in the mood for games. "I have never known you to jest, Mr. Disraeli."

"My dear, I would not construct falsehoods about something such as this, and least of all tell them to you. Tesla's work is, perhaps, the most important thing the Empire will ever do. My own station as Prime Minister has been extended on account of the information these future-men gave, so I can attest to their knowledge."

Outside the carriage, one of the protestors leaned back and hurled an object towards the laboratories. It met the window with an explosion of orange sparks, like a comet tail streaking across the night. Araminta bumped her head on the carriage window trying to see. When the smoke cleared, the building's window was in one piece, and she saw nothing hit the ground.

"Amazing," she breathed.

Disraeli called for the carriage to move on, and they passed a few blocks in silence, his disclosure sitting like a monolith between them. Eventually, Disraeli cleared his throat.

"I hope I have not burdened you with this information."

"Not at all," she said, though her mind had begun calculating possibilities.

"I hoped that perhaps you would write to me. I'm an old man, now, and I would enjoy the opportunity to read your letters. Discuss whatever subjects take your interest. I am too busy for socializing much."

Araminta had no desire to write letters, but she agreed

because she felt she owed him something for the secret he had told her.

"And if you like," Disraeli said, seeming very pleased. "There is to be a private demonstration at Tesla's residence, next fortnight. Perhaps you would accompany me?"

《〇》

Araminta attended the private demonstration at Tesla's residence in a haze of carefully controlled excitement. It would not have done to display any enthusiasm to her mother as she left; such a thing could only be suspicious. But once Disraeli escorted her inside the Baker Street house, she felt she had entered a pleasant dream she had been waiting for all her life.

The downstairs was crowded; a large desk took the center with stacks of papers and equipment surrounding it, like familiars attending their master. The actual master of the house, however, provided his demonstration upstairs. There, Araminta joined the small gathering of politicians and industrialists around an expansive display secreted under a cloth.

Tesla himself emerged without ceremony, for he needed none. He was dressed in a tail suit with oiled hair and a commanding presence that silenced the murmurs in his audience. Araminta realized it was the first time she would hear him speak.

"Tonight, I shall show you something new," he said, in his soft exotic accent, "a train system that will revolutionize travel – quiet, fast and clean."

He drew back the cloth to reveal a detailed model of a cup-shaped track. Tesla reached out to a string of carriages set within the track, and pressed a button. The toy sprang to life, accelerating softly, until it was speeding around the track faster than Araminta had ever seen anything move. All those gathered watched the looping train, heads back and forth as at a tennis match. Araminta wrested her eyes away and caught Tesla's, who was watching for everyone's reaction. She smiled – an uncommon expression for her – and was rewarded with a small nod.

"The train uses no conventional rails," Tesla said. "It burns no coal, uses no water. Electromagnetism causes it to float on its track, making the journey comfortable and efficient, even at great speeds. One could journey from London to Edinburgh in little more than an hour. This is, of course, only a model. But a working model, displaying the exact apparatus that could be realized on a passenger train."

This produced gasps and consternation among the attendees, who began to talk at once.

"What are your thoughts?" Disraeli asked, forcing Araminta to attend again to the train model.

"I think that a world with these machines is very different from ours."

Disraeli seemed to like her answer. Afterwards, he steered her towards Tesla. The man was being addressed from every angle with questions, but he seemed to be able to answer them all at once, and he paused to shake Disraeli's hand.

"Mr. Tesla, may I present Lady Araminta Montague. She is very interested in your work."

Tesla kissed her hand, leaving Araminta blushing. "I am flattered with your interest, Lady Montague. What did you think of this invention?"

On the way home, Araminta could not recall what she had said. Disraeli was telling her how much he had enjoyed her first letter when she said, "I wonder, Mr. Disraeli, if I might write to Mr. Tesla also? If it would not be improper."

Disraeli tapped his chin, and Araminta thought she detected a glint of hurt. "If you wish," he said at length. "Send them to me at Downing Street, and I will forward them with the official correspondence. And perhaps I will see you again soon, if you let me know the next party you would like to avoid."

He smiled knowingly, his good mood recovered, and Araminta chose to ignore any suggestions in his comment. The world had opened its possibilities before her tonight.

Chapter 7

Helen goes back to running numbers on the workstation while Leo sits staring across the abandoned offices, trying to assimilate everything he's been told. David stays with him, ostensibly to organize a pile of boxes in the back corner, but probably to keep an eye on him. Either way, they fall into logistical conversations about the timefield. How long did the facility take to build? How big is it? How is it organized?

"Tesla runs his own areas, and most of the rest of the building supports him. A workshop, with its own foreman, a reagent laboratory that makes anything chemical, and quite a good library. There's a domus supervisor called Forbes who has master control over everything, save Tesla himself."

"Forbes, huh?"

"Think old-fashioned, stuffy butler," David said, still digging. "Came with a recommendation from the Queen herself, so he's a bit pedantic, but keeps excellent records. And tracks all the stock that's delivered, supervises laundering of all the lab cloths, manages a cleaning staff. That kind of thing."

Leo stares at the building plans. "It doesn't seem real."

"Sure. It's easier when you've been there."

"And the building all runs on a steam-driven generator?"

David laughs. "An actual steam engine, if you can imagine. Repurposed 2-6-0 locomotive. Provides the whole building with steam for heating and a few other systems, plus hot water, and it runs the generator for electrical power."

"Okay …" Leo says, rubbing his head, trying to imagine a steam train on blocks in a building basement. "But it's coal powered?"

"For now."

"So what exactly has Tesla changed?"

"Well," David says. "People can heat their homes for free. They can build appliances that run on power in the air. The place has become a hotbed of entrepreneurship. It's like a frontier town …"

David goes on, describing again the new affluence of the borough. Leo had heard this before. "What about the rest of the city?" he says.

"Well, I wouldn't want to give you the idea it's a new world," David says. "It's all fairly primitive, still, what with all the steam engines and the soot, and bad tailoring."

Leo laughs. "You think steam engines are primitive?"

"I'm not diminishing their technology, Leo. It's just hard not to see how far we've moved on since then."

"You know that most power we generate still comes from steam, right?" Leo says. "Coal, nuclear, solar-thermal, geothermal … they're all just different ways to boil water and do exactly the same thing that a steam engine does — use the pressure to turn a shaft around and make power. We didn't get silicon-based solar cells until after the Second World War. Sure, we've made steam processes more efficient, but we're not *that* much more advanced than the Victorians. We've just got a better coat of paint. And sanitation."

David leans back. "Maybe," he says finally. "But there's one thing we're much better at than the Victorians."

"What's that?"

"Killing each other. You have to admit that nuclear warheads and city-fragging particle beams are a long way from muzzle-loading shotguns."

Leo heaves a breath. "Yeah. I'll give you that one."

«‹›»

Still, Leo nurses discomfort with the whole timefield. There's always a rub. His father had always said that the greatest human fallacy was the idea that technology will solve all our problems. Technology always comes with new problems, and it doesn't always solve the old ones. When Leo had been a solider, everyone had been anticipating how drone warfare would keep pilots safely in a building, instead of in actual aircraft, their expensive high-trained arses vulnerable to being fragged out of the sky. Or for robotic soldiers, who could clear a building without loss to your human assets. And drones and robots had done those things … and then they'd also led to decisions that didn't consider the enemy in front of you; that left remote drone pilots with trauma; and most recently, enabled Britain's enemies to hold the city hostage to a powerful weapon high over their heads. No one could have marched an army into London, even now. But they could send drones clothed in light-eating skin, or an unreachable satellite, or a sleeper cell that lives in the flat next door.

Leo stares at the plans of the building on the wall.

"So what weapons are people making in this new timefield?"

"Why do you say that?"

Leo twists around to find Helen standing in the

doorway.

"The first thing that happens with any new technology is someone tries to make a weapon out of it. Come on. You don't think the first guy that picked up a stick didn't see what he could whack with it?"

David laughs. "We keep the technology under strict control."

"Doesn't seem like it," Leo says. "You said you've got wireless power going out into a whole borough, and a hub of new industry around it. The technology isn't contained. Someone's making something with it."

There's a long silence.

"Tell him about the leakage," Helen says.

David shrugs. "The leakage was contained. We haven't had any more problems."

"What's leakage?"

"We need some context first," David says. "In the timefield, the London lighting grid is just starting up, and free energy like Tesla's providing doesn't generate sales for anyone. Edison has had the Holborn Viaduct generator going for less than two years, and instead people are holding out for free Tesla power."

"Thomas Edison?"

"The same. He's well regarded, of course, but people expect the free power that St Alberts has will spread. Some businesses are jittery. They were digging a new Underground right through St Alberts, and the whole thing was just sold because they don't know if they'll turn a profit, if rumors of Tesla creating a new train system comes about."

"A new train system?"

"Only a rumor," David says. "But enough to spook some investors. Not everyone, though. Edison's the one who bought the Underground line. Not everyone puts stock in Tesla."

Leo grunted. "So that's the leakage? Rumors?"

"I'm coming to that. Tesla's rubbish at the business end," David says. "Sometimes his work just escapes his lab. He promised one of the investors a weapons system, some kind of ray gun, I think, and next thing the Met finds one in the hands of a thief. Didn't know how to use it, of course. The Met brought it to Tesla because they didn't know what it was, which is how we found out about it."

Leo frowned. "Ray gun?"

"Rain gun?" David says, snapping his fingers. "Electric driven, magnetic, very high velocity, something like that."

"You don't mean *rail*gun?"

"That's it."

Leo rocks back. Railguns were one of those Holy Grail technologies that worked flawlessly in science fiction and typically disappointed everyone in real life. Where conventional guns used explosives, railguns exploited electromagnetism to accelerate projectiles. That made them cleaner – less sitting around scrubbing gunpowder residues out of barrels – and able to throw out projectiles at speeds that put conventional guns to shame. The applications weren't just weaponry: railguns might put payloads into orbit, slashing the cost of accessing space. All this was enough for anyone with the science-nerd brain circuit to experience a body tingle at the possibilities, which is definitely part of what Leo is experiencing now.

The other part of what he feels is a paradigm shift, as his knowledge of the weapons world broke up and imploded. Because for all these advantages, railguns weren't real. They certainly weren't carry-around-in-your-hip-holster real. Sure, you could make one with basic materials, but to achieve the kinds of projectile velocities that were promised, you needed to solve the complexity of the power supply issues. Government programs had demonstrated working prototypes, but they were the size of ships. Hand-held ones weren't something that existed, even now. But if they did exist, they could throw a bullet in his direction at twice the speed of any conventional rifle, which would probably be enough to blow a soft target clean apart. He swallowed audibly.

"Jesus," he says. "Did it work?"

"No, just a hack job," David says. "Probably made to plans by an enthusiastic amateur. After that Tesla became very cagey. I almost wonder if it was him that leaked it, just to thumb his nose at the investors. That's why I say leakage doesn't matter. We had one incident, and nothing came of it. Tesla's on top of that now, he understands the stakes. The fact is this timefield has been running for ten years in their time. We have the changes we need. We're just confirming the stability, and then we'll close it down and reap the benefits. Do we need reminding that just a few days ago, someone lanced through this city with a particle beam? Thousands of people are dead and you want to know what pea-shooter someone might be cooking up in a slum a hundred years ago?"

Leo takes a breath. There's not really much he can say to that without sounding like a jerk. All the same, he looks around the room, at the bits of paper stuck on the walls, the archive boxes held together with duct tape.

"Ok," he says. "When it comes down to it, you're telling me that this R&D outfit – that no one's ever heard of, with two remaining staff, located in a poorly plumbed basement in Blackfriars – has a time machine, and is planning on readjusting the fate of humanity on the basis of some calculations on dot matrix paper and some lab experiments with paint?"

"Three staff," David says, with a wry lift of his lips. "And I wouldn't put it like that."

"Right," Leo says, impossibly conflicted. "Excuse me while I go prepare for the end of the world."

《〈〉》

By the time the London sunrise is leaking in between the buildings, Leo is up on the roof again, shivering in his shirtsleeves and clearing the hand-of-god debris with short swipes of his boot. Out here, he can still pretend that the shit going on in the basement is some kind of fantasy. But he can also see how ripped up the city is, and it puts a knife in his heart. The air isn't smeared with sirens anymore, because emergency response is maxed out, and there's no one on the street to warn.

Instead, there's columns of smoke rising into the silent air. They'll never be the same again. It'll be one of those cultural moments that roots into the marrow of public consciousness and is remembered, generation on the next, if there even is a next. Leo looks up into the brightening sky and wonders if somewhere up there, that particle beam generator is still lurking. So, he can understand why a physicist like Helen, with that immense power she has, would use it for something like this.

Leo's powers are tiny, but he's deploying them anyway. In his fingers is an ozone detector unit he found in the nuclear decommissioners' lab, linked back to an obsolescent laptop that the nuclear research guys haven't used in a year.

He jumps when the door creaks open. It's Helen, in a thin hooded jumper, the cuffs pulled down over her wrists, so only her fingers are visible around a chipped red mug. "I didn't know you were up here," she says. "God, it looks awful."

Leo doesn't have to look up to know she's referring to the local apocalypse. A lone siren upwails in the distance, a sign of life. She must be thinking about the beam over their heads, too.

Leo finishes with the rig, and stands. He towers over her like this, at least a foot taller, but she seems to have a weight now far greater than the unassuming bookworm sister he's always known. Now, when he looks at her he thinks about the simultaneous genius and terror of what she's made.

"You don't think what we're doing is a good idea," she says, proving she can read his face just as well as she used to.

"I think it's so complicated I can't see how anyone can know if it's a good idea," he says. "I think you ran some equations, and it can't possibly capture how the people will behave. I think you're sampling to measure stability, but you haven't done this before and who knows if you're measuring the right things."

She doesn't argue back immediately, like Leo suspects David would. Instead, she wipes a film of fine ash from a duct and sits under the lightening sky. "I think those are valid concerns," she says. "But the Grid is mathematically robust, and still says we have stable changes."

"The Grid?"

"That's how we measure the changes."

Leo winds the ozone sensor out. "You ever do any game theory?" he asks.

Helen wrinkles her nose. "Not since Dad. More his thing. It's not my field."

"Mine either," Leo says. "Game theory is about why people cooperate. The simplest models just work out what strategy someone should play given certain rules in a game."

"I do remember the prisoner's dilemma," Helen says. "You don't have to remind me."

Leo grunts. The prisoner's dilemma was the classic game theory concept, one their father had taught them while they were still in school. Two people are arrested for a suspected robbery, but there's only enough evidence to charge them with trespassing, so the police offer a deal. Each suspect has to choose whether to keep quiet, or to rat out their accomplice for the robbery. If they both keep quiet, each receives a minimal sentence for trespassing. If one of them rats out the other, the rat goes free and their accomplice takes the fall with ten years in prison. If they both rat, both do five years. The dilemma comes from the fact that while both suspects would get the best outcome from keeping quiet, the best game strategy is always to talk, because it produces the best result no matter what the other prisoner does.

"So you remember the problem is with behavior," Leo says. "A suspect is always going to be sitting there, thinking about whether the other guy is ratting him out, and if he's going to go away for a long time. Better to talk and maybe go free, or at least cut the sentence in half. Cooperating to keep quiet becomes unstable."

"But our timefield is nothing like the prisoner's dilemma," Helen says. "Our people can talk to each other."

"Sure," Leo says, setting the sensor on top of a vent and duct taping it down. "All the basic game theory examples are too simple, that's exactly my point. Life has countless choices, and the system is open. Circumstances change.

Unforeseen forces come into play. People's strategies change over time. Even if someone is cooperating at the start, in time, they try something else to better their situation, or to help someone. Just because they can talk to each other doesn't mean they will. Talking in itself is another game. The strategy you start with is never stable. Strategy is always in flux."

Helen is frowning, watching him. She chews her lip. "Why the hell did you go and join the army?" she says.

Leo feels the old steel security shutter slam down behind his ribcage. He can't exactly answer her; he hasn't interrogated his decisions to the point he has words for them. But he knows his lack of interrogation is partly from fear – that if he looks too hard, he'll realize it was all a huge goddamn mistake. So he keeps his head down, until she lets it go, and feels shitty for doing that, too.

"So you don't think it's a good idea because Tesla will stop cooperating?" she says, clearly pissed.

Leo plugs his sensor into the laptop and boots the data logger, which on an old brick like this takes an inordinate amount of time. Helen's question hangs in the air until he confirms the sensor is reading fine.

"No," he answers. "I'm saying there's more people in what you're doing than Tesla. Who else is being affected by the things you're changing? How are they going to alter their strategies? When could that bring the whole thing unstuck? You can't possibly account for all of that."

"The Grid is stable. Whatever we're doing is working."

Leo exhales. "I don't just mean in the timefield."

This clearly surprises her. "You mean here?" she says, slowly, her frown deepening.

"There's only two of you left, now, but how many other people have been involved in The Machine project? I'm guessing you had at least one military team."

The long pause tells him that he's guessed right. When he was waiting for the old laptop's system to defrag, Leo read up on Tesla. Leo's father had idolized the man, so Leo knew something of his later life – the rivalry with Edison, his Colorado Springs laboratory, the Wardenclyffe site on Long Island. The man had left a legacy of incredible invention, mystique, and unrealized dreams. The archetypical mad scientist. But in the late 1870s, Tesla had been barely out of school, and he'd nearly died of cholera deep in the Eastern Bloc of Europe. Nearly ten years would go by until Tesla worked for Edison, and began the career that would lead him to iconic status in the history of invention. And that meant this project must have somehow extracted a teenage Tesla from Eastern Europe and brought him to London, travelling only by steam train and horses. Not exactly the kind of mission Leo had experienced in his military service, but he'd once been the kind of soldier they came to with bollock-mad missions like that. Now, the idea gives him palpitations.

"Yes," Helen says. "We had an assigned section and commander who helped us in the set-up, and ran security for Tesla, before the laboratory was built and Tesla brought his own security system online. Now the place is run entirely with local timefield people."

"But those military guys know about your Machine."

"Yes."

Leo shifts on his haunches. He's got a nice baseline zero reading from the sensor now, and hopes it stays that way. "Did you hear the reports about the sweeps before the hog?"

"Hog?"

"The beam. They're calling it the 'HoG', for *hand of god*," he says. "Lovely isn't it?"

She grunts. "What sweeps?"

"Before the HoG, people were reporting seeing soldiers," he says. "Or at least, highly coordinated people moving through the area, posing as security and taking transportable valuables. Gold. Artworks. Equipment. Data. They knew where the HoG was going to hit. They swept through first, taking what they wanted."

Helen's face is as pale as the sky. "So?"

"You've got men out there – military men – who know about The Machine."

"You think they could try to take it?"

Leo shrugs. "A soldier should know how to keep his mouth shut. But then, strategies change. People get plastered and talk. Then, someone else knows what they know. Information gets out. Half the missions I did in the army came from leaked information."

"It's not like The Machine's transportable."

"Maybe not the whole thing, but maybe they just need plans. Your computer. Some critical parts. Or maybe they just want to stop you from doing what you're doing. If someone knew about the strategy, they could just come and destroy the microtorus. There's a dozen ways for you to lose the game here."

Helen stands, mug abandoned, and hugs herself against the sharp, after-sunrise cold.

"Plus," Leo goes on, "The Machine draws a lot of power. If someone wanted to know where you were, they could work it out. It's not a difficult thing to monitor a power grid. Maybe they already know."

Leo feels the skin crawl over the back of his shoulders even as he says it. Helen's lips close, and her throat bobs a swallow. Her gaze swings to the computer. "What is that thing?"

"Ozone sensor, for early warning. People over in Westminster were tweeting about the fresh smell just before the HoG, and I smelled it here, too. The detector is more sensitive than a nose. I'm running the wires down the stairway to give us an alarm in the basement. Might give us some time."

"How much time?"

Leo shrugs. "If you have to ask, you should leave now. Maybe half an hour, guessing from what happened last time. Who knows if it would be the same."

Helen nods, resigned. "Should we barricade the doors?"

"I've got hammers and nails, but anyone with training could make pretty short work of that."

She ghosts a smile. "You need training for hammers and nails?"

"I mean, training in explosives."

"Okay." She looks up one more time at the sky. Time hangs, suspended between them.

"Do you ever think that we're just in decline?" Leo asks suddenly.

"Decline?"

"You know, that we peaked some time in the past as a species. That everything since then has just been worse. So tomorrow is always going to be worse than today, which was worse than yesterday."

Helen stares at him for a long second. "How can you say that?"

"Isn't it possible? All epochs have a fall. Maybe we're just in ours."

Helen snatches up the old red mug. "I'm going to go check the numbers. If they're good, I'll prepare to close the timefield down. Then we won't need an oxygen sensor, or a Machine, right?"

Leo stands and looks down on her. She's angry; she's being sarcastic, not looking for reassurance. "You're the brilliant one with numbers. Theoretically," he says.

She stands a second, then she says, "Leo, all civilization is unnatural. There's no central control on morality. It's an illusion, a consensus. We have to decide what's best for us to do."

"You don't worry about the hammer-nail problem?"

She rolls her eyes. Their father always used to bring it up: *when all you have is a hammer, every problem looks like a nail.* It was his way of sticking it to specialists, to encourage them to look around and see how other people did things, too. So now, Leo means *he who controls a time machine sees no other way to solve a problem.*

"Yeah, well, the hammer's what we've got left," Helen says, and storms back to the stairs. "When you've shaken off that arsehole black cloud, come down and I'll show you the Grid."

Leo considers if he will, after he's run the wires. But all the time, he's also thinking about who out there knows about The Machine, and what they might decide to do about it.

Chapter 8

Disraeli's letters were usually substantial and interesting enough, but it was Tesla's brief notes that Araminta opened first. He wrote in a rushed hand, simple thanks for her good wishes, and sometimes plans of what he was working on in that moment: 'an apparatus for the future train engine', 'an improvement to the wireless power system', 'a new experiment with radio waves'. These, she read over and over.

As she established this rapport, Araminta worked on the courage to ask Mr. Tesla if he would employ her in his laboratory. She would take anything in such an environment, even if it were cleaning floors. That was the first step in removing herself to a life in St Alberts, or perhaps even in a future time, where she imagined the suffragettes had finally achieved a victory. This hope, she kept locked very deep. One step at a time. The fear of his answer – or worse, of no answer – held her back.

Eventually, she settled on asking if she might see his laboratory at the Tesla Royal and thus make the approach in person. The newspapers reported he had done this for other friends. When the answer came back that he would be pleased to, and naming an evening the following week, Araminta's joy flew into panic: how would she leave the house at that time of night under her mother's eye? It was Disraeli who provided the solution, offering to chaperone her to an evening party as a cover.

Unable to contain her excitement, she had let slip to a maid of the plan to go into St Alberts. This was a grave mistake, which Araminta realized the day before the appointment, when she returned to her room after luncheon and smelled smoke.

It was not the smell of a coal fire, it was something bright and clean, as if hope itself had been set alight and burned to ash. In a cold creeping panic, she limped to the secret void behind the dresser that held her books, and found it empty, but for one lone copy of the Royal Society transactions. In the fireplace, still smoldering, she found the remains of the *Principia Mathematica*'s cloth-bound cover, along with the rest of her library, their pages curled into blackened petals.

Araminta remained kneeling, staring at the dying fire oblivious to the cramp in her leg. Volunteering to attend a social event in the first place was so out of character, it could only make her mother suspicious, and the maid would have confirmed the rest. She knew with superb clarity what would happen now. Her mother would never allow her from the house tomorrow night. Her mail would be intercepted, if it hadn't been already. What had been a prison would become so tight, so binding, that she would never emerge from it again.

Suddenly, she couldn't breathe. Couldn't even shout to call the maid to unstitch her from her corset. In desperation, she plucked the gold-hilt scissors from her dresser and slit the satin from waist to chest. She threw the corset onto the fire, and watched it skeletonize in the flames, the whalebone laid bare for the second time in its existence.

Then, in a calculating rush of intent, she waited for

nightfall.

Between the layers of curtains, she had pinned up an old suit of her father's, lifted from the washing cart two months ago. It swamped her at the ankles and wrists, but a few turns of the fabric and she could limp, and turn and raise her arms, unhampered by skirts and corsets.

Then up went her window sash, and down she climbed to the street. She was really a much better climber than she was a walker, or perhaps it was simply the terrified exhilaration of her own audacity. No doubt someone on the street would see her, an ungainly figure on the outside of the building, but no one chose to call out. Perhaps in her ill-fitting suit, she passed as a sweep.

She stood on the pavement recovering her breath, and her courage. She was the only daughter of a wealthy peer, and stood to inherit his considerable fortune. Yet she was choosing to leave this house to throw herself on the chance of a future in Tesla's laboratories, where she could live between her ears instead of between the walls of a comfortable house. She told herself that Tesla would certainly meet her a day earlier than planned, and she had to believe that, because even Disraeli wouldn't shelter her against the wishes of her mother.

She would not be constrained by these forces any longer. One way or another, she would meet with Tesla tonight.

《〈〉》

At the same moment Araminta was hailing a cab to St Alberts, another soul was also intent on reaching Tesla's laboratory.

William Potts, age fifteen, was dreadfully late, and had no coin for carriages. He sprinted over cobbles, dodged through lanes, and climbed through the basements of two former netherskens, before finally sighting the laboratory. He should have been there hours ago, and Forbes would surely murder him.

He wove between the skirts, canes and trousers of the protestors, vaulted the fence, and paused only briefly to ensure that no tiny licks of blue fire were visible on the building walls before he rapped on the staff door. He pressed his ear to the wood, but could hear only the pounding hammer of his heart. Then the door cracked open, and a long nose appeared, crowning a body resplendent in black and white livery.

"Yes?" said the man, as though the building's domus supervisor had never seen William before.

"Mr. Forbes, sir. I'm so very sorry I'm late, sir." William shoved his palms down inside his trousers, trying to tuck his escaping shirt.

In the dark inch beyond the door, Forbes tilted his long nose to inspect a worn fob. "You are beyond late, Mister Potts. You are unkempt and tardy. Your trousers are falling down, your shirt is stained, and your face encrusted. Others have done your work, or left it to fester until tomorrow. You are—" he paused to replace the fob "—a disgrace."

William made no answer. He knew it would do no good to explain his shirt had been soiled when he ran into a crossing sweep by the Borough Market, or that he was late because of the photographer, who had taken an age to arrange his sister's body for the photographs. Such things could not be rushed. Indeed, the only thing that could have displaced William's dedication to his work, was his dedication to his family. "Please sir," he said. "I need this work."

The door did not move. "Mr. Potts, the Queen herself

patrons this establishment. I may have been overruled on taking you on in the first place, but I can find someone to take your place who will present themselves respectably, and *on time*."

William's stomach heaved at the prospect. He imagined going home across the bridge, to the dark detritus world outside St Alberts, and never returning, his dreams dashed like glass on stone. He would never again see the Queen watching him from her gilt-rimmed portrait in the foyer. Never have the chance to sneak through the building again, to touch the slide rules and machinery in the workshop. Not be able to keep his mother fed, so he could remain in school and become a great engineer like Mr. Brunel, who was capable of building the world Tesla's imagination created. "No, sir, please," William said. "It will never happen again."

But the door had closed.

William hovered, a frozen shadow of desperation under the bright lights of St Alberts, wondering how to recover this loss. In the pre-timefield version of this moment, his response might have been different. Class divide at this time in history—in our version of it—was still so palpable that someone of Leo and Helen's time would struggle to appreciate it. Middle classes had been growing for nearly a hundred years, but the effort and perseverance of lifting oneself from humble beginnings came with a rub: those who failed had only to blame themselves. The upper reaches of the British Beehive had little compassion. In the most impoverished parts of London, that attitude sent the poor to workhouses, and shattered families. This was before the great wars, conflicts that through sacrifice of millions of lives drove a hammer through the siloing of privilege. However, this was not pre-timefield London.

This was Tesla's London.

In Tesla's London, William, and countless others like him, could see a borough transformed through technology. St Alberts was not perfect, but no one suffered cold and hunger or workhouses here. William saw the daily example of the industry of the people. His dreams were not far-off fantasies of changing medieval stars. They were palpably close, and he carried both the determination that his future lay in his own efforts, and the belief that it was more than possible.

That was when he saw the woman in the suit.

He could tell she was new here, uncertainly standing at the end of the lane, watching the laboratory. She had the fine skin of a well-to-do, and while it wasn't uncommon to see women in St Alberts wearing trousers and coats, the clothes were too large for her. She wasn't one of those sharp women in the store fronts who could size you up in one glance. Perhaps she was a new teacher, brought in for the schools, or a fine lady with money on a jaunt. For certain, she wasn't a protestor. Perhaps, she needed a guide.

"You lost, my Lady?"

The eyes that fixed him were sharper than he'd expected. "No, thank you," she said.

"Carry your bags for you? Shilling for a tour of the borough?"

"I am quite fine, thank you. I know my way."

She moved around him, limping towards the laboratory gates. William found himself perplexed: this woman had the bearing and skin of a wealthy lady, and the fine (if worn) clothes of a noble man, but the gait of a street beggar. Something amiss with her leg, he guessed.

"They'll not see you without an appointment," he called after her, testing if her declaration was true. "And if you touch the door uninvited, you'll be sewer food. The bolt from Tesla's field can cook a horse from the inside out in two ticks of the clock."

That stopped her. Slowly, she twisted back towards him. "I have an appointment," she said, but she sounded unsure. "With Mr. Tesla."

William felt his eyebrow curve. "You'll have the codeword for today, then," he said, making up some barrier to entry just to stall her.

She frowned at him, glanced towards the building, then back again. "You came out of the gate," she said. "Do you mean to say you work there?"

Now it was his turn to hesitate.

"I thought as much," she said, and turned away.

Stung, William drew himself up. "I do, too. You want to hear me recite prime numbers? Or calculate a Fourier decomposition?" he said; no reason to mention what he had actually done there was to clean floors and be the general whipping boy for Forbes.

She narrowed her eyes at him, as though he were a street dog who just invited himself into the Queen's coach. William held her gaze, hoping she wouldn't take him up on the transforms; he'd tied his tongue just to pronounce 'decomposition' – it wasn't like he could actually do one. Or at least, not yet. Feeling he might lose the battle, he said, "You don't look the type Tesla would want to meet."

She drew backwards and reached into her pocket, and for just a moment, William thought she was about to draw out a barker, or one of those new sound-breaker specials, the ones that could split a man in half.

Instead, she produced a letter. "How much will it take for you to provide me your codeword?" she asked, showing a gold coin under the letter. "I have an appointment with

Tesla, for truth, but for tomorrow. This note attests it. Now my business with him is urgent and I must see him today. What is it worth to you?"

William stared at the offered money, stuck, because there were no codewords. He had better think of something, and fast. "I can do better than that," he said, his mind racing with possibility. Through this woman, he could have direct contact with Tesla himself, remain in the circle. Maybe even improve his prospects, if he proved himself valuable. "I can take you inside."

He reached for the coin, but she drew back her hand. "You'll have it when I see Mr. Tesla," she said, and turned again for the gate.

William caught her sleeve. "Not that way, my Lady. Follow me."

《〉》

Araminta doubted the bargain from the moment it was made, her unease ballooning as the urchin took her further away from the front of the Royal Laboratories. She had indeed seen him come away from the door, and his waistcoat bore the Royal Laboratories coat of arms above the left breast – even if the waistcoat itself was somewhat soiled and askew. Even so, her doubt grew the further they retreated towards a narrow lane. "Where exactly are you taking me?"

"The direct way," he answered. "The, ah, insiders' way."

Finally, she stopped. "I shall go no further, until you explain why we cannot go to the front door."

"Because of Forbes, my Lady," the urchin said, as if she should understand this. "Forbes? Surely you know he's the domus supervisor, and that he won't admit you without an appointment. My work shift is over, so he won't even allow *me* back inside today. He's extremely strict. But Mr. Tesla spends all his nights in his laboratory, on the top floor. I can take you directly there, avoiding Forbes completely."

Araminta folded her arms. "This is underhanded."

The urchin shrugged. "Once Forbes leaves for the night, he activates Tesla's shock field."

"You said before the shock field was already functioning."

"Did I?" The urchin grinned. "You must be mistaken. No, my Lady, the shock field is Tesla's protection for when he works alone at night. It operates when everyone else is gone, and Forbes is the last to go."

Araminta scowled. This boy was nothing but a hustler. "I have changed my mind," she said, thinking perhaps it would be better to approach this Forbes directly. She was fairly experienced in dealing with servants. A compliment, a demonstration of her letter, and even perhaps playing to her disabled state may be all that was needed. She hobbled back, cursing this boy anew for causing her to walk further than she had needed.

"Best to be going home, then, my Lady," the boy called after her, perhaps a little desperately. "For Mr. Tesla cannot stand Forbes. He will never admit you in his company."

She paused. "Mr. Tesla does not like the man who runs his own laboratory? Preposterous."

"For Forbes is always trying to see inside Mr. Tesla's laboratory," the boy said. "Mr. Tesla willingly shows his friends, but Forbes ... no. Forbes came to his post from the Queen herself. Mr. Tesla had no choice in the matter."

Araminta would perhaps have disregarded this, if Disraeli had not mentioned in one of his letters a tension between Tesla and a man on the staff of the laboratory. She was suddenly unsure of her reception, if she was to appear a day early of her appointment, and in the company of a man Tesla did not regard. Her hopes were too high to risk such a first impression; she was a poor enough first impression as it was. But she could not come back tomorrow. Disraeli would not shelter her overnight; the scandal to him could be too great.

"What do you even know of Tesla's laboratory?" she asked.

The boy launched into a recitation of wonders that the laboratory contained, making it plain to Araminta that he had as loose a grip on science as Disraeli did. But the actual pieces he described ... apparatus for creating giant electrical arcs, components for a new kind of train, sounded plausible.

She sighed. "Very well. But I will have your name, and your position."

"William Potts," the boy said, extending his hand very modernly. "First footman of the Royal Laboratories."

Hesitantly, she shook the offered hand. "Araminta," she said, straightening as much as she could and looking expectantly at the hulking mass of the building. "Now, where are we going?"

William disappeared down the narrow lane. When Araminta caught up, he was hauling open a grate in the street. Below she could see a dark cavern, from which came the sound of trickling water and the smell of a fuggy pond. A ladder dropped away from the edge.

"After you, my Lady," William said.

Araminta stared down. All she could think was that if she was about to die, it would still be preferable to going home.

Chapter 9

Twelve feet under the St Alberts streets, the tunnel was dark and damp and long, and thick with machine noise. To reach this place, the Masked Man had descended two construction ladders for the new Underground line, and continued along the tracks to an unfinished platform. He nodded to a man with a white neckcloth standing by a pile of covered crates, then unlocked a door behind a sheet metal panel and held his lamp high. A sturdy ceiling-mounted gantry ran away into the dark.

The Masked Man did not remove his coat despite the heat radiating from his collar. He did not acknowledge discomfort; he only tried to prepare for everything.

For that reason, he had tried to sleep before setting out. But even after deploying his considerable force of will, had found somnolence impossible. He had been up since before dawn, beset by nerves. He wrestled with the useless emotion as he went, and though he had not conquered it by the time his other men came in view, he betrayed nothing of the feeling to them. He was right to do this. He may not have been able to convince Ford to join him, but Ford and Firestone were barely grown. Only the Masked Man knew Tesla had stolen their future, and he alone could provide prospective restitution, and a full realization of the potential of St Alberts. Therefore, he pressed on.

The air grew cloudy with dust, the machine noise a roar.

The Masked Man pressed a cloth over his mouth. His wireless light began to glow: faintly at first, then as the dirty outlines of the men emerged from the soupy dark, with a strong blue-white hue. They were close enough now.

Blue saw him first, and the drill clattered to a stop. The Masked Man did not like the progress interruption, but he liked these men. They were identified only through the color of their neckcloths. Yellow, short with narrowed eyes, the strongman. Green, missing two fingers, the boring machine specialist. Black, with a heavy brow, was the rig's back-up. White, who he'd passed on the platform, was responsible for the animals, and supplies.

"Where is Checks?" The Masked Man asked. Checks was the weapons man.

The Masked Man himself disliked guns. He believed that war was wasteful, but he planned for all eventualities, including the undesirable use of force. And so he had commissioned the best weapons, from the newest plans. He had blueprints and sketches for the whole building, the schedule of all concerned, and a carefully laid plan. He and his men would be gone before dawn, with the world restored to balance.

Blue responded. "Gone for the clean clothes. We're nearly through."

Pinkerton had done a good job with these men. In top hats and great coats, their beards trimmed to the Albert style, no one would suspect they were knee breakers and cutthroats. Tomorrow they would all board a ship out of London, with their prize in the hold. While others wasted their lives in sleep, the Masked Man would not. The waiting was bad enough. Wasted time, so much waste. He tried to comfort himself by thinking of it as an investment, one that would pay back in time itself.

"How long?" he asked.

"Twenty minutes to break through," Blue said. "Another twenty to make a big enough hole to squeeze in. Then it's making fast the gantry rail, and starting on the inside."

The men waited on his instruction. The Masked Man pulled a thick disc from his coat pocket and depressed the button on the side. It was time.

"Red," he said into the disc.

《〉〉

On the other side of the building, nestled into the end of a laundry lane, Red had been watching the Royal Laboratories most of the day. Anyone who saw him could assume he was waiting on his clothes being de-stained, washed, dried and pressed by the latest electromechanical machines, mangles, and heated drying rails in the industrious lane, while being idly entertained by the ill-organized protestors who gathered each day before the Royal. But Red had no laundry to do. He kept his hat pulled low to conceal the chunk of metal fixed to its brim, above his ear, and kept out of the freezing wind. That wind wormed through the open weave of his shirt and trousers, biting at his ears and the tender outside edge of his nostrils, and bringing gusts of the London stink that could near cleave a man's skull in two.

A crusher strode by on his beat, and Red clicked off the stopwatch in his palm. Twenty-two minutes. The man who replaced this one at the change did the round at a more leisurely twenty-four minutes. A long beat. Consistently the same. Red watched the policeman disappear around the corner. They were always lax in this borough with their circuits, on account of the lights.

He let his eyes fix on a protestor, a woman in a black dress. She was one of those anti-suffragettes, all corseted and big-skirted and bonneted, with a placard that said something like *a woman's place at home*. At least, he guessed it said something like that. Red had never learned letters, but he'd been in London long enough to know the gossip. Mystics were awash with rumor about the future coming early, about wars and women rising up, and flying carriages and other fanciful nonsense.

Red blew on his fingers. Devil's talk, all of it. He only used the wireless talker because his employer wanted him to. He admitted that it made nefarious work easier, and the guns White had supplied were fearsome effective. But when it came to raw truths, he really cared about his pay cheque, where he would spend it, and what that woman might look like under all those petticoats. These were the thoughts of a man who didn't know he would die before the night was out.

"Red."

The voice was a hissing whisper right behind Red's ear.

He slid a thick disc from his pocket, which could have been a snuffbox, and pressed its button.

"Twenty-two minutes on the crusher," he said. "Still no Tesla, and no signal from inside neither."

Across the street, the left sheaf of the Royal's double front doors slid inwards, and a man in butler's livery appeared, holding a broom. Forbes. Red wrinkled his nose. Forbes was a weasel with a pinched face and pockmarks, a stuffy Englishman Red had no time for. Forbes looked out over the street, gave three quick sweeps at the threshold, and returned inside.

"Signal," Red said into the disc. "Workers must be on their way out. I'm movin' to the rear."

"Keep your eyes open," the Masked Man said. "And meet us downstairs."

Red didn't bother to reply. He didn't overthink, he just did his job.

《〉》

As Forbes returned in the front door, he heard the clatter of Tesla's machinists packing up for the day, and sent mental disapprovals for their boisterous volume and free use of curses. He climbed all the way up the grand internal stairs and emerged finally into the attic space, lit only with the three windows on the long sides of the roof, and the blinders over the water tank. He had been charged with ensuring the building was empty, and that was what he would do.

Forbes extracted a portable blinder from his pocket and shone it around. No one here. No one on the second floor, either, which didn't take long to examine. It was only a few unused rooms besides Tesla's lab, which was locked. It always was, even when Tesla was here, no matter how much Forbes tried to impress the virtues of cleaning. The man was so suspicious.

The bell rang across the building-wide speakers for the end of shift, and Forbes waited on the landing above the first floor as the men filed out, taking their volume with them. Once they had gone, he checked through the workshop. He did not go into the partly concealed door in the workshop wall, because Her Majesty herself had bade him not to, just last evening, when she and Brown had come to oversee something with Doctor Blakeney. Forbes never questioned her word, nor what they had been doing. Instead, he knocked on the wall all along that side, and received no signs of life. He rapped on the door of the

Doctor's office, just for completeness, and swept through the reagent lab alongside. No answer, and no movement. He considered the floor clear. Two remained.

He descended to the entry foyer, moved through the library and the goods dock, and inspected finally the rooms behind his own office. Then, down to the basement. Nothing moving there, save the reciprocating arms of the boiler pistons, and the spinning shaft of the generator, and the constant rising steam from the captive locomotive. He sagged with relief. Finally, he climbed the half-flight to the rear-door landing, and put his hand to the peep flap.

He experienced hesitation, the culmination of a week of thoughts on how he could put a stop to this agreement. He counted himself an honorable man, who had served faithfully all his years. He was a custodian of traditions. He did not approve of the way the world was turning, but it was not his place to question the Queen. The honorable thing would have been to hold his station, to decline any violation of the vast trust that the Crown put in him as the defender of this building.

But his debts were larger than even his honor, and he could not go to the workhouse as his father had done. So he opened and closed the panel, twice. A few seconds later, a hard bootstep fell on the threshold. He cracked the door open and without a word, admitted a man in a greatcoat with a red kerchief at his neck.

The man said nothing, simply slipped past Forbes, dark and slick like oil, and disappeared down to the basement. Forbes rebolted the door, knowing he had made a grave mistake. But what was done was done. It would soon be time to leave and pretend he knew nothing about it.

‹‹››

At that very moment, Araminta was considering the folly of her decisions. After the cramped pipe, and the indignity of a blindfold, she was inside the Tesla Royal. A vast space stretched in front of her, stacked like a ship's dock under its high ceilings. It smelled of exotic wood with a hint of coal fire, and another clean and metallic scent behind all of that. The blinder lights glowed down, and she glimpsed bookshelves through a mesh screen.

She should have been relieved. Only, William was apprehensive. He'd heard something. Now she was listening, too, and wondering at how large a mistake she had made.

Chapter 10

"Helen says you have reservations?" David says.

He doesn't ask it in a belligerent way. David reminds Leo of an emeritus professor, drawing out the reluctant student, knowing he has decades of clout to head off any questions. They're back in the lab now, and Helen is supposed to be showing him the Grid, these numbers that give her such confidence. But David's hanging by as she checks something in the data, almost as if he's waiting for something. Leo supposes he doesn't have anywhere else to go.

"You know, Tesla's paranoid about what he's doing. Has this whole security system, commands amazing loyalty," David says. "And the military team were involved in this more than a year ago. Nothing's destabilized since. Helen will show you."

Before Leo can start to wonder why David sounds like he's trying to convince himself, Helen points at the screen, covered in the shifting numerals. "This is the Grid," she says, scrolling through a table of numbers, which expands to fill the whole screen. "Or at least, a sample of it."

Leo scans the first four lines, which mean nothing to him. "What am I looking at?"

"The Grid measures the stretch in the timefield's universal functions, compared to the conditions in our time-space," Helen says. "When it's non-zero, it means that the timefield reintegration would create a lasting change in our universe."

```
0.0006700   0.0000000   0.0000000   0.0000000   0.0006700
            0.0000000   0.0000000   0.0000000

0.0043890   0.0000588   0.0000000   0.0000000   0.0006700
            0.0000000   0.0000000   0.0000000

0.0006390   0.0000000   0.0000000   0.0782500   0.0006700
            0.0000000   0.0000000   0.0000000

0.0000000   0.0000000   0.0000000   0.0000000   0.0006700
            0.0000000   0.0000000   0.0000000
```

Leo stares at the numbers. "But the universe is made of billions upon billions of pieces of information. *What* are you even measuring?"

"The Grid doesn't measure everything, of course," Helen says. "It's a comparative data only. It shows the difference in electron spins in entangled atomic pairs echoing along the light trajectory path."

"Jesus, English, please."

Helen grabs her mug of cold coffee and sets it in front of Leo. Then she plucks a spare tack from the wall and drops it in the cup. "You see the ripples in the surface?"

"Yes, okay," Leo says.

"So imagine now that it was possible to drop the tack the other way, from under the coffee into the air, so that the ripples it made were exactly the opposite of the ones when it was dropped from above."

Leo frowns. "Wait, what? Drop a tack from underneath?"

"It's a hypothetical, Leo. I'm trying to have you see that the ripples from the reverse-tack are the opposite of the first, relative to the same surface. They cancel each other out. If we superimposed them, we'd see nothing." She scribbles on a piece of paper and shoves it towards him.

"Like this. Do you understand?"

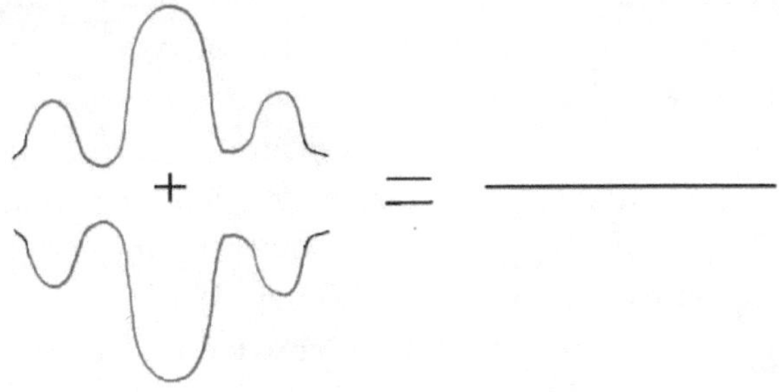

"Yeah, I guess … like combining a negative and a positive image."

"Yes. When we send a ping down the light trajectory path of an open timefield, we get an echo back from the same equivalent space-time of that ping. The same as us, here, that is. When that echo is coming from a universe with no difference to ours, we see nothing. The waves just cancel out. We get a Grid of zeros. But when the universal functions have altered, we see changes. That's the non-zero Grid. It's a sample, but it tells us that the timefield will produce a different reality to ours as it is now. That's why you saw the Grid spikes on the paint experiment footage."

"But you put Tesla in London in the timefield, but he wasn't there in our universe in that year. That's a difference."

"We aren't measuring the timefield at the point we're manipulating it. We're measuring equivalence to our space-time, remember? The timefield's version of *right now*. So a zero result means anything we did failed to change the *future* world in the parameters we're measuring. Now we have a non-zero Grid, we know that we've made changes that last until our concept of *the present*."

"All right," Leo says, though his mind feels all frayed

from trying to wrap his head around this. It's been a decade since he dealt in physics. "How do you know the change is good? Maybe your timefield London-of-today is worse than this one."

"We have some specific measures, comparing the entropy signature for particular event sites. Westminster, for example. Entropy is much lower in the projected timefield, consistent with the houses of parliament still existing, so we conclude the bombing doesn't take place in the timefield. Remember that it's really hard to produce lasting changes. Most actions are just too small to amplify through historical inertia. It took five years in timefield time just to get a non-zero Grid."

"What she means is, this project is a monumental achievement," David says. "This is King-and-country stuff."

"I'm familiar with the idea," Leo says, dryly, reckoning he's spent more hours with a rifle in his hands for the cause of King and country than David has. "So why haven't you closed the loop?"

"We have a protocol to ensure the result is stable for a few days of our time before we close it," Helen says. "There's a time dilation, see, about ten to one. A year here, ten years in the timefield. We can transmit into any sequential time after the last transmission, but there's a hysteresis, too – after we make changes, it takes some time for those to be consistently reflected in the Grid. The protocol just ensures beyond doubt that we're stable. Another twelve hours, and I'm happy we're there."

Leo stares at the coffee mug again. "You know, I do remember some of my undergrad engineering maths. That superposition cancellation thing works for linear waves. Nice, smooth, perfect profile kinds of waves. It doesn't work for foaming breakers, with all their nonlinear turbulence. Two opposites of them crash together, you just get lots of little waves. I might have slept through most of my undergraduate labs, but I remember that."

"It's not water, Leo," David says.

"Yeah, it's just the whole universe you're talking about. That wouldn't be more complex at all."

"It's not about complexity. We're dealing in changes. We don't have to measure everything, just the parts we're interested in."

Leo rubs his forehead. That doesn't sound like a recipe for collateral damage at all. "Coffee, David?" he says, offering him Helen's mug.

"Funny," David says, but he doesn't seem to take offence. He seems more anxious.

When Leo looks back at the monitor, he finds Helen has closed the Grid and is looking instead at a three-dimensional graph in rainbow shades. It looks like a topographical surface, only drawn with lines that smoothly undulate up over hills and down into valleys.

"What's that wiggle there?" he says, pointing to a jagged little wobble in the surface.

"I'm looking," she says. "It's a Grid value that's oscillating."

David leans in. "Amplitude is small. Probably an artefact?"

"Maybe," Helen says, clicking through screens, zooming in, blowing up the lines. They wait as she does this, David tugging down on his waistcoat. "I don't really like this," she says, finally. "I should check the data over the last day again, and run some transforms, to see if this is like anything we've tracked before. And I'll prep The Machine."

David, who is turning away, swings back. "Another transmission?"

"We may need to observe the timefield directly."

"But we're about to close."

"I'm not closing with a possible instability."

"Could it just be hunting?" David says. "That's happened before, and it sorts itself out."

Leo stares at the little wobbles in the lines, each going up and down. *Hunting* put images of old-school steam locomotives in his mind, along with a buttoned-up professor's voice that said something like, *Hunting can occur in any system where dynamic forces cause an oscillation around a steady state.* Then some slides he must have seen once, of train wheel pairs fixed together on their axles, and the swaying motion on the tracks. All very dry and clinical. He'd probably slept through the lecture. It didn't give you the full catastrophic picture of that train at speed, where a hunting wobble became violent, and the whole shit and shaboodle derailed, with consequent ugly death and destruction. Whatever the time machine version was of that, it couldn't be good.

Helen and David are still discussing.

"If this *is* hunting, then there's a too-fast change," Helen says finally. "Could be something Tesla's doing. We need to resolve it. I can isolate the origin of the oscillation and we've enough hours to prepare. The wobble could settle before then."

She gives Leo a glance as she says this.

Leo senses that tacit agreement has sprung up between the two of them, something built on uncertainty about how this game could play out. Despite her earlier confidence, she might have actually listened to him, which he finds quite frightening. Leo hauls himself up.

"Where are you going?" David asks to his departing back.

"To check the HoG sensor and do a sweep," he says, and walks out. He has the sense that the world is starting to spin out of his fingertips. The same, uneasy feeling he had just before the mission that ruined his knee and put him out of the army. And that job didn't even involve a fucking time machine.

❮❰❯

As soon as Leo's gone through the doorway, Helen turns to David. "What aren't you telling me?"

He doesn't answer immediately, just chews his lip, demonstrating doubt she's never seen in him before. Having worked with the blinding confidence of Doctor D these last years, the change in him drops her stomach to the floor.

"David?"

"I don't know," he says. He sounds nervous. Helen never used to pick up on things like that, but she does now. "I can't remember the last trip."

"The last three," she corrects him. "You think something happened?"

He chews his lip again, tugs his waistcoat. "Probably something Tesla's working on," he said, confidence wicking back into his words. "That has to be it."

Helen turns to stare at the jumping numbers. "You know that blip in the data from the other day? I think this is related."

"You said that was a Machine echo."

"It looked like one. Only, the timings didn't quite work out. We didn't transmit any data when it first appeared. Unless …"

"Unless what?"

She shrugs. "I could have missed the first appearance, if it was very small, or lost in another signal."

"But you don't believe that's true."

She shakes her head. "David, I don't want to lose all this work. It's a massive thing we've done here, and I don't pretend it's not sometimes questionable, but …"

"I know." He's staring at her hard now, focused, as if he's decided something. "Helen, how long have we worked together?"

"Four years, three months."

"Then you know that I can fix this. That's what I do. I mean, come on. We've brought a brilliant scientist across Europe. We've established a new research facility. Built it, funded it, produced results. In another time! Whatever this is, it's a detail. We might be down to our last men, but I will do this. Trust me?"

She can't do anything but believe him. "Okay, then."

Chapter 11

By the time Helen is ready to transmit, David has become stoic, focused as if he's about to walk on stage. Leo has no idea what's boiling under the surface … if Leo had to get into one of those metal coffins in The Machine, he'd be wigging out.

The wobbling in the Grid numbers hasn't changed since this morning, except that another of the values has started oscillating. Helen's lips have disappeared into a thin bloodless line.

"How's David going to know what he's looking for?" Leo asks, when Helen has been staring at the unchanging screen for ten solid minutes.

"Huh?"

"You said you could localize the problem. How does he know he's found it?"

"The console." Helen reaches across the bench for the pocked-sized tablet. "Transmissions into the timefield are precise vectors. We align the beam to a specific point in time and space, so we have a space-time map of the timefield. David can have the console locate the oscillations, a bit like following a GPS navigation."

Leo is frowning, looking at The Machine again. "If you align the beam so precisely, you must have had to calibrate it."

In fact, Leo has been thinking about this because he's just done that calibration of the ozone sensor on the roof. Any calibration needed at least two known points. Zero was easy — he'd just sat the sensor in a container he'd flushed with pure nitrogen from a cylinder in the workshop. A non-zero data point was harder, until he found an ozone generator in the geotechnical laboratory on the third floor, which conveniently produced ozone at a known concentration. Hook that sucker up to the ozone sensor, and Leo had his two points. All he had to do then was put both values into a spreadsheet, fit a line through it, and out fell a calibration for any reading of the sensor. Only after he'd gone to all this effort did he realize that he didn't know what reading level to set the alarm at. When it comes to measurements, knowing what you're measuring is everything. And Helen isn't talking about calibrating something as simple as a sensor, which is just a straight line between two points. She's calibrating a photon beam angle to thread the needle of space-time. One would think it was a more demanding exercise.

Helen points to two printouts tacked on the wall, the ones Leo noticed the first time he came here. The graphs curve in an elegant spiral, like snail shells, beginning at the margins of the paper and vanishing into a point on the axial field. "Those are the time-curve calibrations. They feed directly into the program on the computer, of course, but I like having the pictorial on the wall. The maths isn't actually too complicated—"

Leo snorts, and she gives him a dirty look.

"—but whenever I think about The Machine, I think of that curve. There's a unique spiral calibration like that for each point in three-dimensional space. That's why we re-use the same transmission points. No need to keep changing the numbers."

Leo pulls the tack from the left-most sheet and takes down the paper. If he stares at the spiral for too long, it will send his eyes crossed. "Where is this one for?" he asks.

"Our second transmission point inside the Royal, on the second floor. It's in an unused room that we keep locked."

Leo tacks the paper back in place, and points to the next. "And this one?"

"A large outhouse, in St Alberts. We haven't used it in a few transmissions."

Leo mulls on the graphs, feeling queasy. "How did you work out where to aim it at the first time? I mean, what if you cast someone into a wall, or into the moon or something."

"The calculations got us pretty close. Then we sent a camera with a compass and some other instruments and a timed-recall, so we could work out where we were, although we had to do it a few times to achieve a return with actual measurements. Also, when there's an obstacle, the back-pressure on the transmission tends to push the beam, which we don't want. That's why we're using the point inside Tesla's building – nothing moves."

Leo grunts. "So somewhere in the timefield there's a farmer who swears he saw an alien device just appear in his field, and no one believes him?"

Helen laughs. "Maybe. I guess. I never thought of that."

David comes out of the office at this point, tugging down a waistcoat on a very brown suit. "You have those locations?" he asks. "I don't suppose the oscillation is dampening?"

"Still the same," Helen says. "And yes. The first oscillation originates in the basement of the Laboratories. Maybe Tesla's made a change to the generator system? If so, you can meet Tesla and have him roll it back. He understands the implications. We don't need the rollback actually done, just his intent to do it. I'll transmit you after day's end, so you won't have anyone in the building besides Tesla. I'll put you in the second-floor transmission point, so you can go direct to his lab."

David huffs a breath, as if he's about to argue. Then he just says, "I'm putting the kettle on", and stalks out.

"He has a tea drinking ritual before a transmission," Helen says. "Getting in character, I assume."

"How likely is it he's going to be able to fix the problem?" Leo asks. "I mean, what if it's big, or it takes a long time to resolve?"

Helen shakes her head. "It might blow your mind, but information is what's important here. In quantum systems, cause and effect and space-time descriptions are complementary, but mutually exclusive."

"Which means what?"

"The timefield universe already has a past and a future, and intentions are enough to alter it. The appearance of cause and effect is just our human-centered experience of it …" Then she sees the look on Leo's face. "The point is, this is not something unresolvable – the oscillation is too small. Whatever's happening isn't unstable yet."

Yet, Leo thinks, is such a loaded word.

Despite his reservations, the transmission itself feels like a non-event. David returns from his tea drinking, tugging on his jacket lapels, and when Helen tells him to climb into the coffin spaces, he does so without complaint. Leo has to look away, and think thoughts of open pastures and rolling hills.

"The oscillation is damping," Helen says, peering at the Grid graph. "That's good news."

"So David doesn't need to go?"

"No, I mean we're right to do this transmission. Before we use The Machine, we sometimes see an intention spike in the Grid. When we see that, the odds of our changes sticking are much higher."

"How can that happen *before* you've made them?"

Helen gives him a sidelong glance, "You're rusty on quantum effects. Remember: space-time and cause-effect don't exist in the same view of the universe. Effects can propagate backwards."

The computer displays scrolling numbers, reporting statuses and asking for inputs, and Helen authorizes each screen in sequence. The Machine sits, humming as it always does, until a count-down begins, from ten to zero.

"Why the clamps?" Leo asks, through gritted teeth. "On the hatches?"

"You remember what I told you about superposition?"

"Yeah?"

"Would you want the hatch to open accidentally while you're in a here-and-there state? There's a fair amount of vibration in the outer chassis when we transmit."

Then, there's a *whump, whump, whump!* and the high whine of several fine control servo motors, overlaid on the raw, rib-rattling hum of magnetic power.

"Jesus," Leo says. "You never asked me if I had a pacemaker."

"You don't have pacemaker insertion scars, and if you have any bone plates they're probably titanium," Helen says, distracted, scanning the numbers. Leo spends some seconds thinking about when she might have had chance to look. Oh yeah, that's right, when he was concussed after the particle beam burned a hole through London.

"Besides, we aren't inside the field, here. It's extremely contained. Transmission looks good," she says, still frowning, tabbing through screens. Leo watches the dual clocks running above the Grid screen, counting the seconds. Above each is a plain white card. In Helen's block capitals, they say: *Now* and *Timefield*. She opens what looks like a chat window, types a single number. The word "Status?" appears, and she waits, drumming her fingers, until a single number returns.

```
Now> Status?
TF> 1
```

Helen's shoulders relax. "He's there, all fine," she says. "We just used two of the qubits in the console. That's why the coded responses. Zero for negative, one for positive."

"How long is this all going to take?" Leo asks, wondering how much time David would spend inside that tiny space.

"We account for the time dilation effect," Helen says, "A minute here is about ten minutes in the timefield. David was transmitted to right outside Tesla's lab, at a time Tesla is usually there. He'll probably call on Tesla first, then go down to the basement, before returning upstairs to recall. I think a half-hour in the timefield, at most. So he should recall within the next few minutes."

"All right." Leo feels the steel tension ease around his ribcage. He watches the transmission timer, large red numbers at the top right of the screen, scrolling through two minutes, approaching three.

When it ticks over three and a half minutes, Helen goes back to the chat screen, and stares at the response.

The cursor sits, blinking, as another two minutes scroll by. "This is taking too long," she says, and queries the status again.

```
Now> Status?
TF>
```

"Can't you call him back?" Leo says, as the question remains ominously unanswered.

"If he's not in the transmission radius, nothing comes back," Helen says. "And once the qubits are gone, we can't communicate at all."

She lets another ten seconds fly past, then the Grid graph pops to the front, a warning flashing.

"Shit," Helen says.

"What?"

"The oscillation just exceeded a ceiling level I set."

The room contracts in on Leo. He's very aware of The Machine, hulking over the pair of them, the soft fragility of their bone and muscle. Outside, there's a death ray hovering in the sky. In here, there's a powered-up time machine that might be about to upend space-time. He doesn't know which is worse.

That's when they hear the alarm, a *whoop-whoop-whoop*, blaring from the hallway.

Helen jerks. "What's that?"

Leo feels his insides liquify into some non-functional molecular arrangement. For a long second he can't make words. "It's the ozone sensor," he says finally. "For the HoG."

They look at each other as the alarm whoops its incessant ascending notes. Helen's eyes are round with horror. They both know what that means. The HoG is out there, charging with particles, stripping atmospheric electrons and leaving a trail of broken oxygen, their pair-bonds mashed into threesomes.

"How long do we have?" Helen says, pulling back the chat window. Her hand shakes.

"I have no idea," Leo says. "Half an hour? But really, no idea." His heart is a blacksmith's hammer against his ribs.

Helen sends the status question again. After a ten-second pause, this time she gets:

```
Now> Status?
TF> 99
```

Helen sits back in her chair.

"What?"

"It's an automatic code. It's sent if someone without fingerprint access tries to unlock the console."

"Someone else is trying to use it?"

"I think we could assume David no longer has it. Possibly it's Tesla, but he knows about the consoles. Or David could have hurt himself. Or … or …"

The ozone warning alarm blares again.

"So you're going to shut it down?" Leo says.

Helen stares at the screen, shaking her head. "I can't. That oscillation is too large. It needs to be stabilized. If I do an emergency microtorus destruction, we'll lose everything – all the work in the timefield, and probably David as well. It'll all be gone, Leo, do you understand?"

Leo's mouth is dry. "You can try again."

"Not if we're wiped out. And not without David … he's the one who made this all possible. I can't just leave him there."

In those words, Leo feels that kick in his heart, the one that says you don't leave people behind. Helen's eyes swing around to him. "You're a soldier, Leo."

And he knows with horrible certainty what she's going to ask.

"There's a second transmission chamber. You can take another console back, find David and sort this problem."

"Look, um," he says, stalling, because walking into

unknown shit-storms is well behind him. "Um."

"If you don't go, that's it," Helen says. "The HoG wipes us out. We're already dead, Leo. Whatever reason you're cleaning floors instead of still wearing a uniform, you need to put it aside and do this. For all of us. You don't have a reason to live? Fine. The rest of us do."

And just like that night in his apartment when she'd called him out of nowhere, he looks at her and finds enough reason.

"Shit," he says. "Damn you, Helen." He stands, walks across the hall into the abandoned office, and tears the building map down from the wall.

Chapter 12

In a part of his mind that's currently dissociated, Leo remembers a few hours ago, when Helen tried to explain to him what was in the microtorus, the core of The Machine. A small torus, she'd said, and he'd given her a withering look for stating the bleeding obvious.

"It's best to state the obvious sometimes," she'd said. The microtorus is not just small, it's very very small, so that it would more resemble a long noodle joined in a loop, and thousands of times finer than a human hair. It was a single atom-thick loop of gold, on which was mounted an intimate assembly of molecular gears. A kind of nanotechnological charm bracelet. Those molecular gears were spun by a glancing beam of light, in much the same way that a mill wheel turns in a stream. But The Machine's microtorus could spin with so little friction, that the surface rotated almost as fast as the light. And that was what made the time travel possible.

Leo had looked at his hands and wondered at the scale of it. Helen was talking nanometers and angstroms and probabilities, things with a purity he could never match. He could design a torus out of sheet metal; she'd designed one that could send a signal through time.

He'd asked then, who made the molecules? Bacteria, she answered. Factories encoded in DNA. This was the part she'd borrowed from David, because the artificial brains he worked on used the same kind of process to repair themselves. But The Machine took that technology and made a new universe. Spin the microtorus, and a path around the outside would arrive back in a timefield. All you had to do was shoot a string of information – a beam of transcendent light – on the right course, and you could send anything back.

All you had to do. She'd actually said that, which was the point at which Leo lost track of the conversation.

Now, The Machine is a dim outline of chrome and coils across the lab, and Leo's heart is thumping behind his ribs like artillery fire.

Against all this noise, he hears a new sound, a thumping of rotors in the air outside. Leo feels it, but he doesn't know if it's real, or a memory drawn up by the idea of getting into that small coffin space. Then it's gone, leaving an uncanny silence, a horror movie soundtrack just before the attack.

"You're going to arrive inside the building," Helen's saying to him now. "On the second floor, in an empty room. I'll get a fix on David's location just before transmission and send it to the console. Use that to find him, then deal with the oscillation together."

She presses the console into his hand.

"Run your finger across here to code for access."

He does, but this is all moving too fast now.

"When you find David, both of you need to come back to the transmission room, or within a few meters of it, to recall yourselves. This is how you do it."

Leo only catches the barest of the steps she shows. A particular icon, labelled *Recall*, a number of steps asking for confirmation.

"Do you want this?" she says, pausing to open the drawer of the control desk. She points to a Glock 17, nonchalantly resting beside a spare box of pens.

He shakes his head, thinking about the sound of the

helicopter. "You might need it here."

"You'll be back in three minutes, our time," she says.

Then he's facing The Machine, the crawl space through the door into the coffin chamber looming larger and larger. Leo goes through the doorway, almost outside of himself. He presses a shoulder against the hard roof and even though it's bigger in here than he anticipated, he has to swallow the panic that says get out get out get out.

Just like when he was trapped under that building, his leg broken, and thinking he would never see sky again. He has to focus on closing that clamp, his fingers slipping.

His last glimpse of Helen is her leaning across the hatch, then it slams and he's in the echoing dark. He thinks he hears her footsteps departing, but everything feels a bit … odd.

Time simply ends.

Leo feels his ears pop. The walls distort. A *whomp* reverberates through his chest, like an explosion has gone off in his heart. For seconds, he can't breathe. His body is stuck, fused rigid and hung impaled on his last thought. Then comes a smell: hot metal, burning slag, the smell of foreboding, like standing outside the gates of hell. His vision vibrates and comes apart in a pixel swarm. Then his body simply loses awareness, and the critical things that make him Leo suspend, and are copied into light.

《〉〉

Once The Machine has transmitted, Helen closes down everything except the systems that keep the microtorus spinning. There's a big capacitor in the system which helps even out the current, and the UPS, but those can't sustain The Machine for long. Besides, the UPS hasn't been tested in a long while, and The Machine transmissions suck electrons like a demon vacuum. Her skin still thrums from the vibration, as if the entire laboratory is airborne and just flew through turbulence. Mirage heat ripples from the cooling vanes.

She eyes the running clock. Leo should need only three or four minutes. Then he better be back, because he was right. She knows it's no big thing for a foreign nation to monitor the power grid. Someone will have noticed.

The elapsed time approaches two minutes, then three.

Doubt burrows into her mind like a tap-root through a stone. Any second now. Any second, they'll be back. But the Grid keeps dancing and there's been no intention spikes this time. Nothing has changed. Nothing.

Shit.

Then one of the calibration sheets vibrates loose, the one Leo took down before. Helen hears the fallen drawing pin *tink-tinking* across the desk, a tiny noise that saves her. Because while she crawls under the desk to retrieve the paper, a shadow falls under the lab door.

She sees that shadow as she's emerging with the calibration sheet in her hand, and her blood freezes. Instantly, she's back under the table, her heartbeat a hummingbird in flight. She senses a shape outside the door. A dark shape. Searching. Hunting. Someone.

In that moment, she thinks of Leo. Of all the times she wondered if he was doing this kind of thing, somewhere in enemy territory. Camouflage stripping his identity as her brother, as anyone's brother, a faceless agent with a rifle in his hands. She shouldn't have thrown that beer in his face. But he shouldn't have left either, not then. She needed him, and he wasn't made for killing things.

Then again, if he hadn't gone, would she be here right now? With The Machine? With this chance to assign so much destruction to never-happened?

Then comes an electronic pop, and the door bolts *thunk*. Security overridden. The door swings open, revealing a man in black, holding something long and down-pointed.

Helen glances at the desk drawer, where that Glock sits. She has to decide. Can she reach that drawer? She judges the distance, the lines of sight from the door, the shadows and cover. She doesn't know.

The soldier pauses, as if he's waiting for an order. He has nothing to mark him, no sign of his allegiance, just like the man Helen used to imagine Leo had become. She holds her breath in burning lungs, anticipating his move. All the time, the clock is ticking. A second here, many more in the timefield. What the hell is happening there?

PART II

1884 St Alberts Royal

Trans
Room

Tesla Lab

Second floor

Reagents

M-1
M-2

VOID

Workshop

M-3

First floor

Lift

Library

Dock

Forbes

Ground floor

Boiler

Gen

Basement

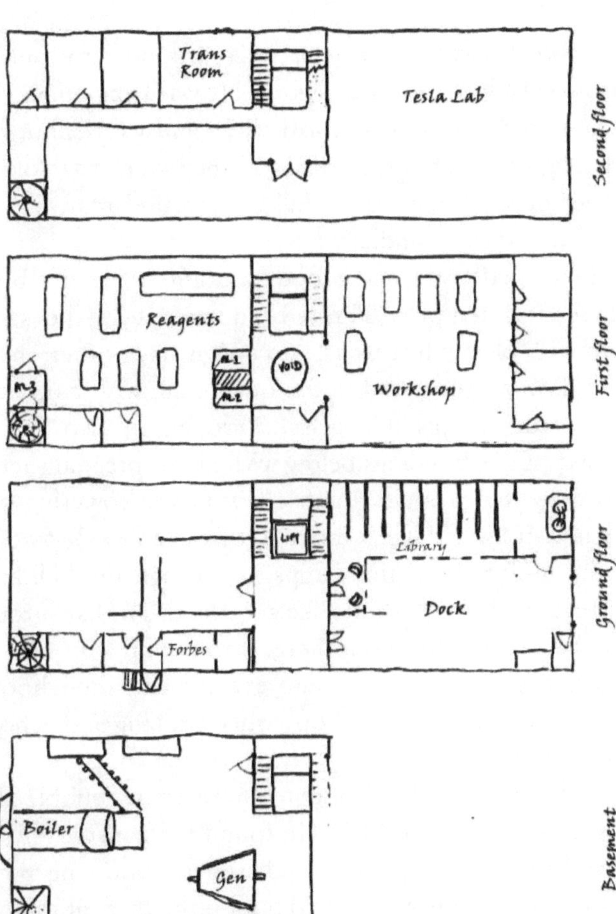

Chapter 13

Leo came to with a sense of walls around him, but the crushing claustrophobia was gone. He was lying on his side, hearing mechanical noises, soft clicks and whirrs, but they had a lightness about them, as if they were toy sounds. Deeper beyond that was a dull background roar, like the crowd of a distant stadium.

He turned over and stood, kicking off a throbbing between his temples. Through squinted eyes, he saw a room with plain white walls, and a high stack of tea chests. A window was centered in the outer wall, with bars fitted outside the unopenable glass. Through it, Leo saw an expanse of low buildings below with night spreading across a grey sky. He was clearly up a few floors, towering over the view. It looked like a movie set from *Mary Poppins*, but for the multitude of tiny lamps lit through the buildings. The lanes and streets shone like a starfield. The background roar was coming from out there. It took him a moment to register the horses. They were everywhere, their hooves clashing against the stones, cart wheels rolling and echoing in the streets.

He shook himself, disoriented in this calm bubble after the pressure of Helen's lab. He found the console and the creased map in his pocket, and turned about the room, orienting himself to the X he'd put on the map, at the spot Helen had said he'd arrive. It was while doing this that he caught sight of the table behind the tea chests.

On that table was an intricate layout of rotating rods and gears, clicking and ticking around like clockwork. It indeed looked like the innards of a giant watch, spread out and interlinked, something Leo might have built with Meccano when he was a kid. This one even had a single sheet of thick paper clipped to a stand, and a pen drawing a pattern from the mechanism. He knew what this was: a rudimentary calculator. He thought of Helen, with her calibration graphs, before he stopped and wrenched his focus back. Find David. Find the problem.

He was supposed to be on the second floor, in a small room near the main stairs. The same place David had been transmitted. Only David wasn't here.

The wooden floor creaked under Leo's footsteps as he approached the door. It was unlocked, so he eased the door open, and found an empty hall, opening at left into a wider foyer. The lights were bright, cold white, set at regular intervals on the walls, throwing hard shadows across the plain wooden floor. The walls softly hissed and sighed around him. It was creepy as hell, but he saw the double doors into what must be Tesla's laboratory to one side of the foyer, and the elevator doors and the wide wooden stairs on the other. He seemed to be where Helen had said he would be.

Leo turned to the console. It had two tabs to select. One read "David"; the other, "oscillation". Leo chose "David", which brought up a little red circle with a long arrow pointing down underneath. As Leo turned around, a crescent of green grew into the circle, shifting through a whole phase of its moon before returning to red. Leo guessed that green, pointing towards the foyer, was good, and that the arrow meant he had to go down.

He crept across the boards, past sheet metal elevator doors, and onto the descending stairs. Then down, down the first flight, and across the landing behind the elevator. He felt himself fall into a muscle memory pattern, keeping close to the walls, placing his feet with care and quiet. Only it felt awkward and wrong, like wearing a too-small suit.

At the head of the next flight down, he paused to glance at the map. Yes, that was the first floor ahead with its void in the center. Through the void's railing, he could glimpse the checker tiles of the foyer below. No sign of anyone around.

Leo relaxed a little as he stepped carefully into open space, and then around into the next flight down. As he reached the top of the stairs leading to the expansive ground-floor foyer, his eye caught on an enormous framed portrait over the front doors.

"Jesus," he breathed. He'd seen plenty of pictures of Victoria in the pages of his school books, and this one wrote the hooded eyes and dour cheeks and chin into an enormous visage. The only difference was, this monarch wasn't dressed in black. She wore white lace, a blue sash and diamonds visible at her shoulder. While she wasn't smiling, and her eyes were a disapproving shade of steel, there was something soft and youthful about her face. It thrust into Leo's head the image of Queen Elizabeth II, who'd reigned during his early army career. Her 1950s portrait had still been smiling from the wall of some far-flung briefing rooms he'd sat in. Just not this big.

He shook himself and glanced at the console, and found the arrow had flipped around, pointing up. He'd gone too far. With a backward glance at Victoria, he returned to the first floor above and looked around.

On the left was a workshop, an open space stretching

back to what looked like the full depth of the building. He could see lathes, saws, grinding wheels, presses and drills, all quiet, but the smell of machine oil and grease pronounced this a working shop. There were no cobwebs, no signs of neglect. The raw wood floor was scratched blonde timber, and piles of metal swarf and wood shavings collected around the bases of the machines. It was oddly comforting that not a lot had changed between this Victorian machinery and the equipment in workshops he was familiar with.

Leo stood inside the shop, where he could see the stairs. There were three other doors on this floor. Two were across on the other side of the floor void, heavy-looking and set into the wall – *Reagents*, the plan said. Another much more ordinary door was to his left – David's office.

Leo consulted the console. The arrow had disappeared, so he must be on the right floor, but as he faced David's office, the circle remained red. He had to spin back to the far corner of the workshop for it to be green again. Leo frowned, and moved in that direction.

The floorboards sounded different here, more solid, the hiss and sigh of the building muted. Large windows opened in the far wall, but the right wall had none. He looked between the stock racks, behind each machine, until he reached the back corner and found nothing. The green circle steadfastly pointed into the wall.

He retreated, scanning, looking for something he'd missed. In the nook beside the grand staircase was a small hatch, probably a service access or a store room. Wait.

Leo straightened and turned back to stare at the windowless wall. It was hung with stock racks and cabinets, but at the end closest to David's office was a blank space. When Leo approached, he could see the door, its hinges and handle made flush and unobtrusive with the wall. Leo carefully lifted the pull-out handle. Behind the door was a long narrow hallway – smuggler narrow – and with another door at its far end. It smelled of dust and damp.

All Leo could hear on the walk down that hall was his own heart hammering. The green circle told him he was going the right way, but he had to pause and really listen. That was when he heard a chair shifting on the floor. But nothing else. No voices. No steps.

He decided against knocking; at least if he just opened the door, he wouldn't be the one surprised. But then he was, because the first thing he saw against the far wall was David, tied to a wooden chair and with a tartan gag in his mouth.

Leo glanced around the rest of the room, trying to orient himself. He knew already this wasn't on the plans, but it didn't look like the rest of the building. It had a tiled white floor, white walls, long benches and two metal sinks, and in the center, a narrow leather-covered table.

It looked just like an operating theatre.

❰❮❯❱

Leo stared at David. Turning through his mind was a realization that he has not the least idea of what was going on in the timefield. Both David and Helen had made it seem a benign place, but Leo hadn't seen someone tied to a chair since some deep shithole in the Middle East he'd rather forget about. And nothing about this room made sense. The surprise on David's face suggested Leo was the last person he expected to see.

Leo checked the hall again and closed the door before untying David, who then engaged in a good deal of sputtering, and picking wool fibers out of his teeth.

"Leo," he finally croaked. "Helen sent you, then? And with a console? Thank god."

He mopped at his forehead with the tartan gag, then chucked it on the floor. He pulled a fob from his pocket and consulted it. "See anyone on your way down?"

"No one," Leo said, still staring at him. Something here didn't fit.

"Good, excellent. We'd better make tracks while it stays that way. Easier with two of us." David headed for the door, then paused. "How about you go first."

"Wait a minute. What happened? And who trussed you like a turkey?"

David waved a hand. "Let's just say there was a misunderstanding with one of the investors. I lost the console, so I couldn't recall. But time's tight. We should go."

"Stop," Leo said. His fingers had started up a fine tremor. Helen had sent him to find David, and sort out this oscillation problem. Now, the whole mission had shifted with unknown threats. "Who are we talking about? How many men, and where are they now?"

"Two only, and not so very professional," David said. "They're gone away for now, so as long as we're quick about correcting the oscillation, we can be out of here in a few minutes."

He turned for the door again.

"Wait." Leo heard that old steel come back in his voice, the tone that cops use on drunken disorderly pub patrons to inspire sobriety, the one that he didn't know was still in him. "I just found you tied to a chair, and Helen's counting on us. The HoG's charging up."

David did actually pale a shade. "Over us?"

Leo nodded. "It's the proper pointy end of urgent. So

let's be clear what we have to do here. What weapons do these investors have? And what do we have to do?"

David backed up a pace, raising his hands. "Look, easy there, big guy. You have it all wrong. There are no armed adversaries here, just pissed off investors. It was one man got the better of me, wearing a kilt and carrying a dirk, of all bloody things. But I'm not exactly an expert in hand-to-hand. He grabbed me as soon as I came through on the last transmission. Didn't even have time to react."

"And what's he pissed about?"

"More of the same. People out there in the borough don't buy coal anymore, blah, blah. One of them just choose to make a point, a bit of a scare tactic. He's gone now, so we need to move."

Leo heard what David was saying, but something here still didn't mesh. He looked around again. To one side of the sink was a low trolley, fitted with draws. Resting on its surface was a length of looped yellow tubing. In a small tray to the side was what looked like large bore needles.

On the other side of the sink was a vessel with a pressure gauge on the top, and an insulated pipe leading into the wall. If Leo had to guess, he would say that was a steam sterilizer. The lab in Blackfriars had an autoclave, and this looked like it, just a tad more primitive.

Then, on the wall were three small metal taps, one hung with a facemask. The mask was made from something opaque and vintage looking, but the shape was undoubtedly intended to go over the face. Leo had been underneath an oxygen mask like that more than once. "Why is there a medical bay here?" he said.

"This isn't a medical bay," David said, which was such an outrageous lie that he almost immediately recanted. "Look, it was a side project, for someone's sick kid. It doesn't matter for what we have to do. Now, we need to go."

"Does Helen know about this?"

"Kid needed transfusions and some enriched air. It's not high-tech. It never created any blips in the timefield. All we needed was oxygen, steam for sterilizing, and suction for clean up. The suction's clever, actually. Uses high-pressure steam from the basement boiler, expands in this pipe all the way up to the roof, so any contaminants get cooked before being vented. Tesla's design, of course."

"You have oxygen? Coming from where?"

"Downstairs," David said. "Why are you looking at me like that?"

❮❰❱❯

The thing about oxygen is: it makes things burn. That might sound obvious, reductive, but that's because most of the time we think about garden variety fires. They need fuel, and they need oxygen. In that context, we mean atmospheric oxygen, the not quite 21% of the air we breathe. That 21% is the part of air that keeps us alive, that also slowly kills us, and that some people attempt to mitigate with kale and goji berries. Oxygen is inextricably linked with life, and with fire. Being alive is a little like burning to death, just very, very slowly.

In the late Paleozoic — 300 million years ago — atmospheric oxygen was higher than today. Aided by all that oxygen, insects were gigantic and fires the natural order of things. Dr Ian Glasspool from the Chicago Field Museum says, "at levels significantly above 25% even wet plants could have burned, while at levels around 30 to 35%, as have been proposed for the late Paleozoic, wildfires would have been frequent and catastrophic". *Catastrophic* means intense, and hot, impossible to extinguish. The coal laid down during that period of history – the very same coal that Helen and David were trying to avoid burning so exclusively in the next hundred years – contained huge quantities of charcoal from those ancient catastrophic fires.

And those were fires that burned in just 35% oxygen.

Catastrophic was also the word pulsing around Leo's brain as he looked at that humble oxygen pipe in the wall. A fire in an oxygen system is nothing like a garden variety fire, nor even a Paleozoic fire. Oxygen systems port around pure oxygen, or near enough to it. That much oxygen can make metals and flame retardants and wet blankets burn like acetylene. Leo had been unfortunate witness to the fact, having seen that delivery tanker burn it to the ground. Stuff like that still happens in modern times.

Because of this propensity to destruction, tubes that carry pure oxygen must be molecular clean. You can't use oil to lubricate joints, because oil is highly flammable. Can't use ordinary valve seats or gaskets, because all it takes to blow a valve into a fireball is a fleck of paint, picked up by the flow when someone turns a tap, and slammed into one of those gaskets, igniting merry hell in all that beautiful oxygen.

Staring at that pipe, Leo had absolutely no clue how much respect for oxygen whoever built this system had. Put that together with finding David bound and gagged, in this freaky-arse building, within a medical room that reminded him a little too much of black and white Frankenstein movies combined with his own traumatic experiences, and Leo was beyond ready to go. He was out of practice, too long out of uniform, and he wanted all of this over. He closed his eyes. Only, he couldn't think that way, not when Helen had an axe of high-speed particles hanging over her head.

"Okay," he said, swallowing. "Is this oxygen rig the thing that needs disabling?"

"Not exactly," David said, a little too quickly.

Leo thought of the time running on the clocks in Helen's lab, and again suppressed the need to run. "Let's make sure."

Chapter 14

David led Leo down the stairs and into the ground-floor foyer. The void in the roof gave the space a soaring cathedral quality, accentuated with three pairs of ornate double doors, one under the portrait, the other two in the left wall. From under the middle pair—which led to the dock on Leo's map—a clear wear track emerged across the tiles, and disappeared into the elevator gate. David headed for the closest of the left-wall pair.

The air beyond those doors smelled of stored books, reminding Leo of long nights studying at Cambridge. And around a corner he beheld an extensive library, full of high shelves in smoky wood. Books were crammed in double-height, others piled on the floor in irregular stacks, which intruded into the walkway. The walkway itself was corralled behind a mesh wall, beyond which the view of the rest of the floor was blocked with stacks of tea chests.

"The rig's in the space down the end," David said. "Why don't you take a look, and I'll duck downstairs, be back here in five, and then we can go back to the transmission point."

"Hold it," Leo said. "Helen sent me here for you. We're not splitting up."

Leo pushed on to where the bookshelves ended at a rim of white plaster wall, intruding like a tumor into the library's plush gothic vibe. Beyond, in the corralled space, was an exposed brick wall with an industrial frame bolted to it. The frame held a tank shaped like a squat sausage, made from two hemispheres flanged together. Two rods like aerials stuck out of the top, connected to wires that ran somewhere down behind it. Leo guessed they were electrodes, and that the tiny pump he heard whirring intermittently was keeping a water supply topped up.

That was all you needed: water, and electricity. Apply the energy, and hydrogen would bubble from the positive terminal, oxygen from the negative. Two holding tanks were duly bolted to the wall to receive the hydrogen and oxygen rising up on each side.

It also looked remarkably like a bomb. "Why's it here?" Leo asked.

"Tesla's orders," David said. "The hydrogen is for cooling the generator downstairs. Better than water apparently. The oxygen was collected for the reagent lab. I co-opted a bit for medical use."

Leo grunted. Not a word of that really made sense, because the generator and the reagent lab were both at the other end of the building. This had the look of an afterthought. Maybe there just hadn't been space for it anywhere else. But not-on-the-plans retro-fits made him nervous. It meant unforeseen need. Lack of planning. His eyes jumped to another set of double doors with glass peep panels to the right. "What's through there?"

"Receiving dock. Go through there, you come out those others doors in the foyer."

Leo peered through the glass, and saw a palette of metal tubing, and another tall stack of tea chests. It all looked fairly ordinary. He heaved a breath, and consulted the console and chose *oscillation*. The dot was spinning through green and red, the arrow pointing down. This wasn't the oscillation source; he was just wasting time. "Alright, let's go down."

"When we get down there, best thing is if you keep watch at the base of the stairs," David said, as they approached the library doors into the foyer. "I'll duck in and sort this problem."

This time, Leo had the distinct impression that David didn't want him to see what was in the basement. He didn't reply, just let David lead the way towards the double doors and back into the foyer.

He hadn't gone two steps across the tiles when figure appeared on the stairs below. Leo started, and reached for a pistol he wasn't carrying, before he registered the details.

The man wore tails, and polished shoes. His forehead was high, hair receding. He climbed the stairs with the bearing of a three-star general, his mouth pulled down tight, as if stitched in place. The man saw them, and shock passed through his features.

"Can I help—oh, Doctor Blakeney. This is *most* unexpected," he said.

"Forbes," David said, with obvious surprise.

"I expected you had gone with Mr. Brown yesterday," Forbes went on. "Or you had … gone away." Forbes raised his eyes to heaven, as if the future was akin to god.

"I won't be here long. I'm just here to … see Tesla."

Forbes' mouth visibly relaxed. "Then allow me to summon a carriage for you, Doctor. Mr. Tesla departed a number of hours ago to entertain a friend. You and your … companion can find him at his Baker Street address." Forbes' eyes roamed over each of them. "And might I also be introduced to your colleague? I must have oversight for those who visit Her Majesty's facility."

"No problem," David said, smoothly. "We have only a small matter to attend to in the basement before departing. We won't be in your way."

"The basement?" Forbes eyebrows dropped like anvils. "I'm afraid I cannot permit that after hours, Sir. Also, there is a delicate matter to discuss with you. Mr. Jarvis's men were here again, making threats. Perhaps you will follow me to your office upstairs, and I will place a call to Mr. Tesla with the telephone."

He pronounced "telephone" as if using such a device came under some duress, but nevertheless, he was off, striding up the stairs and clearly expecting both of them to follow.

David glanced at Leo, then down the stairs, before turning to pursue Forbes. As he reached the first floor again, Leo glanced at the console: he'd been in the timefield now for just over half an hour. He imagined Helen watching the time-elapsed creeping past three minutes. Forbes was heading for the door on the far side of the floor void, and wrestling with a key ring.

David raised his voice. "Forbes. This is not necessary. We can organize ourselves."

Forbes stopped, but continued to sort through the keys. "I really must insist, Doctor, that the building is fully evacuated before being secured for the night. Mr. Tesla is very particular about that, especially on a rare night when he is not in residence."

Leo watched the two men, dueling for power over who would do what. Finally, David said, "Forbes, I appreciate your concern and admire your sense of proprietary, but I do not need supervision, nor do my actions here require your scrutiny. No doubt it has been a long day and you've executed your duties admirably. So, I ask you very kindly to *take your leave.*"

Forbes drew himself up. "Very well," he said, slowly, clearly defeated by rank. "If you are certain." With obvious and great reluctance, he carried himself away across the foyer, and down the stairs, backward glancing for as long as line-of-sight allowed.

David blew out a breath. "Bloody meddlesome man," he whispered. "There's no reason for him to ever go into my office. He has his own line to Tesla downstairs. He should have gone home by now. Give him five minutes to leave the building. Then I'll go down and sort all this out. Though I wouldn't put it past him to lock the basement doors out of spite."

Leo was consulting the crumpled map. "What if he does? Can we go down this maintenance stair?"

"We could. Or down the service shaft behind the lift. There's a hatch leading to it, right over there."

Leo glanced at the narrow wall panel leading under the stairs and felt a chill. "Down a service shaft?"

"Of course not." David clapped Leo on the shoulder. "I just saw the look on your face. Don't like small spaces, do you?"

Leo made no answer.

"Relax," David said. "We'll be on our way in five minutes."

❮❯

Forbes descended the stairs, then retraced his steps, then descended again. Should he tell Red that the building was not clear, after all? Should he do what the Masked Man had charged him with: activate the lock-down system, and go home?

But if he did that, he would be leaving the Doctor and that other unfamiliar man, who looked like a boxer, inside. Forbes contemplated the consequences. If he failed to do what he'd promised, he was no stranger to the rough tactics of powerful people; the Masked Man was certainly one of those. But if he tried to warn Red about the Doctor and the other man, Forbes would be admitting his failure. He paced the first-floor landing, a rat in a cage of competing consequences.

It would be unfair and reductive for us to judge him. More than a century from this moment, social neurologist Jean Decety would say, "we are the most social species on Earth, and also the most violent. We have two faces because these two faces were important to survival". Cooperation, such that Helen, David and their timefield were aiming for, is possible. But resources are always limited, so as a species of individuals, we have also evolved to act against opponents. These shifting incentives make game play unstable, and subject to rapid change.

Forbes had not yet done what the Masked Man had asked. Because of this, Tesla's building was still open. Forbes had decided to go to his office, thinking he had the time to wait, and ensure the Doctor departed.

He did not have such time. The Queen's carriage was already drawing up outside the rear doors, its occupants free to enter and change the game entirely.

❮❰❯❱

As all of this was playing out, the oxygen rig maintained a steady electrolysis, tiny bubbles of hydrogen and oxygen collecting on the electrodes sunk into its water tank.

Leo's concern about oxygen was well-founded, but he paid less attention to the hydrogen side, because everyone pays more mind to the problems they're intimately acquainted with, and can forget those that are buried deep behind their thoughts. For Leo, the Hindenburg was a buried thought.

At that moment, inside each tiny buoyant bubble in the tank, millions of hydrogen atoms spun in chaotic pairs, their dance wobbling with foamy quantum uncertainty. It sounds crowded, but each pair system enjoyed enough space to be like planets in a vast solar system, aware of their neighbors only through the spring-like push of atomic force, a kind of molecular ESP. The simplicity of these tiny solar systems – two proton suns with two orbiting electron planets – made hydrogen the lightest gas and the one that could most easily transmit heat. This conferred advantages. As David already knew, Tesla had been able to build his generator more efficiently because the hydrogen cooling worked so well.

But that simplicity, that tininess, unencumbered by larger nuclei or more orbiting electrons, also made hydrogen slippery slick. It passed through spaces that other gases couldn't. It leaked, or escaped, depending on your point of view. Then, lighter than air, it rose and gathered into inverse pools on ceilings and inside wall spaces, gathering collections of pure explosive.

That was what was happening in Tesla's building. The connection between the tank and the rig was loose, because two days before, David had called away the technician changing a valve, to do something for him. For hours and hours, hydrogen had been slowly seeping up, up, into the space between the ground and first floors, the space created by the reinforcing under the workshop. No one noticed, because the tank itself had kept up with the generator's system demand. But every bit of new hydrogen was escaping. A stream of it was, at this moment, tracking around the wall space, creeping nearer to where the basement locomotive's boiler sucked air into its coal furnace. Every moment, gathering more.

Chapter 15

Helen waits no more than a few seconds, but her hyperacuity dilates those moments to hours. She sees nothing but the man in the doorway. She assumes it is a man, the angle of his thigh bone suggests it, as does the proportions of his torso. Somewhere in the deep animal part of her brain, those dimensions have formed an established pattern and brought forward that one conclusion. He might be dressed in black, or she might simply be so terrified that her brain won't resolve more that his silhouette.

Silhouettes, silhouettes. When she'd been young, on a rare weekend he was sober, her father had shown her stencils of aircraft on the wall of a WWII command bunker. An enemy plane betrayed its identity in those outlines. But this man does no such thing. Maybe he's one of the American separatists, whose considerable military resources and grudge against Britain over the whole we're-not-getting-involved-in-an-Asian-war thing would place him logically here. But it's not the only theory. London has always been attractive to invaders. And Leo was right … maybe it's The Machine itself that's drawn him here.

She doesn't quite believe it when the soldier steps back. She remains stuck and stupid as he paces away down the hall, footfalls making the tiniest *snick, snick* on the floor. A tiny hope breaks the ground of her terror. In the workshop next door they have three-phase-power machines. If the solider is looking for a power surge, maybe he will think it came from in there. And if not, the workshop has infinitely more liftable valuables. Copper tubing, even gold stock for making tiny inert screws and fixings.

Now, straining to hear the soldier's movements, she scrambles across the floor on cramping legs. The desk drawer squeaks, every chink of metal on metal echoing in her brain. Her hand closes on the pistol, top-heavy without the clip. She finds the magazine and restores the balance, easing it home. The weapon is stupidly heavy in her hand. Her fingers shake as she clicks the safety off. She hasn't done this in a long time, not since the program was fully funded and she'd done the basic training like everyone else. She imagines Leo has done this far more times than she has, and she wonders about all those empty years she doesn't know about him, what proportion of them he spent with a gun in his hand. Had he done this so many times he wouldn't have to think about it? Because now she doesn't remember what's next. Something is next.

She presses herself into a dark space beside The Machine, the information sliding away at the edges of her memory. She's never been under pressure like this before, and it makes all her thoughts slippery. She cradles the weapon, fixing on the possibility this will all be over in a minute or two. She's close to the microtorus destruction button here. All she needs is for them to come back and open—ah! She's supposed to chamber a round. For that, she has to pull the slide, which will make a *snap*. She edges out, grabs her hoodie off the back of the chair, and smothers the gun with it, muffling the clicks. There. Locked and loaded. Green lights still on.

And now, she has to wait.

Chapter 16

At that moment across space-time, William and Araminta were also pressed into a small space, listening to footfalls. Their venue was a cupboard in the back of the ground-floor offices, a much less gracious place than what William would have wished to impress Araminta with, especially after their journey through the tunnel had been difficult for her. Still, this could not be avoided.

William's senses were honed from a lifetime of threats in every shadow, and knew Forbes—in his leather-soled, patent-polished shoes—anywhere. The man had just a trace of a limp, a tiny delay in the regular *click-click* of his heels that gave him away. There had been a moment when William was sure he could hear footsteps upstairs, too, but for now, Forbes was all that mattered.

"You didn't say that we would have to secret ourselves from the *servants*," Araminta hissed.

"Shhh."

The leather heels clicked to a stop, and William heard the snap of Forbes' fob. That was it: the sign he was preparing to depart. William knew that Tesla worked late, often all night, alone in his lab, as regular as the clocks themselves. William had used the fact to enjoy free rein in the building.

Forbes kept a meticulous routine. He would check each floor of the building from top to bottom, return into the foyer, check the time, then collect his hat and coat, and lock the building down on his way out. William waited to hear the footsteps head for the office, but they didn't.

The footsteps paced again, back and forth, and then receded into the stairway, heading down.

This wasn't the usual way of things.

William poked his head out of the airing cupboard. No one was in this area, with its row of flushing privies lined up along the rear wall, making a set square angle with the washing sinks against the south wall. William's eyes tracked the thin streams of steam that leaked from the ironing shoes, stacked above boards to the side of the airing cupboard. The steam drifted across two giant mangles dotting the center space next to two coppered soaking tubs, one of them full of towels for tomorrow's wash. Two trolleys were lined up square along the far wall, loaded with clean linens for the laboratories, and workers' overalls.

William could hear nothing more than the usual shift and sigh of the laboratory itself. Imagining himself a furtive lane mouse, he signaled to Araminta to stay where she was, and crept to the foyer. Victoria stared down from her gilt frame, high over the front doors. William knew she was the monarch, but there was something about Victoria that made him crawl, especially when she was staring at his back.

He paused, thinking he heard her voice, drifting up from the basement stairs. He shuddered, moved faster. Across the tiles, the dark cave of the library beckoned, its volumes of knowledge set on towering bookcases that disappeared into infinity.

Everything *looked* quiet and normal, but if William had learned one thing, it was that you didn't accept what anything looked like. It had to feel right. And he knew, as long as Forbes had gone downstairs, it wouldn't feel right. They couldn't use the elevator to reach Tesla's lab. Luckily, it was not the only option.

He crept back to the cupboard, and drew Araminta out. Then he led her through a door into a long hall, past Forbes' own office, and the staff door he had been dismissed from only an hour or so before. They did not go as swiftly as they might have; she was slower, hampered by her lameness. By the time they'd reached the maintenance stair door, he was glad to have chosen this option; he only hoped that she could manage the climb.

《〈〉》

Araminta climbed the stairs believing at any moment she might die in pursuit of her foolish choices. Though she had imagined herself capable and desperate for adventures, she hadn't quite bargained on the adventures being foul-smelling, dangerous, or quite so subversive.

She'd kept on only because going back was impossible now, and because William promised they were only a few steps from the second floor, and Tesla's laboratory. Step, she went, step. Step. Up the spiraling stair filling the narrow walls; at least, it was a skeleton of a stair. Each run was formed from thin metal bars, such that she could see the dim light, which persisted down through the floors. She was gasping and clutching the rail by the second landing, where William waited at another open hatch.

The wedge of light delivered Araminta from the stairs, and into a spare white hall. Clearly forgetting himself, William clasped her hand and drew her along, past closed doors, until they emerged into small foyer of plain wooden floorboards. Here, they were back at the elevator, and the main stairs. Directly across the foyer was a set of high, double-width doors.

"There is Tesla's laboratory," William said, with a flourish.

Araminta straightened her back, her heart a thumping beast, and limped to the doors. She knocked.

Not a stir, not a step, no sign that anyone had heard. She glanced at William.

"He's always here," William protested. "Try again."

So Araminta did, with the same result. She then tried the door, and while the handles turned, the leaves were locked fast. She stood back, frustrated, and knocked again, loud enough that the sound carried all through the unassuming lobby.

"Maybe he's somewhere else in the building," William said, in the helpless kind of way that indicated he didn't believe it. Araminta took a step back, then forward, unsure of what to do. "In fact, I actually hear something, don't you?"

Araminta frowned. In the quiet of the lobby, it didn't take long to perceive the mechanical clicking. It was almost like the jangling of a harness, but far too regular. William went back into the hallway, head cocked like a bloodhound.

Araminta noticed the light under the first door as William opened it. Inside was a room the size of a bedchamber, half filled with tea chests. An unadorned window was dark with night sky. Beyond the chests was a large table holding a mechanical device. Her eyes ran over the slender square sections supporting thin rotating rods and gears, which articulated with each other. These connected to six flat discs at the far side of the table, then through further mechanisms to a single sheet of flawless parchment propped on a plinth near the front. The parchment was stapled in place, and drawing on it was a pen, poised in mechanical fingers. Rods and gears across the table were variously turning, pausing or stepping inside their housings, as if the mechanisms were dancing to music playing in a range inaudible to human ears.

Araminta started at it. She had once seen factory jacquard machines running looms at frightening speeds, the machines heavy and menacing. This machine looked oddly similar, only delicate, understated, intricate.

"This is a calculating device," she said, slowly.

"The mechanical differential analyzer," William said proudly. "For making complex calculations. Mr. Tesla said it's faster than by hand, and more accurate. At least, that's what I heard."

"Like Babbage's engine?" she asked, fascinated.

"Umm," William said. "I suppose?"

"Well, more Lovelace's work," Araminta said, running her finger along the table. In fact, she was distantly related to Ada, the Countess of Lovelace, and that kinship had driven much of her early interest in mathematics. Disraeli had told her in their first conversation that while funding had been given to Babbage to develop the difference engine, Ada's work had been instrumental. Like all women, however, her contribution had been largely forgotten amidst that of the male Babbage, and all the work had fallen foul of escalating costs and Babbage's move onto a new project, which the government saw as abject failure. Ada's early death had not helped. The government had bought plans for difference engines from other inventors, but only really valued the output tables, not the process of the invention. Short-sighted fools.

Araminta stepped back, feeling the weight of defeat, both her own, and that of generations of her female ancestors. She would have to go back out to the street, and find some way to spend the long hours until morning, when she might be able to appeal to Disraeli for sanctuary until their genuine appointment.

"You'll show me back outside," she said. "And I'll not give you the money. You promised me Tesla, and he is not here."

"Not yet, my Lady," William said, as if an idea as bright as a new coin had lit in his mind. "There's a telephone, in the offices on the ground floor. You could call Mr. Tesla from there."

"I have no knowledge of telephones."

"I've seen Forbes use it many times. I can show you!"

Araminta stared at him, caught on his tendrils of hope. "Then you had better come and operate this elevator, too. I will not climb down those stairs."

❮❰❱❯

Three levels below, the tunnel swirled with noise and dust. The Masked Man resisted the urge to check his fob, to catalogue the minutes flying past. To eliminated wasted time, he'd had the men bring the equipment carts into the tunnel, and ready the animals.

The two dogs crouched in crates on the unfinished platform, still and patient, their long limbs folded. They looked to be dark slabs of short fur with oversized heads, like living versions of the Egyptian Sphinx. Only with teeth. And breeding. And training. The dogs scared even these rough men. The Masked Man saw them as useful tools. He teetered on the cusp of action, the lure of work baiting him like wily rabbits baited these dogs. Nearly. Nearly.

The drill wound down, and he heard the *crack crack* of falling stone. Green came jogging down the tunnel, giving the dogs a nervous eye. "We're through," he said.

"Take out the animals," said the Masked Man.

Everyone had to face their fears. The dogs uncurled themselves, sleek and silent, stretching their backs and legs after the long sojourn in the crate. When unfolded, their shoulders reached the Masked Man's thigh, and the skin of their gums was red as blood.

The hole in the underground wall into the Royal Laboratories was barely large enough to squeeze through, the room beyond a dark vault. There were no lights here, in this secret room. Even so, the Masked Man sensed the bulk of the object waiting for him. He smiled into the darkness. They had broken through in the right place, in the hidden chamber alongside the basement's boiler room. The prize would not be kept from him.

Such times required utmost care.

On silent feet, the Masked Man slipped through the room, his prize glinting enticingly to his left, and entered the under-stair passage to the boiler room. The air heated, again thick with mechanical noise of the steam engine. He slowly pushed open and absorbed the scene, searching between the boiler, the mass of cables and pipes, and the generator, for what he wanted.

He found his quarry on an instrument panel: a gauge that read the water flow rate to the boiler. He stood there, silent and unmoving, watching the needle hold on its reading. The water flow was steady and stable, just as he was. He noted the figure, and retraced his steps. As he pulled the passage door closed, he stopped. For just a moment, he could have sworn he'd heard voices, somewhere above.

He closed the door.

Red approached with a blinder held high.

"Are we on track?" The Masked Man asked.

"No problems."

"Guard this passage, then. The others will set about enlarging the tunnel, and completing the other tasks." Checks and Yellow appeared in another halo of blinder light. "You know what to do," he told them.

Silently, the two men returned to the tunnel, bound for the outside world again. The Masked Man was taking no chances: along with his mission in the building, he had to nullify any interference from Tesla himself.

Chapter 17

Now – Helen

Helen crouches in her hiding place as the seconds tick by. She tries to count them in her head, but she's probably counting too fast, thrown off by her heartbeat. Her only comfort is the steady vibration of the idling Machine through her fingertips. The microtorus is still spinning. Otherwise, nothing changes. Maybe the solider is still in the workshop. Or maybe he's waiting just out in the hall where she can't see, with a thermal imager trained on the room, watching her.

Her stomach twists into its own torus. The control computer screen is dark, the hidden Grid luring her to check it. She has to know. She stretches up, balancing the gun against her leg and peers through the open door. No movement in the hall. She's halfway back to the desk before the blood flow returns to her legs and a cramp seizes her calf. She stretches her leg out, and awkward tripod crouch before the keyboard. Checks the hall again. Wakes the monitor. After the dark, the display saturates her retinas. It takes two, long, panicked seconds for her vision to return.

The Grid values are still moving, bouncing, some exceeding the display field size. The possibility of failure forms like cold iron in Helen's chest.

She stares at the numbers as the elapsed time increases. There can be only one reason why the numbers are still moving like this: nothing has changed. Whatever is in the timefield basement is still there.

And then she hears the faint whine of the workshop door hinges. Hot panic melts the iron. She's right out in the open here, an expanse of bare floor between her and The Machine. She doesn't have time to retreat; she only has a second before he'll be back in the doorway.

She turns off the monitor before she drops under the table again, pressing herself into the wall among the cables and the dust. Then, the man is back in the doorway.

Seeing him the second time is worse. A revisit displays intent that the first time does not. He's seen something to make him look again. Just then, she remembers her hoodie, left in the space beside The Machine, which he would have seen earlier on the back of the chair.

The gunmetal has warmed against Helen's skin. She holds it in her right hand, resting her trigger finger along the side, and points it towards the legs in the open doorway.

One black leg swings forward. Then, the other. Slow steps. From the angle she's at, she can't see where he's looking, only the direction he's walking. The legs turn away a little. She guesses he's watching the green lights on The Machine. In the part of her mind that deals in higher theory, Helen wonders if this has to happen, somehow. If an unsolvable timefield could be resolved by The Machine being destroyed here, if the universe could somehow bring that about.

This is pure nonsense, as if the universe has consciousness, a purely human conceit. But then, she is still human. She bites her lip, fighting against the hopelessness that comes from a deterministic theory of the universe. The Light Trajectory Theory isn't incompatible with determinism, it only adds that the universe can exist as any stable solution. This made it possible to change the past or future without invalidating physics. But the key word is *stable*.

That's why the bouncing Grid values are certain doom. It's oscillation, the marker of instability. When you spin a top, it wobbles before it falls. And now, the Grid is wobbling. Something is happening in that timefield that can't be allowed to be.

The soldier takes another step, the weight transferring to his far leg. He's leaning, looking around the far edge of The Machine. Maybe he'll walk down there. If he looks across at the desk, he's far away enough now to see her underneath. Helen works the fingers of her gun hand, keeping the blood flowing. Sweat is rolling down her temples, off her top lip, and blooming across her palms. She has to be ready if he sees her, or if he touches the power cables that jut from the wall. Only she's suddenly unsure she can even move.

His weight rocks back onto both feet. A step forward, his body square. In that instant, somehow she knows: he is going to see one of them – the power cables, or her feet. And either way, she has to decide what to do.

Chapter 18

Three minutes had gone by when Leo heard the shot. It sounded like a tenth dan master breaking a wood board into a screaming jet turbine. Or, at least, what that would sound like from some distance away. A peculiar, piercing rip that he felt in the bones of his spine. His head whipped around as fast as David's.

"What the hell was that?" Leo asked. A minute echo bounced through the air between the steel reinforced doors of the reagent lab, and the workshop machines.

David was very still. "The building makes noises," he said.

Leo couldn't localize the sound, he just knew it had come from within the building. Perhaps the generator system downstairs had blown a line; a high-pressure rupture could make a sound like that, especially if it threw some ejecta across the room. Leo swallowed.

David motioned to move back towards the stairs, casting frequent glances at the empty foyer below. He seemed to have lost the reluctance to go downstairs, and now he wanted to go in a hurry.

The ground-floor foyer was still empty when they crossed it and went down again to the rear-door landing, where Leo noticed the door standing out of its catch. When he pointed it out, David pushed the door open, took one look out into the lane, and blanched. He rushed down the remaining stairs before Leo could look back, only pausing outside the basement doors to listen.

The air warmed, and a *chuff-chuff* sound grew as Leo came up behind him. Then David pushed open the basement doors, and Leo beheld a behemoth. On the map, the space was marked *boiler room*. In reality, it was industrial chaos.

At first, he could only see parts of it. The steam train ran as if it had never been off rails, its pistons flying, pushing steam and soot into the shaking flue that ran upwards against the far-right wall. Even with the high ceiling and generous clearance, locomotive seemed far too large for the room, the noise reverberating from every surface. Jesus Christ, it was like looking at a continuous controlled explosion that might escape its bonds at any second. On the far side of the room, a covered conveyor rattled from a chute all the way into the steam train's cab. He knew an automated coal feeder when he saw one; this engine didn't need anyone to shovel fuel into its belly. It would keep the generator spinning as feedback adjusted the rate the coal came in.

The walls and floor were adorned in valves and pipes, many of them disappearing into the engine, others snaking into a grate under their feet. Through this mess of metallic snakes, Leo made out a door in the far corner, set into a blocky column that stood proud of the walls, about the right size for a stairwell.

In fact, the only thing in the room that wasn't bulky and industrial was the generator, a tapering polished metal capsule, mounted on its side and half sunk into the floor.

Leo frowned at the generator. He'd seen all those lights outside, and David claimed a wealth of industry was out in the borough, including smelting, which was power intensive. Generators in modern power stations dwarfed a man, even a man the size of Leo. This generator wasn't powering a city, but it was supplying a lot more than just this building. It looked too small, much too small. Unless it was some kind of Tesla magic.

Was this what they were here for?

Leo looked for David and couldn't see him, not until he turned all the way around, to a niche, punched back to give access to a door under the stairs. David was standing, looking into the open doorway, his face pale and his mouth ajar.

"David?"

Leo approached, until he saw the body of a man lying beyond that doorway. He was dressed in a kilt, long socks and leather shoes, the sporran hanging down because of the way he'd fallen on his side. Leo could have guessed from just the way he was lying that the Scotsman was dead. Two more steps, and Leo perceived that the man's body basically ended at about his waist. What had been his torso and head had been vaporized. Leo had the impression of a well-dispersed spray of organic material fanning up and out, onto the ceiling and through into the space beyond the door he was propping open. In a detached mode, Leo assessed, whoever had shot the man had stood about where Leo was now, and had probably shot him high in the chest with the power of a several-inch mortar.

Jesus H. Christ.

David ran for the stairs like a rabbit racing from a hound pack.

Leo charged after him, only to find David had stopped on the landing and had again hauled open the building's back door.

"Shit," David hissed, and turned upwards for the lobby.

Leo peered out the rear door and saw nothing but the low expanse of the bright-lit borough. In the cobbled lane, a few children chased each other through the gutters, dodging around a large dark carriage waiting on the pavement. To Leo, it meant nothing.

"David, *wait.*"

Leo caught David in the foyer, mostly because he was hesitating on which way to go. "David. What the hell is going on?"

"Brown," David got out, flapping his hands in a panic. "That was Brown."

"Brown who?"

"*John* Brown. Don't you get it?" He gestured up at the portrait. "She's here!"

"What?"

"We have to leave *at once*," David said, turning about in a circle, his top lip beaded with sweat. "I mean, we have to *recall.*"

Leo was trying not to catch David's panic, but images of that mutilated body were setting up camp in his mind. He had to fist David's collar and haul in a breath. "What about the instability?"

With this question, everything seemed to unravel at once. In slowest motion, the first thing Leo noticed was Forbes, emerging from a hallway across the foyer, mouthing protests.

The next was a chime from the elevator, where the doors slid open, revealing two people he had never seen before – a woman in a very bad suit, and a rough-looking teenage boy. They had time to step out into the lobby, each looking in different directions, before the woman's gaze fell on Leo. Her limping gait froze, just as the boy flinched at the sight of Forbes across the foyer.

Leo had an out-of-body experience, seeing the whole thing as an endgame of chess, where he was well outclassed and watching an opponent slide pieces into an unseen checkmate.

The last, and most critical move came from the stairs, where ascended another man, wearing a red kerchief.

❬❮❯❭

William had forgotten about Forbes, and now the man was coming straight for him.

He heard something like, "Mister Potts. I distinctly remember giving you notice," but William had frozen like a city rabbit who sees a fox, and consequently found himself collared.

He smelled a stench of fearful sweat as Forbes hauled him towards the front doors. William's neck pounded like a drum. The grip was too tight, his vision clouded oily black. As William twisted to relieve the pressure, he saw a man in a red neck kerchief rising up from the basement stairs like a demon from a crypt.

This man raised his arm, pointing something heavy right at William's heart. Forbes abruptly slackened his grip, and in a plaintive voice William had never heard before called, "No, don't, I'm securing it now!" and lunged for the reception counter.

Then came an air-splitting crack, like a pneumatic engine driving a steel bolt into a beam of oak.

❬❮❯❭

In Red's hand, the railgun scribed a rising arc, like the orbit of the summer sun across the sky. Under a finger whose ridges were back-filled in grease, the button depressed into its cradle. This closed an electrical circuit.

The high-energy capacitors lodged in the gun's handle were like a besieged castle, packed with an energized army. Outside, the besiegers sat about, immobile—this was the charge-sea in both the gun's pair of rails, and its cross-piece projectile of machined iron. Together, the rails and projectile resembled an H. From the perspective of a commander on the castle battlement, the button closing the circuit breached the castle wall. In an instant, all that energy released, shoving against the charge-sea with an acceleration approaching the speed of light.

The army analogy breaks down here, so let's simply say that an immense current flowed in the gun's rails and projectile. This produced a magnetic field as the fabric of the universe spun around the charge-sea. And because the up-rail and the down-rail charge flow was opposite, the magnetic fields both turned into the center, where sat that iron projectile, the crossbar of the H.

At least, it *sat* for a bare fraction of time, before the magnetic field flung it from the railgun muzzle. The velocity was so extreme that, had it not encountered obstructions, it could have crossed the night and shattered the stained glass in the rose window of St Leonard's church two hundred meters away, all in two hundredths of a second.

But the flight was not unobstructed. Fractions of a millisecond after achieving maximum velocity, before the collisions with air molecules could do much to slow it down, the projectile met skin, then bone. In so doing, the iron lost velocity in shear, the same force that makes your palms warm when you rub them together.

This projectile was designed to fragment and deform, converting its considerable energy in pulverizing flesh and shattering bone. Not unlike the HoG that had redesigned future London, it heated the tissue to vapor, before a few remaining iron fragments slammed into brick wall of the reception office.

Red released the button. At the same moment, Forbes's finger released the button under the reception counter, which had triggered a different cascade. A relay closed under the basement floor, activating electromagnets at the exits, pulling closed the rear door that David had left ajar, and dropping bank vault bolts through the steel-cored doors. The generator wound up.

In the basement, the Masked Man paused when he heard the shot, and then listened to the whine of the generator's perfectly balanced rotor accelerating. He knew that the generator was electrifying Tesla's grid all over the building, even across the locked gate of the coal chute. Tesla was paranoid, and that paranoia was the Masked Man's advantage. It would keep out anyone with a meddling interest long enough for him to complete his business. That had always been the plan.

These intruders in the building had not.

"Red," he said into the disc.

No answer.

He ran his eyes over the woman who'd come barging in here with the Scots muscleman. She had spirit, this woman, fighting against the bonds despite the futility of her efforts. The unattractive ones often had spirit. Even now, White was busy adding more stiff cord about her ankles and wrists. The Masked Man did not believe in killing, but he couldn't allow her, or anyone else, to compromise his plans. He needed to know everything, even if the plan would ultimately not change.

"White," he said. "Take an animal, find Red, and report back. I want to know what he's shooting at."

These developments mattered a great deal. Someone was dead. The Masked Man and his Pinkertons had the only weapons, and they had a prisoner. Leo and David could not reach their object in the basement. And now, the building was locked down.

Less than a second on the clock, and everything had changed.

Chapter 19

Across town, in the genteel surrounds of Baker Street, Samuel Clemens leaned back in his chair and twirled the stem of a wine glass, wanting very much to light the cigar in his breast pocket.

"You don't think this time-walking business is bizarre?" he said.

Tesla, who was shuffling papers into orderly stacks on his desk in the sitting room, gave Clemens a look that was quick, direct, and appraising.

"I have ceased to question it," he admitted, his hands still stacking. "I only learned about it after they had already approached me. When I first heard the details, I thought it a fabrication, but any doubts were overwhelmed with the evidence. I simply stopped my circling thoughts and kept on with my work. It's hard to argue when you're given the opportunity to stand on your own shoulders. Of course," he added, almost as an afterthought, "I'll admit that the power it promises makes me nervous. But I'm not meant to speak of it. This is a confidence, you understand."

"Of course." Clemens scratched at his whiskers. They'd only just now retired downstairs from the laboratory, which occupied the whole second floor, where Tesla had been demonstrating levitation with magnetic fields, a technology he assured would revolutionize the railways within ten years, even make it possible to launch men into space.

Clemens was a clever and perceptive man, but even he was given to a giddy faintness in the face of Tesla's mind and ideas. As a man whose business was words on paper, Clemens was even more astounded that Tesla did not do much work on paper himself, preferring to form his inventions in his mind and only write them down when he had to send plans to his machine shop.

The laboratory upstairs was crowded with what Tesla called 'old' equipment, and so prodigious were his elderly devices that there was only enough room to squeeze between the apparatus, and duck below racks hanging from the ceiling. Clemens counted it lucky he was shorter than Tesla, else the place would be a hazard. He had no idea how so much could come from just one man.

Even on this level, Tesla's work forced out other uses of the rooms – Clemens's wine glass competed for resting space on the side table with two unopened parcels marked with grimy fingerprints, and Tesla had presumably sat in the desk chair because the two other sitting chairs were playing host to stack of parts for wireless lights, and a basket of what could have easily been a cranial stimulation device.

"Ah, yes, your work," Clemens said, recovering his manners. "I don't suppose these Time Walkers could have given me the manuscripts for my next several novels? Have they no compassion?"

Tesla's smile was brief, but full of humor. Clemens liked the man immensely. "I did not think you would want to look, my friend, after you admit it makes you so uncomfortable."

"Very true. My life might become too easy. The artist has to struggle. I'd prefer to know about my investments."

"Yes, I suppose," Tesla said, distracted, and never very

interested in money. "I acknowledge my advantage has been great. I know more about what my life should have been than any man does. I feel a great responsibility. I am using that advantage to push ahead. London will have power free of encumbrances, a dream I did not make happen in my first life. After London, then to the world."

Clemens grunted. Tesla had taken to calling the things the Time Walkers had told him about himself his 'first life', and the one he was presently living his second. Clemens found it absurd that a life that hadn't been lived at all could come before anything. "And what of New York? Are you not meant to move there within a few years?"

Tesla shrugged philosophically. "Eventually, my inventions will be available everywhere. I am already far beyond my first lifetime's achievements. America might be better served to wait for the levitation invention to be ready, and upgrade all their systems at once."

Having finished stacking, Tesla now kept a pencil in his hand, writing out a letter as if he wasn't also carrying on a conversation.

Clemens had been taken aback when the now-famous scientist had contacted him out of the blue, inviting him to visit his laboratory in London. Clemens had almost not come that first time, but his writerly interest eventually had won out. To his surprise, he and Tesla had become fast friends. Clemens appreciated his brilliance; so much so that he hadn't been overly surprised to hear about the Time Walkers, or that in a different version of history, he and Tesla had been friends in New York. Tesla seemed easy with this 'first life' and 'second life' scenario; Clemens hadn't yet managed such a neat way of rationalizing the information.

"And what about that destructive terror you spoke of

last time?" he asked now. "The one that fleets and armies would be helpless against?"

The strokes of Tesla's pencil paused. He put the implement down. "The death ray? I confess I blustered a lot about that in my first life's work. Seems I wrote nothing down of its operation, so I suspect I became aspirational in my old age. Either that, or someone removed my notes. I've corrected those issues now, of course, but ..."

Tesla was rarely lost for words. Clemens abandoned the wine glass. "But?"

Tesla took another long pause, searching Clemens's face. Finally he said, "Beyond my own life, I know some of what this next hundred years will bring. What men will do to each other is ... staggering. In view of that, I should perhaps re-direct my efforts."

"Really?" Clemens asked, though he often avoided asking directly about the future. He suspected that Tesla would tell him what he knew, but he found the idea of knowing about your own life to be at once unsettling, and useless. After all, Tesla's life was now completely different. He'd come to London, instead of the United States. Made inventions appear ahead of their times. He was making decisions based on the known future, not the aspirational one every other man used, and where could that lead? Madness? It was reason for any rational man to avert his attention. But now, Clemens found himself with the twitching sensation in the back of his mind, which usually heralded the beginnings of a good novel. "What sort of things?"

Tesla paused once more, and then redirected. "I have something quite incredible I must show you, my friend, when you are next able to come to the main laboratory. What I have here are just triflings, items obsolete, or that I wish to keep away from the prying eyes in St Alberts."

Clemens drew the cigar from his pocket and stood. "I am always honored to see your work. St Alberts and your laboratory are fine achievements. I heard Edison bought up that Underground line through the middle just to keep tabs on you."

"I'm not concerned with Edison." Amusement then came into Tesla's voice. "Did you know that I worked for him, in my first life?"

"You did?"

"Yes. And then he failed to pay me a promised bonus, and then we entered into a protracted argument about whether direct or alternating current was the superior method for power distribution, with much useless showmanship on his part. And yet, see! Because I have avoided all that in this second life, we have wireless energy in London, and many more inventions to come."

"And yet you have an Edison-Bell telephone here."

"I don't care for telephones anymore. Let Edison make them. They are good machines, but they belong to the past."

Clemens smiled. Tesla's lack of territorialness about his work was strange in an ambitious man; but then, for a man who worked so fast, why would Tesla be threatened? No one could hope to keep up with him.

"I don't doubt it," Clemens said. "But now, my friend, you must allow me to smoke this cigar. Don't fear – I'll spare you the smell and take it outside."

Clemens didn't make it more than two paces before the lamps in the townhouse flickered, and a single red light flooded the sitting room with an ominous, bloody hue. Until that moment, Clemens had not even known about the light, and it produced an instant change in Tesla. The inventor pushed from his seat and ran to the far wall, where several gauges, lights and switches had been mounted in a decorative brass panel.

"I've been meaning to ask you what that was," Clemens said, arresting his journey to peer over Tesla's shoulder.

"Telemetry," Tesla said, distracted. "It reports the status of the laboratory." He picked up the telephone receiver. Twenty long seconds went by before he replaced it. "No answer."

"Is there a problem?"

Tesla pointed to the red light. "That light says that the main laboratory building has been secured."

"Is that not usual?"

"This is the first night in months I have not been in the main laboratory. Forbes knew I would be here until our time was over. He was to stay in the laboratory until I returned. The system should not have been activated before that."

"Perhaps he forgot."

"Forbes is exceptionally fastidious. I find the idea exceptionally unlikely."

"You are concerned?"

Tesla paused, considering the red light. "I do not like being in the dark, my friend. Probably, nothing is wrong, but my instincts are often good."

Clemens gave a short laugh. "I would trust your instincts, too. I hope the man hasn't locked himself in and gotten up to mischief. Anything dangerous in there?"

"Advanced electrical apparatus, a high-pressure boiler and steam system, numerous chemical reagents and experimental inventions, and an unknown situation. No," Tesla said, "nothing dangerous."

"I see." Clemens, sobered, put the cigar back in his

pocket. "Presumably you can open the place back up, make sure this Forbes fellow hasn't fallen down the stairs, or some such?"

"I have of course an access key," Tesla said, dangling a key in the air between them. "But the system is only meant to be turned off from my laboratory. Probably best I take a field disruptor at the correct frequency." He walked to one of the equipment racks and commenced rifling.

"That sounds … complicated."

"We have many enemies, Clemens. I designed a system to keep the building safe from anyone who might seek to profit from my inventions. I activate the system once the workers have gone home, to allow me to continue working through much of the night in my laboratory. Something secured with a mere key would be cracked in a day. Ah."

Tesla drew out an object resembling a medieval mace. Flicking a switch on the base, he pointed it at one of the wired lights, which instantly ebbed out.

Clemens raised his eyebrows, and resumed progress towards his coat. "Shall I hail a cab?

Tesla shook his head and picked up the receiver again. "I will try one more call. Then do me a favor, my friend? Stay here and—"

《〉》

Tesla stopped, feeling the pressure of someone else's attention on him. Two men were coming down his hall, two burly-looking men in great coats. Both wore neckerchiefs, one patterned with checks, the other a sickly shade of yellow, like the British winter sun. Checks raised a weapon. Tesla's eidetic memory recognized the design at once: this was one of the leaked railguns. He appreciated the irony of having his own design pointed at him.

"You'll be replacin' that doodad, there's a good lad," Checks said.

Tesla let the handset fall back into its cradle. Clemens had already reached his hands for god.

"Interesting," Tesla said, inspecting the gun levelled at his neck. "Not quite the elegance of the design I made. But still, a dual-rail, capacitance driven ballistic firearm, if I'm not mistaken."

"You won't be," Checks said, "when it puts a hole in ya. Away from that thing."

Tesla complied. He knew full well the power of the weapon this man carried, and had no plans to end his second life today. "What happens now?" he asked.

Yellow barked a short laugh. "Nuffin," he said, with no trace of a smile. He gestured to one of the sitting room chairs.

Tesla caught Clemens's eye. His friend was maintaining his composure, but all Tesla could think was that this seemed too much of a coincidence. First, his main laboratory locks down without a call from Forbes; now, these men were here.

"If you're looking for money," he said. "I don't have any. But that copper tubing there will fetch a good price, and there's a small ingot of gold upstairs, if you prefer."

"We ain't interested. Siddown."

Tesla lowered himself, remembering to kick out the tails of his jacket.

Clemens spoke up. "You fine gentleman wouldn't know anything about a situation afoot in the Royal Laboratories this evening, would you?"

Checks stared back, stony faced. Yellow scratched his neck. "We ain't here to talk."

"I see," Tesla said, softly. He knew it, then. Whatever

was going on at the main laboratory involved organized men of the nefarious kind. These two were down the tree of authority, so someone higher had thought to send them here, with the sole purpose of detaining him. Nothing more, nothing less. And that could only mean he was being kept from interference. He was the only person who could remove the lock-down at the laboratory, so it followed that whoever was there wanted it to remain secure. Wanted to be locked in. For what purpose?

It could only be to give them time.

Tesla thought of what the laboratory contained. He rarely felt fear, but he felt it now, a pure gut-emptying chill, like falling in an elevator. For there was only one reason to have time, and that was to steal. Destruction was accomplished in a moment; theft, especially careful theft of large and important things … that took time.

Yellow was poking around the papers on Tesla's desk, setting the pages askew. Tesla ground his teeth.

"How much would it be worth to you both," he tried, "to walk out of my house and disappear tonight?"

Checks took a threatening step forward. "As we said, we ain't here to talk."

Chapter 20

Leo came out of automatic pilot face down on a hard floor with something soft pressed against the side of his neck. The hard floor belonged to the library; he recognized the wooden boards supporting the bookshelves. The something soft turned out to be the woman in the suit. They were in one of the first stacks of the library, a full height shelf between them and the foyer doors. The unfriendly crack of the weapon discharging still reverberated in his head. That hadn't been the sound of a Victorian firearm; it was the air-slicing note of a supersonic bullet.

Leo crouched, his eyes split wide, searching the library for movement. The room receded into more dim shelves, and back there was the doorway into the oxygen rig, and then doors through to the receiving dock. Ahead was the foyer. To his left, the stack ran past the central aisle to the wall; to the right, it ended at another wall, this one with a hatch that looked like the one David had joked about upstairs – to the services shaft. The best choice appeared retreat, for the loading dock presumably had a door.

Leo felt every gap through the shelves like a portal for a sniper shot. He looked around for a weapon, and found nothing save a hefty *History of the Roman Empire*. Hardly practical. He strained to hear anything beyond building creaks. Where was the man with the red neckcloth? Where was David?

As the woman pushed herself up, Leo started at a *thud,*

then spotted David cowering in the stack behind, a fallen book on the floor.

Leo snuck right, towards the hatch-wall, and around the end of the stack, placing his feet on the nail line to minimize creaking. The woman followed, limping. Leo wanted to look at the map, but that would create rustling. Instead, he gestured to David that they should move down the wall towards the back.

David gave a furtive peek through the stacks at the foyer and then lunged for the wall hatch. Before Leo could do anything, David had opened it and disappeared inside like a fox down a hole.

The woman was watching this, too, her eyes wide and a tremor in her jaw. Leo had no idea what they should do at this point, except find a safe place, and David did know the building better than he did. He didn't feel like he'd felt in the army, prepared at least in some way for what he was doing.

He heard every squeak of the floor, every creak of the woman's boots as she ducked through the hatch ahead of him, which entered a mercifully short tunnel. Leo squeezed through awkwardly legs first so he could close the hatch behind, and feeling his ears pop when he did. A breeze moved across his sweating skin. He tried to block everything out except the thought of Helen for those few seconds, then David was pulling him out into a vaulting space.

They were standing in a services riser, a giant void from ground to roof with space for pipes and access ladders. Here on the ground floor, they stood at the bottom of the shaft, with just a large square penetration at the wall allowing a ladder and pipes to continue down to the basement. From that opening, Leo could hear machine noise and occasionally, voices.

Lights dotted the high wall; he could see the next floor clearly, and another light set for the third, but it looked as though this shaft continued further. Leo was surprised to find the woman had already started on the ladder up, her flat boots hooked into the rungs, though she only pushed up with her left leg. She swung round and gestured questioningly up. Leo caught David's eye, and David seemed to hesitate before he nodded, and pointed *up, up, up.*

They were going all the way to the top.

❰❮❯❱

Araminta regretted going first. Her idea had been to achieve a head start, knowing she would be slow. But then she felt the pressure to go faster, well beyond a climb she was capable of. When she finally reached the tiny landing underneath a hatch in the roof, she had to lean on the rail, her head spinning at the precipitous drop below, and allow the man in the suit to push the hatch open. She was shaking so badly he then also had to pull her up, the bigger man boosting her from below.

She collapsed to the ground, gasping in the attic. It echoed, all hard spaces and emptiness with only a little night light bleeding in through high windows. She felt a queer detachment from what had happened down in the lobby, as if the dramatic departure from her evening's plans could not yet be reconciled.

"Are you hurt?" asked the man in the suit. Araminta jumped.

"No," she managed, still breathless.

"You are limping," he pressed. "I'm a doctor."

Araminta shrank away; she had learned an early caution

against doctors, who meant pain and invasions of her person. This one wore tailored clothes, the mark of a man successful in his profession, with a noble face but an expanse of forehead that she thought would be more becoming on a bull. She didn't much like him. "I am not injured," she said firmly, folding her arms.

The Doctor stepped back, eyeing her suspiciously. "And just who are you, then, madam?"

Araminta paused, stuck, because she didn't know who these men were, or what had just transpired downstairs. She snuck a glance at the bigger man, who had closed the hatch and was now slowly pacing a line away from it. She noticed his arm shaking, and the way he gripped his hands together to conceal the tremor. He wore no waistcoat or jacket, just a shirt that must be inadequate against the chill. She judged him as a man who's raised himself up from the working classes, without stuffy affectation. Perhaps he was a craftsman, working in the machinery shop. And after what he'd done for her downstairs, he had bravery. She looked back the Doctor.

"I am Araminta, Lady Montague," she said, leaning on her title for the first time in her life. "I had an appointment with Mr. Tesla."

"Bollocks," the Doctor exclaimed, rudely. "Tesla isn't here."

"As I am now aware," she said, and pushed herself up. The bigger man had turned a corner, and was now returning on another straight line, further away from the hatch.

"Not so fast," the Doctor said, jumping away from her as if she were a dangerous quarry. "What are you doing here? It's past shift end. The building is supposed to be empty, and we're being attacked and here you are."

Araminta caught the insinuation. "I have never seen that man before in my life," she said, indignant. "I am Araminta, Lady Montague. I have an appointment with Mr. Tesla. See here."

She pulled the crumpled letter from her pocket and brandished it at the man, her own hand shaking. He paused to peer at the text, but when he reached for the letter, she did not relinquish her grasp. No need for him to see the appointment was for tomorrow until absolutely necessary.

"Where did you get this?" he asked.

Araminta snatched the page back. "Through Mr. Disraeli. He facilitates our correspondence."

The Doctor straightened. "Disraeli?"

"The Prime Minster," Araminta said.

"I know who Disraeli is." The Doctor's voice had become thin, cautious. He glanced towards the other man, then slowly dropped his head. "Great," he muttered under his breath.

"Shhh." This from the big man, who had now crouched at one corner of his pacing box and put his ear to the floor. He had a rumpled piece of paper in his hand. After a moment, he stood. "That door," he asked, pointing to a door dimly visible in the far corner. "That's access to the maintenance stair?"

The doctor nodded. "And this other door leads to the main stairs."

"I figured." The big man scrutinized the paper in his hand, then said, "David, there's someone shooting a high-powered weapon down there. You're not going to tell me he's a disgruntled investor?"

"I have no idea who that was, but he isn't one of ours," the man called David said, tugging at his waistcoat. He began pacing again. "Jesus, this is not happening."

"That wasn't a standard-issue handpiece," the big man said. "In fact, I'm fairly sure that was a railgun."

David nodded slowly.

"I thought you said they were all dealt with."

"They were. Look, I don't remember every trip here, okay?"

"Then how—"

"Because Disraeli told me as much."

At this, Araminta finally gained traction on the conversation. So, this David knew Disraeli. She remembered when Disraeli had mentioned problems with Tesla's work, and the weapons that had been recovered. She limped a short distance, under a skylight, trying to remember what else he had said. She could see a faint purple glow to the light, and tiny tongues of blue flame at the edges of the glass. Evidence of the active security system. So where was Tesla? Clearly, that man downstairs was one of his enemies.

She returned to find the big man still pacing in the square pattern. "Why are you doing that?" she asked.

"Marking out the shaft we came up so I wasn't standing on it," the big man said. "Didn't fancy someone taking a shot up from underneath."

Araminta swallowed. "Is that man here to hurt Mr. Tesla?"

"All right, I need to think about this," David said, interrupting her with a silencing hand. "I can fix this. Just find another way to finish the job and leave." He continued pacing, muttering to himself.

Araminta shot a questioning look at the big man.

"I think we can safely assume," he said to her, "that whoever that man is down there, he is not friendly. David. David."

"Hmm?"

"I'd like to return to the subject of an armed combatant shooting a railgun," the big man said. "So what's down in the basement? This map only shows the boiler room. Or don't you remember?"

"It doesn't matter, Leo," David said.

"Yeah, it does. Because the whole game just changed. You do realize Forbes is dead."

What little color was left in David's face bled away. "Forbes?" he said, as if not comprehending.

"I know where he aimed," Leo said. "And he hit his mark. That makes two men down for starters. Forbes was on your side, right? So that's very bad news for us. So what's so important down in that basement that two men are dead for it?"

There was a long pause, where both Leo and Araminta looked at David. There was something about Leo that Araminta trusted, and she didn't do such things easily.

"A device," David said finally, under their scrutiny. "Look, I might not remember absolutely everything, but I know this. There's a device that needs to be destroyed."

"Why would a device of Tesla's need to be destroyed?" Araminta asked, confused. "Who exactly are you gentlemen?" she asked, a little sparkle of fear in her chest, as much that she might find her trust in Leo was a false one.

"We're here to resolve … a technical problem," Leo said, cutting off David. "One with a tight timetable."

"What kind of technical problem?"

"When David lets us into that knowledge, we'll both have it."

"I see," she said, a little more hopeful that David may also be an ally, one in the first circle of Tesla's employees.

"Mr. Tesla sent you?"

"You could say that," David said. "We have to salvage the situation, somehow. Have to salvage it. Leo, you're a soldier, right? This is your department. You can go down there and, you know." He waved a hand.

"And what? This isn't *Die Hard*," Leo said, looking around the dim attic. "There's a guy down there walking around with a *railgun* that can atomize a man at fifty paces. If we stay in the building with him, we're going to die. I know because if I were him, I'd start searching the building systematically for us. Tactics haven't changed that much since this time."

"It's just one man."

"You don't know that. Hate to break it to you, Doctor D, but one unarmed man against a group only works in the movies. And this one has the equivalent of a canon. What do we have?"

David's throat bobbed as he swallowed. "But we have to fix it," he whispered. "Helen's counting on us."

Leo shook his head. "How on earth did you run operations here, if some of the transmissions you didn't even remember?"

"I keep comprehensive field notes in my office," David said, looking at the ground. "Usually Helen transmits me there so I can consult them before heading out. It's not perfect, but it works."

Leo grunted. "Regardless of that," he said. "The Grid is still unstable, so we can assume this railgun guy isn't here to do our work for us."

"So ... this other man is here to steal Tesla's device?" Araminta surmised, trying to follow. "And you want to destroy it before he can?"

A moment's silence indicated that everyone believed

this was the most likely conclusion.

David tugged on his waistcoat, then straightened his body, seeming to pull his thoughts together at the same time. "Even if that's true, the security system's been activated, so he can't go anywhere. Besides, the device is large. He'll not be able to remove it alone."

"All the more reason to expect there to be more men," Leo said. "And so we're stuck, in the same building with them and their superior firepower, until we work out a way to destroy this device. And we have to do it in the next few hours at most or Helen is going to be a pile of ashes and all of this will cease to exist. Am I correct so far?"

"Yes, I suppose." David's voice was tight. "There's another thing I should mention. One other problem."

"What?" Leo asked.

David looked down at the floor, his jaw quilted with tension. "The, uh, the Queen is also in the basement."

〈〈 〉〉

Queen Victoria acquired many labels, both during and after her lifetime, in addition to those owed to her by birth and rank. These included the 'widow of Windsor', the 'grandmother of Europe', and 'Mrs. Brown', a reference to her trusted Scottish manservant. This Brown was one of her solaces after the death of her beloved husband, Albert, and the same Brown who had both terrorized David, and who now lay dead in the basement. For anyone like Victoria who lives so long with such high profile, official and unofficial titles accumulate and compete with the reality of the person. Perhaps this affected former Prime Minister Gladstone, of whom Victoria complained spoke to her more as "a public meeting" rather than as a woman.

David had been blindsided, too, in their first meeting,

but in a different way. Struck by the diminutive and physically unimpressive Victoria, he had avoided the tongue-tie she could often induce. Instead, he'd bantered with her, and she had been initially impressed with his intellect, his observations, and what he could reveal about the future. David had assessed her as easily-steered, and learned too late that underneath all the titles and labels, Victoria served her own agenda, though that agenda often aligned with the good of the country.

She had extracted sufficient information from David to prop up the ageing Disraeli in the Prime Minister's office, because she preferred him. But from David, she had extracted a much greater object, something her money and power alone could not buy.

It was true, David did not remember all the transmissions he'd made into the timefield, including the last several. But he'd had a very strong feeling that it would be bad luck to come back again. It was an idea implanted in his subconscious that had somehow resonated across The Machine's quantum divide.

"The Queen?" Leo was saying. "You think Queen Victoria is in the building?"

"That's what I was saying before – that man on the basement floor is *John Brown*, her most trusted manservant. Her carriage is in the lane. Believe me, she's here."

Leo pulled his console from his pocket and checked the Grid numbers, which were jumping around in a particularly violent fashion. He dug his fingers into his scalp. Complication on complication. "Shit."

"The Queen is here?" Araminta asked. "But whatever for?"

Why didn't even figure in Leo's thoughts. Victoria was one of the most important public figures of this era.

Perhaps the most important. If she was at the mercy of armed gunmen, if her life was in jeopardy, that could explain a hugely irreconcilable difference in the timefield. Maybe that was the reason for the instability.

"Great," he said. They were in worse trouble than he'd thought. "We can't deal with this situation. We have no weapons. We don't know how many of these men are in the building, but they know we are here, and eventually they're going to find us."

Araminta looked as though she had really lost the thread of their discussion now, but she understood the implications. "So we must turn off Tesla's security system, and go for help." She looked at the two men expectantly.

"She's right. There's no other option," Leo said. "You can't bring a knife to a supersonic gun fight."

He stalked across to the large water tank, and after searching around, finally bent and came up with three short, thick lengths of discarded pipe. He then moved to the maintenance stair door and locked it, passing a pipe through the handles. He kept the last pieces for himself.

Araminta frowned. "So you're going to take a pipe."

Leo nodded, his mouth grim. "Well I don't have a knife." He could still feel the cracking sound of the railgun, that tearing note as if the bullet could rip the air apart. "We get out of the fight first. And, I don't know, call the Met."

David snorted. "Not the Met. Disraeli has a private force being trained for just such things." He then snuck a look at Araminta. "Apparently he got the idea from the Boers."

Leo gave a short laugh. "Commandos," he said, with a weird sense of connection. He'd worked with green berets in his military career, and now here he was, at the inception point of the concept in the British Armed Forces. But whatever weird it was, at least they would have weapons and training, which was a damn sight more than Leo had now. "So we get out and contact Disraeli."

David shook his head. "The only place we can turn off the security system is from Tesla's laboratory."

"But his laboratory is locked," Araminta said. Then her face lit. "When we were climbing, I saw small doors into other floors. Does one lead into Tesla's laboratory?"

"Doesn't look like it on this map," Leo said, looking at David, "only lots of things aren't on here."

"No," David said. "Tesla removed it in the plans. There's none on level three. The only way in is through the main doors."

"You don't have a key?" Leo asked.

"Tesla's lab has a combination panel for the deadbolts, and a key for the door. I have the combination, but not the key. Tesla would never negotiate on that."

"What kind of lock are we talking about?"

David shrugged. "Skeleton type key into the door handle."

"What about the deadbolts?"

"All around the outside of the doors. They retract when the combination is entered. Some kind of electromechanical system in the wall."

Leo squared his shoulders. "Then that's where we go. You retract those deadbolts, I can take care of a basic door lock."

"Take care of it how?" Araminta asked.

"I'm going to knock with my sizeable boot," Leo said. He'd broken down more than one door in his life, and a double door was even better; the leaves weren't as solid a connection as a door and a jamb.

"Yes, good," David said, brightening. "And there's a

phone in Tesla's lab. It only calls Tesla's townhouse, but we could lock ourselves in and call him to put the commandos in motion."

Leo didn't like the problem-solved tone in David's voice. Nothing about this was good.

"If we can get in so easily, won't that man be able to enter also?" Araminta asked.

Leo caught her eye. "Maybe. All sieges are a bad idea. But it's a better position than here. And we only have to go down one floor."

"If we do turn off the security, how do we then leave the building?"

Leo privately thought that if they got that far, they'd be doing well. But he looked at the map anyway. "We'll need a way to the front door. David, you said that reagent lab on the first floor has interlocks?"

"Yeah, on the airlock doors."

"Then that's our secured position on the way out."

They all stared at each other a moment. Then David said, "that lab has an interlocked door into the maintenance stairs, too."

Leo nodded. "Then that's also our plan B." He got up and strode towards the maintenance stair.

"What are you doing?" Araminta's voice came from behind. She sounded like Helen used to, whenever he did something she wasn't included in.

"Putting another pipe bar in the maintenance stair door," he said. "We don't want these guys coming up behind us."

Chapter 21

When Red returned downstairs, the Masked Man was with Green in the boiler room, while White and the dog stood guard just inside the stair doors. The body of the Scot had been taken away. The Masked Man could have allowed the complication of a body to unnerve him, but he was focused. He was verifying a sketch Forbes had provided, showing the central locomotive boiler, the generator to one side half sunk in the floor, and the supply lines snaking to and from the units. Along the west wall, pipes with various diameters from a finger-thin to a thigh-thick rose up out of the floor and into a control manifold, before diving back down into the grating. The Masked Man observed Red's confusion when he looked at all this machine architecture. Who knew what on in such a man's mind; if Red could read, he would have seen order in the chaos, the lines variously labelled: *Steam – east wing, Steam – west wing, Steam – extraction, Water – boiler, Water – waste* … but would he still have made any more sense of it?

But Red did know better than to interrupt. The Masked Man had impressed that this task was mundane but essential – the fast drill needed water. So Red waited until Green began shutting valves and re-directing the line. The Masked Man then turned to Red.

"What happened to your radio?"

Red shrugged. "Just getting' a lot o' hiss." And then he laid out the situation. Four people sighted upstairs, two men, a woman, and a boy. Forbes was dead.

The Masked Man twitched in irritation. "That was not the plan."

"He proved himself unreliable. He told us the coast was clear when it weren't. He's a loose mouth," Red argued.

"Bodies create questions," the Masked Man said. "More bodies, more questions."

"Dead men don't talk, though."

The Masked Man did not betray any outward sign of his amusement or approval. Such a thing was not wise. Instead, he catalogued his progress. Besides the unexpected people, and the loss of radio — probably interference from the building — all else seemed in order. He took out a stopwatch. As soon as he heard the rush of diverted water, he started the timer. A minute later, the rumble of the drill was audible, so he knew Black was in his stride, handling the fast drill to widen the hole, and make it large enough for their prize.

He beckoned White to join Red, and placed the stopwatch in his pocket.

"Where are these people now?" he asked.

"Went into the library," Red said. "Blue's waiting at top of the stairs, in case they decide to come out. It's a dead end."

The Masked Man's nose wrinkled. He would never have been an inventor if he believed in dead ends.

"Make sure they are still there," he told White. "And then, Red and Blue: go up to the top floor and begin the search for the calculation machine. This is what it looks like."

He unfolded a hand-drawn sketch that Forbes had provided.

"What's that?" the men asked in unison, leaning in to scrutinize the pencil marks.

"Doesn't matter what it is. It's what it *does*. I want it found. Now."

When they had gone, the Masked Man took up his folding chair again, sitting opposite the woman Red had caught. A short, dowdy, dumpy woman, wearing a brown dress. He extracted a knife from his pocket, but she didn't flinch.

The Masked Man leaned forward. He played with the knife as he spoke. "You spend a great deal of time looking at this," he said, nodding his head towards the bulk of metal in the room. "Tell me what you know of it?"

She gave him a scowl so fierce that the Masked Man could almost smell her tenacity. He smiled.

❰❮❯❱

White experienced instant relief on leaving the basement, even with the animals pulling so hard his arm bones stretched out of their sockets. He sympathized with them. He hated the tight, underground space, too. The noise of the drill as it bit the rock, the constant drone of the generator and the roar of the boiler. The strange smells of oil and metal leaking out of every seam in the tunnel. The skin-crawling creeps of the Masked Man who directed them. And the animals felt the same. They wanted to be in open space, and hunting.

He joined Blue and Red as they threw open the library doors. They advanced inside, the dogs surging. White dropped their leads. They shot into the labyrinth of shelves and furniture, like oiled seals through water.

White expected a quick find. But when the dogs found nothing, he and Blue began their own search. A minute later, they established the library was empty. They swept the shelves again and found no one, not even lurking in the strange set-up of pipes and tanks, partly walled off at the far end. They even broke the lock into the cavernous space of the receiving dock, and searched through the pallets of supplies and tea chests and shelves. All was crushing silence. The only evidence anyone had been here was the dislodged book, on the floor near the front of the library.

The Masked Man would not be happy.

White had his first moment of crippling worry. He had no primer to give the dogs, and dozens of people came through this building every day. Tracking would be difficult. But he could not go back downstairs with nothing.

It took ten long minutes of searching to note the hatch in the wall, its seams blending with the molding. White hauled the door open and found a tunnel, running under the stairs and into a vaulted space behind the elevator. With a portable blinder, he could see the scuffs in the accumulated dust on the floor and on the ladder rungs. They had gone this way. A route the dogs could not follow.

He smiled. The hunt might take a little longer, but it had just become interesting.

《〈〉》

By the time he had formed a coherent thought again, William's back had taken on the shape of the wall underneath the reception desk, complete with a long indentation for the skirting across his bony behind, and a sharp notch into his scalp from the angled desk support. His joints had seized painfully, and yet he dare not move. The blood on the boards had ceased creeping towards his drawn-up toes, but it formed a barrier that may as well have been a moat.

He had been in this position since first hearing the footsteps of the Red Man approaching. William had heard a *chink* of a belt buckle and smelled the stench of a long-worn coat as Red had leaned over the counter.

Forbes, or what was left of him, had not moved in response. The former domus supervisor was lying on the floor, having tumbled over the counter. The wall beyond was covered in a bright spray of atomized flesh, and a ragged edge of white shirt was now soaked deep red. Forbes was really only recognizable by his suit, and was no longer capable of moving.

William sat paralyzed with scenarios in his mind. Was Red still out there, waiting for him to emerge? Had Araminta escaped, or did Red have her? There had only been one shot, so William assumed she must be still alive. But there had also been no screams.

William experienced a tiny twinge of responsibility, but his urge to flee was like an animal in his chest, straining to be let out. He just had to summon the courage to crawl out of the office, across the foyer, into the dock and out of the building. Then he could slip away into the lanes of St Alberts.

He'd just moved his foot when he heard new steps, and gruff men's voices again across the foyer. Three different voices, and something else: a huffing, panting breath, like a resting steam train. William didn't know what that was until the smell of dog reached him. He knew enough about the tenacity of stray mutts to be alarmed. And so, he stayed where he was, frozen, waiting for another chance to move.

Chapter 22

Across space-time, Helen exists in similar limbo. In the few exposed moments while she waits for the soldier's move, she doesn't have time for thoughts. There's only time for a sense she may have missed something about the timefield.

If she had had time to consider all the numbers, and chew an apple, and really *think*, she'd have gone back over those first blips she noticed in the data. Revisited the idea of a Machine echo being the cause. Because it can't be coincidence that a problem developed in the timefield, one that kept David there, and that now is keeping Leo there. Coincidences don't happen in this kind of sequence. They happen in lots of other places, but not this one.

The only thing is, the dots connecting the pieces often aren't penciled in until later, when someone else is sifting through the rubble. By that point, you're only good as a textbook case for some later practitioner to study, perhaps voyeuristically, because everyone thinks they won't fall prey to the same problems. Helen knows she's in this situation now, in the middle of a causal chain, but she hadn't yet seen the problem. Part of the reason is that these chains don't have single-point origins. They are branches of factors that twist together to create the disaster. The systemic safety failures of the *Deepwater Horizon* were like that. So was the O-ring fault and decision making for *Challenger*. The design faults and procedural violations that preceded *Chernobyl*.

The textbooks pull them apart, but they always exhibit chains of lost opportunities to avert the crisis.

Well, this timefield, this Machine – it's the last shot. There won't be a textbook about this, not if they don't pull it off. She doesn't have to see the whole chain, just has to grab one of the links before it's gone.

So, she focuses on what she knows: The Machine, something about The Machine. What could it be doing that produced that instability signal?

This is what she would have been doing if she could. But Helen didn't have time for these thoughts. Every molecule of her body is concerned with staying alive, and protecting The Machine. Waiting for the solider to make his move, and waiting for Leo to make his.

Chapter 23

It took all of thirty seconds to re-enter the stairs from the roof, and edge down the two flights to the second-floor foyer. Leo considered rigging a mechanism to lock the door after them, perhaps creating the impression they were still hiding somewhere in the attic, and thus giving them more time. But he knew he might regret that later – locking both doors to the attic could lead to dead ends of the literal variety.

Every footstep down the stairs seemed to creak or groan a note that must sound all the way to the basement. Leo expected at any moment to be confronted from below, until his heart beat so hard he couldn't hear anything else. He was almost hyperventilating, with the short length of pipe too insubstantial in his hand, as they crossed the corner of the second-floor foyer and took refuge in the transmission room.

There, he lowered the pipe, and looked around with a sense of déjà vu. He was back in the room he'd first arrived in, with its stacks of tea chests and the softly whirring and clicking table-top machine behind. The calculating machine felt like the only thing that hadn't changed, obliviously tracing its graph with steady precision through the whole time that Leo's circumstances had been upending.

David took two steps towards the calculation machine, peering at it, his footsteps slowing and the posture of his body suggesting apprehension. Maybe the calculating machine had been running when David had last been transmitted, and so he too was fixated on being back where he'd started, but in so much worse a position.

Leo crept to the door, and slowly cased the empty hallway and what he could see of the foyer. No one there. He edged down the hall until he could see the neat brass panel by the doors to Tesla's lab.

"David," he hissed when he returned.

David was still peering at the machine.

"*David.*"

David shook himself and turned back.

"Be as fast as you can putting in that combination. As soon as we hear the deadbolts release, you make yourself flat against the wall while I push through the door. I'll try to keep the catch intact to close again, but it'll make some noise, so Araminta, you be ready to move. We get in there fast, I close the doors, and David re-locks the deadbolts from inside."

David straightened his waistcoat. His skin had tinted grey.

"And take your shoes off," Leo said. "Those leather soles make too much noise."

David slipped off the shoes, straightened his waistcoat again, and snuck out of the transmission room. Leo crept into the hall mouth so he could keep watch on the stairway. David reached the brass panel, and flipped it open. Leo could see his arm working as he entered the combination.

Nothing happened. David paused, his arm motionless, then tried again.

Leo counted the seconds. He'd been out there more than a minute. Finally, after a third attempt, David closed the panel and made a retreat.

Back in the transmission room, the Doctor shook his head. "It's not working. Tesla must have changed it. I'd have that recorded in my field notes."

"Could you break down the door anyway?" Araminta asked, giving Leo a look that said she thought him capable of it.

"Those doors are held with bank vault pins," David said. "And the walls and doors are reinforced with steel plate."

"Even I have my limits," Leo murmured. "Don't suppose you have a spare sledgehammer and an oxyacetylene torch."

"Maybe in the workshop ..."

Leo shook his head. "It would take too long, standing out there, making that much noise. Tell me about that combination lock."

"It has eight switches. Each one can be top, center, or down. You have to enter the combination from left to right, and all the switches spring back to center after the last one is entered."

"Had to be a weird-arse system," Leo muttered.

"Six-thousand five-hundred and sixty-one," Araminta said softly. "Combinations."

Leo blinked. "You just worked that out in your head?"

Up until this point, he hadn't given Araminta much thought. He was awkward enough around people of his own time, let along this Victorian native. He didn't know how to take her; she was nothing like the women in the period dramas he'd sometimes been subjected to watching, and when she'd said she had an appointment with Tesla, somewhere in his brain he'd shelved her as a librarian or an aide, someone caught in the crossfire but not significant to what he was doing. Now, he was forced to reappraise her,

her eyes lit up with numbers. She reminded him of Helen, correcting his A-level maths homework even though she was watching a documentary on cosmology and eating a TV dinner, because Helen could do those things simultaneously in her head.

Araminta appeared to blush. "Not exactly. I memorized power tables one summer."

"You memorized power tables?"

"I was staying at my aunt's country residence. It was that, or contemplate how deep the pond was. I memorized powers of two and three with particular diligence." Araminta gave him a small smile.

"Your aunt must be a riot," he said dryly. "But that's too many combinations to guess."

"There's still the telephone in my office on the first floor," David said. "We can call Tesla from there. He must be able to re-enter the building. Or perhaps he has a way to turn the system off remotely. We could go down the maintenance stair at the end of the hall, then through the reagent lab to stay off the main stairs."

Leo didn't like the idea; it meant travelling a much greater distance, and through parts of the building he hadn't seen. "No system is impregnable," he said.

"How does the mechanism work?" Araminta asked.

"David?" Leo said.

"Why are you asking me? I'm not a locksmith."

Leo sighed. "Might be time for plan B. Get the new combination from your field notes and—"

He stopped. He'd heard something, a barely out-of-place sound. An echo? Or something else?

He signaled the others to keep quiet and slipped into the hall, placing his feet to avoid creaking, the pipe in his hand. In a few steps he emerged into the foyer. After the dark of the hallway, he felt bathed in luminescence. The doors to Tesla's lab were silent and closed, the stairs up to the roof empty and dim.

Then, something moved at his vision's edge. If Leo had paused to allow his mind to assess the information, to process it, react to it, he would have been dead. The brain is an organ that recognizes patterns. The information that floods in through our eyes and ears and skin is so immense that processing it all in every moment is impossible. It would be like a post-master drowning in mail as he tries to read each individual address. Instead, the brain uses its experience and the broad patterns of information to assume what is happening. It is a system with expectations, and those expectations have the inertia of heavy-haul train. Should something unexpected enter the field of view, the brain can take a long time to register the departure. This is how drivers fail to notice a strange object on the road. Seconds can pass, enough time for everyone to be dead.

Leo did not think. His animal brain short-circuited complex reasoning and wrung his adrenals out into his arterial blood, lifted the brakes on his heart rate, and drove blood past the scar tissue of his knee and into his calf muscles. Those instincts were the only reason Leo made it into the hall before Red, White, and Blue were in view of the foyer.

It was not enough to prevent Leo being seen; just enough for him not to be dead.

David and Araminta were standing in the doorway of the transmission room when Leo came flying on rails. He only had time to point. David and Araminta ran, too, but Leo was at speed and ended up pushing David, low in the back, and scooping up Araminta under the arm. She would never keep up with her limp.

He ran like that, hardly feeling the effort, or the pain in his knee, not hearing anything over the roar of his breath. Every nerve was focused on flight. *Adrenaline is magic stuff.*

The hall curved around to its end and David was the one who reached for the door, throwing open the maintenance stair. In the eons this seemed to take, Leo heard barking.

Barking?

He pulled up and spun back. A black mound of fur loomed in the mouth of the hall, snapping out the oddly suppressed noise, as if the animal were behind a glass panel. The three men stood behind, watching. Leo glanced to see David and Araminta disappear through the stair doorway.

The dog surged forward.

Leo bolted through the door and pulled it closed. There was no way to lock it from the inside; all he could do was run. As he scrambled down the spiraling steps, nearly blind in the low light, he heard the dog scrabbling at the door, and that same far-off barking sound, making it seem the dog – if that's what it was – was much further away. The perceptual distortion crept gooseflesh down Leo's back.

More frightening still was when the noise abruptly ceased. Then silence seeped into Leo's chest and curdled into terror. He half expected to find the men and the dog waiting on the next floor down. His mind regressed, and he was a soldier again, unarmed and behind the lines of the enemy, looking for a way out, hearing nothing but gunfire and the shouts of his team, tasting dirt and rot. Training had been what saved him, then. He found that training again now, and caught up with David and Araminta, holding them back on the next landing while he pushed on the door, the pipe thrust out before him.

The door was heavy, and stiff, with thick seals around the frame. They gave with a sucking sound, and immediately came a pneumatic *thunk* from inside the walls. Leo flinched, but the space ahead was empty.

He stepped through into a small airlock, with a door at either end, the cool, silent air smelling faintly of chemicals.

《〉》

When David pulled the stair door closed behind them, Leo heard the same *thunk* again. This time, he recognized it as a solenoid driven lock operating inside the wall. He pulled out the map.

"That's the reagent lab through there, right?" he asked, trying to suppress the escape impulse from the close space.

David nodded. Leo reached for the inner door handle, and turned it without pushing the door. Another *thunk* sounded from the door behind him.

"Try the stair door please?" He said it through gritted teeth, checking the urge to fly out into the lab without caution. Which would be a great way to get killed.

Araminta grasped the handle. "It's locked," she said.

"Good." Slowly, Leo pushed his door open and peered into the laboratory beyond. At first glance, the desks, benches, and tall cabinets appeared to have no order. They were set against each other and stuffed with materials. Only two blinders shone so the shadows were deep, but Leo could see great banks of brown stoppered jars, jumbles of retort stands, thick coils like car springs, electrodes, tanks, and reels of wire. The place looked well-used, with lab coats left draped over the stools, and stacks of record books — some open at a half-filled page — and boxes of worn measuring spoons and stirrers. He crouched, scanning through the legs of stools and benches.

No movement.

He crawled on his stiffening knee across the space to the far wall. Here, at the foyer end, were two sealed doors, each much like the one they'd entered through, except these ones each had a small round window, about the size of a dinner plate. Two more airlocks.

"Those doors have the same interlock system?" he said, after returning to the others.

"As far as I know," David said.

"Linked with this single one, or independent?"

"Independent. But the foyer pair are linked to each other. Only one door in the set opens at a time."

"Well, that's something." Leo reached for a limp lab coat. He looped it into a thick fold and wedged open the inner door they'd entered through.

"What is 'something'?" Araminta asked.

Leo didn't answer immediately. He signaled for her and David to wait, then crept again across the lab to the double doors at the foyer end. He opened the left-most one, and heard this time a dual *thunk* as the locks on both the foyer entry doors engaged. Leo grabbed another coat, and wedged the left inside door open.

He breathed out, trying to pay attention to what materials they had in here. A cabinet between the entry and exit airlocks held two rows of fire grenades, blown glass bulbs the size of a highlander's fist. The top rows were filled with salt water. The bottom bulbs were marked *carbon tetrachloride*. Lovely. He didn't know if he was more disturbed by the toxicity of carbon tetrachloride, or the rudimentary fire control. In a chemical lab, you didn't really want to be fighting a fire with high-tech water balloons.

"David explained there's an interlock," Araminta said when Leo returned. "So the outer doors lock when the inner is open. And therefore these men can't follow us in."

She seemed needing confirmation from him, so he nodded. She leaned against a bench, relieved, but he saw pain in her expression. "What do they do here to need such a door system?"

"You mean, what are we locked in here with?" Leo asked, moving systematically through the benches, cataloguing and ensuring no one was lying in wait. He passed a rack of strong acids, each carefully labelled with quill pen on paper. On another bench were flasks of cloudy yellow liquid that smelled of fermentation. Which meant growing organics – yeasts or bacteria. None of these were labelled. Retort stands crowded other surfaces, along with stoppered glass jars. He would have had no idea what half of the equipment in here did, and given how little Victorians respected toxic heavy metals and understood bacteria, he gave it all a wide perimeter.

"My guess would be concern about contaminated air leaking out," he said on return. "There's not really any other reason to have airlocks on a lab."

"Air contamination?" Araminta asked. "Are you talking of germ theory? I've read the work of John Snow."

"A precaution only," David interjected. "The Victorians are still so much into miasmas; it was to allay fears of spreading disease."

Araminta gave him a scathing look. "What a peculiar thing to say," she said. "Especially for a doctor. Are you not aware of the recanted views of William Farr on cholera, or Koch's proof on the causation of anthrax? Surely you don't give credit to this antiquated view of miasmas?"

David was clearly taken aback. "I meant that people of your time don't yet fully grasp—"

"David," Leo said, cutting him off. "The people of our

time are still in the same situation, if you haven't noticed."

David straightened his waistcoat. Araminta shifted her gaze between the two of them, her brows drawn down. She hadn't missed David's reference. Eventually, she said, "Are we not simply trapped here, now?"

"We have a little time to think," Leo said, casing the room again. Microscopes on a table. Racks of empty flasks, petri dishes and pipettes, and jars of powders lined the far wall. Next to them were bottles of clear liquid, labelled "buffer" with various chemical compositions written underneath. He couldn't make his thoughts turn any of this into something useful.

"My office is right out there, in the foyer," David said, walking towards that end. "My field notes, and the combination to Tesla's lab are just *there*."

"Stay out of the line of those doors," Leo said. "Unless you'd like to be shot through the port holes."

"That is Tesla glass," David began. "It does not simply break."

"Seen it tested against a railgun?"

Leo had no sooner said it than they heard a rattle of a door handle. They all involuntarily ducked.

Leo listened around his own shallow breaths. Someone was trying one of the entry doors out in the foyer. He couldn't hear the footsteps through the thick sealed doors, but a few seconds later, that rattle came again, more muffled this time. Someone was trying the outer door on the other airlock, now, the one whose inner door was still closed.

The men were out there. Probably that dog-thing, too.

Araminta's voice was soft beside him. "How long do you think it will be before these men work out how to open the door?"

"I don't know," Leo said.

"Will they not simply shoot their weapons at it?"

Leo considered. "They seem reluctant to fire, else they could easily have shot me upstairs. That could mean the guns have limited shots, so perhaps it would not be worth expending the ammunition. As to the doors, solenoid locks can be powerful, and those doors are thin and steel. There's no bulk for a bullet to fragment inside. Shooting the door might just put a very small hole in it. Of course, it could still put a very large hole in one of us."

She swallowed audibly, and then asked, "How does the lock work?"

"Solenoids. That's an electromagnet being used to throw the bolt. There must be a switch somewhere in the doorframe that triggers a circuit when it's open or closed. It could be all electrical, or the magnet might be acting on a hydraulic circuit under pressure."

"What if the power was to fail?"

"It could be set to fail with locks engaged, or open."

"And if it has this hydraulic system, what then, if the pressure fails?"

Leo's mouth compressed. "If they cut a pressure line, all the locks could open. But they'd have to be clever enough to work that out."

"You think they are fools?"

An uncomfortable silence settled. "No," Leo said, softly. "Never assume your enemy is a fool."

They shared a look of understanding, before Leo glanced at David.

"So let's think about what else we can do. Is there any way we could turn off the building security from this room? Find the electrical lines in the wall running to Tesla's lab and cut the power to the security system that way?"

"It's wireless power transmission," David reminded him.

Leo cursed. "You had to build this place with an electrical genius, didn't you?"

"My office is right behind that wall. It's only a few meters across the foyer," David complained again.

"A few meters with direct shot lines from the staircase, the workshop, and probably in some places through the void in the floor," Leo said. "To even see what's going on out there means sticking your head up in that tiny port window. Are you volunteering?"

David responded with silence.

"And then we'd have to get back to Tesla's lab, assuming we trust whatever combination is written down in your book, and hope that these men haven't stationed guards to watch up there."

In this time, Araminta had crept over to the wall separating them from David's office and was sitting against it. Now she ran her hand over the surface. "You said the walls into Tesla's laboratory upstairs were brick and steel," she said. "What about this one?"

Leo ran his own thumb over the surface, then tapped with his knuckle, down low. He expected a solid feel, the wattle and daub of Victorian plasterwork. Instead, it sounded hollow. "Sounds like stud wall."

He set his pipe down and put a hand to the wall, thinking. There were a dozen ways to put a large hole in that wall. The trick was going to be to do it quietly, so that the men out in the foyer didn't know what they were doing. He turned back to David and Araminta.

"Stay low and look around. For prying tools, and anything soft we could use to muffle some noise. Also, I think I saw gas bottles down the back there."

"What are you going to do?" David asked.

"If we're going to try this, we might need to make a statement," Leo said. "Let's get to work."

Chapter 24

Twenty minutes later, Leo had used a small metal chisel to cut a slit in the plaster, and crack away a piece about a foot square. The process had taken an age, the noise muffled with a discarded lab coat. Leo had sweated through his shirt and was white with plaster dust. Then, just when he thought progress was made, he discovered the other side of the wall was lath, with thin strips of wood nailed into the studs and coated in more plaster. He had cursed with free abandon. Araminta's eyes had rounded in shock.

"There's no quiet way through that," he said. "I'll have to break the wood, or saw through it if there's anything in here that could cut. They're going to hear that, and breaking down the office door will be easy."

Araminta stood chewing her lip. All the time he'd worked on the wall, she had been pacing out of the way, as if feeling as locked in as Leo did. Now, she approached.

"The conversation never heard is the one across a crowded ball room," she said. "Can we not make more noise?"

"More noise?" David said. "Are you crazy? That will just confirm where we are."

"I think they know that much," Leo said, dryly. "They have a dog with them, or whatever that thing was." He glanced at Araminta, again arrested by how much she reminded him of Helen when they'd been teenagers, offering up suggestions to improve his go-kart or whatever he was patching together in the workshop that week, even when he thought she'd been paying no attention to him. Helen had always had a calm about her, even when Leo was ready to throw spanners. Araminta had that same quality now.

"Making more noise isn't a bad idea," he said.

"So what do we do?" David asked, while Araminta began searching. "Start smashing beakers into a sink?"

But Leo had forgotten about making noise. He held a hand up, noticing again a shift in the air pressure. He'd felt it the first time in the services shaft when they'd been escaping, and now he felt it through the opened-up wall: a whisper of breeze as the air grazed across his skin. Something about that air movement bothered him, but he couldn't bring to mind what it was.

David finally waved a hand in front of his face.

"Sorry, what?" Leo said.

"I said, I just remembered the extractor system." He pointed to a switch panel in the far corner, near which Leo could see a hood hanging down from the ceiling over a steel bench, much like a kitchen stove hood. "I remember Forbes complaining it makes a hellish noise."

Leo looked at the time ticking by and decided it was the best chance they had. "All right. But we're really going to need to make that statement, now."

《〉〉

Araminta didn't quite understand what Leo meant. She'd been thinking about the way she'd come into the building through that underground pipe, and how she wished she had never allowed William to bring her through. They couldn't even retreat that way; she had no idea where the entry was, but for somewhere in the ground-floor dock, and no doubt it was now protected by the security system.

These thoughts were pushed aside watching Leo carrying a metal cylinder towards the foyer entry lock's open door, which he closed to a bare inch and then poked the cylinder's hose through the gap. Soon, gas was hissing into the space beyond.

"Nitrogen," he said when she asked. The gas that along with oxygen, made up most of the air around them.

Araminta felt a qualm as she put together what Leo was doing. She knew that oxygen was necessary for life; it had never occurred to her to remove it in order to harm someone. Quite the statement.

When the gas filling was done, Leo had Araminta remove the hose, and he pitched in a glass grenade of carbon-tet, and slammed the door home. *Thunk*. Solenoids unlocked. David, waiting at the other airlock, hauled the inside door open, sounding the second locking *thunk* before anyone outside could use the opportunity. Leo then repeated the nitrogen filling in the second airlock, keeping to the side of the door.

"When we finish this one, we go on my call."

Araminta didn't need to be told again. She was thinking that as soon as the door closed, the interlock would release and anyone would be able to open the external doors. Hopefully the noise of the extractor, plus the temptation of the doors, would be enough distraction from the exposed position inside David's office. Because she, as the smallest of the three, was the one going through the hole. Another minute, and Leo indicated to her to go and wait by the hole. David crab-walked across to the switches, and Leo palmed another carbon-tet grenade.

He checked between the two of them, then nodded, and threw in the grenade.

Araminta heard the glass smash this time, and the

releasing *thunk* of the solenoid, just before David threw the switch.

A roar erupted from over their heads, louder than Araminta expected. Her hair blew across her face and stuck to her sweating forehead. Goodness, that was loud. If the men didn't know they were here, they certainly would now.

Leo raised one enormous foot, and kicked the lath. The material cracked like a house of sticks and, as Leo kicked again, a rush of dirty plaster dust and splinters flew into Araminta's face. Blind, she panicked, until strong hands gripped her forearms, guiding her hands to the wall. The air was clearing, and she felt the ragged edge of the hole, and the floor on the other side.

She hauled herself through, too desperate to even be scandalized when she felt hands grip her thighs and push her forward. She twisted to take the fall on her hands, and then twisted her legs through. She picked herself up, blinking gritty dust, her heart thumping in her throat.

The dark office held the shadowy outline of a desk, but it was the papers pinned to the wall that caught her eye, ruffling in the slight breeze and catching the pale window moonlight like roadside ghosts.

Destroy it, read one in large hasty letters. *Leave now*, said another, the ink smeared by a careless hand.

She glanced back to find David peering through the wall hole. He had seen the papers, too, his expression shocked. His eyes found a thick journal on the desk, which Araminta handed across. He disappeared at once.

Then, Leo appeared in the hole. She nodded that she was well, and then crept to the office door, straining to hear anything out in the lobby.

Nothing.

Was no one out there after all?

No, wait. A *scuff* sounded beyond the door. Or was it breathing? Araminta pulled back. The door handle had a keyhole, and was supposed to be locked, but was someone on the other side, listening now, just as she was doing? Someone who could as easily kick a door down as Leo could kick through a wall?

She daren't move. She imagined, with creeping horror, being atomized by a railgun shot, or torn limb from limb by that black animal. She couldn't look. Couldn't do anything except be one with this all-consuming fear. Eventually she dragged her eyes around to Leo. He was watching her steadily, something in his face saying that he understood her fear.

She found the will to move, dropping down as if her spine had undergone a controlled demolition, until her eye was level with the keyhole. Her bad leg jagged, her breath held to bursting, but she forced herself to look.

She saw nothing. No eye looking back, just an empty wedge of foyer tiles. She took a slow breath and rose again, limped to the desk, and searched for the telephone.

《〉》

Clemens spent the first half-hour of captivity studying the two assailants with varying degrees of amusement. Yellow, who seemed the less intelligent of the pair, sprouted a prodigious amount of hair from his nose and ears. Once Clemens had noticed the burgeoning forest, he could see nothing else. The surly one, Checks, kept scratching at both elbows, and from the glimpses of red welts on the man's wrists, Clemens deduced he must be afflicted with a skin condition. Or lice. Or perhaps both. Tesla was clearly suffering in idleness, but Clemens was almost – almost – enjoying himself.

"Perhaps you'd care for a game to pass the time?" he asked now.

Checks sniffed pointedly, and scratched. He'd given up telling Clemens they "wasn't here to talk", and had resorted to the silent treatment. Clemens was encouraged, knowing full well that boredom was friendship's bedfellow.

"Wot kinda game?" Yellow asked, not three minutes later.

Ah, ha, progress.

"Chess," Clemens said, brightly. "Tesla has a board."

"We ain't here to play games," Checks said, roused to assert a new line of refusal.

Clemens reply was cut off by a shrill alarm from Tesla's telemetry panel, where a light flashed above the Edison-Bell telephone receiver. The two thugs bounded up like bloodhounds, brandishing their weapons. "What's tha?"

"Telephone," Clemens said, pointing. "Tesla should answer it."

Tesla rose slowly, but didn't move from his spot.

"Don't do nothin'," Checks said.

"Now, consider," Clemens argued. "Mr. Tesla is an important figure in London. If he doesn't answer his appointed phone calls, the local sheriff comes to check everything is fine with him. In your interests, gentlemen, you should let him answer it."

Checks frowned, but didn't object when Tesla stepped across. He only raised his weapon as Tesla reached for the receiver. "No funny stuff."

❰❬❭❱

At first, Tesla heard only crackling. He knew, just from the sound, that it was the security system's electromagnetic flux interfering with the telephone signal. His telephone had only two sources for calls: Downing Street, and the laboratories. And this was coming from inside the laboratories. But another noise was present in those crackles, something less familiar. "Yes?" he said.

"Mr. Tesla," came a woman's voice, hesitant and whispering. "This is Araminta, Lady Montague. We were to meet tomorrow night with Mr. Disraeli."

Tesla's eidetic memory identified the name from some weeks ago, at his electromagnetic train demonstration, but the rest was a mystery. She paused as if waiting for him to say something about it. When he didn't, she rushed on. "I am presently inside your laboratories in St Alberts with Doctor David Blakeney."

Tesla absorbed the name of the time-walking doctor he had first met in a fevered dream, and who still dropped by the laboratory at appointed hours to update him on matters of the timefield.

"He bids me to inform you that men have entered the building with railgun weapons, most likely with the intent of stealing some equipment. They have already killed a Mr. Forbes and a Mr. Brown." As he listened, Tesla identified the other noise on the line as the extraction system in the reagent laboratory, which meant this call was coming from Dr Blakeney's office.

"I see," Tesla said, affecting boredom, and risking a question. "How many and where?"

At the question, Checks' frown deepened.

"Three that we've seen. And some kind of animal, an enormous dog-like creature. I've been instructed to ask you to remove the security system if you are so able so that we can escape, and to summon Mr. Disraeli for help, not least because the Queen herself is inside the building, and probably at the mercy of these men. They appear quartered in the basement."

"Mmm," Tesla said, masking his deep alarm. "Well, I really cannot assist you I'm afraid. You'll need to call on me at the laboratory, tomorrow perhaps. I have guests to attend now, who will occupy me much of the night."

She paused. "Mr. Tesla—"

But the rest was lost, for Checks had dropped his meaty finger into the receiver's cradle, and pushed the heavy railgun tip into Tesla's ribs. "That's enough of that."

Chapter 25

Araminta relayed the conversation to Leo and David through the wall hole.

"Doesn't sound like Tesla," David said, distractedly examining his field notes. "He would never have brushed us off like that. He's normally so paranoid."

"Which could only mean the he can't talk," Leo said. "Some of these men could be there. We should assume Tesla can't help us call for the commandos."

A beat of silence passed, then David cursed under his breath and closed the field notes. He licked his lips, his face paler than before. "I have some bad news. This combination here is the same one I tried already. But that shouldn't be. The protocol is always to confirm notes before recalling, and the last transmission was yesterday this time. This is not supposed to happen."

"I figure that's coming up a lot today."

David didn't appear to hear, muttering to himself. "This is not good, this is very much not good."

"We're not done yet," Leo said, more so because David had always been such a fixer, this descent into despair unnerved him. "We could barricade the stairs on the second floor to give us time to short the combination lock. Those tea chests in the transmission room could work, and that calculating machine was on a heavy table."

"A moment ago, you didn't want to go up there," David said, but faintly.

"A moment ago there were other options."

The evacuation system abruptly cut out. In the ensuing silence, they both heard the clear *thunk* of the solenoid locks in the wall, and then the *snap* as a heavy door closed into its latch.

⟨⟨⟩⟩

Araminta put her eye back to the keyhole. The far lab entry door was just visible in the narrow view. Through its tiny window, she thought she saw something dark, moving. Then came a muffled *thud*, and a long pause. Each of Araminta's heartbeats sounded like that hollow thud.

"Hey."

Leo beckoned from the hole, and Araminta crawled back through into the lab. David pulled her away while Leo peered around the corner at the inner doors, the pipe held in his right fist, and a screwdriver in his left.

Araminta hated standing back. When nothing happened, she crept up behind Leo and looked out into the lab. The space was empty, both inner doors still closed. No one had come through.

"How long would it take?" Araminta whispered.

"Seconds," Leo murmured. "No oxygen, no life."

"Then why the grenade?"

"To slow them down if we didn't displace enough oxygen," Leo said. "Carbon-tet is poisonous."

"Lovely," Araminta murmured, as Leo stretched up to peer in the first airlock. A quick glance through the window a moment later showed her it was empty. The second airlock was not. A single figure with a white neck scarf lay sprawled on the floor inside, unmoving.

"Only one," Leo said, sounding dissatisfied.

They retreated to the corner, where Leo took out a thin device from his pocket. "Numbers are still spiking," he said to David. "We're going to have to decide what to do."

"Are you sure you can short that panel?" David asked. "That barricades could work?"

But Leo didn't appear to be listening. He was staring at the crumpled map. He looked to Araminta like a man who has been courting a woman for months, only to discover she had held affection for someone else the entire time. Betrayal, pure and simple.

David saw it too. "What?" he asked.

《〈〉》

Leo stared at David. A thought had come to him suddenly, through a tortuous path that cognition sometimes takes. Firstly, it had been looking at the console, and at the Grid and the time-elapsed, which had naturally made him think about Helen, back in her laboratory with The Machine. Then, it had been David, mentioning the barricade. Leo had begun thinking through all the steps such a plan would involve. Which led back to the table in the transmission room, holding that calculating machine and the graph it was drawing. He thought of Helen, perplexed by the oscillation in the timefield. Then all the off-plan features of this building. In the synapses of Leo's neurons, this information coalesced into a different picture of what had gone on here: that David had been prosecuting a parallel scheme.

"You know, you never explained why the *Queen* would have gone down to the basement," Leo said, watching David's face. "You said something about having an appointment with her. Why wasn't the appointment in your office?"

David paused. "The Queen often takes an interest in the equipment." But the statement was weak. Everything had been weak since he'd read the field notes. He knew something he didn't want to say.

"I might believe that," Leo said. "If Brown had been killed next to the generator, but he wasn't. He was killed in the doorway under the stairs. So, it follows the Queen must have known whatever this device is in the basement. The one you wanted to destroy."

When David grappled for an answer, Leo went on, softly. "That mechanical calculator upstairs in the transmission room ... what it's tracing looks remarkably like the calibration curves on Helen's wall. Did you notice that?"

David swallowed, his grip on the field notes slipping.

Leo experienced a cold, sinking nausea. "What the hell did you do, David?"

"Look," David said finally, raising his hands. "When we were trying to keep this place funded. The Queen had a lot of money to invest, a lot of power to smooth our way. It wasn't probably the most effective way to have gone about the whole project, but it was how we did it. By the time we had useful changes starting to come through in the Grid, she wanted something back, just like any investor. I had offer something ... tangible. She could have razed the building to the ground, or had Tesla arrested for treason, and there was only one thing she wanted."

"Which was what?" Araminta looked from one man to the other.

"To change something," David said. "Same thing we wanted."

"I don't understand," Araminta said.

But Leo did, even before David rubbed a spot between his eyebrows. "All right, yes," he said. "There's another Machine."

Chapter 26

Now – Helen

The soldier advances. Assessing, cataloguing. As if he knows he already owns everything and is simply seeing it for the first time.

He keeps his back to the far wall, The Machine to his right. His attention is head-height. Helen knows what he's looking at – the calibration curves, and the photos and maps visible through the open office doorway. Trying to reconcile those things with the immense apparatus of The Machine.

He moves again, towards the office, until he's behind the long end of the desk and Helen can no longer see him. That's when her other senses take over. The soft plastic *snick* as his shoe soles bend. The *schiff schiff* of black fabric between his thighs. Her cheeks burn hot, her hand aches around the gun. He's been paused too long, now, right by the office door. The Machine hums.

The table jerks aside so fast that Helen has no time to react. A leg crashes into her hand, and the gun flies away. She's exposed now, against the wall. The solider looks down on her, his body all black, like a man-sized hole punched in the fabric of space. A calibration sheet flutters down beside her, but all she can see is the weapon, bandoliered across his body.

She is caught.

But The Machine is still running.

Chapter 27

"Another Machine?" Araminta asked. "What kind of Machine?"

"A back-up, a B-Machine, whatever you want to call it," Leo said, forgetting who he was talking to. "Like the one that brought us here. Only it's here, in this time. In the basement."

He was sure he was right, but his head was swimming with the impossibility. Helen's Machine might be ugly, but it ran on thoroughly twenty-first century technology. It had software, computer control. Those things in themselves could be replaced with precision manual systems, but the microtorus that allowed The Machine to work, that was *molecular*. Its parts had been made by gene-doped bacteria, and assembled with atomic lasers. There was nothing in this time that could replicate that.

"How is it even possible?" Leo said finally.

David cleared his throat. "I think we should focus on the problem at hand."

"What do you mean, like the one that brought you here?" Araminta asked. "What machine?" Her expression was suspicious, as if she had put something together in her mind.

"Tell me you haven't used it," Leo said.

David was silent.

"No, of course you have," Leo said. "Because you had

to use it at least once, to record a data point for the calibration, the one that's calculating right now on that machine upstairs." Leo felt cold fingers digging around in his gut. He drew the console from his pocket. "Finally this oscillation makes sense. It's not hunting, it's not some new invention of Tesla's that's ahead of its time. You made another time machine, and you opened another timefield. Not only that, but one of the most important people of this era knows all about it. That's a fucking destabilization if I ever heard of one."

David blanched. "Now look—"

"A time machine?" Araminta said, her eyebrows raised, voice breathless. "So you are they … you are the ones who came here for Tesla. Tesla's Time Walkers."

Leo looked at her, and had no patience for obfuscation. "Yes, basically, and leaving out all the details, but yes. And now we have bigger problems."

Araminta blinked, as though a thousand thoughts were turning over and conclusions dropping into her understanding at regular intervals. "I have so many questions—"

"War," Leo said, guessing what she was about to ask. "They came here to stop a war. And a long litany of problems besides."

"This device in the basement is another time machine?"

But Leo had turned to David. "Jesus, David. Where did it transmit you when you tested it the first time?" He imagined David opening a timefield in the Paleozoic, among the giant dragonflies.

"We shouldn't discuss this in front of time natives."

Leo laughed. "Araminta knowing we're a couple of geezers from a future London is kind of small chips against you building another Machine, and leading the Queen of

England into the hands of railgun-toting thieves, who just as a by-and-by, are planning to steal the whole box and dice. Jesus, David."

Leo looked around this reagent lab, at the wireless blinder lights glowing from the ceiling, at the sea of lights outside the window throughout St Alberts: at all The Machine had changed. "Can you imagine what happens if that B-Machine disappears? What these men stealing it might use it for?"

"They can't use it without the calibration," David said, crossing his arms. "And you weren't here. You didn't have to do what I did."

"Comforting, when that calibration is being determined upstairs as we speak."

"I didn't know about that," David said, shifting his feet. "Look, I knew the alternate Machine existed here, I knew that. But it wasn't supposed to be used. It was never supposed to be calibrated! I didn't know about that—"

"Until you read your notes."

David closed his mouth.

In the ensuing silence, Araminta said, "Disraeli told me once that Tesla was visited by men from the future. I never hoped to see such a thing."

Her eyes shone. Leo saw fear and wonder, and could only feel how inappropriate that reaction seemed given the mess they were staring into.

"Not so impressive, are we?" he said.

"Not at all," she said. "When you have expected nothing ... when all you have is hope ..." She stopped herself. "But that does not change our circumstances, does it? There are still men here, intent on stealing this ... B-Machine."

"Yes."

"And you are concerned what they could use it for."

"Yes," David said, recovering his mettle. "And moreover, that it could destabilize this whole reality. It must be destroyed."

She paused. "So what are you using *your* Machine for? You said to avert a war."

Leo flicked a glance at David, then decided there was no point in withholding. Araminta was smart, a far greater asset to them informed. "I'll give you the condensed version," he said.

Five minutes later, Araminta stood, and limped to the window to look out on the London she knew. Leo had only left out the idea of the timefield itself, because he wasn't sure anyone would be happy to know that their existence was a simulation created by a Machine. Otherwise, she knew what they did. For just a second as they had sat together going over the console, Leo could swear he had seen the Grid stop jumping. The worst wishful thinking was the kind that bled into hallucination.

Now, as he watched Araminta staring out at London, her body in its twisted pose and her hands working the fabric of her suit pants, she said, "So where is *your* Machine, the one that brought you here?"

"It doesn't work like that. The Machine stays in the future, where it is. It doesn't move. We do. Or at least, we're both here and there, neither and both," he said, then frowned. "Sorry, that won't make sense until Einstein comes along in a few decades."

"Then how do you return to your time?"

"We use the console to recall ourselves."

"Recall? So … how is it that you might take something back with you?"

Leo paused, suddenly understanding the hope in her

voice. "We can't do that."

❮❬❭❯

The news was a heavy slug in Araminta's chest. She hadn't realized until that moment how tightly she held dreams of seeing the world to come. Since Disraeli had first told her about the time-walking men, she had acknowledged a hope of entering Tesla's orbit, and escaping the house of both her mother, and her one-day husband. Then these men had revealed themselves, shown her the console, which was unquestionably born of a time far beyond this one.

She had been enraptured with that console. The surface shone like French polish, and light from within showed moving columns of numbers with the crisp precision of printed type. Araminta had only to look at this console to know that the future was a place of mathematics and science, beyond anything she could imagine.

Consciously, she hadn't known the significance of those thoughts. Then, the instant Leo had told her that only things from The Machine's time could be sent here, and that there was no passage for anyone of *this* time forward … then at once had come a disappointment so intense that she knew it was all she wanted. Escaping not only her mother, but this time itself. To have the dream scuttled only moments after imagining such possibilities was a cruel disappointment.

That was when her interest turned to this B-Machine. The one that had brought Leo and David here was lost to her, but this other one …

"What interest does the Queen have in such a Machine?" she asked, taking care to cover her own interest. "She is privileged and powerful, perhaps the only woman who truly is. So she must want to change something that neither power and privilege can bring her."

David didn't answer, but she saw the distaste that flashed across his expression. Araminta could understand such distaste. She herself rather despised Victoria, though she would never have admitted as much to anyone, lest her opinion make it back to Disraeli, who was a favorite of the monarch. Araminta's distain was purely the disappointment of example; she could not imagine why a woman who had power, money and influence, would behave as Victoria did, deriding suffragettes, and acting as though she were beholden to her husband. Wearing black for twenty years because he had died. It was only in the last year Victoria had finally emerged from mourning.

Araminta looked at David, astonished at the thought that had just shot into her mind. "Albert," she said. "That's the one thing she wants. Prince Albert, who died in eighteen sixty-one."

"Christ, Albert," Leo said, looking up from the console. "David, how could you?"

"Look, it wasn't supposed to matter! I've no idea how anyone would know about that Machine, let alone want to *steal* it. I wasn't actually going to allow her to use it! I just had to give her enough to keep her on board."

"Now I understand the operating room. Didn't he die of something treatable?"

David shrugged. "No one knows. But we already had the oxygen – it was a waste product. Prince Leopold has hemophilia, so I offered it originally to ease his treatments. The oxygen high convinced her for a good long while to continue supporting us. Unfortunately, she's a sharp woman. She worked out what we might be able to do."

"Why did you even build it?"

David shook his head. "You don't understand what it

was like coming here, Leo. And we weren't supposed to need to come back again. That bastard Brown was waiting for me outside the transmission room, and took the console away. He was talking some gibberish about going to collect the Queen to follow through on the bargain, and I didn't have a clue what he was talking about. All I had to do was get the console back, and return to the future. Who knows … maybe that's what happened last time, too, for all I can remember."

"So you'd have just left another Machine here and forgotten about it?"

"Helen was going to close the loop. It shouldn't have mattered."

Leo shook his head. "You opened a timefield within a timefield. That can't be stable. You're right about one thing – we have to destroy that B-Machine."

Araminta listened to all this with a cold gripping despair. These men would destroy this machine, and then they would leave for their time, and not come back again. The world had changed from a vast, color-filled canvas to a dark tunnel in a few seconds. "How exactly do you destroy it?" she asked. "Is it large?"

"Yes," David said. "But we only need to destroy the microtorus. That part can't be remade in this time. You could open the hatch, lift it out, and put a boot through it if you wanted to. Or, we could just cut the power."

Leo hefted the pipe, examined it meditatively, and then leaned towards the small airlock in the rear of the lab. "Both of you stay here."

"What happened to not splitting up?" David demanded, just as Araminta felt a qualm of the idea of Leo leaving them, almost equal to the qualm she felt at the idea of destroying this B-Machine.

"We need to know more about our options, and I want to see if we could shut down that generator. Besides, you don't have any shoes. I'll go down the maintenance stairway. Not that I'm looking forward to stepping out blind, but that B-Machine is through that door under the stairs?"

He peered at the blank space on the map.

"Yes, but the service corridor we climbed to the roof is better," David said, pointing at the ground-floor stairway. "The floor there is the ceiling of that basement tunnel under the stairs. That's what we were standing on when we went through that hatch from the library. But you can see down from that space around the pipes. At least you could see anyone coming and going from that room."

Leo nodded. "That's better than me opening a door into the basement. I'll go down one floor, and across the foyer to the library, then back in that hatch. You can open the inside door here after I've gone through and to keep the airlock barred."

"How will we know it's you, to let you back in?" Araminta said, not wanting to be left behind. "There's no window on those doors."

"Code knock," he said, and tapped out a sequence.

‹‹ ›

Once Leo was through the small airlock, the maintenance stair enfolded him in an eerie quiet normally reserved for underground passages. A cave network, perhaps, or a dry sewer. Silence punctured with tiny fractions of noise – a dirt fleck skittering off the iron railing, unearthly whistles always at the boundary of hearing.

He detested being back in here, because he was petrified, and because it was the location of last contact with the men with the railguns. But there were also no good sight lines in the spiraling stair. Less chance of being shot.

Only one floor, he told himself. He only had to go down one floor, then move through the rooms behind reception, cross the foyer to enter that services riser again, and then look down on what was happening in the basement. It all looked so simple on the map. Maps didn't capture the terror of doing it.

His sneakered feet stuck to drifts of uncleaned dust as he padded down the runs. Five steps. Ten. Fifteen. A single Tesla light glowed over the next exit, throwing hard geometric shadows off the risers and railings.

Leo crouched on the last stair before the ground landing, checking his orientation. If he took the stairs down another three circuits, he would come out in the actual basement, hub of the intruders. He was glad not to be going that way. He listened, and heard nothing over the distant *chuff-chuff* of the train-boiler, which would disguise many noises. Maybe there was nothing to hear. But maybe someone else was there, being still, and quiet, and watching him. From one of the levels above, or pressed into a landing shadow below. Leo checked the map one last time and pressed his hands to the ground-level door. It gave with well-oiled silence, and he stepped slowly into a wide hall.

Empty, long, and white. Black tiles on the floor. Tesla lights on the walls.

Half a dozen steps took him past closed doors. He was too exposed here; needed a place to hole up. He passed the landing of an external door, and a branch in the hall left, deeper into the building. Leo moved faster, knowing he must be close to the foyer. His plan was to observe the space, and pick his chance to cross.

Nope, not nuts at all. Leo shook his head. This is just what you bloody got with a brilliant sister. Getting roped into a time machine and grandiose plans. Next thing you knew you were trotting through an electrified building, carrying a lead pipe, avoiding thieves with railguns, all in the service of the Queen of England. Bloody proper stupid shit.

The foyer came into view at the end of the hall, and to the right through a doorway, he saw the low reception counter. He pulled up in the hall as he smelled the meaty tang of a butcher's shop.

Blood.

He crept to the threshold of the reception office.

Forbes' remains were on the floor beneath the counter … and up the wall, and on the ceiling. The largest piece lay in a pool that had been notably smeared on one side. Leo had to turn away and press a hand over his mouth. Jesus, what a mess. So he'd been right about Red's aim.

Eventually, he crouched and pressed his back to the doorjamb. Sucked a breath, and tried to go in again. Nope. He took another breath. Christ, this was bad. There was another body in there, too, or at least half of one. He recognized the kilt and legs he'd seen downstairs, protruding from a bloody mass of what looked like hessian sacking. The man David had called Brown. So the men downstairs had brought Brown up here to be out of the way. A regular little railgun mortuary in the front office. Leo's stomach rolled again. He was out of practice for seeing shit like this.

Finally, he tamped down the revulsion and averting his eyes, skirted around the pool, his knuckles blanched around the pipe. The office was otherwise empty, save a hard chair in the corner, a large book and ink station on the counter, and a clean desk in the back. The counter provided an excellent vantage to peer across the foyer.

No one in sight. He couldn't see up through the ceiling void from this angle, but he could skirt the wall past the front doors, and stay out of sight for anyone up there.

Leo dropped back to his crouch, and then saw the faint outline of a red shoe print, just near the door. It was small, unlikely to be one of the thieves.

He frowned, remembering with a jolt. There'd been a boy with Araminta when she'd come out of the elevator, one Forbes had hauled off across the foyer. Where was he now? Leo risked another peer across the counter, pushing up further to see all the way to the main stairway. Something glinted from upstairs, through the ceiling void, and he pulled back. So focused was Leo on the foyer and the void above, that when he stepped back into the hallway, he forgot to check his retreat.

The dark shape slid into his peripheral vision like spilled ink into water. Leo turned to find the enormous dog filling the hallway, its shoulders braced like cathedral buttresses, and blocking his exit to the maintenance stair.

In those hairlines of seconds, Leo's executive functions were completely offline, in utter contrast to the men who had made this animal. They had planned carefully, inspired by Darwin's ideas of selection and centuries of intimacy between hound and man. They knew how to breed for strength, for loyalty, for vicious defense, and then how to enforce that with training, but after Darwin, their efforts took on exaggerated purpose. At an unseen molecular level, their breeding program crammed together the olfactory receptors in the dogs' noses, generation after generation, evolving an exquisite hunting instrument, that could single out a known person among a million others, and keep on them, relentless, eschewing everything else. There would be no bargaining with these animals, no reason. The Victorian equivalent of a machine mind.

This animal could not just smell Leo, and identify him as one of the recent smells in the basement, he could detect the molecular scent of David on Leo's clothes. And though fainter, he could smell Helen, too, and categorize her scent as not-male. The dog's brain did this in microseconds, comparing the complex data screaming in from its olfactory neurons to circuit patterns already laid down in its neural architecture, until it found a pattern that fit like a hand in a glove. This was how the dog knew something else about Leo, David and Helen. It smelled the residues of plastics in their volatile skin oils, the complex industrial trace chemicals in their breath, all absorbed in lives in the turn of the twenty-first century. This way, the dog knew that they were not of this time. Of course, the animal did not have words for that. It didn't think in terms of time and names. But it identified the alienness about this man and the other scents on his body, and knew its masters wanted this scent above all things. In this, the animal had been well trained. And now, this was what Leo faced.

The dog bared its teeth, creased lips quivering in silent growl, saliva dripping to the floor.

Chapter 28

Leo was not so stupid as to bolt. The dog was close enough that he'd never outrun it, not from a standing start, and especially not if he had to dodge around any corners. He kept the pipe between them and backed away into the reception office. The dog followed, its limb tendons as taut as bridge cables. God, it was big. Leo fixed on the animal's eyes, which watched him with cold, malicious intent. The inhumanness in that stare was the most unnerving. Leo couldn't get around the fact it was stronger than him, with better reflexes, and better weapons.

Yet Leo hesitated in a way he never would have with a man pointing a gun at him. He didn't want to hurt the animal. Putting the pipe in his hand into its flesh was the kind of deliberate brutality he'd left behind. When it came to the heat of attack, he would do anything it took, but now, in this slow, tense retreat, he could only wait.

Sweat slicked down his nose, where his next breath atomized it into his sinuses. The burn made his eye twitch, and he almost stumbled. In another three or four steps, he would have to act, because he would run out of room. All the options seemed doomed to failure. Vault over the counter and hide underneath the other side, hoping that the dog would jump over him? Lunge for one of the cupboards and hope to close the door in time? Ease across the counter, then make a run for it, hoping the counter would slow the dog down enough to have a head start?

Leo never got the chance to find out, because he took

one more step backwards, and his foot slid out from under him.

He hit the floor with a lung-emptying crash. Leo had an instant to wonder what had happened, and then the attack was already in motion. The black head lunged at him in a cloud of rotting meat breath. Leo swung the pipe across his body, a defensive blow that caught bone and muscle and knocked it sideways. A tearing pain burned through his shoulder, and then he was scrambling, slipping, something wet soaking his shirt and slipping through his fingers.

Blood. He'd slipped on the pool of blood.

Some dim corner of Leo's mind was revolted. The rest was in flight, desperate for purchase on the floor, for escape.

The dog was upright, half turned away, shaking its head, dazed. A single stagger. He would have only a second.

With self-preserving strength, Leo propelled upwards, vaulted the counter on his good leg and fell awkwardly on his hip in the full glaring exposure of the foyer. Victoria stared down. Leo crawled, frantic crab-steps, hearing the tacky squeak of blood prints he left in his wake. He rounded the corner back into the hall. The dog hadn't come over the counter, but now he would have to go back, past the open office door.

He sprinted, high on the balls of his feet, as silent as he could be with ragged breath, down the hall towards the maintenance stair. Behind came the *clack clack clack* of claws on the tile. The stair door was coming towards him fast. Too fast to stop gently and haul the door open. He had no time whatsoever to fumble. And the pipe was no longer in his hand.

His hand met the door latch with perfect grip, twisting his body so his shoulder crumpled against the wood. His vision swam with black spots, and he was sure he would feel teeth sinking into his calf as he hauled the door open. Then he was around the corner, seeing a flash of black as he yanked it closed again.

The latch seated.

Leo crouched, holding up the handle. He could hear nothing through the door. No thump, or panting, or scritches of claws. Nothing in the spaces between one breath intake and another. Was it out there, snarling silent at the door? Or had it never chased him at all?

He couldn't know. All he could do was return and regroup. His heart rate settled back to regular fast. One stair up, he went, then two. The face that came around the corner surprised him.

Leo had swung his fist up before he realized it was the boy from the elevator. He averted the blow in time, his circulation doing its best to blow a blood vessel through the center of his forehead.

They stared at each other.

The boy's eyes were wide, a slick of blood showing down his shirt. He said nothing, but motioned with his shaking hand. *Up?* or *down?*

〈〈〉〉

In the basement, the Masked Man sweated, great rolling droplets beading at the base of his neck and tumbling down between his shoulder blades. A pool collected in the small of his back. He betrayed no sign of it. His attentions were on more disagreeable developments.

Firstly, the woman he had captured, who had known this Machine was here. He had been hopeful of extracting information from her. About The Machine, or about the future itself, because he was convinced that she knew something.

She was a servant, the Masked Man guessed, with a surly disposition. For her eyes had angry flint in their depths, the type that grew from a life of service, or perhaps with an anger over the shooting of her fellow servant, the Scotsman, for whom she no doubt held some affection. She was a housekeeper, perhaps one that, like Forbes, had come with the building, and who wore a fine but worn dress, likely cast off from a mistress. She was a self-sufficient type – something he appreciated – but fancied herself a manager of others, because she watched the coming and going of the men with a hawkish disapproval.

"Thieves, then, are you?" she asked at one point.

The Masked Man didn't answer. He checked the stopwatch, assessing the remaining time.

"American, too," she said. "I should have thought we had sufficient light-fingered expertise in England that we didn't need to import it from the colonies."

The Masked Man reconsidered her. She spoke in a confident, well-educated way, but the Masked Man and his Pinkertons did not associate with the English to know more.

"Why do you wear a mask?" she demanded next. "Are you deformed?"

"No, madam," he replied, curtly.

"Then secrecy is your pursuit," she concluded, then nodded at Green, whose misshapen hand was visible as he worked. "Have you tortured this poor creature? Is that why they follow you? Are you that sort of man?"

"That, madam," the Masked Man responded. "Is a faithful employee, motivated to better the world through my endeavors."

He was rewarded with the woman's pursed

compression of her lips.

"And what do you know of this Machine?" he demanded of her again.

"Machine?" she responded, gesturing to the hulk of metal. "What do I know of such things? I was coming where I was bid. And instead you have shot the one man who could have answered your question."

The Masked Man frowned, knowing that she was being untruthful, but not exactly how. He retreated to watch her, which was where he still was when Blue brought him the news that White was dead.

"How?"

Blue shifted. "He went through them double doors on the first floor. Can see him in there, lying' face down. I wanted to go get him, but Red said leave him there. Door might be rigged, or som'thin'. We already tried to break the glass, and it don't break."

The Masked Man frowned, deeper.

"I swear, it don't. Never seen glass like it."

"Leave him there."

At least Red had a half-pound of sense. The Masked Man had planned for unexpected staff left in the building, but not ones who posed any real threat to him. White's death could not have been an accident. "What about the animal?"

"Found her on the ground floor," Blue said. "She's taken a blow, but sound enough. She was all a-whining at that spiral stair in the corner. One of them went up there."

"And then where?"

Blue shrugged. "Trail divides, but the double door on the second's still locked. Didn't want to go in there anyhow. Not after Whitey."

The Masked Man considered. These few people,

whoever they were, were hiding in the sealed laboratory, he was sure of that, but now they had put down one of his own men. That invited caution.

"Relieve Black on the drill," the Masked Man said. Then, he called Red, Black and the dogs to him. No one would be going anywhere until the Masked Man had what he wanted. He checked the stopwatch; there was still time.

He took a railgun from the trolley, looked it over. Considered taking it, but he detested the feel of a gun in his hands. He handed the spare to Black, who slipped it without question into his holster.

"Red, take the dogs and start a search from the ground floor up. Black, you come with me to the top. It's time to collect the calibration."

❬❭

Back inside the reagent laboratory, David checked William over. He seemed physically unharmed; the blood on his arm and shirt must belong to Forbes.

Leo had to admit defeat. "I didn't make it to the services riser," he said, talking about it made it somehow less real. "One of those dogs was on the ground floor. So we still don't know what they're doing down there."

"I do," William put in.

All three turned to look at him.

"How's that?" Leo asked.

The boy shrugged. "There's a spy lens in the receiving dock that looks down on that room in the basement. I watched them a while through it. They've a woman tied up, and a bunch of men coming and going around that big Machine. You know, the one with all the metal parts."

"A spy lens in the receiving dock?" David spluttered. "What the devil?"

"I didn't put it there," William protested. "It's in a cupboard, on the side wall, behind one of those racks of tea chests."

"Forbes," David said, as if the name were a curse. "But then they definitely have the Queen."

"Wait a minute," Leo said. "How is it that you know about The Machine?"

William's expression guarded. "Um, well, from Forbes," he said. "He keeps these sketches in his office. Rather good. Most of them are of birds or the Thames, or that sort of thing, but there's a number from inside the laboratories. That's the reason I started looking around the building, you see. They were so interesting, those sketches. So I, uh, started going looking for the places I didn't know, and then I overheard him talking about a machine in the basement with someone on the telephone."

"But that's impossible," David spluttered. "*Forbes* didn't know about it!"

Leo didn't dignify this with an argument; clearly, the super had known about far more than David realized.

"Anything else?" Leo asked William.

"No," he said. "Oh, except all the men have a different colored neckcloth."

"How many altogether."

William counted on his fingers, mouthing colors. "Five I think, plus the Masked Man."

"Masked Man?"

William shrugged. Leo looked at David. "That calibration you're calculating – tell me it's some kind of ruse. You just told Victoria you were calculating it."

David was silent.

"Why," Leo burst out. "How moronic could you be?"

David's eyes hardened. "Well, let's imagine someone's

holding a gun to your head and telling you to get in a time machine. Would you go, knowing the calculation was wrong? I didn't think so."

Leo turned back to William. "Was there ever a sketch in Forbes' collection of a calculating machine, it's sort of like a—"

"Spread out clock, on a large table? Oh yes, of course. It's on the second floor."

Leo rubbed a hand over his face. "Jesus," he said. "Shit. Then they know about the calculation, too."

"I still don't understand how they could possibly have known about the B-Machine to begin with," David said, still stuck on his point. "It was a closely held secret."

Araminta was the one who responded. "Doctor Blakeney, I never thought that London society would teach me anything, but I did learn that secrets are the possession of one person. The moment another person hears your secret … it will find its way into gossip, and then it is public. There's no way to stop it."

❬❭❭

If David had been honest about the business of the B-Machine, he could have told the story of what really had happened. It would even have been an achievement, had the consequences not been so dire. The microtorus itself had been the easier part, because it was small enough to secret in a satchel, carried on one of the routine transmissions. He'd been able to exploit the change in a machinist position in the research program to gain an access to the workshop. There, it was not a complex matter to have the computer-driven machine reproduce the housing plans from Helen's computer. And while David had to painstakingly construct the molecular parts himself, he could do it alone, assisted by computers and high technology. After all, he was the originator of the technology that had made the microtorus. That part was his province.

Making the rest of The Machine was another matter, and had taken months. He'd employed a specialist metalworker, a careful craftsman who would curve and polish the metal as precisely as the plans he had copied from future London.

What's it for? The man had asked, once.

Sculpture, David had replied.

The man didn't ask again, but his apprentice did. *Come on, then, how's about it*, he'd said. *We know it isn't no sculpture.*

Experimental flying machine, David had said eventually, goaded and just to be ridiculous. *And my employer says to stop asking questions.*

You're a tight one, the apprentice declared. But the boy knew that David worked with Tesla. He'd seen him leaving the laboratory one morning. His sister was in service at one of the well-to-do mystics in St Alberts, who said Tesla's laboratory was being built by Time Walkers, so the apprentice told his sister about the part his master was making, and she told her mystic mistress that some strange secret was being manufactured for Tesla.

A few days later, the mystic told a client, an industrialist who'd visited her as a drunken titillation. He repeated the story at his club, which was where the Masked Man had heard it himself. The Masked Man was already investigating Tesla; it was his sole purpose for being in London, and for buying the defunct Underground rail line that ran underneath the St Alberts streets. The story had become fanciful by the time he heard it, all manner of unnamed experts speculating that the device was a healing apparatus, or a transporter, or the very fountain of youth, and powered by the semi-magical electromagnetics that Tesla communed with.

The Masked Man knew only that he desired to know all the details of any new invention. He had a nagging sense of wrong about Tesla, after the man had coldly rejected an offer of a position at a very generous salary. The Masked Man dreamed of Tesla, and the Masked Man did not like his dreams to be invaded by his competitors.

Through a frustrating mire of rumor, the Masked Man eventually tracked the story to the workshop, but the pieces had already been delivered, all drawings removed. The craftsman would not speak with him, but the apprentice took a coin to describe it in detail. The Masked Man still did not know what it was, but the more he heard, the more he suspected something strange was afoot at the center of St Alberts. Something that threatened his business supremacy.

In the last few months, the Masked Man had been busy. Acquiring useful assets, pushing forward the business of the Underground line he had invested in. Following leads, placing coins in the best hands, all the way to the palace itself. Until finally he discovered Forbes, and his debts, and exerted pressures. Forbes had finally cracked and spilled like a soft-boiled egg, and become the inside informant the Masked Man needed. Soon he had learned of volumes of future patents, which Tesla was exploiting to his advantage.

So the Masked Man was convinced that these rumors of assistance from Time Walkers was not rumor, but fact. Tesla had unnatural advantage. These future-men were aiding a rival and impairing the Masked Man's business. And the device that had been made in the workshop was something critical — even perhaps for the transporter that had brought the Time Walkers here.

The ultimate crowning to this investigation, however, was one evening when he followed a man from Tesla's laboratory, a man who took a carriage to a fashionable club. The Masked Man paid his way in at the door, and casually introduced himself, worried about this man recognizing him, but he gave no sign of doing so.

Tesla's man was partial to drink that night. The Masked Man had pretended to drink with him, to stroke the man's ego by asking him about his medical profession, being sociable until this man was so drunk he could not stand up. And into the miasma of whiskey, the Masked Man asked his questions.

Your knowledge seems incredible, he said, *how did you learn?*

Well I have incredible stories, the man had said. *You would not believe them.*

Try me, the Masked Man said. *Are you going to say you're from the future? For I'll tell you I've read all the works of Verne*, and he laughed.

David had given him a broad, drunk smile. At the end of the night, the Masked Man left knowing all he needed to, and David remembered nothing.

Chapter 29

Helen scoots backwards from the soldier, equal parts propulsion away from his raised weapon, and attraction to the lost gun. Both objectives straying towards electromagnetic metaphor. Even in a crisis, her brain works like this.

Her back collects the wall with a *thud* that knocks her lungs empty. This corner is shadowy, full of detritus from the upended table, the air cold from the open door. Her hands fumble behind, feeling the carpeted wall, the floor. There's something long and thin ... a pen. A tough wibbly loop of rubber band. The slimy cool of an apple core. The pinprick end of the fallen drawing pin.

"Hands, high."

His voice is male and flat, unplaceable mid-Atlantic accent. She shivers.

Her hands rise, but not before she's swept along the floor and felt the hard, heavy barrel of the handgun. Then she's gripping the top of her head as the soldier stares her down. She has a bare second to feel the crushing importance of this moment. This is really where everything could end.

The computer is a crumpled mass beside the upended desk, the main screen lying on its face behind the soldier. The screen is still on. She can see the glow of it against the carpet. What she can't see is the Grid. Is it still oscillating?

So what if it is? What she has to do is protect The Machine. Protect the power. To give Leo and David time. Because they have to do it.

Then, something weird happens.

She doesn't know if it's real, or if the stress of what's happening has tripped a hallucinatory circuit inside her head. Because everything just ... shifts. The soldier, the power cables, the walls, ceiling, the scattered papers and tools, all of it just jumps a foot to the left, then jumps back, as if the whole room is a giant CRT projection whose electron beam just wobbled under the touch of a powerful magnet. Only The Machine stays put, an ominous constant in the glitch.

Weird.

The soldier's blunt boots stop. His head cocks, as if he's wondering what the fuck just happened. Did he see it, too? Helen decides it wasn't hallucination. It's the physical reality of a discontinuity. Mathematically, such glitches are possible when the universal functions approach an invalid solution. This is what Leo had asked her about, the bad-case scenarios for improperly integrated universes.

It's a really bad sign.

She wants nothing more than to see the upended monitor now. If she allows this to go too far ... if The Machine keeps running, holding the timefield open, there could be uncontrollable consequences. They could be closed off in a quarantine loop, lost forever from this reality she is trying to change; or the timeline could fracture, and contaminate reality with scattered debris of individually reconcilable loops. And worse, Helen will still fail to change anything about this warfare reality, or the particle beam guillotine currently hovering over their heads.

Helen doesn't want to die, doesn't want to fail. But she

will destroy the microtorus before The Machine can create disaster. First, she will send a message to Leo. Use those precious qubits in the console to tell him to recall back here, and now.

She waits only until the soldier's head tips to the other side. Then her hands fly down to the floor, fingers scrabbling for the gun. She'll try to aim her shot, fast, and then roll away. She hopes to hit him, or distract him, even if she doesn't kill him. She needs just enough time to put a message through.

Her fingers close on the metal and she lifts. But something's wrong. She can't move, as if the gun has become a block of concrete. Too slowly, she realizes — it's not the gun in her hand, it's the leg of the upended table.

Chapter 30

The Doctor had sweated through his clothes. William could see a great translucent patch under each arm through the white shirt. Araminta's hair had come undone, and the back of Leo's shirt was completely red with blood. William particularly tried not to look at that; the color brought him uncomfortable memories of what he'd seen downstairs.

"I have to go up to the second floor again," Leo said. "Wreck that calculating machine before they can get their hands on it. The B-Machine can't be a fast thing to move."

William listened to all this with wide eyes, having been rapidly filled in on the state of affairs in the laboratories. He hardly knew what to think. One moment he'd been fired, and within hours, he was a fugitive in the company of Tesla's Time Walkers.

Leo strode into one of the back-wall offices and peered out the window. He looked like no man William had ever seen, a body heavy with muscle and with a mind that preferred action. He offered a quiet assurance though; when William had seen him in the stairwell, relief had washed him like a bath.

"What I wouldn't give for a tactical team with assault weapons," Leo muttered now, leaning in towards the glass. "Or at least someone to go and relieve Tesla of whatever situation he's in."

"Leo," William said. It came out as a squeak. Only

Araminta glanced in his direction. He cleared his throat. "I know a way out."

Leo made no response.

"What did you say?" asked Araminta. "Speak up."

"I said: I know a way out." This time, his voice was too loud, bouncing off the hard space. William winced, imagining the men in the basement would have heard him.

"There isn't a way out," David said. "The security system is on. The exits electrified! I'm sure you want to help but this is no moment for conjecture."

William knew what that word meant. He'd already been accused of spouting it, in the classroom just this year. "But I do! I brought Lady Araminta in to the building through the very same way."

"Whatever way you entered, it's secured now with Tesla's field," David said.

"No, it isn't."

"You can't possibly know that."

"I know from when I was locked in, one night."

That drew a silence. Leo and David exchanged a glance. "You were locked in?" Leo said.

William shrugged. Since he was already fired, this mattered little. "A month back, more or less. A Monday, I think. Quite late. I was supposed to have gone already, you see. Forgot the time because there was this slide rule in the workshop—I mean, I saw Mr. Forbes come down and press that button, and then let himself out in the delay. I would have been trapped here all night if I hadn't found a way out. That blue fire don't go across the hole in the pipe."

"What pipe? Where?"

"You have to go through on he ground floor, in the dock. Quite a squeeze it is."

Leo shook his head. "Even if that's true, that's a long

way for all of us to travel avoiding people with railguns and dogs. And all the while, giving these men time."

Araminta straightened. "By which, you mean, to steal this B-Machine. And you think they want this calculation, too."

"I could go," William said. Everyone stopped to look at him again. "While you go for the calculation upstairs. I could find Mr. Tesla."

William broke off, looking hopefully at Leo, whose expression was unreadable.

"No," Leo said softly. "I'm not sending you. You saw what happened to Forbes."

William swallowed, the image of the domus supervisor and that spreading crimson pool flashing unwanted behind his eyes. It wasn't that he wanted to go back out into the building, but he wanted to be useful. When he saw opportunity, he moved to it.

"I agree," David said, quickly.

Only Araminta was still staring at him, something appraising in her look. It didn't prevent a bright spot of shame burning in William's chest that the men were saying no. It was somehow worse than how Forbes made him feel, because he'd never liked Forbes.

"Leo is the soldier," David said. "He has the training. The best thing we can do is remain here and let him do this work."

"I'm going upstairs too," Araminta said.

"Of course you aren't," David said.

"Oh, but I am. Leo will need someone to stand guard while he … tends to the calibration machine, and I imagine he will want to again assess the foyer while we are up there, to see whether you might try again to enter Tesla's lab. I am, however," she went on, "very glad that you are taking the initiative to guard our home base. And I'm sure that someone with your skill in planning and direction could be more ably employed in formulating an escape route to the ground floor while we carry out this task."

William glanced at Leo, whose face during this speech had transformed from abject refusal to amusement.

"You can't possibly entertain such a notion," David said.

"It's a bad idea," Leo said. "It's safer to stay here."

Araminta glanced at the floor. "Leo," she said, quietly. "I don't know if you can imagine a life where you can never leave the house without judgement and scrutiny, where no one will credit you with a rationality and a desire to be useful, but that is my fate here. I want to be useful, and make some effort. I came here seeking Tesla for that end. I would rather die in this endeavor than return to the life outside these walls. I am quite brave enough. Please."

William saw some appraisal cross Leo's face, but he mentioned neither Araminta's limp, nor the stupidity of her suggestion.

"It's your skin," Leo said finally. "As long as you understand that you are risking your life. Given a choice between protecting you, or my objective, I *will* choose my objective."

Araminta's lips pressed together. "I'm glad we know where we stand."

"Fine. But first, I need a weapon." Leo drew himself up.

"Are you going to make one?" William asked.

Leo shook his head. "I don't have to. We have one. In there." He pointed into the airlock. "So I need all of you as far away as possible, down the other end of the lab, while I open that door."

"Don't you want the extractors?" David asked.

William raised his eyes to where grills were set into the ceiling. Similar ones were installed in the washroom, and Forbes had yelled at him more than once to turn them on when the sheet boiler was operating.

"No," Leo said. "No reason to attract them here again."

As Leo and David conferred on what he would do, Araminta drew William away, down the long workbenches and into a corner. At first, he thought she was concerned they were too close, but then she turned to face him. They were almost the same height, William realized, her bright blue eyes only just above his.

"Listen very carefully," she hissed. "This must be quick."

《〉》

Red began his sweep at the maintenance stair in the basement, which he had Blue chain closed behind him. In the dim hole of the stairwell, blood pulsed in his temples, and his shoulder strained to hold the dogs. Only a few hours before, he had been standing outside this building, counting this job as straightforward nightwork. Sure, maybe some heads would be knocked, but that was standard practice. White's death had given him serious pause. He saw ghosts in the shadows of this building, now, unknown and dangerous things.

He emerged into the ground-floor hallway, letting the dogs lead. The hall was empty but for faint bloody prints. He released the animals, allowing them to speed ahead, one sniffing at doors, while the other bounded around the bend in the hall into the washing area. Red followed, ears primed for the dogs' muted barks.

None came.

He slipped past the front counter, eyes dispassionately

running over the blood pool in the office, which was now separating, a border of yellow fluid around the darkening red center. There, alongside, a piece of pipe lay on the floor. That had not been here before. Were they down here, now?

He crouched before venturing into the foyer, following the confused arc of bloody prints, imagining the chase that had taken place here. To his left, he could hear the dog snuffling as it searched through the nearby rooms. The other had drawn up beside him, waiting for a command to move on.

Red sent her forward, and followed. No one was in the foyer, and he couldn't lock off the section easily, so he settled for placing a heavy wooden chair into the mouth of the hall.

He prepared to send the dogs again through the library when he chanced to glance up. A portrait hung high on the wall, above the front doors. He'd not noticed the details before; the picture wasn't visible to someone walking in the rear doors a half floor down, and whenever he'd been up or down the stairs he'd been intent on his task. The one time he'd faced across the foyer, he'd been aiming at Forbes. Now he stared at the painting with a shock of recognition.

It was the woman they had tied up downstairs.

❰❮❯❱

The maintenance stair had not changed, but Leo's apprehension was deeper than before. Every time he thought about that calculation machine sitting upstairs, his hands would sweat and the railgun slip in his fingers. He tried not to think of what he would really do if they were confronted, and it came to saving Araminta, or himself. He had to think of the mission, but it would not sit easily to sacrifice someone else.

He had been stupid to let her come along. But that look she'd had in her eyes … it was the same one he saw in Helen's, that passionate want to be *allowed*. He could admire that about her, and suddenly, he realized why Helen had worked with David. It was because he'd believed in her, probably when no one else would. Leo had no idea what it was like to live as her in the world. But he knew what it felt like to be weak, and that was what the whole world did to women. He'd watched it happen to Helen as she grew up, being passed over, for no other reason than that men were used to being the winners.

So, he had said yes. A limping, untrained woman could come with him.

Jesus.

Thankfully, Araminta kept her mouth shut, carrying a sturdy retort stand in one hand. At least she couldn't shoot him in the back.

Their progress up the stair was uneventful, and when he pushed the door open into the second-floor hall, nothing moved. Leo's heart hammered looking out down that short white hallway to the blind corner. He closed his eyes and thought of Helen, alone in the lab, watching the clock, probably wondering what the hell he was doing.

He propped the stair door open, hearing Araminta's uneven steps behind him, and adjusted his grip on the railgun. It was heavy for a handgun, but all the weight was in the handle, so it wasn't hard to balance it. A short rack on the body held two remaining iron pellets, but had space for four. The sights were rudimentary, but the mechanism was straightforward enough. Barrel loaded with no safety switch to confuse things. No, firefights were confusing enough.

He crept forward, railgun out, around the corner and towards the thin slice of empty foyer at the end of the corridor. Then came a *scuff*, a shoe on a floor. Leo stopped suddenly and Araminta's arm braced against his back.

A man stepped out of the doorway to the transmission room. He wore a suit, Leo would guess later, but at the time, the clothes were a grey smudge below the man's face: a round, almost child-soft face, with thick hair, framing a mask. A goddamn mask, like a superhero. Leo looked – actually looked – to see if he was wearing a cape, too.

The Masked Man didn't move, just stared at Leo like a judging priest. That stare … Jesus, Leo could feel it like laser beams, heating up the back of his skull. He stood there, dumbly, railgun aimed, while this unarmed man betrayed no surprise at having a weapon levelled at him.

"Back away," Leo growled.

The Masked Man tipped his head. "Come closer," he said.

Leo paused. Of all the things an enemy can have, confidence was the worst. It's a sign of not being quite in a right mind, and therefore being willing to do crazy things, like stare down a weapon without due regard for the danger. He had seen it before, in combatants so satellite-high they were walking around with wounds he didn't care to remember. But Leo could swear this guy was stone cold sober.

Leo took another step forward, watching, listening. He wanted to know if there were more men up here. There was nothing – no sounds, and the Masked Man's eyes never wavered from his.

"Yes," the Masked Man said. "Come closer. I want to see you, future man."

Okay, so *creepy* confidence was the worst, especially in

that born-again soft southern American accent. Leo stopped advancing. "Hands up," he said. "And back away."

This time, the man's hands lifted, just away from his body. "You know what you hold there, future man?" he said. "Or are there weapons with still greater power in your time?"

Who the fuck was this? Leo knew, without doubt, that this man was the instigator of the operation to steal the B-Machine.

"Yeah well, this mince-maker's in my hand, so how about backing the fuck up?" Leo said.

"But do you know how many times it has fired?" The Masked Man asked. "And, will it fire again? Sometimes two. Sometimes four."

"There's one left for you," Leo said, hoping it was true.

The Masked Man leaned sideways to peer around Leo, no doubt looking at Araminta behind. Then, very slowly, he took a step backwards. "I do not care for weapons myself," he said.

"Said the man who doesn't have one," Leo responded, advancing another step. He wanted this man away from the transmission room, wanted him standing in the mouth to the foyer so that Araminta could slip into the room and lay the pipe into the calculating machine. Leo was only a few steps from the doorway now.

He had the barest warning when the Masked Man flicked his gaze towards the room. In an instant, Leo knew he'd misread the situation. Another man appeared, black kerchief about his neck, his own railgun raised.

Leo fired, and the recoil knocked him backwards. Holy hell, the thing had a kick, and the world sounded like he was under a down pillow. He couldn't tell if the other weapon had fired back, only that Black was down on the floor, one hand thrown over his head, but unfortunately whole. That was what you got for being out of practice and with a new weapon: missing the mark at pointe blank range. The Masked Man had vanished.

Leo surged forward, kicking at the gun still in Black's hand. It clattered away, but a snaking arm caught Leo's leg and he toppled like a concrete column, his bad knee wrenching as he went.

Before gravity was finished its work, a blow landed on Leo's head, and his vision danced with psychedelic chicken wire. His railgun hand was empty, and something hard like a knee was driving into his middle, pushing against his gasping lungs just as rough fingers squeezed his throat. As Leo watched the oily swim of unconsciousness move across his vision, he heard a dull *thud*.

The grip slackened, just long enough for Leo to escape from under Black and rise, with heaving breaths. Drunk on returning oxygen, he saw Araminta – with the retort in her hand – standing over the stunned man. Her hair was stuck to her forehead with sweat.

"They never notice the woman, do they?" she said, breathless, before bending to take up Black's dislodged railgun.

"You'll forgive me for being grateful for that right now," he said, and recovered his own weapon. He pointed it at Black, who was pushing weakly off the floor, and glanced inside the transmission room. There was the Masked Man, watching them.

Leo licked his lips. He didn't know who either of these men were. Didn't know how injured the man on the floor was. It wasn't in him to be an executioner, even more so now, in the timefield, where actions affected stability.

But what if killing this man would actually resolve the

oscillation? Leo adjusted his grip, and thought about that conversation with Helen about Hitler. It was one thing to talk about changing the past, to do it academically. Quite another to look people in the eye and assign them a bullet point in a bigger strategy. No wonder generals were sociopaths.

He waited in the suspended decision space, Schrodinger's cat inside the box, waiting for whether an atomic particle would decay and decide fate for him: would he end this man's life, or not?

Black groaned, and swaying, pushed himself to sitting.

"Hands," Leo said.

Black's hands crept atop his head. The creases at his wrists were full of black dust, and the cuffs of his shirt were thick with dirt too, as if he'd been crawling through mud. Leo nodded to Araminta, who limped through the doorway and towards the calculation machine, her railgun unsteadily levelled at the Masked Man. He admired how she held her aim, despite the rock of her limp, the determination she had.

The Masked Man did not watch this, or react. He kept vigil on Leo, as if he was filming with his eyeballs. Even when Araminta pulled the calculation sheet off the now silent machine and hesitated before taking up the retort again and swinging it through the slender gears and rods. They scattered like toys.

"I wonder at the things you have seen," the Masked Man said, in a voice that was smooth with wonder, as if he knew secrets that would fill great chasms, and that he was here to steal the means to more.

Leo didn't answer. It was time to get away from here. Every second that ticked past was more danger. Leo pulled Araminta back into the hall and behind him, and they began backing towards the maintenance stairs. *Faster*, he thought. They had to get back down to the others.

The Masked Man appeared in the doorway.

"Your friends are all dead," he called. "So is this place."

Leo tried not to imagine Helen's body beside The Machine in the future, its uncaring steel and solenoids oblivious to her fragility. The Masked Man could only mean Forbes, and maybe Brown. Not the Queen. Not the monarch who was to reign for another seventeen years, whose dynasty shaped European courts that still existed in Leo's time. Not Helen. He itched to draw the console from his pocket, to examine the Grid numbers.

"Your actions are futile," the Masked Man continued, with a conviction honed enough to split atoms. "You cannot succeed."

Leo stopped, suddenly thinking *he's right*. Everything Helen calculated could be a fallacy, an elegant theory that had no reality at all. She and David had done all this for nothing.

Then they reached the corner of the hall, and Araminta was pulling him to the stairs, leaving the doom of the Masked Man's certainty hanging in the hall.

Chapter 31

The Masked Man met Red on the main stair, as the dogs were pulling Red up. He could feel his ear tips radiating heat, his mind burning as it processed all that had happened in the past few minutes. The faces of the two people he'd met were etched in his mind, like acid on a zinc plate. The lame woman was of little interest, some progressive type of the borough with her man's clothes and confidence. But the man ... the Masked Man knew he was a Time Walker just as the dogs did. And they'd taken the calculation as if it were gold from an ancient tomb. The Masked Man mined all this for meaning, for strategy, and only paused at the look on Red's face.

"You're goin' to want to see this," Red said.

A minute later, the Masked Man stood in the ground-floor foyer, staring at a gilt-framed portrait. For the first time in years, his nostrils flared in surprise. That defiant face. The Queen of the Land.

What luck.

What fate.

The Masked Man hurried, his feet blurring over the stairs back to the basement. He shoved aside the door and there she was, in her dowdy brown dress, her hair with looping sidepieces that matched her jowls, her back drawn up straight, her eyes hard chips of tungsten. It was certainly, undeniably her.

"You are the Queen," he said.

She pursed her lips. "And you are a Godless American

who will not show his face," she said, with a small sniff. "I knew there was a reason we let you have the colonies. It must be the only suitable place for such men."

The Masked Man smiled. Nothing she could say could bother him, because however dowdy, however diminutive and unassuming she might appear with her hands tied behind her back, however sharp her tongue, she was all he needed. He checked his fob, which said eleven twenty-five, and then the stopwatch. They were running out of time to do this as he'd planned. Soon, there would not be an option to stop the events he'd put in motion.

He told Green to shut down the drill for a minute, then strode to the control bank in the main basement. He lifted the distribution mouthpiece, the one that connected to speakers all over the building, for sounding the end-of-day call.

"We seem to have the basis of an exchange," he said into the mouthpiece. A crackling echo of his voice came back to him. "You have a piece of paper. I have your Queen. You have five minutes to bring that paper to the ground-floor foyer, or you will be singing *God Save The King* tomorrow."

Click.

Silence settled, until the Masked Man told Green and Black – still woozy – to return to the drill.

"What if they don't give it up?" said Red.

The Masked Man checked the stopwatch again. "I want them out of that lab," he told Blue and Red. "Take the dogs and the dynamite. If they haven't opened the door in five minutes, break the damn thing open."

At the same moment, David was pacing and flapping his

arms between the benches of reagent lab, his face approximating a beetroot. "We have to give it to them," he said. "She's Victoria, the Queen. She's awful, but we can't let them kill her."

Araminta glanced across to where Leo was checking over the second railgun, the one she had carried. She was shaky after what had happened upstairs, and was trying to focus on something else. She still had the calibration sheet in her fingers, folding the spiral curve repetitively in half, and half again, then unfurling it and starting over. She made herself stay her hands.

Black's gun was configured differently to the one Leo had taken from the man in the airlock, with a run of crude, scrimshaw-like etching down the handgrip. She wondered if the man who wielded it carried it on some long journey and did that work to pass the time, a man's version of cross-stitch. Leo lay the second railgun with the first, as neatly as if in a shop cabinet. William watched with an awed expression.

"We can't hand over the calibration," Leo finally said. "Without it, they have no idea how to align the beam, which makes The Machine a scattergun at best. If we give it to them, they could work out the underlying maths."

"You don't understand," David said. "Victoria cannot die. It would be irreversible."

"But you thought it fine to promise her the return of her dead husband?" Araminta asked, surprising herself. "You men think you know how to *fix* everything."

David made no answer. Leo smiled in a way that Araminta could not interpret, then said, "What bothers me most is that masked man. How did he know to call me a future man?"

Araminta pointed. "Is it not obvious?"

Leo looked down at himself. "What?"

"No man in this time cuts his hair like yours or dresses like that. I would have known you were a foreigner no matter where I had met you."

"Oh, right." Leo ran a hand over the close cut of his hair, in a self-conscious way. He didn't seem a man who cared much about appearances. He cared about what was real and immediate. She wanted to tell him that she would have known he was different because he answered her questions, because he treated her as she wanted to be treated. But that part she would keep to herself.

"Still, he was too confident, like he knows something we don't."

"He did seem familiar," Araminta said, because it had been bothering her. "I'm sure I've seen his face before."

"Yeah, in *Phantom of the Opera*?" Leo said, then, "Sorry, that's a joke. But we need to think of a way to disable the B-Machine. There's enough chemicals in this lab to make some kind of bomb, and deliver it down that gap between the pipes in the services riser. Or—"

He stopped abruptly, and held up his hand for silence. Araminta then heard muffled clicks and a low hum.

"They're in the elevator," Leo said. The hum stopped, and Leo's eyes tracked to the foyer wall of the lab. He motioned for everyone to move back against the wall in the corner, out of the direct line of the airlock doors. Araminta's heart stumbled over itself as she pressed her back to the cold surface. Leo peered around the window of the airlock where the White man still lay inside, then a moment later, he stepped across to look into the other airlock window, before returning to the corner.

"Are they trying to get in again?" Araminta whispered. He smelled of machine oil.

"Not sure. I can't hear anything," Leo whispered back. "Can't see anything, either. Wait here."

《〈〉》

Leo pulled open the entry lock's internal door, and carefully stepped around the man on the floor, holding his breath against residual nitrogen. The interlock *thunked*, locking the external doors. The clear glass window out into the foyer was a formless brown, until Leo had his nose almost against it. He ducked as he made out a dog sitting, ears pricked.

He inched back up, chest burning for a breath. Men were out there, too, doing something to the right, towards the other airlock. He couldn't see what, but then one came into view, walking backwards and unspooling a reel along the floor. The image matched a familiar pattern in Leo's brain.

He turned and ran around White's body, hauled open the internal door, and slammed it closed. Det cord. They had fucking det cord.

He hauled in a breath, then sprinted. "Run," he yelled. "They're blowing it up."

He had time to snatch up the railguns, while William hauled Araminta towards the maintenance stair. David reached it first and fumbled with the door, taking two goes to open it. Leo pushed everyone through, before taking two long seconds to haul it closed and activate the solenoid. They stood in the too-small space, their breathing loud. Araminta hauled on the stair-side door. It didn't budge.

"Try again!" Leo called.

She dropped her shoulder and hauled down on the handle, struggling against the seal.

Out in the foyer, an unassuming short cylinder wrapped in dirty brown paper trailed two wires across the tiles. Red and Blue had enough wire to descend to the next landing of the stairway. They glanced at each other, Red's hands gripping the wire ends near the capacitance device. Blue shrugged, and Red touched the ends.

The electrical signal, like the one that drove the railgun, seemed to arrive in an instant. Within the grotty, paper-wrapped cylinder, a tan paste enveloped the wire ends. It looked like clay, and mostly it was, but within it was a pocketed distribution of oily nitroglycerine.

Nitroglycerine is an ironic explosive, because it is also a medicine. Spray it under the tongue, and it can dilate blood vessels, so potently and reliably that it was still, even in Leo's time, the first-choice treatment for chest pain. It's a chemical stent, a prying bar that forces vessels open and allows blood to flow past dams of packed cholesterol. More blood to deprived tissues means more oxygen delivered, and therefore an end to the pain of a diseased heart. But the nitroglycerine inside the paper tube was intended to do no good.

Leo, Araminta, David and William had just tumbled through into the maintenance stair at detonation, and the odds were not highly in their favor. The door was closing behind them, nearly in its latch, but that closing door was racing the speed of light and sound.

In the detonator, a tiny burst of electrons arced the wire gap, their energy escaping into a waiting bead of nitro, its molecules already wobbling and vibrating on the edge of stability, like a twitchy hothead ready for a fight.

The first molecule that broke apart created an atomic shock wave, a miniature supernova that obliterated its neighbors before Red and Blue had even blinked. The shock accelerated, outstripping sound, propagating through the doped clay like a ripple on the surface of water, just a thousand times in fast-forward.

An instant later, when the shock left the brown paper, the stick no longer existed. In its place was an irregular ball of compressed searing hot gas. If the moment could have been frozen and zoomed, it would have been an alien beauty, all swirls and eddies of char black and flame red, collapsing fractals that vanished as the ball violently expanded under its own heat.

The shock met the outer lab door with the force of a speeding eighteen-wheeler. The door tore from the hinges, and the air inside the lock compressed so that the inner door shot out like a champagne cork, battering a path through the benches before it hit the far wall, just where Leo had been moments before. The shock lost just enough energy through the lab that the maintenance stair inner door deformed, but held.

Inside the stairway, the roar was like a jet engine, sending shivers of dirt down from the upper stairs. Leo's ears popped as the floor trembled.

Leo looked up from under the hands he'd thrown over his head. They were huddled against the central spine of the spiral stair. He imagined the destruction inside the lab. The foyer wall breached, upended tables, smashed glass, and fires. Including chemical fires. Their fortified position was lost.

Not to mention any structural compromise to the building – cracks in critical supporting walls, or the floor.

Leo pushed past Araminta and looked up the stairs, trying to suppress the panic of exposure. They still needed to destroy the B-Machine, and go home; that was the only endgame. They had to regroup in a new space.

Leo led them all the way to the attic door, and found it wouldn't budge. Only then did he remember he'd locked it, to prevent the intruders catching them on the roof. He tried shoving with his shoulder, but the pipes he'd used were thick steel. They'd have to go back down to the second floor, take the exposed route to the main stairs.

He turned back to the two faces behind him.

"Where's William?" he asked.

David looked about, surprised. Araminta leaned down around the stair. "Will!" she hissed.

But William had disappeared.

Chapter 32

William had never felt fear like he did crossing the ground floor. It was nothing like when earlier today, he'd faced Forbes at the staff door. Nothing like the last winter, when his mother had coughed every night until he was sure that she would die. That had been a prickling, insidious rot in his guts. When his sister had died suddenly this month, he'd been seized by that rot again, only it came with hot despair that only tears, shed quietly at midnight, could temporarily wash away.

He often feared what would become of them if he failed to bring an income. But now, he feared something larger than all of that – the loss of a future for them all, and the idea burned hot, a fire that pushed his resisting body through the hall with its bloody footprints. He had tasted the world larger than the poverty and desperation his sister had known. Araminta had promised to give him a chance if he could do this. She had said they were similar creatures. He had nothing else left to believe in.

He reminded himself of that as he paused at the office where Forbes and Brown were still resting in bloody slumber. Forced himself to look on them, and resolve to escape their fate.

When he finally faced the open expanse of the foyer, beyond a chair in the hall's end, he squeezed the note tighter in his fist. The air was hazy with dust, and chunks of wood and plaster had fallen through the void in the ceiling. Seeing no one, he scuttled across under Victoria's portrait, and found the receiving dock doors chained and locked.

He dodged left, along the wall towards the library, every shadow shifting with impressions of dogs or armed men. His heartbeats were louder than his feet, his senses scrambled. He fell against the library doors, and felt them give.

Mercy.

Inside, he crouched. Peered down the long length of the floor, through the mesh wall to the tea chests and palettes of materials. Then, he scuttled down to the oxygen rig room. Here, he expected to be trapped, but the doors into the dock had been unlocked.

He breathed. Once. Twice. Then, eased through into the dock.

In ten seconds, he reached the far corner of the building, where sat a small store room, mostly used by spiders and mice. He slipped inside. On one wall were shelves of tubing and valves, a container of odd nuts, and a lonely pipe wrench. William cared for none of this. Instead, he squeezed beneath the shelf and eased out an unsecured hatch low down in the wall.

The air beyond was frosty, the light so dim he could only just make out the glinting metal edge of the ladder. Time to retrace the steps he'd made with Araminta earlier this night.

Twenty rungs down he met a packed-earth floor, and another low door, which he knew from experience was locked. Instead, he lifted the grate in the floor, holding his nose against the stench that rose up. Thankfully, only a thin trickle of water still flowed in the center of the pipe, and he could shimmy his feet to either side, bent over in the low space.

It was true dark in here. The savage kind of dark that William rarely experienced in London, which drew images of ghouls on his eyelids, and amplified noises into twisted things. He huffed his breaths, talking to himself in short little words, as he might have once soothed his sister. He only had to go as far as the pinprick of lamp light that shone down from a street grate. Then, he would be free.

It took longer than he expected. Sure he had missed it, he tracked back, his flanks burning from his stoop. Ten paces back and he didn't see a single crack of light. William stopped, the darkness suffocating, the note sticking to his sweating fingers.

The beam of light fell suddenly on the fetid tunnel water, right before his toes. William twisted to look, and saw the corresponding oval on the ceiling. Someone must have been standing over it, or a carriage blocking the light.

Five minutes later, he scraped the round manhole cover back into position. It seemed devilishly heavy now; he could only lift it by locking his arms straight and pushing up with his legs. The V of the VA monogram cast into the lid pointed towards the river. William straightened his aching spine, feeling the grime between his fingers. The cuffs of his shirt were black, his hair hanging down in his eyes.

He sensed eyes on him in the darkness, probably watching from the windows that lined the long lanes of St Alberts. He had no fear of walking the streets here. Well-lit, warm homes with opportunity for enterprise created a bonded society that largely pushed out exploiters. He was more worried about being confronted for what he was doing.

Down the way, in front of the Royal gates, the crowd of protestors had swelled with gawkers, now pointing to the roof. William followed their gazes and saw a dirty thread of smoke rising from under Tesla's tower.

Carriages still flowed past the broad street, each with their blinders lit. William pulled his damp jacket about himself, and picked his target: a large carriage heading to City Road. His arm jerked as he swung himself onto the rear bench, unnoticed by either occupants or driver. The wind on the wet fabric turned him to ice, and his teeth danced together. He knew when he arrived, he would look exactly like he had been crawling through a sewer.

He would have doubted, then, his ability to carry this message. But this carriage had come at just the right moment. William's mother believed firmly in signs, and for that moment, William did, too.

After transferring across two more carriages, William ran the last block to Tesla's Baker Street address. He'd been here once before, driven by curiosity. A crusher had chased him out of the street that time, so now, William checked carefully and found no one on the footpath. The Commissioner of Sewers' night brigade had finished, and the advance guard who would start at two not yet around.

William slipped along the iron palisade fencing, and across the entrance to the address. He was surprised to find the front door ajar, a thin column of yellow light spilling from the crack.

"Hello?" he called timidly. "Mr. Tesla?"

No answer. William's trembling fingers pushed at the door, which swung on silent hinges. He could see, then, into the short hall. He could hear a shuffling, but no voices.

He edged inside. "Hello?" he called again.

This time came an immediate creak, and lumbering footsteps.

A man with a yellow neckcloth bowled into the hall,

wrenched the door full wide, and scanned the street. William, his heart hammering in his hiding place on the cellar steps, bit down on his own lip. Lucky Araminta had told him to expect intruders.

A burden then settled on William's grubby shoulders like a great bird, but unexpected resolve flexed to take up the weight. Curtains were drawn across the street-level windows here, so William ran the half-block around to the rear, stood on a fence, and leaned in to a gap in the drapes.

Mr. Tesla sat in a desk chair, facing in William's direction. Yellow was not visible, but another man with a checked neckcloth was, a heavy railgun denting the flesh of his trousered thighs. They didn't seem to be doing anything, just sitting, waiting. William tucked the note into his damp pants pocket and looked up. The next floor balconette was a foot away, the wall blockwork a perfect fit for his toes. William stretched, his weight on one wedged shoe. He couldn't quite reach.

He took a breath, and leapt.

《〉》

Leo made the others wait while he checked through all three floors of the maintenance stair. No William.

"Did he say anything to either of you?" he asked when he came back to the top landing.

David shook his head.

Araminta hesitated. "He's gone to try the way out, and on to Mr. Tesla."

Leo cursed, imagining the boy faced with one of the intruders' dogs, or blown into a molecular cloud with a railgun. But it was done, and their window on the B-Machine was closing.

"How are we going to save Victoria?" David said, his

voice low and urgent.

"I'm not sure that we are," Leo replied. "Dealing with the B-Machine comes first. Maybe she doesn't matter."

"But we have time," David argued. "They're not going to just escape with something so large. They're going to have to move it to the elevator, and what about the security system? They are trapped here too. They could easily be caught. All criminals make mistakes."

Leo was silent. That part of the whole proceedings bothered him. Since he'd looked into that masked man's eyes, he knew he was missing something. That man wasn't the kind who made grave mistakes, who hadn't known about the security system.

"That man isn't a pick-pocket," Araminta said as if hearing his thoughts. She caught Leo's eye. "I'm so sure I've seen him before."

A breeze pulled the fine hairs on Leo's skin in that moment, air that had sucked in under the door above them, and that rushed down the stair to some escape below. That breeze, again. Why was the air moving like that, here? It reminded him of the Underground, when a train came through the station and pulled the air with it, creating a wind tunnel as you tried to negotiate the stairs. This wasn't as powerful, but still the same effect. Air had to have somewhere to go. It didn't move like that in a sealed building.

"You feel that?"

"What?" David said.

"The air is moving."

"So there's a draught," he said.

"There shouldn't be. Not in a closed building." Leo experienced a moment of clarity and swore under his breath. "Didn't you say there was a new Underground line running near here?"

"Yes, why?"

"It travels under St Alberts," Araminta said, then her eyes widened. "Oh … Edison. That's who he is!"

"Edison?" Leo said.

"Thomas Edison," Araminta insisted. "The American inventor. I've seen his face in the journals before, and he bought the Underground line interest when it experienced financial difficulties. Disraeli said as much."

"He was wearing a mask."

Araminta raised her eyebrows. "And you clearly have not experienced a great many masquerade balls. It's him. I am sure of it."

Leo absorbed this. Christ, Thomas Edison? They were fucking around in a timefield, in a building built by Nikola Tesla, where Edison was holding Queen Victoria hostage? He couldn't make this shit up. But with grim clarity, he was sure he knew what was happening.

He raked a hand over his head. "They don't care about the building security, because they're tunneling it out."

David laughed. "But the tube line doesn't connect to *us*."

"That man upstairs in the black neckcloth? He had river dirt on his arms. They're tunneling to the tube line, I bet you that, and they've probably been doing it for a while. They had inside help, don't forget. They've chosen a night Tesla isn't here, and when his own system can protect their work. They never intended going out the front door."

David's mouth had formed a perfect circle. "What do we do now?" he said.

"We do what Helen sent us to do. Disable that B-Machine, and get back to the transmission room."

David scowled. "What about Victoria?"

"Screw Victoria."

From somewhere far below came a wrenching metallic creak. Leo tensed. He waited to hear footsteps on the treads, knowing the three of them were in a dead end. He'd hoped to have longer before the intruders realized they hadn't been killed in the explosion. But Leo didn't hear steps. Didn't hear anything except an occasional *tink* and *swish*.

Leo didn't like those sounds. He descended in a crouch, guiding David and Araminta behind him to the second-floor. As they reached the landing, he heard a panting breath, a *chink* of a claw against steel.

He was about to throw open the door when the dog leapt from the lower stairs, a hurtling mouth of teeth that aimed straight for Leo's arm. Leo felt bone slip against his flesh, and the wet smack of jowls as the dog just missed. His finger sought the railgun trigger, but the space was tight to swing. His shot flew wide, deafening in the close space.

The dog flinched. David was through the door before it righted itself, so it lunged for Araminta. She wasn't fast enough, even with Leo lifting her. He felt the animal's dead weight dragging her back. It had a lock on her leg. Leo braced and aimed a kick at the dog's soft under-neck, and felt the hard tube of its windpipe give under his toe.

The animal released. Unbalanced, Leo pushed Araminta through the door as he fell. His neck struck the hard edge of the door threshold, and he threw up his hands. The animal was on him again. He felt cords of tendon under its coarse fur, his arms near buckling under its weight. He pulled his knees up and shoved from underneath.

The push didn't land square, but the dog lifted to the side, rolling over on the landing as it went. Leo scrambled through the door, his shins crashing on hard edges.

Someone tried to shut the door, but the dog had nosed through, its neck caught in the gap, jaws snapping. Leo found Araminta leaning her body into the door; David was nowhere.

Leo added his weight to hers, noting the door latch was gone, sheared off at the wood surface.

"Go," he gasped, and with the point of his boot in the dog's soft throat, he pushed the animal back inside. The door closed on fur like pine needles, and Leo felt the growls through the wood. "One," he counted, trying to calm himself as the animal shoved. He pointed the muzzle of the railgun at the door, hoping the dog would stop. He didn't want to do this. "Two … three."

He fired, and the shoving stopped.

With his ears ringing, Leo stepped back and looked at the hole punched in the door. *One down*, he thought. *One of two*. But something in him died. He stumbled back, and forced himself into a jog.

Down the hall near the transmission room, he caught up with David, who was aiding Araminta's painful shuffle. Her leg was bleeding freely. Leo scanned the foyer ahead.

"Go up the stairs to the roof, then down the shaft to the first floor," he said, breathless.

He could think of only one place to go, trusting that the other dog couldn't climb ladders.

❬❭❭

They half-fell down the service ladder. Araminta put no weight on the bleeding leg, but Leo didn't hear a word of complaint. After the tight crawl through the connecting tunnel, he cracked open the hatch into the second-level foyer.

Leo leaned out. The view disappeared into a haze of

plaster and wood dust. Each breath had a thick, sour taste. It smelled like another building he didn't want to remember. A ring of splintered wood chunks had sprayed into a tide-line of debris, which had blown across the workshop, collecting in front of the door to the operating room. Yep, looked like that building, too. Thank fuck he had something to do.

David had to pick his way across the glass in his sock feet while Leo carried Araminta down that secret hall to the medical room. Then he set about barricading the door as David got to work.

"Take the boot off," David told Araminta as he rolled up his sleeves.

Leo prowled around the room, looking for useful materials. That steam autoclave in the corner, its brass lid still gleaming, was too small to hold a door. The wall-mounted pipes delivering oxygen and steam were useless: both firmly bolted to the wall. Finally, he settled for a stout steel rod, liberated from a trolley, to wedge in the door handles.

Then he paced around, one railgun hanging from his hand, the other shoved in his pants pocket—unloaded—thinking about how he could disable the B-Machine.

The services riser they'd just climbed down ran all the way to the ground floor, and to the basement through the hole for the pipes. The simplest thing would be something that could be dropped down through that space. An explosive rolled close enough to the room could do enough damage. Or maybe—

"I need sterile wash," David said, holding out a dish. Leo broke his thought and glanced at Araminta's bare leg. A row of oozing punctures ringed her calf, the skin already swollen and red. David wiped at the marks with a wad of cottony gauze. He shook the dish again. "Put some water in there and stick the steam wand in it for a minute, will you?"

Leo took the dish and stepped towards the tap, distracted. Explosions could do a lot of damage; just look at the reagent lab. But maybe that pipe space meant they couldn't get a bomb close enough. Or make one powerful enough. Or …

"David, is that B-Machine using wireless power?"

"What?"

"Is it wireless?"

He looked up. "No. It's hard-wired. Cables run into the generator switchboard."

"Where do they run?"

"On the floor, through the passage under the stairs. I need that wash."

"Where's the fuse on the B-Machine?" On Helen's it had been low, near the ground.

David glanced away. "Same configuration as the original."

Leo felt a stir of hope. Those pipes in the services riser connected to the big tank in the attic. If he could flood the room, he could short the B-Machine. Helen had said if a Machine lost power, the microtorus would stop spinning, closing down the timefield. But would that destroy it?

He held the dish under the tap and turned, thinking about the logistics. A gush of yellow water came out. No one had used the tap in a while. He tipped it out and let the tap run until it was clear, then turned to the autoclave steamer. He took out the steaming wand, sunk it into the liquid, and opened the steam tap.

Nothing happened.

Leo frowned. His eyes automatically moved along the

wall, looking for a tap or valve. He found it, flipped it. Still, nothing came out. Had the supply been damaged in the blast? Or had the intruders turned it off?

"Where's that wash?" David asked.

"No steam," Leo answered.

David marched across and tried for himself. "They must have turned it off."

But why would they turn off the steam system? Leo followed the pipe back to the wall pushed his finger inside a joint in the lagging. The pipe was still warm. So the steam hadn't been off for long.

"Make do with what you have," he said. "I need to make a bomb."

Chapter 33

Araminta listened to the conversation while David finished the bandage. "A bomb?" he said, frowning. "What for?"

"For the B-Machine. To flood it and fry the electrics."

"How?"

"The services corridor we've been climbing up and down carries those big water pipes. They're cast iron, non-ductile. Easy to fracture. All we'd have to do is blow out a joint flange, and all that water will pour straight down into that room."

David shook his head. "Sounds too simple. I'm telling you, we should try to negotiate—"

"Of course it sounds simple. Because there's also thugs with railguns looking for us right now. We have zero chance of getting close to the B-Machine itself. But that thing is electric. Helen said she lost a Machine to a short-circuit, so that's a viable option. Water plus power equals *zap*."

Fascinated, Araminta said, "In your time, have they proved Grotthuss's mechanism?"

Leo paused. "Grotthuss's mechanism?"

"Yes, the mechanism proposed by Grotthuss. On how electricity conducts through water."

"I'd have to get back to you on that," he said, after a pause.

"I mean to say, are you certain this would work? Would it be enough water?" She pushed aside a protesting David to test her leg. Her calf was throbbing. The bandage felt overtight, and the boot would not lace over the top of it.

"That tank in the attic should be full," Leo said. "I saw a jockey pump up there to feed it."

He dug in his pocket and handed her some kind of stick, then continued to prowl around, looking. "Need to run some figures. Write this down?"

Araminta discovered the stick had an inked tip, excellent for marking figures on the wall.

"Say thirty meters of line on each side of each floor, plus another three between ... say average hundred-millimeter diameter pipe," Leo said.

"Metric units?" Araminta asked. "The future has adopted metric units?"

"Mostly," Leo hedged. "So that's ..."

"Wait," Araminta said, scribbling the calculation. "Nearly five cubic meters of water in all the pipes."

Leo peered over her shoulder, inspecting the figures. "Okay," he said. "You're fast."

"Is five cubic meters enough?" Araminta asked, trying not to burn from the praise. "How big is the room?"

David shrugged. "Maybe twenty feet square."

Leo caught Araminta's eye; he gave her a small smile. "I did say 'mostly' metric. But that's tight."

He began prowling the cupboards, taking down selected items and sliding them onto the top of a wheeled cart. A canister with a screw top lid. Two syringes with thick needles. A wad of muslin.

"What exactly are you planning?" she said.

⟨⟩

In truth, Leo was thinking they were all screwed, because whatever he thought of he couldn't make from this room. His first thought had been thermite, but he didn't have any metallic powders, and while there would be swarf in the workshop, it wouldn't be fine enough for powder. There wasn't anything old enough to have rusted into iron oxide dust.

Second, he'd considered a simple overpressure device – a chemical reaction inside a closed container. Acid and bleach mixed together would do it. He bet he could have found both in the reagent lab … before the explosion. Not to mention he might end up killing himself with chlorine gas, and he wasn't convinced the explosion would be sufficient to get the job done.

He didn't have time for complex chemistry, even if he'd had anything with ammonium nitrate in it and a recipe to use. Leo rifled the cupboards again. They were full of surgical instruments in sterilized trays, drapes wrapped in waxed paper, spare ether masks. Now actual ether – that would have been useful, but there wasn't any, or even petrol or fuel oil. Everything in the building was electric, except for the coal, and that was in the basement.

All he really had was oxygen. He could probably fill that autoclave with the stuff and something flammable, but that would require a wick, which meant a leak in the container. Hardly practical.

Quite frankly, it would be easier to just go and steal some explosive from the intruders.

"That's your plan?"

Leo wasn't aware he'd spoken aloud. He looked up to find Araminta and David both staring at him. "No," he said quickly.

"Can't you just undo the bolts?" David said. "Those pipes have lots of joints."

"Those couplings have twelve bolts each," Leo said. "Each one would take several minutes to undo. You want to go and hang out in one spot in the service shaft making noise for forty minutes? Not to mention I'd need the right size shifter."

David was silent.

"Look," Leo said. "There's a hydrogen tank on that oxygen rig downstairs. I can make something out of that and it would do the job. Just have to figure out the details."

He circled around, looking for wire. Damn Tesla. Everything was wireless. The railguns had wires in their handles, but only a few inches long. No way he wanted to be that close. He envied the intruders, who'd used a long spool of det cord. He should go and see if any of it had survived the explosion.

"What about using the railgun?" Araminta asked.

"I'd like to avoid being in direct aim of an exploding cylinder. We're getting nowhere here. We need to go to the oxygen rig first."

"We?" David said. "I think it would be much better if Araminta and I stayed here."

"No," Leo said. "You might have to move and we don't have any way of finding each other. We go back the way we came to the services shaft, because the other dog can't follow in there. Go down one floor, then through the library to the rig. Can you walk?"

Araminta gave him a nod, hefting the second railgun. She had a look of determination in her eye, but she was also terrified, and obviously in pain. As he stared at her, Leo had one of those moments of his childhood overlaying on this moment. A memory of Helen, her body cramping from the hours at her desk, plugging on with her work. That was the natural state of a soldier, of anyone who believed in something bigger than themselves.

"What are you looking at?" Araminta asked.

"You remind me of someone," Leo said.

"Who?"

Leo glanced down at the floor. "Someone I used to know."

He took a deep breath as they formed up inside the operating theatre door. This was it, he thought. If he fucked this up, a great inventor from the nineteenth century would take possession of a twenty-first century time machine. A man who was pre-quantum physics, who didn't have a clue about timefields and stability of the universal functions. He lifted the railgun. *Just another glorious day in the corps.*

The hallway was white and silent. Air flowing around the door to them was cool. Leo put a hand to a radiator under a window: a fading warmth. Steam definitely off.

They crept across the wreckage of the floor void's railing, through the bars of streaky Tesla light falling in distorted shapes across the floor. They reached the hatch door into the service shaft and Leo took a moment to look for det cord, then he heard a *thunk* and long *hummmmm.*

"Lift," he hissed as the whine of the elevator motor sounded upstairs. But where was the car?

Before Leo could think any further a man with a Blue neckcloth stepped down from the stairs, raising his weapon without a word. Araminta was already through the hatch, but Leo and David were caught in the open. A shot sliced the air and Leo felt a solar flare by his cheek. His own weapon flew up and the men stared at each other in momentary impasse.

"Hands," growled Blue.

Leo held, even as hot liquid ran down his chin. David's hands crept over his head, one of them clutching something. "Now, let's just be calm about this," he said, in what he probably thought was a reasonable tone.

Shut up shut up, Leo thought. These were not reasonable men. He looked round for the dog. Where was it? One man he could maybe best, if he could just bring himself to pull the trigger.

"We all want the same things," David went on, slowly stepping forward. It was field notes in his hand. "And I think we can negotiate a reasonable outcome."

"Stop where y'are," Blue growled.

David paused, then took another tiny step, right into Leo's line of fire. *Shit.* "David," he hissed, trying to force him with syllables to stand the fuck down.

"If you'll just give us some time to discuss what you want—"

The atmosphere was an overstrung guitar string. Leo heard the pinging warnings with every move David made, with every twitch at the corner of Blue's eye. Leo had no idea where the back-up was, but it couldn't be far away.

David took another step.

The railgun cracked. Leo saw David's pant leg ripple. A few splintered words fell from his lips before he crumpled. Blue's cocked the gun to reload and aim again, but Leo was moving. He fired wide as he dove for the hatch and hauled arse through to the shaft. His bad knee jagged as he fell out the other end, scrambled around and reloaded, aimed, then pulled the trigger again. This time, the railgun didn't respond.

Leo could see a square of the foyer though the hatch. David lay on the floor out there, clutching a spreading dark stain on his thigh. Then Leo glimpsed a snout and forelimbs before he ran.

Araminta was on the ladder, waiting. "Up, up!" he hissed.

The climb went on forever, his knee uncooperative.

Finally, he saw Araminta's hand reaching for him through the attic hatch. Leo burst onto the roof, gasping shallow breaths, thighs burning. He lay out, unable to move, until he felt a buzz in his pocket.

Slowly, he extracted the console. Over the top of the dancing Grid numbers was a single message.

NOW – HELEN

The blow lands on Helen with no warning, and for what seems an age, all she can see is black in her vision, the room tilting to the side.

Slowly, it registers. He'd hit her, with something hard. Probably the butt of his rifle.

She is lying on her side now, part of the lab door and the upended computer in her field of view. The monitor has moved, that's why she can see the Grid. See the numbers hold, for just a second, before they begin dancing again. But that pause in the instability … that's something.

But something is wrong with her face, too. It doesn't feel right, all numb and achy and unresponsive, her eyelids moving too slowly as she blinks. The soldier is still there, investigating The Machine, touching the fat power cables.

He glances back, towards her. She wonders if he can see that her eyes are open. She doesn't move, but then she realizes moving isn't so much an option. Commands she sends to her fingers fizzle out, like meteors burning up across the heavens. She flops onto her back without meaning to, and feels a fluid shift inside her nose, a thick gush into the back of her throat that induces gagging swallows. A retch comes, and her jaw clicks in a place it shouldn't click.

She manages with huge effort to turn onto her other side so that a thin trail of fluid runs from her mouth. She hears the *schiff* of the soldier's uniform as he twists to watch her floundering, but his footsteps don't come. He talks in a low voice into a radio. He's unconcerned.

She wonders then if her skull is broken, if she is bleeding inside, her brain swelling in its immovable casing. The thought is curiously detached. She lies still, mulling it over, one arm flung out, fingers resting on the keyboard.

The keyboard.

She remembers what she was supposed to do.

She has to do this by feel, with hands that are blunt instruments of her deadened senses. Her pinky finds the space between the letter keys and the arrows, slides up all the way to the top. F12 opens the messaging program. F5 will load the emergency phrase code she wants.

She counts across seven keys; loses count and has to start again. Hopes the key under her finger is the right one. Pushes it. She imagines the dialogue that comes up, the warning that she's about to use precious qubits. Her hand flops down, searching for the arrow keys now. Left arrow, she hopes, to select *send anyway*, and then enter.

Over on The Machine, a green light flashes. At least, she thinks she sees the reflection of it in the glossy curve of a table leg. At the same moment, the soldier's radio is cracking in an insistent way. Short bursts. Giving directions. She knows, somehow, that those directions will not be good for her, or The Machine.

She fixes her eyes on the Grid. She doesn't want this to be how it ends, to leave Leo in the timefield. She needs him here, to preserve The Machine when she can't any longer. And it's more than that, because if he dies in the timefield, there can't be any redress. He can't work with her the way they were meant to, can't even do it with her posthumous notes. They'll be forever separated, no longer just in space but in time, too.

So, let him get the message, she thinks. Let him understand. At least if he is here, he has a chance.

Machine compromised. Recall. Recall. Recall.

Chapter 34

Timefield, 1884 – William

The second floor of Tesla's townhouse resembled an overcrowded storeroom, apparatus and pieces thereof, and tall shelves, filling air from floor to ceiling. William padded between the towering rows, which only cleared around a vast table placed before the balustrade topping the stairs. Tiny Tesla lights burned on the wall above the stair, making a pattern like a ghoulish fishing net. William was thankful for the shadows.

He considered what he was about to do. It was, he decided, not only stupid but sacrilegious, and more than a little frightening. Who knew what all these machines were, and what Tesla might have in place to deter would-be thieves? If he had protected the Royal Laboratories with a lock-down system that could explode an egg, what would be lurking here in his private home?

Still, William had gotten in, and that gave him courage.

He scanned the shelves and selected something heavy and metallic that fit in the curve of his palm. After a slow backwards lean, he flung it at the far window and ducked, his heart galloping. He heard the object hit with a soft *chink*, and then bounce, landing on the floorboards with an odd dull thud.

William popped up, his ears burning like radiator fins. The glass was intact, the black lump of the object resting on the floor. How could he have missed?

He tried again. Retrieved the heavy metal thing and pitched it at the glass. This time, he watched the thing sail into the window. Again, that soft *chink*, then the muted fall to the floor. It barely made any noise at all. Certainly there were no voices or creaking from downstairs that might signify the men coming to investigate.

William knew when he had met sufficient resistance to a plan. So when he retrieved the object this time, he simply hurled it down the stairs. At least gravity could not be argued with.

The object bounced over the treads, gaining speed and clatter volume as it went. Long before it had met the low point in the foyer floor, William heard the scrape of chair legs as someone heavy and unrefined scored the polish in a rapid bid for verticality.

Heavy boots approached the stair. William waited only until he'd seen the barest hint of an arm — a thick arm — reaching for the banister before he crammed himself in a narrow space beneath a shelf. A long pause came. William imagined the man picking up the object, peering up the stairs, a pair of thick brows perhaps drawing together. *Come up*, William willed.

Silence. A long, long silence.

In desperation, William opened his mouth and let loose the call of a mallard he'd once heard on the bank of the river, a heavy guttural cry, which came out strangled in his nervousness.

A pause, then finally the first stair groaned under a heavy boot.

The man took his time coming up. Finally, William saw the bald edge of a large head shining under a Tesla lamp, like a melon in a night-time market stall. The face under it rested on a yellow neckcloth, the neck itself so thick that only the ends of the fabric had met.

"Oi," came a rough voice from below, near the foot of the stairs. "Anythin'?"

"I'm not up there yet, am I?" growled Yellow, pausing to glare back down at his companion.

William took this as his cue, flinging a steel washer he'd taken from the table across the room, which softly pinged against the window's seemingly indestructible glass. Yellow's head turned towards the rattle as the washer skidded into a corner and commenced a decaying spin. The big man stalked around the vast table in pursuit, promising gruesome murder to the assumed rat. Once he reached the far side, as far from the stair as possible, William made his move.

He scuttled out of his hiding place, bent low like a cripple, up to the crest of the stair. Down below, another man gripped the banister, his body turned towards the downstairs sitting room. William let out a soft coo, a pigeon call.

The man downstairs peered over the banister, up the stair. His neckcloth was a scrap of checks, like it had been torn from a tablecloth. "Oi!" he called again. "Yella?"

William glanced up to where Yellow was still prowling in the far corner. Caught in the eerie silencing quality of Tesla's lab, he didn't respond. William cast down a louder, more plaintive coo, then added a soft groan.

"Yella?" the man called, shifting his body along the banister, so he could stand square at the foot of the stairs.

Come on, William silently begged. Now he could see the man's other hand, the thick body of a railgun glinting in the long fingers. William swallowed. He needed both of them to come up here, and he realized he had probably blown it. Yellow would tire of looking over in the corner and come back. William would have to show himself.

And do what?

He still had no idea even as his feet touched down the treads. If he stuck to the wall, he could make four, maybe five stairs in a shadow, but Checks would soon work out that William was not Yellow. At that point, William hoped for two things. Firstly, that when he turned and ran, Checks would give chase. And second, that William could outrun any thought Checks might have to shoot him in the back.

Two treads. Three. Four.

William watched Checks body shift in surprise at seeing a ruffian boy, then the split second of trying to decide what to do with unexpected information. William took one more step, trying to force an equal look of surprise onto his own face. Then, just as William could suppress his need to flee no longer, Checks abruptly crumpled.

William threw himself against the wall as the railgun hit the boards of the hall with a heavy *thud*. Then he saw another man standing over Checks with a stout length of wood in his hand. This new man had a thick moustache, his brows drawn together in a concentrated frown, his hair making an artful sweep behind his head.

This man glanced up the stairs. "You're awfully big for a duck," he said, dryly, as Tesla also appeared, his hands flicking back the panels of his jacket, fob chain catching the light, his face curious and furious at the same time. Spotting William, a recognition swept over his features and he beckoned.

William picked his way downstairs on legs shaking like celebration jelly and drew Araminta's note from his pocket. Inelegantly, he thrust it at Tesla. The other man picked up the railgun and aimed it up the stairs as Tesla unfolded the paper.

"From Araminta, Lady Montague," William whispered.

Tesla scanned the lines, then glanced at William. "Tell me exactly how you managed to leave the laboratories, and evade the security system?"

They were interrupted by the footsteps nearing the top of the stairs. The other man's eyes narrowed, his gaze becoming intent and watchful, focused on his aim.

"Are you confident with that thing, Clemens?" Tesla asked.

"I may have only been a solider for a fortnight, but it was a rather singular experience," Clemens replied. "As long as this works much the same as the rifle I had then …"

"S'going on?" Yellow called down the stair, a waver in his voice.

"Your companion has fallen idle at his task," Clemens called up calmly. "And unless you place your gun on the ground and come down that stair with your hands raised, I will shoot that ridiculous head from your shoulders right now."

A pause. Finally, Yellow's heavy legs appeared, slowly descending, then his elbows and hands. His face bore a mean scowl.

"There's a good fellow," Clemens said encouragingly.

"You know, I do have an electric gate at the top of those stairs," Tesla said, as if musing on several different ways this event could have played out. "We could have just locked him up there."

Yellow spat. "You dunno who we work for," he ground out. "You wouldna think this was so smart if you did."

"Threats," Clemens said, nodding, as if this was both expected and approved of. "Now let me tell you something. I was born under a comet, and I'll die under one many years from now. That tells me my part in this goes rather well. Tesla?"

Tesla had thrown open the doors of a cupboard that rested in the sitting room, drawing out and discarding items as he searched. Coils of brass and copper tubing, small gauges dragging disconnected wires, two small baskets stuffed with washers and circlips. Finally, from the very back, he pulled out a squat lantern, and with some grim satisfaction, laid it on his work desk.

He flicked a switch, and the lamp glowed with ethereal brilliance. Another click, and it vanished.

Clemens shook his head. "I never quite get used to that etheric transmission," he said.

"This is merely a capacitance device," Tesla said, quickly. "In the case they tamper with the power transmitter, I cannot rely on the lighting in the laboratories. I must leave you a while, Clemens."

At this, Tesla put a firm hand on William's back and propelled him out the back door of the townhouse.

Chapter 35

"Jesus," Leo panted, still lying on his back, reading the message over and over. Breath was coming back into his lungs. He tried to sit up, and a murderous pain stabbed him in the left side. "*Jesus.*" Maybe he'd cracked a rib.

"What happened to David?" Araminta's face leaned over him, her voice trembling.

Leo shook his head. "Either he's dead, or they have him. Help me up."

Araminta tried, but it was hardly like help, more like tugging on the end of his good arm. This is where, Leo reflected, being the big guy was not an advantage. He managed to sit and tried putting weight on his knee. Painful, but still usable. He touched his cheek and found bright blood on his fingers. There was another wound on his upper arm, but both of them were superficial. Certainly not as worrying as the message on the screen.

Araminta watched him with knotted brow. "What's does that say?"

"It's a message from ... our physicist, with The Machine," he said finally. Saying *the future* felt ridiculous.

"What does it say?"

"That The Machine's under threat, and that we should recall as soon as possible." Leo's blood ran cold, thinking of what that really meant. *Helen* was under threat, which meant he should do exactly what she'd said. Only he couldn't, not with the B-Machine situation. And what about David?

Araminta stared at him, as if trying to decide something. "You mentioned the water tank," she said.

Leo pointed to it. Araminta limped across; her gait was slower and more painful now, and Leo wondered how much longer she could walk. She rapped her knuckles on the metal, as high as she could reach.

"Seems full," she said. "Why are there three pipes?"

Leo twisted. "Where?"

"One goes into the top, another at about halfway, and another at the very bottom. The last two connect together."

"Is there a valve at that connection?"

"The thing with the handle?"

"Yes. Turn it so that it points to the pipe at the bottom."

There was a pause before Araminta limped back. "The pipe at the top is the feed, yes? That fills the tank?"

Leo nodded. "The other two are outflows. Usually they'd take water from the middle pipe, so the tank is never dry. But if we're trying for a flood, we want it all."

She nodded. "What now? You said we were going back down to the oxygen rig."

"Yeah." His brain seemed to be working so slowly, preoccupied with the pains in his body. He attempted a stretch, and his ribs felt as though they were popping out from his sternum. He sank back; lactic fatigue was setting in. "I'll have to go down to get that hydrogen cylinder."

"You can barely walk." She hesitated. "I'll go."

"Don't be silly."

"Oh, I'm silly?" she rounded on him, indignant. "You think I can't do these things?"

At another time, in another place, Leo could see her in a uniform like he'd once worn. He'd seen soldiers who seemed small, or weaker, do incredible things and he bet like them, Araminta had been told what she couldn't do enough times in her life. "I think," he said, "there's armed men and dogs downstairs and that I can't have you leaving me here."

He ghosted a smile and after an uncertain moment, she smiled back. "I thought about it," she admitted.

"I know you did." He looked away. "Neither of us are in good shape. But when you don't have any choice, you do what you have to."

Something passed between them in that moment, some kind of understanding that transcended time and difference. She gave a single nod. "Then you need a binding on that arm."

"You'd have made a decent nurse," Leo conceded when, three minutes later, Araminta was wrapping his bicep wound with lengths torn from the lining of her jacket. "Efficient, and a little bit cruel."

She snorted a laugh. "Like Miss Nightingale? If I'd had a father like hers, I suppose."

Surprised, Leo said, "You know Florence Nightingale?"

"Not directly. Our family was acquainted with hers. My father forbid me to have anything to do with them, because her father educated her. Mine doesn't believe in that sort of thing. My mother, either." She paused, pulling on the strips with renewed vigor. Leo winced.

"Where did you find out about that mechanism, the one about conduction through water?"

"Grotthuss?"

"Yes."

"I read his paper. I don't have as many as I'd like, so I've read most of them many times. My library is too small and now ... "

She trailed off, working a moment in silence before her hands stopped. "Tell me the future is really better for us?

That those protestors outside actually have something to worry about, because women do find a better place in the world than we do now?"

Leo took a shallow breath, and didn't know quite what to say.

Araminta pushed on. "Because it doesn't escape my notice that both you and David are men, and that you came here to help Tesla, another man. Are you still so unbelieving that we are capable of anything, even a hundred years from now?"

"Not at all," Leo protested, but then he stopped, because he had to really think about it. "Look, it changes. But slowly. The physicist who built The Machine is a woman."

"Really?" That seemed to give her thought.

He nodded. "If I was going to ask anyone about Grotthuss, it would be her. Do you really want to know about what's coming in the next hundred years?"

They looked at each other then, Leo finding her eyes brilliant, blue and hungry. "More than anything," she said.

"Wars are coming," Leo said. "Two in the first half of next century so long and bloody that will seem like the world is ending. Millions die, not just on the battlefield but exterminated in camps by evil men. Then many smaller wars come afterwards. More despots, more suffering. Then warfare changes, and when the next big one kicks off, which is just a few years before my time and The Machine, it's so different we don't even really know what to call it. There's no trenches anymore, no fronts. Just bombs going off in the middle of the cities. Unpiloted aircraft dropping more. That's what we were here to try and change."

"I asked about women," she said after a pause.

"I'm getting to it. In these big wars-to-come, so many

men go to fight that women at home have to do everything. Run machinery and businesses, play sport and everything else. And so many of those men never come back, or if they do, they aren't the men who left. There's a whole generation of men and boys lost to these wars, and women have to make up for all of it. There's a profound shift after that. Women don't want to go back to how they were before. They've seen what else their lives can be about. A few decades later, there's a social revolution. Doors open up. Women can do almost anything."

"Almost?"

Leo shook his head. "Like I said, it takes a while. When I'm from, there's a few things that have only just become open, like front-line soldiering. A lot of people are uncomfortable with the image of a woman with a rifle in her hands, or dying with an enemy bullet in her heart, or blown to pieces by a mortar, more to the point. We seem more comfortable if these things happen to men, even if those men are very young."

Araminta swallowed, and lifted her chin towards the railgun. "Carrying rifles like those?"

"No." Leo shifted uncomfortably. "Those we don't have. A consequence of Tesla's work here. Very new."

"So these weapons might change time, too?"

"I don't know. With Tesla, David and Helen were trying to make the world less dependent on oil and coal. That new war I mentioned … the Warm War… it started because … well, for a lot of reasons. But one of the big ones was countries started mucking with the weather. The world's climate changes because of all the coal we're burning, and that we're still burning when I'm from. Summers are drier. Winters harsher. Crops fail, but still no one seemed to be able to do anything about it. The big governments that could have were too slow, and then it was too late. Some smaller, poorer countries that had dreadful droughts, or catastrophic floods, they were the ones who looked for mitigation. They started atmospheric seeding to change rainfall and temperature. But air doesn't respect national borders, and then suddenly if their neighbor had a bad drought—"

"They blamed it on the other country and went to war."

Leo nodded. "Right. Some of the big governments by then – America, Russia – they were isolationist. They didn't want to get involved in the conflicts at first, then they decided they wanted to call the shots on who to attack. It was unpredictable. China was tense. And North Korea. And Russia. And the Middle East. Then there was a famine in America, and the government blamed the Chinese for that, accused them of changing the weather."

"Did they?"

He shrugged. "Maybe, but it doesn't really matter. The climate had been changing for decades, but no one could agree to do anything, because the businesses that provide coal and oil are so powerful. Protests about it in America turned violent, then the government tried to disarm the country, and that provoked rural militias, and it all dominoed and fractured into another civil war. It was complex and ugly, and long in its brewing. That was the reasoning in starting this place, in working with Tesla as I understand it. They were trying to push the technology in a different direction, avoid the climate crisis in the first place, before it all gets ugly."

"But it didn't work?"

"That's not really my area," Leo said. "Helen—that's our physicist—knew something here was becoming unstable. Risking time itself being unsolvable. That's why that B-Machine can't be let go. Helen knows the maths of these things. I understand what I can see and touch. Time is her specialty. She's the clever one."

"There is a great affection between you, I think," Araminta said slowly, as if she were jealous. "The way you talk about her."

Leo felt a small smile bend his lips. "She's my sister," he said, simply, feeling so proud of the fact he could have cried. "I'm doing what she asked me to do. No one else could have got me inside that damned Machine."

He gave a little involuntary shudder.

"And why is that?"

Leo looked up at the dark roof of the attic. "Six years ago, I left Cambridge without giving her any warning, or any explanation of where I was going. Then I was in the madness of the army. I didn't think about what things were like for her when I left. Then a bit over a year ago, I was on a mission in a delightful sandy city, in a building. There was an explosion, and the whole thing collapsed."

Leo paused, sucking a breath against the memory of the dark. "I woke up hearing fire. Smelling fire. My leg broken under a pile of rubble. I thought I'd never get out of that place. I regretted then, leaving Helen by herself like that. I knew she was lonely, and she wanted us both to work on her ideas. I knew I'd run out on her. And thinking about that was the only thing that kept my head together while I was waiting. So when she found me again, she could have asked me to do anything. But I still see small spaces and fire, everywhere. You have a bad experience … you remember. But I still came here, trying to fix it, because I believe in her. That … or because I'm an unsavable idiot."

Araminta's expression was curiously sad. She sighed. "If only I could have a brother such as you," she said.

"You don't want me. You'd want someone smarter," he said. "Less battle scars."

She paused a moment, then rubbed at her hip. "But scars are at least some evidence, that one has done something."

"True enough. But not the only evidence." Leo hauled himself to standing now her bandage was finished.

"Wars are dreadful things," she said slowly. "Women and children die in them, too. They died in camps in the Boer War, but of course no one polite will talk of it. Men fight each other and know everyone pays for it, and yet still they seem to think such suffering is inevitable. Tesla is the only man who sees the world in a different way. Maybe there is more reason to do this than just your sister."

Leo blew out a breath, her words making tiny sparking connections through his thoughts. "Everything about the next hundred years starts here. Maybe that's what Helen meant, and I'm not sure I appreciated that until now," he said slowly. "I'll keep trying. With everything I've got. Even if it's not enough." He tested the binding. "This is good," he said.

Araminta appeared not to hear him. She was staring into the middle distance. After a pause, she said, "Even with all you've said, I think I still should have liked to see this future after all."

Chapter 36

Leo did not want to retrace their steps, so they went down using the maintenance stair. It was a deep well, dark and foreboding. Araminta gripped the stock of the railgun, pointing the tip down and away from her path, resting her finger along the side as Leo had shown her.

He had warned her they may come across the body of a dog in here, but Araminta noticed no signs of it. Leo's shoulders were knotted with tension, his movements stiff with his injuries.

She had felt indifferent to the intruding men at the beginning, and their objectives. Now she understood how she was inseparably part of something they had created. Or, more specifically, that this physicist Helen had created.

Leo was in Helen's service. And that meant that now Araminta had images of war and death, and another century of fighting to be treated as well as a man. And even the woman who had made a time machine thought it might not be changeable.

For the first time since she'd walked out of her home today, she was viscerally scared. Scared of what men could do to each other. Scared of the low odds of success. Scared that she was not capable of living in the world when Leo and his future were gone. And yet, as they crept down the stair towards the ground floor, she felt emboldened, as if courage could only exist when hope had nearly vanished.

She kept following the steps down, as if she was descending the vacant halls of her own heart. Leo was right;

there was no choice. Edison could not have the B-Machine. No one could.

Every step, she expected to see an enemy face around the next bend, to hear the huff of animal breath. These ideas kept her blood pumping, her eyes open, her nostrils flared. She felt like the horses she'd seen after a hunt, the whites of their eyes showing, the blood-red membrane of their inner nose visible with every heaving breath. With grim humor, she remembered that they shot lame horses. The idea gave her a charge. She would show them what a lame horse could do.

The air warmed as they reached ground, tinged with a metallic scent, something bright and sour and new that burned up high in her skull. Leo paused in the glow of a Tesla light, his brow furrowed. She raised her eyebrows, and he returned a slight headshake; he didn't know what it was. He opened the landing door carefully.

Araminta held her breath. The door itself had been dented and scratched with long parallel marks, but the hall was empty but for faint red marks. They crept forward, passing door after door until they reached the reception room. Araminta saw the blood on the floor and walls and clasped a hand over her mouth. Gently, Leo turned her attention to the foyer ahead.

A chair blocked the way, but the foyer was empty, as was the main staircase. Leo pointed out signs of the intruders: the chair, the dock doors that were chained shut, but those of the library itself appeared unchanged.

Leo went first, crossing the expanse and pushing backward through the library doors. Nothing happened. Araminta followed.

Inside, the library looked the same, except for a few more books on the floor. They passed through to the back to where the oxygen rig was a gathering of dark shapes – domes and elbows and glinting surfaces. Someone had pushed open the doors into the receiving dock, so now a great expanse of space opened to Araminta's left as she put her back to the wall.

Leo began turning a red-painted wheel on a thin pipeline. Araminta watched the library, her railgun raised, her body rigid, glancing around only to check Leo's progress.

On her next look, Leo was reaching for one of the lines when he paused, staring at a gauge on top of the tank. That frown again.

"What?" she whispered.

His reply was mumbled, something about the pressure being a little low. He seemed to waver in indecision, as if considering searching for the cause of this problem, or remaining on task.

A muffled sound stole through the atmosphere, making the skin on her arms prickle. Then again – the sound of a rattling, as someone tested the dock entry doors against the chain. Then it stopped, leaving ominous silence. She wanted to run.

"Leo," she hissed. "Hurry."

She leaned out, to see further through into the library. Nothing seemed to be out there. She leaned out the other way, into the receiving dock. Nothing there either, among the stacks and palettes and store cupboard. The top of the library's double doors were just visible, dark rectangles in the distance through the mesh. Had one of them moved?

She had the sense something was there. "*Leo.*"

He had finished unhitching the tank and was attempting to lift it, his railgun set aside on the edge of the rig. He winced, shifted the weight, tried again. Araminta's neck broke out in sweat.

She glanced back through the library. Something had changed. The door. The door was not quite shut. Had it been like that before?

Fear clawed its way up her spine and sunk its talons into her scalp. She shifted, searching between the shelves for any movement.

Nothing.

Nothing.

Wait.

She froze. Something moved, something black not two shelves behind the door. Araminta tried to swing the railgun, but she was too afraid to move and betray her position. All she could do was watch in horror as the black shadow hovered there by the shelf. The shape darted, and Araminta stumbled back in surprise.

"Lord Almighty," she swore, steadying herself against the wall. A rat. A black rat. Her hands prickled as the shock ebbed away, her muscles weak with relief. A bubble of laughter pushed into her throat. Leo had found the rat too and was tracking it as he rolled the cylinder with his toe, one hand gripping his ribs. They caught each other's eye. His lips tugged in a half-smile.

The shot came from nowhere.

Araminta froze dumbly, until Leo shoved her in the back and she landed, sprawling, her chin cracking on the floor. The room wobbled. A pain flared in her jaw. She tried to rise, but Leo held his arm across her shoulders. She could hear him gasping as if he couldn't quite draw his breath.

Another shot cracked overhead. Araminta heard the round destroy a hole in something metallic nearby. They were cornered, she realized. The hydrogen tank rolled on its curved side across the floor, softly ringing.

Leo was now pushing her to crawl into the dock and down the long line of goods stacks close to the wall. Araminta dragged herself, her injured calf and bad leg both stabbing protests. She pushed the railgun before her, terrified of being vaporized by the gunman at any moment.

They paused behind a table. They could hear steps now, careful steps, separated by long silences. Leo stared intently through the table legs and stacks. He glanced at Araminta and nodded to her railgun. His own was still where he'd left it.

Araminta handed the gun over. Leo took one of the heavy pellets from the side. He motioned that he was going to throw it back towards the rig, and that when he did, they would move down to the end of the stacks, towards the foyer doors.

Right into a dead end.

〈〈〉〉

Just before Red loosed shots on the floor above, Green relaxed his cramped fingers on the drilling rig and stepped back, wiping away the sweat with his three-fingered hand. He shut the cooling water flow and without looking at the Masked Man, or the captives, retrieved the sledgehammer from the equipment cart.

The Masked Man inspected the mess of the offending rock while the last of the cooling water ribboned into the drainage pit under Black's swift broom. A rough arch of two-inch holes had been punched through the rock. "Will you need to blast it?"

"Nah," said Green, hefting the hammer. He'd worked all his life in the mines of the Black Hills, before the incident with the explosives that had mangled his hand.

This meant that he knew rock like he knew his mother's face, and that he was resolved to avoid explosives unless absolutely necessary. He'd begun working for the Pinkertons precisely because it didn't involve going down mines with the risk of being blown up or buried alive every day. The last thing he wanted was to tempt fate here. And he was convinced it wouldn't be necessary.

He swung the hammer, and a fracture opened between two holes. One more hit, and a block between three points cracked. The third blow knocked it out into the space beyond. A drag of air cooled the sweat on his cheeks. Ten more blows and he had the portal half open. Little pieces of mud stuck in his eyelashes, making ghosts in the darkness beyond.

A few minutes more work and the portal would admit the prize, and carry it down to the new Underground line, where a train would take it away.

《〉》

The Masked Man walked away from the manual work of the hammer. His portable generator was ready to take over when they unhooked The Machine from its hardline to the building. Green and Black were, at this moment, attaching rolling jacks and slings. The only thing remaining was to obtain that calibration. He checked the stopwatch. Still enough time, especially as now his adversaries had no refuge. Any moment, that piece of paper would be his. So near to his objective, the waiting became intolerable. He slipped out into the boiler room.

Immediately, he sensed something was wrong.

A smell assaulted him, one that he only associated with metal works. An ominous *tink tink chink ... tink tink* was coming from the boiler, a tell-tale note of material expanding under heat. A mirage rose from the locomotive's flue.

Now, if you could ride the coal conveyor towards the locomotive's firebox, it would be like riding the road to hell, the pavement all black and flammable, the destination a maw of flame and incandescent coals. This conveyor was still moving and feeding the firebox, while Green swung his hammer, and the drill's cooling water lay puddled on the floor. Thames water. Critical water.

That water, before the intruders diverted it, was the pipe supplying the boiler. The Masked Man had been timing the descent of that water level, managing their time here as he managed the progress of his men.

Because when the water inside the boiler was gone, it was like a kitchen kettle without a cut-out switch. A massive industrial kettle. The locomotive's boiler was a big cylinder full of nested pipes, where water holds the temperature, preventing its rise to that of the hellfire itself. When the last droplets shake off their liquidity, lifting off the tube surfaces like atomic jump jets, there is only air on the other side of that thin tube, a pan left on a range with nothing inside it.

All while the firebox hellfire was still being fed.

There should have been an interlock – a cut-out that noticed when there was no water flowing and stopped the coal. But the switch was fixed on the line before the diversion, so as the water had flowed through Green's drill, the switch detected no problem.

So the firebox heated, and the tubes heated, the slippery electrons in each metal atom swapping their places at an increasingly rapid rate. The crystalline structure of the metal lost its strength, bonds stretching like Dali's clocks, painted four decades hence. The metal liquefied at the hottest spots, wicked into drops. The structure could no longer support its own weight. The boiler tubes bowed, and the firebox plate buckled like a soda can under a foot.

So now, with a long conveyor of coal snaking away from it like a line of gunpowder, the Masked Man smelled impending disaster.

He reached the instrument panel in an instant. Zero pressure on the steam line. The boiler was dry. He checked his stopwatch. No, *no*. They were not meant to be at this point, not yet!

Feverishly, he thought back across all the calculations, all the assumptions, looking for what he had missed. Something had required more output from the steam engine, had used more water than expected. But lights had not changed. Security had not changed … but, ah. *Yes*, it had. He'd taken his reading of the water flow before security had turned on, because Forbes had been late.

The oversight enraged The Marked Man more than the calamity unfolding before his eyes. He had always planned for this to happen. The boiler would run dry, melt, and weaken. And at that critical point, he would turn the water back on, cold water that would hit the superheated metal and flash boil, guaranteeing an explosion. An explosion that would spread fire all through the basement, and beyond. It would cover their tracks, explaining away the dynamite blast that would seal the escape tunnel.

Just not *yet*. Not while their tasks were incomplete.

Slowly, the Masked Man gathered his temper. He would have to accept that the calibration sheet was gone and move to an alternate strategy: Forbes had been an excellent artist. He had drawn the calculation machine that produced the calibration, so in theory it could be re-created. In a few minutes, the prize would be in the tunnel. There was really no reason to wait.

When he re-entered the secret room, he closed the door behind him and called Black and Green.

"We have reached the hour," he said, which meant Black was being sent into the boiler room to turn the water back on. If he was going to blow it, he would do it now.

❰❰❱❱

Upstairs, Leo prepared to throw the pellet. Araminta saw his grimace as the throw stretched his ribs. She heard the *tink tink* as the railgun pellet glanced off the hydrogen tank and bounced sideways into the oxygen rig structure. She had a random thought that she would never wear a skirt again if she could help it.

Then the world simply ended.

Chapter 37

As Leo threw the railgun pellet, a cascade of unexpected events sent the Royal Laboratories on an irreversible damage track. Leo intended to distract Red, to give the shooter a sound to aim at while he and Araminta made it to the other end of the dock.

But just as Red was aiming across the library, Black threw the valve on the boiler water down in the basement.

Red assumed that his quarry would be keeping low, so he dropped to a knee and aimed his railgun at a flash of movement far through the shelves. At the same moment, a floor below, Black bolted for the stair door.

The first water that flooded down the pipe hit the incandescent metal plate separating the coal fire from the now empty overheated boiler. It flash vaporized in an instant, tearing open the heat-weakened metal walls with an anvil of overpressure. The steam train's torso ripped apart like a firecracker, spewing glowing ejecta in a radial burst across the basement. These bolides—fragments of superheated water tubing, glowing coals, and liquid metal—slammed into walls, ceiling and anything attached thereon. One of them had the right trajectory to punch through the thin metal of the furnace air-intake, and skid all the way up the duct, and ping into the space between that duct and the external wall of the Tesla Royal, right where the expanding pool of accumulated hydrogen was waiting.

Hydrogen is not particularly shock sensitive; the

dynamite detonation of the reagent lab two floors above had not affected it. But a glowing rock above ignition temperature was another matter.

The explosion propagated at roughly Mach 8, about four times the speed of the Concorde, tearing apart the hydrogen filled space, all the way back to the oxygen rig itself. The force ruptured the lines and spewed out pure oxygen gas, transforming anything it touched into flammable tinder. This was the double-punch in the explosion. Floor joists splintered, until they could no longer hold the weight of the workshop above. The pressure in the interfloor cavity blew out through a weak spot in the wall of the services void, sending a plume of smoke directly towards the roof.

All this happened in a fraction of a second, the same second in which Red fired at that flash of movement. That flash was the hydrogen cylinder, rocking against the open door to the dock.

As ever, Red's aim was true.

The railgun pellet ploughed into the cylinder long before the sound of it leaving the railgun had even reached Red's ears. The energy the pellet carried converted into heat, sending a spray of molten metal in a graceful fractal pattern that would have earned a computational dynamics student a doctorate. A microsecond later, when the hydrogen inside the cylinder reached five-hundred Celsius, it also detonated.

Contained within the cylinder, the pressure ramped until the container failed like a pulled Christmas-cracker, fragmenting into twisted pieces of flaming debris that shot across space. The ejecta from the cylinder and from the back-propagating explosion from the boiler met in a definitive turbulent hellfire.

Through this flame, the burning workshop floor fell, crushing the mesh library-dock wall, creating a sinkhole into which flowed lathes and saws and timber and anything else the workshop had held.

When the debris settled, oily rags and timbers made burning spot fires, lighting a new world on the ground floor, a dystopian mess of broken pieces, where Leo and Araminta had just been.

《〉》

Green was heaving on a lever under The Machine when the ground shook. His feet failed him, the steel prying bar flying away in the tunnel. The wall before him shimmied, streaming rivulets of dust and then, all at once, a sheaf of dirt in the mouth of the portal collapsed.

When the world had stopped shaking, Green peeled his hands off his face, shedding dust, expecting to be shortly explaining his unchristian choices to his maker. But the tunnel was still open. They would have to dig out the collapsed dirt, but they'd make it out, as long as the roof didn't fall down on their heads first.

"Devil almighty," he cursed, and spat into the earth.

The Masked Man appeared in the blinder light, but his usual steady and impenetrable conviction had cracked at the edges. His eyes were wide. Green didn't have to be told that whatever had just happened wasn't what was supposed to happen. If it had been a mine, Green might have wondered about a pocket of mine damp blowing a set charge sky high. Because that explosion was bigger than it should have been, and it had been above them and all the way down the other wing, too.

Where the shots had come from just moments ago.

"Continue moving The Machine," the Masked Man

directed, but in a voice that had lost its mettle.

"What about Red and Blue?"

The Masked Man licked his lip. "Black can search the stairway if he cares to."

Green knew in that moment he would not likely see Red and Blue again.

"What about 'em?" Green asked, thumbing at Victoria, tied to her chair, who not that long ago seemed so important; and David, the cloth of his trouser leg wet and scarlet.

"Leave them," the Masked Man said, in a voice that cared for no one. "They are not needed."

Chapter 38

Tesla's carriage was like nothing William had seen before.

"Do we have time to wait for the horses?" he said dumbly, seeing the unhitched cab. It had such small wheels, a fully glass-enclosed body with forward and rear benches, and a bank of blinders set into the front. "Won't it be faster to take a hire?"

Tesla made no answer, but climbed into the front bench, and pushed the opposite door open. William felt like a fool sitting in the unhitched cab, until he noticed the wheel mounted before Tesla, and then the carriage sprang forward of its own accord. Tesla twisted to watch over his shoulder as he backed out, talking the whole time.

"This is a prototype model," he said. "Greater flexibility than horse-drawn vehicles. Not much good on country roads with the smaller wheels, but suitable in town."

They burst from the laneway at what William considered a terrifying speed. Any horses they passed gave the electric carriage wild rolling eyes, arched necks and pricked ears, blowing steam clouds from their nostrils.

"And, of course, no droppings," Tesla said, veering around a monstrous pile of horse dung. "The capacitance battery charges from the wireless chain generator I have at the townhouse."

He continued on the technicalities for some minutes, William quite unable to pay attention through the eddies of fear and awe.

"Do you think we should have left your friend alone

with those two men?" William asked, white-knuckled as the carriage sped into the St Alberts borough limits. Rain was starting up, covering the forward glass in a vision-limiting spray.

Tesla didn't answer. He was leaning out the window, so that the drizzle collected on his eyelashes and beaded on the oil in his hair. He had neglected to take a coat against the chill, and the hand he held on the wheel was pale with cold and tension. "Of course, there can always be improvements," he muttered. "Some kind of glass wiper, for instance."

The Royal Laboratories loomed through the spotlit evening. As they approached the corner of the lane where William had made his escape from the sewer, Tesla pulled the carriage to a screeching halt. He had the door open almost before the wheels had stopped turning. Moments later, William was following him to the pit lid.

"Clemens is more than capable," Tesla said over his shoulder, as if the question had only just been asked.

"Mr. Tesla, you knew about this pipe?" William asked.

"I know everything about my building. Now—"

A muffled boom thumped the air, like a falling sack of mill flour had just landed on a nearby cart tray. William gawped at the Laboratories. The windows on two floors closest to them glowed with orange and yellow, and plumes of dirty smoke leaked out under the roof, as if the building were a smoking pot with the lid crammed on. An audible metallic crash broke the silence into pieces.

William swallowed. Those were flames inside. And in other places, the light of the Tesla lamps had gone out, so that the windows were just dark dead eye sockets in the façade. Without wanting it, his sister's face came into his mind, her eyes closed, the face of the eternally resting. And then her eyelids opened, and there was nothing at all behind them. Just dark falling depths.

William stumbled and put out a hand to steady himself. When his fingers encountered a leg, he jerked back, momentarily delivered from his nightmare. Tesla's face was bleached, too, like a sheet in the copper boiler, his bloodless skin luminous in the streetlight as he watched his creation burning.

"Quickly," he said to William. "I must reach my laboratory without delay."

❰❮❯❱

In the maelstrom of the ground floor, Leo's consciousness dappled back, like sunlight penetrating a smoggy winter morning. He heard ringing, like a distant fire alarm, high and constant. He lay on his side, one arm up over his head, at the far end of the dock.

His skin was tight, and covered in dust; he could feel the grit on his lips. His breaths came short, the pain in his ribs a lancing jab. A dull ache defined his thigh and shoulder.

He opened his eyes, and saw haze and ruin. He was lying against a wall; the foyer wall, he eventually worked out. The mesh dividing the library and the dock was gone, replaced with a chaos of rubble. He tried to rise and the agony in his thigh put him down again. His shaking hand found a jagged shard sticking from his shoulder, and a wet patch on his thigh.

Shrapnel.

He lay in disoriented shock, staring at the rubble, thinking he'd seen this before. Finally, he realized. Explosion. There'd been an explosion.

It was hard to see because many blinder lights had gone

out, leaving only the glow of spot fires. A stack of tea chests had been blown into a heap a few feet away from him, many cracked and spilling sawdust and straw. The floor above had collapsed down like a chute, leaving a pile of twisted machinery in the center, and the broken ends of the supporting timbers were lit like torches. More flames licked along toppled shelves in the remains of the library. Paint bubbled off machine surfaces like festering boils, and a smoky haze was gathering on the broken edges of the ceiling.

Leo coughed with a stabbing pain between the ribs. Broken now, that was for sure. The binding on his arm had slipped and was restricting his elbow, so Leo undid it with a surge of effort. He tried to tie it around his ribs, but it was too short, his left-hand fingers barely able to maintain a grip. He looked around for Araminta.

She wasn't there.

He tried next to tie the strip around his thigh, and gave up when he had to swallow the upchuck. He was wasting time. And while his lungs were stiff when he drew breaths, he was technically mobile, and he had to move. Had to get out of this burning room.

He crawled a few paces, but the action put too much pressure on his shoulder. Once on his feet, he could only move by leaning on the wall, coughing as he stumbled for the unchained library doors over the debris. One leaf had been blown from its top hinge and sagged against the frame.

The foyer beyond was a rectangle of light, just a few toppled shelves away. Then Leo's foot hung up on something solid and he stumbled. He tried to step over, and encountered more obstruction, which sank in a fleshy way under his foot.

Leo stopped and sank down, his heart shaking as he felt for a pair of leather boots, and a bad suit with a woman's body inside it. He found the leather boots, but they were much too heavy and large.

Further down the library, a broken beam shifted, dumping a mass of burning timber onto the floor. In the light flare, Leo made out the Red scarf about the man's neck, and the irregular hole that a piece of shrapnel had punched through the center of Red's face. Leo stared at the wound in the dancing light, each breath burning with smoke.

He had noticed two things. The first was Red's railgun, which had fallen not far from the man's hand, nestled against a fallen book. The second was that Leo's pocket, the one where he kept the console, was ominously flat.

He patted himself down; his pockets were empty. No map. No console.

Despite the heat, Leo's heart froze into brittle ice. The link with Machine, with Helen, was gone. He attempted to retrace his steps, but he found no sign of it, and the thickening air blinded him and drove him back towards the library doors.

Cooler air flowed through there, drawn by the fire, but the fresh breaths brought no relief. All hope of going home was gone. He tried not to think of Araminta, lying dead somewhere in the room behind him, of the waste of her life.

He stood alone in the foyer, trying to rally, but he seemed to have nothing to hold onto. Everyone else was gone. Everyone but Helen.

He lifted his eyes. Maybe he could not return, but he could save her.

He could climb to the second floor and short that lock

into Tesla's lab as he'd planned near the start. More of the intruders were dead now; that would improve his odds. With the building unlocked, help could come from outside to catch the thieves and put out the fire.

Leo held himself together with this bare plan, until he stepped further out towards the main stairs. A soft sound, almost like popping corn, was coming from the rooms behind reception, and a new gust of char and ash came thickly up the stairs. Not the smoke of a wood fire. It smelled of slag at a steelworks, of things going terribly, terribly wrong.

The same thing he had smelled just before Helen had sent him through time.

Leo gripped the banister, an ill feeling sweeping through him. This was what he'd smelled earlier, in the maintenance stairwell. Or, at least, the beginnings of it. The warnings. The steam had not been off upstairs because the intruders had turned it off; the damn boiler was dry. It had melted down, and set the coal hopper on fire.

Wait.

If the boiler was dry, then the generator would stop spinning. Ergo, the power would be off. Which meant …

Buoyed, he limped through debris in the foyer to the double front doors, thanking the gods of time machines for the luck, and expecting to throw the doors open. But he found them still pinned shut, the blue arcs of Tesla's security field still licking between the sheaves.

Leo straightened, knowing he was now on a suicide mission. He didn't understand how, but he was still trapped, and in poor shape – ribs, thigh and shoulder were each a giant stitch of pain, and his cough left him breathless. If he went upstairs, then the fire would suffocate him there, before the building burned to the ground. A coal fire wouldn't be put out.

And so, Leo started down, step by agonizing step.

The last thing he could do—and it probably would be— was to put a railgun bullet into that microtorus. As he went, he thought maybe he'd never been meant to get out of that last burning building. This was just the universe, correcting itself.

Chapter 39

Despite Tesla's immaculately waxed hair and tail suit, he showed no reluctance whatsoever to entering the stinking pipe. He had insisted on going first, dropping his tall, slender body through the manhole, not even caring that he tore the shoulder out of his jacket.

Once they had negotiated the pipe, and were back beneath the ladder, on that earthen landing with its small locked door, Tesla turned and took William by the shoulders.

William had been expecting this, waiting for Tesla to demand *how did you find this?*, but instead the inventor said, "Have you ever kept a secret, William?"

Wrongfooted, all William could reply was a befuddled, "Sir?"

Tesla's hands squeezed, his voice urgent. "Invention serves everyone, my friend. I believe a finished and ready invention benefits no one if it sits idle, waiting for someone to buy it. But that does not mean that *unfinished* work should be everyone's property, no! Quite the reverse."

Tesla released his grip, and dug in his own collar, bringing out a chain, with a long key dangling from the end. He unlocked the small door, then stuffed the key into William's hand.

"Here, take this. Go up the ladder and then the stairs to the second floor, and enter my laboratory. You can turn off the security field from there, and perhaps save those souls still within the walls."

"Where are you going?" William asked, dismayed.

Tesla briefly glanced up. "This laboratory has served me well, but I have surpassed its contents. It is all in here." He tapped his head.

So, Tesla planned to leave.

"Sir, wait," William said, digging in his own pocket. "Here. It's like the one that the Time Walkers had."

He handed across the slim console, the polished glass screen shining even in the low light.

"Where did you find this?"

William didn't want to say that he had spotted it peeking from the side of Brown's sporran when he'd stopped at the front office on his way out of the building. Instead, he said simply, "Brown had it. I thought you would know what to do with it."

Tesla gave William a slow, approving nod. "I wish you a long life, young man. Now, remember this," he said, and gave William a code for the laboratory. Before William knew it, he'd been shoved upwards onto the ladder, and Tesla had closed the door behind him.

William dared not go back. Instead, he climbed, alone, his breath catching in his lungs, his mission heavy in his heart. Up four turns of stairs he crept to the ground floor, where a seam of light showed around the entry hatch.

He smelled the smoke. Trepidacious, he almost pushed open the hatch, before remembering the intruders' dogs, and what had happened to Forbes. Far better to be alone in a secret stairway than out there with those things.

He had just stepped up on the next riser when he heard a faint cough.

William paused, the tread creaking under his foot. No, he was hearing things. It was just the staircase.

Another cough came, clearer this time. It sounded like

a woman.

❰❬❭❱

Araminta came back into her senses with a foul shock. For the longest time, she was convinced that she was dead, and been sent to the hellfires that her grandmother had been overly fond of reminding her existed for headstrong young women like herself.

When she opened her eyes into the ruin of the dock and library, the hellfires still seemed real. Orientation took a long while. Eventually, she saw the dock's huge double outer doors were along the wall to her right, the blue licks of security charge still visible in the seams. She was wedged inside a storeroom door, and blocked in with debris. The debris, she eventually worked out, was the floor collapsed down from upstairs. Crawling forward and leaning out, she could see nothing left of the oxygen rig.

In only firelight and smoke and shadows, it was hard to see anything else, just jagged edges of broken tea chests, and glass glinting across the floor.

A memory returned: the sound of the glass crunching under her feet when she'd first stumbled around, looking for Leo, the railgun still heavy in her fist. She'd tried to call out, but her voice was gone. Eventually she'd retreated from the smoke and the groaning remains of the ceiling, crawling into this small room.

She must have fainted then. Now, her lungs squeezed, as if she were in a corset. She had nowhere to go but back into the smoky haze.

Then a hand grabbed her from behind.

Araminta yelped and threw herself away, only to find William inexplicably staring back at her.

He was filthy, out of breath, and fervently tugging her

towards an open hatch just visible under a low shelf. After she stumbled through and he'd closed the door on hell, she surmised where she was.

"This is the way we entered," she said, once she was done coughing. They could escape. But William pointed up.

"Stairs," he said, trying to haul her to her feet. "To Tesla's lab."

She craned her neck. It looked much like the maintenance stair on the other side of the building, only narrower. A smattering of light filtered down through the punched metal treads. Neither Leo nor David must have known about this.

William was already climbing. "Come on," he said. "I have the key."

By the time they reached the second floor, her lungs felt like roasting coals at Christmas. William put a code into a small panel, much like the one that had prevented their entry from the main foyer, and a key in the stair hatch. Locks *thunked* in the wall and the door opened into an entirely new world.

In Araminta's mind, this laboratory had been until now a blank space, a vague white emptiness she couldn't begin to imagine. Now, she saw walls lined with high shelves, densely packed with devices in shades of grey and black and silver, with occasional flashes of gold or copper. What looked like a giant cage occupied the far corner, like a holding fence around a thick cylinder topped with what looked to Araminta like a capped silver service dish. Alongside was another table-top apparatus, this one suspiciously man-sized, with overhanging arms. Beside that was another, this one a vertical cylinder with a tall door. On and on, different inexplicable pieces, things so strange they seemed conceived for a time beyond this one. Another wall contained shelves of parts. Motors, she thought, recognizing one item among the many. She took a moment to appreciate that this was Tesla's laboratory, their goal from the start, and hers for much longer. Only the world wasn't what it had been, then.

"Where do we turn off the security?" Araminta asked.

William stood in the corner, shifting on his heels like a weathercock in a stiff breeze.

"Uh," he said, turning the key in his fingers. "I'm not exactly sure."

Chapter 40

Helen is still lying on the floor, listening to the garbled chatter of the soldier's radio. She doesn't like it. Doesn't like the progress of his footsteps, moving so assuredly. He doesn't scan around anymore. They've told him to do something, and he is carrying out the instructions.

She watches out of one, half-closed eye. Watches as he reaches for the black power cables and pulls them from the wall.

Helen feels as if he's pulled out her heart.

He takes two steps back towards the door, and pauses to glance down at her. She can feel the swelling in her face in the tightness of her skin, the pain in her bones. Can feel fluids leaking from her nose and mouth. She feels like the soon-to-be-dead.

The soldier's judgement clearly matches hers. He walks out the door.

This should be the end. The Machine has lost power. She is dying. There will be no victory for the small, incredible mission, just more of the same kind of history, where overwhelming force snuffs out oppositional hope.

This patriarchal dismissal ignites some reserve in Helen. If that were certain, then the Grid would never have moved.

She knows she has a minute or two at best. The UPS battery can only spin the microtorus for so long and retain enough power for recall. If the acceleration beam fails, then David and Leo's path back will be lost.

The room glitches again. This time, the plane of the shift is horizontal, so that it seems for a short second that the roof has translated downwards, to a few crushing inches above Helen's head. There's a fizzing sensation in her brain as this happens. This time, it might just be hallucination.

She commands her limbs to push her body up. She wants to sleep; needs to sprint. Wants to die; needs to live.

Irrationally, she thinks of her father. Aside from being a mathematician and a drunk, he was a yachtsman. The kind of man who stood on the helm during a storm while the other crew huddled below decks. He didn't expect that kind of thing of her, he'd said once. Courage was not everyone's calling. She had been such a shut-in, a bookworm, a recluse, who never fit with anyone except Leo. And then Leo had broken that bond and gone off to war, leaving her to become what their father had seen as antisocial, and weak-minded, a creature of theory and paper and threat-less things.

Was that what had been in her mind when she'd pushed Leo into The Machine? To punish him for how he hadn't been like her?

Perhaps.

And yet, now she was here, with her skull bloodied and bleeding, her Machine disabled. Two lives depended on her; maybe countless thousands more. She was in the middle of the storm. A single pair of hands to grasp the wheel. Courage, she thinks, is easier when no one is watching you. When you can be sure that the only soul accountable for your actions is your own.

She can't rise, but she does move. By shoulder and hip,

like some kind of landed eel, across the two meters to The Machine, and another foot more to the wall. The power cables are as thick as her wrists, their ends studded with the wanting pins. She looks up at the sockets, so far above. Reaches a hand to The Machine's side, and braces to climb.

Chapter 41

In the deepest, darkest corner of his building, Tesla's feet made no sound across the dirt-packed floor. The walls in this room were covered in soft pyramids of felt, shifting geometric shadow banks in the beam of his lantern. No one was here.

Tesla sighed, intensely relieved. For he had worried that the device the men were stealing was not the one in the next room, but this one. The one he had told no one about.

He flicked the lamp switch and went on in the dark. He didn't need the light anymore. Ahead, the soft blue glow of the pool from his first-generation fusion device was enough to see. Beyond it … there was another device, a fuller realization of his vision.

This device, he knew, would be called ugly by anyone who could see it. A dull torus, pocked with square blebs on the outside. But on the inside, it was a conglomerate of magnetism, a pure contained energy at its core, with electromagnets modulating the frequency and vibration of the field, maintaining stability. That was true beauty, hidden within the beast.

Tesla was the only man to ever have seen it complete. He knew, better than most, that anything another man's eyes saw could escape out into the world. He had even relied on that fact from time to time.

But not this. This was the secret of one. In truth, ever

since David Blakeney had first appeared in his fevered vision and told him about the future to come, about his first life and the world that would extend beyond it, Tesla had been haunted. In his first life, he had not left the legacy he had intended. The future had not profited from his inventions in the way it should have. His own government had stolen his plans, millions still lived in poverty, needless scarcity.

So now, in his second life, he must go further. Must ensure that the same nightmare did not happen again.

That was why it had been necessary to let some of the inventions promised to the investors to leak out. No one was served by monopolies, by realized inventions held close, for profit. That was not the way to improvement. Those investors might just as soon sit on the inventions than use them, or hoard them to reinforce their position as oppressors. If the figures on paper did not look promising enough for the first year, for instance. If profits seemed unlikely.

Figures.

Profits.

Money.

No, no.

This was the problem with business – it was near-sighted, and ultimately blind. Without the foresight Tesla enjoyed, business could be a long blunder of small steps in utterly the wrong direction. Someone needed to provide a vision, and those technologies must be out, in the market. Being improved. Ensuring the future was electric and clean and the poor not objects of profit.

And so, this. Tesla put his hand on the rim of the apparatus. This would be the one that changed the paradigm. Who knew that the same technology that had conceived those hideous railguns would also lead to this device? Within ten years, every train would haul its cargo with one of these in its locomotive. Every city power its lights and heat its homes with one.

It was nearly ready to go into the world. Nearly.

Just a few issues of occasional instability to iron out. A few issues of fluctuation. Issues that couldn't be allowed to run away if the building was inaccessible.

Tesla flicked the switches that disabled the particle accelerators. He would have to wait a few minutes for the core to cool, before turning off the magnetic field.

As he waited, Tesla concentrated on hearing anything from the next-door room. Nothing much transmitted through the soundproofing, but he thought he heard the occasional guttural note of a shouted word.

Araminta, Lady Montague's note had made it clear that the intruders were stealing the valuable Machine from the concealed room next to the boiler. She was the same woman who had called his townhouse from the phone in Doctor Blakeney's office. Tesla's had momentarily puzzled over her, for he had no idea who she was, save some associate of Disraeli he had met at a demonstration. But he had moved past that confusion, into the information she'd brought.

Tesla disapproved of theft, but he was more concerned about setbacks in his own developments. Whatever happened to this building, his apparatus must remain secret. After these years in St Alberts, he appreciated the peril of his designs being appropriated. From now on, he would take a different path.

Araminta and William had been three times around Tesla's

lab without luck. William had become distracted by a thick device the length of a walking stick laid out on a bench. He hefted it, examining a forked end and its handgrip. Araminta was on her second pass of the work desk, which contained only a double inkwell, and a stack of seemingly blank paper. She flipped through the sheets, and came across one that appeared to be the start of a note, with the date at the top, and a few lines requesting a modification to a part. Something about it bothered her, but she put it aside, and stood back from the desk, and the plain brass wall plaque above it.

Odd.

Araminta ran her fingers over the plaque, pressing to see if it was solid. The surface gave with a click, and the panel dropped down. Facing her now was three small dials, each of their needles hovering in a green zone in the center top. At the end of the row was a switch with a keyhole alongside.

William yelped as his stick emitted a crackling *buzz*. Araminta spun to find him shaking out his fingers. "It shocked me," he complained.

"I think I found it," she said, but her eyes slid back to the note on the stack of paper.

"Oh." William appeared beside her, the fingers tucked under his arm. "I guess that's what he meant."

Araminta stared at him. "Tesla told you it was here?"

"Not precisely. He just said 'it's under the panel'." William gestured helplessly around the laboratory, which Araminta acknowledged contained many things that could qualify. "Does it need the key?"

"It seems to," Araminta said, finding the switch locked in place. She paused to look again at the partial note. William gave her an enquiring eyebrow. "Go ahead," she said, but slid her own letter from Tesla from her pocket.

As she compared the pages, William sank the key into the slot and turned the lock with an oiled *thunk*. The heavy sound could have come from Araminta's chest, because the handwriting in the two notes was utterly different. Whoever had been writing to her in his name, it was not Tesla.

"Shall I press the switch?" William asked.

"No, I will," Araminta said. Her finger depressed the perfectly set metal tab, as a key construct of her life also sank.

A hum that had been imperceptible before was abruptly obvious in its absence. The three dials in the panel floated towards zero, and Tesla's laboratory silenced.

"There," Araminta said, feeling no relief. "It's off."

PART III

Chapter 42

Leo was on the last step of the main stair before the basement when he heard something like a far-off jet engine winding down. He looked back to the rear-door landing, to the door that had been impassable for the last hours. Was that the system turning off? He wanted to run up those few stairs and check. Irony was that he didn't think he could climb them, now. And besides, what would he do if he found the door open? Escape out into the street? Not to mention that if he opened that door, any fire downstairs would greedily suck the oxygen-rich air to feed itself.

He could hear the persistent ticking of hot metal, the creaks and groans of structures twisting and buckling in the heat, and a roaring base note of pure flame. The air was hot, sour and vibrating.

He propped his body on the rail and leaned out, pressing a torn corner of his shirt against his nose and mouth, bracing himself. Perhaps it would not be as bad as he thought. He pushed open the door.

The view inside the basement shattered this idea into pure traumatic memory. The roaring was the draw of the fire spreading across the basement, sending flame up the wall and across the ceiling. Leo pressed his back to the hot bricks. It was exactly as bad as he'd thought; there would be nothing left at all except the bricks of the outer shell. Everything would be destroyed, including Tesla's work, and the generator.

Wait.

Leo leaned out again and scrutinized the generator, resting in its sunken floor position. Even through his watering eyes, Leo could see that the shaft was not turning. Of course it wasn't. As soon as the boiler stopped providing steam, the turbine would have lost all its drive. Just as he'd thought upstairs.

It had been dark up on the ground floor, where the explosion had probably shattered the lights. But the steam had been off for longer than that, and the lights had kept burning. And down here now, even with the evidence of the hobbled generator, the lights in the stairway were still on.

Where was the power coming from?

Maybe Tesla had installed some kind of back-up power supply, a capacitance bank, or another generator, one he hadn't told anyone about. More secrets.

Leo swallowed and looked towards the doorway that led under the stairs, and to that room that held the B-Machine. Was it still there? Was Victoria? Was David?

How much time did he have?

He remembered an argument he'd had with Helen once, at Cambridge, when they'd been at a pub one night, him drinking Guinness and her doing equations on a napkin.

"You don't have anything better to do with your time?" he'd said, only half-serious, because he wanted her to have a drink with him.

"Time is the only true currency," she'd said, distracted and not looking up. "All other measures of wealth or production are tied to it. You want something cheaply? Then you exploit someone whose time is valued less than yours. You want something of quality? Then you find the person whose time creates the most beautiful things."

Leo had swallowed his Guinness. "What if I want

something fast?"

"You would," she said. Then Helen had simply gotten up and left, heading back to the lab and her ideas, which tried to bend entropy and time and other rigid stalwarts of physical reality.

Leo had followed her that time, and leaned in the door of her lab. "You could just say you need time to work," he'd said. But he'd known even then it wasn't just that. She'd wanted time with him. And then he'd left.

Now, when time was all that was left, he really needed something fast.

《〉》

"But where are you going?"

William's plaintive call came down the stairs as Araminta stumbled from tread to tread, bracing her hands on the rail. Behind her, Tesla's lab doors were thrown open to the second-floor foyer. Ten seconds ago, she'd been following William to Tesla's secret stairway for the quickest path outside. Now, she wasn't.

"I have to look for Leo," she said. "You go and find help."

Her right hand used the railing, the left holding the shock stick, which did an admirable job as a walking stick. It also emitted an arc of purple power from two prongs at its tip, which Araminta decided was as good a defense as any.

The edge of the first-floor foyer was still passable, but the air thickening with smoke. The atmosphere improved as she descended, until at the junction into the ground-floor foyer, a stream of smoke was spilling visibly from the stairway.

Araminta held her breath as she descended through the

drift of it. She thought she could see flames licking the walls of the hallway beyond reception, the serene jowls of Victoria reduced to shades of grey in the gilt portrait.

To the left, the library doors both hung from a buckled frame.

Araminta tried to hurry, but it was more a drunken lurch. The first thing she saw inside was a man's body lying on the floor.

No, it wasn't Leo. It was one of the thieves, the one with the Red neckcloth, lying flat on his back, a great dark patch in the center of his face. Araminta pressed herself against the wall, watching for companions, for dogs.

None emerged. She peered over the tip of her nose at him. She saw no weapons, just a simple leather satchel still tucked against his body.

Araminta left him and tried to climb across the debris into the dock, but she only reached the chained doors before the air was truly unbreathable. She retreated towards Red's body, keeping to the wall, pressing the prod's trigger, which shed electric purple light to see by.

The next time she pressed for the light, and saw a glint on the floor. She almost didn't investigate, but she had to turn that way around a fallen tea chest. So she unexpectedly came across a smooth glass rectangle, a little larger than her palm. Too regular for broken glass. *The console*, she realized. The one that Leo had always carried in his pocket.

With shaking fingers she touched its polished surface. A grid of numbers glowed back. A few of them were changing, but others held for several seconds before they changed again. But she could do nothing else; every touch of her fingers produced nothing but a small oval. She had seen Leo press his finger to it to open other views, but when she pressed her finger on it, the screen only glowed red, with the word LOCKED flashing above.

Araminta tucked it in the pocket of her trousers, then stopped. Not far away was a shredded piece of material, still knotted from where she had bound it around Leo's arm. He had definitely been here, but now he wasn't.

He was alive.

Or he had been.

A crash came from the foyer. Araminta jerked as the air shifted, the flames flaring and singeing her hair. She must move. She reached the library doors, and was horrified to find the main stair rails now alight. She reversed, coughing, caught her foot and sprawled backwards.

She'd fallen over Red, tripped right on the dead-staring head of him with that gaping wound. She scrambled away but he'd trapped her ankle. In irrational fear, she twisted and thrashed and finally something snapped and she tumbled free.

His satchel. Her boot had been caught in the strap, and now the contents had tipped all over the floor, including David's notebook, and three short sticks wrapped in brown paper. Araminta picked up the notebook, and then gently touched a stick.

Then she looked across the demolished library to the hatch in the wall, the very one she had gone through when all this had started, the one that led right to the water pipes.

《〈〉》

The milling crowd outside the Royal Laboratories had doubled in the time William had been inside, but none of them paid him any attention as he pulled himself out of the manhole for the second time tonight. All were focused on the flames behind the laboratory windows, and the sooty plumes rising from the roof. Some huddled together, others chatted in excited voices. The placard wavers were particularly jubilant; William thought he could hear scripture being recited. Two enterprising men were even selling refreshments from trays slung around their necks, braying the virtues of their Cornish pasties and mugs of ale at vastly inflated prices.

William paced, the hollow in his chest growing with the flames.

How could he have left Tesla in there? How could he have left Araminta?

When she had gone on ahead of him, he had only been relieved to get away. But he'd expected to find Tesla outside already, the situation coming under control. But the inventor's electric carriage remained in the lane, where he had left it.

Two fire engines had arrived, but the men were taking their time approaching the front doors, perhaps because the doors were puffing out little clouds of black smoke, like a gentleman sucking a cigar. When one finally swung an axe at the lock and the door popped open, the crowd ventured a cheer. The lobby was glimpsed momentarily, with its expanse of tiles and grand staircase dressed in orange flame.

The firemen's coats ruffled, as if a stiff flight of ghosts had rushed past them. In the moment after, one fireman stepped through the threshold, shielding himself from the heat. Unaware of what he faced.

In the bowels of the building, the fires of the boiler and the library-dock had long been depleting the oxygen, so the coals burned more and more incomplete. The sealing of the building was too good, the intruders' tunnel too small, to supply a fire of its size, and it had reduced to an unhappy equilibrium, puffing out dirty sooty smoke.

Opening the front door changed everything.

The immense heat from the fire rose like the updraft of a tornado, and the cooler, heavier night air – rich in oxygen – rushed in underneath, straight into the heart of the combustion. The oxygen met the superheated gas and fuel like a sledgehammer on a firecracker.

The ensuing blast wave picked up the man standing in the doorway like a manikin, and threw him down the front stairs. The crowd, momentarily stunned, erupted into screeches and shouts. This was the moment that the fainter of heart, who hadn't bargained on their night-time entertainment turning serious, left the scene. But they were few. The rest were looking around for some authority to step in, to whom they could deputize their impotent desire to help. A bare few – though none of the placard holders – rushed forward to drag the firemen back from danger.

William watched it all, crouched and horrified, his hands over his mouth. He was desperately afraid. Desperately frantic. Waiting, too, for someone to do something. Someone. Anyone. Anything.

When nothing happened for two long minutes, it dawned on him that the person he was waiting for might be him.

Chapter 43

Leo was in the under-stair tunnel, just outside the door to the B-Machine room, when the backdraft rocked through the building. Dirt hissed down from the ceiling but he was beyond pause. The door lock here had been cracked out, probably with a heavy hammer. Leo took a breath of clearer air, and slowly pushed it open.

Peering through, he saw rough-cut walls and a packed-earth floor. A little further, and he glimpsed the edge of a chair with a leg propped on it.

David. Leo felt a surge of surprise.

The Doctor was lying on his back, his injured leg bound and elevated, eyes closed and skin pasty pale, but he looked alive. Otherwise the men would probably have stashed him with Forbes and Brown upstairs. Alongside him sat another chair, holding a stout woman in a rough brown gown, her lips pinched, watery eyes scowling at whatever was going on out of Leo's view. He blinked, realizing this was the Queen. This unimpressed, belligerent, prisoner.

He saw no men. Or dog.

He edged out.

Nothing else seemed to be in the room, except that the dirt floor was cut with parallel lines. Wheel marks, like fingers raked through sand. Had they already taken it?

And even though he thought he'd accepted he would never leave this place, Leo felt the grip of panic. He didn't want his life to be worth nothing in the end.

He took another step, putting himself in full view of the

captives. Victoria saw him instantly. Leo knew it from the shift in her shoulders, the tightening across her brow. He knew what he must look like: ragged and covered in grime and blood. He would look to her like a man who had no place to do what he was doing.

Leo half agreed. He was damaged. Unsure he could lift the arm holding the railgun. He sure as hell couldn't carry anyone out, let alone run if the situation demanded it. And yet, he held her stare. In return, she tipped her head just a fraction, a signal he was clear.

Leo stepped out, so that he could see the punched-out portal in the side wall. From within its darkness he could hear grunts and scrapes and something creaking. He would free the people first, then storm the tunnel.

He took his chance, hobbling down the wall, and then across behind the chairs. David had spotted him now, and was glancing at him fretfully with one wild eye. Leo wished he would stop drawing attention.

The bonds on the Queen's hands were rough hemp rope, tight around her wrists but only lashed to the chair with a hitch. Easy to remove. The Queen stood and, with surprising grace, disappeared at once out the access door.

David was not tied at all, but could he walk?

Leo jerked his head at David, with a questioning eyebrow. The Doctor returned a tiny nod, his face then folding into a grimace as he swung his leg down and pushed himself to his knees. Leo grabbed a fist full of David's jacket and provided what uplift he could. David struggled, sweating and stiff-legged with Leo's help. They were almost to the doorway when Leo felt a chill across his shoulders.

He stopped. Glanced around.

Edison was watching him from the portal, still in his mask, a black dog alongside.

《〉》

"That's far enough," Edison said, when Leo turned towards the door. "I will release this animal if you move again."

Leo stood there, exposed. "You don't know what you're dealing with," he said. "That Machine isn't for you."

Edison made no reply. Leo wondered what the hell he was waiting for, just standing there, smiling.

"And what is it you think I'm dealing with?" he asked, finally.

"It's not of this time. You don't know what it does."

Edison's expression shifted, intensity in his eyes. "And what do I think it does, future man?"

Leo's guts sank. It wouldn't matter to Edison what he said. The man could re-do calculations. They might take time without modern computers, but it could be done. And now, the man was waiting again. Just waiting.

It drove Leo mad. He wanted to know why Edison didn't have someone shoot at him, or have men go after Victoria and David; why he didn't release the dogs.

Edison checked his watch, as if waiting for a tardy train to pass a station.

Then Victoria flew back in the door, levelling full regal force at Edison. "You do know the building is on fire?"

"Just on time," Edison muttered, checking his watch again as David also hobbled back in the door. Edison looked between each of them, as if prepared to simply wait.

"Rear door's been barred," David said to Leo. David's face was beaded with sweat, the tight bandage around his thigh soaked dark red. "I can't break it. And the foyer's consumed. No way to reach the front door."

"And so now, we wait," Edison said. A muscle ticked in

his cheek. "No witnesses, you understand."

Leo finally did. Edison was simply waiting for the building to collapse down on their heads, while his men went out through the tunnel.

Leo fingered the railgun. Odds were, he could shoot out whatever had been used on the door. But he had to get out of the room first. His arms were both weak, one from his cracked ribs, one from the shrapnel. The railgun was heavy. Too heavy for accuracy.

Sod it.

He raised the railgun straight at Edison. At least, he thought he had. His arm refused to come quite level, and when he pressed the trigger a plume of dust erupted from the middle of the wall. Reload.

Then the dog was bounding forward.

Leo pointed the gun, but the animal peeled to the side. Leo swung, but he was slow, his shot missing.

It was closing as he reloaded again.

He realized, in a grim slow-down moment, that the dog was going to get him, and there was nothing he could do about it. He tried to dodge and felt a crushing pressure across his calf. At the same time came a *whomp!* that made his ears pop. He twisted, trying to throw the dog off, but he was falling.

The dirt floor rushed up and struck him in the ribs. The pain snapped him into a protective ball, and then the animal was diving at his raised arms, aiming for his throat. Teeth sunk into his arm, and all he could hear was that low, near-soundless growl, the animal insistence that Leo would soon be no more.

Chapter 44

Moments earlier, Araminta had been feeling the slight breeze in the services shaft. It chilled the sweat on the backs of her fingers as she fumbled with the paper-wrapped stick, trying to wedge it behind the two thick pipes bolted to the back wall. It wasn't that the space was tight, but that she had to reach out to place the stick on top of a bracket, otherwise it would fall all the way down the shaft. That reaching unbalanced her. Then there was the fact that this was *dynamite*, a substance that earlier had blown apart the reagent laboratory. Oh, but she was doing this anyway, feeling almost giddy about it.

The paper was oily on one side, and her fingers slipped once. She nearly dropped the *damn* thing. She was swearing in her mind now.

Concentrate.

"Damn, damn, damn," she muttered, in open defiance of her mother. If she was going to die, she would have a try at obscene language first. The outburst cleared her mind; she really must swear more often. Finally, hanging precariously from the ladder with one hand and one foot, the other toe balanced on the lip of a slightly mis-laid brick, she pushed the stick into place with the tips of her fingers.

Now, hurry up.

Easier said. Araminta had no idea how big a bang this could make. How much had the intruders used to wreck the reagent lab? She had no idea, and Leo wasn't here to ask. She couldn't open the ground-floor hatch again; the flames had probably intensified. She shouldn't be down low anyway. If the plan worked—*when* it worked—she would be right under the deluge. The only option was to climb, dragging the prod along with her.

She tried the trap door exit on the first floor, but found it hot, so she was forced to climb all the way to the attic hatch. From her position, the dynamite was like a speck in the darkness, her angle so oblique she wasn't sure she could even hit it. She would have one shot. Maybe two.

Her first, cowering back from the open hatch, did nothing but strike a spark off the pipe somewhere far below and nearly throw her backwards. She paused to cough. "Grotthuss, smotthuss, cannot shoot for motthuss," she muttered, when she could catch her breath, feeling a little hysterical.

Ah, the hell with it.

She lay on the attic floor and leaned into the hatch, fixing her aim on that speck down the shaft, blew out her breath, and fired. A thin silver stream erupted from the pipe. Close. But would the gun fire again? Jaw set, she held her aim, and squeezed the trigger.

Araminta's next awareness was being flat on her back under the attic roof. She pushed up, feeling all the hurts in her body, her ears ringing, and peered into the hatch. The air down in the services riser was milky with smoke, and smelled sharp and greasy. As the ringing in her ears subsided, she thought she could hear rushing water.

Araminta retrieved the prod and climbed down into the space. The two pipes had bent out from the wall like rearing snakes, the joints broken and spewing water like a weir.

She sagged against the ladder, feeling no sense of celebration, only a dull kind of relief. One thing was done. But only one.

She hung the railgun off her suspenders, shifted the prod, and continued the climb down.

❬❭❭

Leo couldn't hold his hands up much longer. He smelled his own blood mixed with the dog's rotten meat breath. Then came a roaring noise.

Water rushed over him, a tidal wave of force. It drove into his mouth and nose, and he tumbled over in the dump, collecting the far wall. Choking and gasping, he struggled to his knees. The pull had gone out of the water, and it was now filling the room. The dog was wetly shaking in the far corner.

Leo's hands were empty, the railgun lost. He heard the *slosh, slosh* as the dog shook itself and bounded across the water, coming to finish him off. Leo tried to stand, and failed. He couldn't move. Couldn't do anything but want for different things to have happened.

He saw an apparition, then. A woman in torn clothes, with a staff of purple fire. A battlefield angel … or the first Valkyrie come to circle his body. He bowed his head, ready to be taken, and heard her scream into air that crackled with lightning.

❬❭❭

The dog was enormous up close, its shoulder well clear of the water, upper lip shuddering with inaudible growls. Araminta aimed the pulsing electric shocker straight at its nose.

The dog moved with grudging respect, not wanting another dose of the stick, but circling around as if waiting for her to make a mistake. Araminta tracked it in a slow arc, until she was facing the portal.

That was when she saw Edison, watching from the tunnel's dark mouth.

Araminta could imagine her grandmother crossing herself at the sight, forgetting that she was meant to be a protestant now. But she couldn't see the B-Machine. She was too late. The water, too late. It flowed over Edison's shoes and into the tunnel, his face a pale rim around the mask.

"Stop this," she said, though her voice cracked. "You will not do this."

"No, Lady," he said, "it is you who will not." The mask melted back into the darkness.

Araminta was blocked by the growling dog, who backed up slowly. Then, as if called by inaudible whistle, it too vanished into the tunnel's maw.

Desperate, Araminta limp-sloshed to the mouth. The air was surprisingly cool and fresh, the darkness absolute. She hesitated. She would never see a corner where someone was lying in wait, or giant holes in the floor, or hell-dogs waiting to pounce. But it was also underground, which limited the places the thieves could emerge. Immediately, she saw another chance to stop them, and all the steps she must take to apprehend them … and it began with leaving this damn building.

Then she felt a wire under her hand on the wall, running away down the tunnel. And then, another. Those wires gave her a bad feeling.

She backed up. Leo had managed to make it to the door and was sitting on the stoop, leaning on the frame. He was soaked through, his arms red with blood. David sat by him, leg bleeding through the tourniquet, his face a shade of jersey milk. She looked between the two men, at the defeated brokenness of them.

"I think there's explosives in the tunnel mouth," she said.

Leo sagged and David slapped at his face. "Leo," he said. "Pull it together. Stay awake."

"I know how to get out," Araminta said, leaning on the shock prod. "We go up, across to Tesla's lab, then out."

David gave her a sharp stare, and shook his head. "He won't make it that far. He's barely conscious. He's taken some lung damage, I think. And I can barely walk."

"Then we take him to an infirmary—"

David shook his head. "Not here."

"I know not here. The building's on fire! But once we're—"

"I mean, not *here*."

Araminta suddenly realized what he meant.

"I told you, I lost it," Leo whispered. "The console."

"You lost it?" David sagged too, then, and seemed to lose all motivation. "That's it, then. That's the whole game." He raised his eyes. "I tried," he said softly. "Shit, Helen. I tried."

Araminta's hand shook as she extracted the console from her pocket, the last link she had to them. "I found it on the floor, back over in the dock."

David roused from his bleakness, color and hope coming back into his cheeks. Araminta felt a tiny surge of possibility, a bright shooting thing straining for light. David moved his thumb over the screen, and froze.

"Oh, shit. Leo?" David said, voice tight, a flash of red blinking on the curve of his corneas.

Leo didn't respond.

"What?" Araminta asked.

David tipped the screen towards her. It flashed red. Flashed again, over a bank of red numbers across the screen, counting down the time.

❰❬❭❱

Now – Helen

Helen is no longer conscious. She tried, strived, to the end of her ability, but consciousness was the first thing she lost. The second was the cables she was trying to plug back in. And by virtue of those two losses, she is now losing a third thing, even more critical.

Power.

The UPS is almost used. Sensing the tiny drop in voltage, the warning circuit in The Machine's controls uses the five emergency qubits to communicate a grave malfunction code, which is as dead-set-serious as it gets, and a guaranteed time remaining. Here and now, the guaranteed time remaining is calculated in seconds. With the dilation, it gives Leo and David the hard deadline to get-the-hell-out.

Helen's part in this is done.

Leo and David have a little more chance. Not much, but it's all they have.

Time remaining: *00:10:26*. A little over ten minutes, and counting.

Chapter 45

00:10:02

Leo stared at the numbers, not quite registering what David was saying. He was having a hard time breathing, having to concentrate on each sucking lungful of air.

"The Machine lost power," David said, trying to haul him up. "There's no more time. We go or that's it."

David hasn't a hope of lifting him. "Victoria," he said suddenly, knowing he's missing something. "Where did she go?"

"To hell, with any luck," Araminta said.

For some reason, Leo found this incredibly funny. He was about to laugh, but he caught Araminta's eye. In it, he read a dozen conflicting emotions that shut him up. "I'm going to stop them," she said. "You can leave now. I'll make sure The Machine is recovered."

"What are you going to do?" David said.

"That is my affair." Araminta smiled. "How do you … *recall?*"

David nodded. "We need to return to the transmission room on the second floor. If we can still get there."

"Then we had better hurry."

Leo blinked, his lungs like two thick slabs of meat. He had a strange feeling he owed Araminta a debt, one that would stretch across space and time. He tried to say thank you, but it sounded like a gurgle. Araminta hefted the shock prod over her shoulder. "Well," she said. "Let us not stand here just conversing about it. I'll summon the elevator."

David pushed himself along with one leg over the wet mud floor, hauling on Leo's collar. "In case you haven't noticed," he said, "this building is going to be a pile of ashes. Move your oversized arse."

⟪⟨⟩⟫

00:08:46

The short distance between the secret door and the basement lift was like traversing a roasting oven. The coal chute was a shooting furnace of flame, the ceiling an angry churning of smoke and fire. Some of the water from the burst pipes had flooded out here, but the pool evaporated in the time it took Araminta to limp, coughing, to the wall and call the elevator car.

Nothing appeared to happen. She stabbed at the button again, then held it down, holding her other arm up against the fire, the leather of her boots hot against her skin, her injured calf throbbing pain. Finally came a tiny jolt under her finger. The building groaned, timbers creaking and cracking somewhere far above.

She leaned her weight against the handle of the bi-leaf door and it gave abruptly with an oil-greased slip. Araminta struck her temple against the frame before she could catch herself, and for a moment the heavens were dancing in her vision, her knees threatening to buckle beneath her.

No.

She would not fall now.

She stumbled back to the doorway, helping the limping

David and Leo, who could only push along with his legs. They fell inside the small smoky car and she hauled on the door, momentarily shutting out the fire. An overly cheerful ping sounded, and the internal automatic cage door rattled closed.

"How long?" she asked, as they began to move.

"Eight minutes, twenty seconds," David said.

As the elevator shuddered up against gravity, it sounded like long enough.

"And the building?"

It was Leo who whispered, "Don't know. Depends how long … the load-bearers. Once they go … the floors will probably pancake. You need to … get out."

Araminta looked away. She didn't like the way he sounded, and she couldn't have sentiment hanging off these last moments. These two men had shown her that time had not given science magical powers. Had not given women full liberation. And yet, she would not see them again, and that made tomorrow somehow dim and unfaceable.

They crept past the first floor. The air was less heated on her skin.

"Will you try again?" she asked, knowing they were in their last seconds. She tried to not let her words contain too much hope. Hope of making a different ending to this one. "Will you re-strategize, use your Machine to return again?"

Leo took a breath to speak, and then, everything stopped.

《〉》

In the darkest corner of the Royal Laboratories, Tesla lifted his hand from his apparatus. The core was cool enough now, so he opened the circuit.

Instantly, the device lost its large-wave hum, as if a mechanical heart had ceased to beat. Tesla allowed a last grace of his fingertips over its surface. He sensed, in the way a mother knew the welfare of her child, that the laboratory was in its final moments. True shutdown was now complete, so there was no reason to stay.

It was time to escape.

Chapter 46

00:07:19

The elevator abruptly stopped, and the lights went out. In the darkness, the air smelled strongly of sour blood and machine oil, sweat and smoke.

"This is what we get for using the lift," David said. "You're never supposed to use the lift."

"Was waiting for this," Leo said, his voice a whisper. "No … generator."

"Maybe we are near the second floor," Araminta said, straining to see anything in the dark.

"Close, but not close enough," David said, consulting the console. "We're not in the recall radius."

Araminta patted the cage door until she found the handle, but it would not budge. She tried again, even with the now-expended shock prod as a lever, but the door was so fast that it was clearly locked.

"Won't move … between floors," Leo whispered. "Interlocked."

"How do we get out?" she cried. God almighty, they weren't going to end up stuck in here, while the building burned its way through them.

"Look for release lever," Leo said, softly.

"He says there's a release lever," David repeated. In the blinding blackness, Araminta felt along both sides of the cage door, then over the walls. "What am I looking for?" she asked, having no idea what she was feeling.

"Leo says a panel with a lever, something like that," David said.

"I can't see anything."

It was hopeless. Another half-minute scrolled by as she fruitlessly searched. David tried handing her the console, but the red numbers were so dim, they didn't provide enough illumination.

"I need a light," she said, then stopped. "Wait ... there's a hatch in the roof. I saw it earlier, when I rode down with William."

Araminta couldn't reach the elevator roof, but David managed to struggle up and find the hatch near the back edge of the car. It folded back onto the roof with a reverberating thud.

Araminta had to climb on the car's rail using the prod, then lean on David. He winced as she stepped on his shoulder and he pushed her up on the roof of the car.

She heard cables creaking and her fingers met a taught steel rope that wimbled like a halyard. She inched towards the shaft wall, and her fingers met the smooth steel of the second-floor door. In a flood of relief, she felt along its edge and found the handle low down, a foot above the car's roof. That meant they'd stopped just half a car height short of the second floor.

She gripped the handle and dragged it back, a hideous screech of metal in the darkness, then most inelegantly turned on her stomach and dropped her feet down to the foyer. Just across the boards was Tesla's laboratory.

As she straightened, Araminta had a flash of insight, as if she had channeled her father. She was in the position of power, now. She could walk away from these broken men, leave them to their fate. Just as she might have taken the B-Machine once, if that had been possible. That's what her father would have done. He had no compassion, little loyalty. A favorite horse who broke a leg on a hunt was shot without regret.

This moment showed Araminta two things. Firstly, she was uncomfortably marbled with ribbons of both her parents, traces that she would never likely remove. Secondly, that she would spend her life suppressing them.

"The foyer floor is here, just a few feet up," she called through the now visible top of the internal cage door. Now, she had only to fetch a light.

《〉》

00:05:05

Araminta took a step forward, the floor creaking. She stumbled as something shifted in the building; it was like walking on a swaying ladder.

She caught herself and noticed a light coming from the door to the calculation room. It was so much easier to walk to that light than grope across to Tesla's lab and search for a lamp. As she pushed open the door, she saw the light was some part of the broken calculation machine. She really needed more light than this tiny glowing bulb, but it would be enough to aid her search in Tesla's lab for something better. The floor groaned under her foot.

"Who's there?"

Araminta froze. It was a woman's voice, trembling. There was a dark shape near that tiny light.

"It's Araminta," she said. "Lady Montague."

"I thought you were my Albert," said the voice. "It's so dark. I so loathe the dark. I couldn't get out. Couldn't get out."

"Your Majesty?" she asked, incredulous.

Now she could glimpse the outline of the woman's face in the glint of light. Clearly, the Queen was not in her right mind. Araminta reached out her hand.

"Take my hand," she said, feeling momentary pity. "It's all right now."

"And just where are you taking me?" Her voice cracked.

"Out," she said.

In the little light, Victoria looked over Araminta's shoulder, her eyes wide. "There are things out there," she said. "Terrible things. Beasts and fire."

"Yes," Araminta said, edging forward, her skin crawling. Another groan sounded from under the floor.

"What's that?"

"It's nothing to worry about," she said, but then she stopped, hearing a *click, click*. Soft, but startlingly close.

The hairs on Araminta's neck curled and prickled. She looked out, holding the light with a shaking hand, and saw the coarse fur of the dog in the corridor.

Chapter 47

00:04:25

Araminta couldn't breathe. She was trapped in the doorway as the dog approached, a slinking shadow along the wall, the whites of its eyes and teeth glinting wetly. It left dark patches on the floor, maybe mud, maybe blood.

Her hands were empty. She backed into the room. "Victoria," she hissed. "*Move.*"

Araminta felt a brush of a hand on her shoulder. "Is it there?" Victoria whispered.

"Shhh."

Araminta backed up, desperately groping for anything she could use. Her hand closed on something blunt but long, with some weight in it, about as long as her forearm.

A man's shoe, she realized.

She thrust it out anyway, shaking.

The dog hesitated; caution in its step. Maybe it was injured.

It lunged.

Araminta's arm snapped back as the dog knocked the shoe square on its end. Victoria had a death grip on her arm, threatening to pull them both over.

The dog feinted back out of the room, and Araminta took the chance. She screamed like a banshee, thrusting the shoe, and dragged Victoria with her into hall. The foyer was behind them, then. The dog in front.

It lunged again. Teeth clamped down on the shoe and

wrenched it from Araminta's grasp.

"Go!" Araminta yelled. "Run!"

The hand lifted off her back. Araminta waved her hands, making the tiny light dance but when the dog lunged again, all she could do was throw her hands up.

Its body knocked her down and hot breath was in her face, her wrists sliding through the daggers of its maw. Biting pressure came, then abruptly came a crackling flash, and the jaws released.

Araminta lay bewildered, until she realized someone was standing over her, the purple fire of a shock stick sparkling in the darkness. It was William.

The dog shook itself, gathered for another attack, deterred only by the warning sparks … which abruptly vanished.

"Uh," William said. He shook the useless stick. The dog snarled.

Then came an ominous rumble, a mighty crash, and the hall floor and dog simply fell away together into an orange glow.

Araminta slid, screaming, the air full of dust and confusion. Her fall arrested with a jolt, something squeezing around her ribs, tighter and tighter, cutting her breaths to gasps. Her fingers scrabbled across splinters. Below was a giant pit of yellow and red flames.

She saw where she was now: on the sagging edge of the disappeared floor, her legs hanging into the three-story abyss. The only thing preventing her fall all the way to the basement was the shock stick in William's hands, hooked on the edge of her waistcoat.

The sagging lip shuddered.

Araminta saw her death in a fall into the inferno.

She caught William's eye, glinting orange. He was

leaning back against her weight, his knuckles blanched around the prod's handle, face sweating and fearful. For a whippet-thin boy, he had surprising strength.

She threw her right boot forward, digging her elbows against the boards. Fabric and skin tore, until she thought she had no more effort to give. But she would *not* die. She would not. She flung her hand out and caught the body of the prod, pulling up her other knee, and then William could reach to help. Finally, she scrambled up out of the hole as new flames erupted below.

00:02:49

They stumbled away. When they reached the foyer, Araminta could see that the whole western end of the building was caving in. Only the stair and lift complex held, supporting the edge of this floor's foyer. The eastern wing of Tesla's lab remained up, but for how long?

"We must leave," William said, snatching up a lantern he must have left on the foyer floor. He pulled her towards the lab.

"Wait. Did you see Victoria?"

From the blank look on William's face, she knew the answer was 'no'.

"I didn't see anyone."

"All right. But bring that light to the elevator."

Through the cage door, David and Leo appeared washed out in the lantern's beam.

"There," she said, breathless. "Can you see now?"

There was a long, long pause, then she heard a mechanical *click* of a release.

"Try it," David called.

Araminta hauled on the cage door, and it rumbled open.

〈〈〉〉

00:01:03

Leo had been watching, no *feeling*, the time running down, retreating further into the nightmare of that night he'd spent in the collapsed building, waiting for a rescue he didn't know would come. Now the elevator door was open, and he didn't know how he would make it up the four-foot cliff.

Then he was hallucinating William's face, and a rope passing through that David looped around him, and that he was being hauled, up and up.

"Jesus," he heard David say when they were in the foyer, because the western end of the floor was just gone. They could not re-enter the transmission room. "Get us to the stairs, as close as we can."

The best they could do was the far edge of the stairwell.

"Will this work?" Leo said, feeling drunk.

"One way to find out," David said, waking the console. The timer was diving under a minute now. David shook as he selected the options to *recall*.

A confirmation screen appeared. *You have selected to be recalled. This cannot be reversed. Yes or No?*

He hit 'Yes'.

Last chance if this is a mistake. Yes or No? Like this wasn't all a mistake.

Yes.

Checking qubits, it said. Leo felt a drop of sweat trickling down his forehead.

Another screen appeared. *Within radius. Execute when ready.*

David caught his eye, then hit *execute*, less than twenty

seconds on the flashing timer.

    Recall in 5 ... 4 ... 3 ... 2 ... 1 ...

His ears didn't pop this time, and his reality was already distorted. His chest felt hollow, as if he were an emptied-out jug. He smelled smoke, strong smoke, and realized he could only move his eyes. The drop of sweat has ceased trickling. The last thing he sees is two figures across a foyer, framed by the doors of Tesla's lab. He's across time now, he knows that, and yet he's sure she's still looking at him as all of this happens. Then the pixel swarm blots out his view, and his body and David's are remuted into light.

Standing in the foyer, Araminta experienced a crackling energy across her skin, and a momentary aurora. Then the sensations were gone and so were Leo and David. She turned away as a shudder bounced through the building. It was done, this part. She tripped after William into Tesla's lab and to the secret stairs. She had one last look back at everything of Tesla's that would not survive the fire, and then she and William closed the door, and stumble-stepped down and down, to the only way out.

Chapter 48

00:00:00

Helen is not quite aware to hear the HoG siren stop. She had lost her consciousness because her blood pressure had bottomed out as soon as she'd risen off the floor. The tiny control switches in her carotid arteries had noted the loss of pressure. Their signal to her heart (pump harder) was fast, but not fast enough. Her brain, greedy for oxygen and nutrients, and to ship out its wastes, flipped out the lights to ensure she returned to the much more sensible position of lying on the floor.

A selfish organ – especially when in charge of all essential life-sustaining functions – always knows best.

Now, in the steadier blood pressure conditions flat on the floor, her grey matter has enough blood to be satisfied. She is dimly aware, in the marrow of her subconscious, that something important has happened. That trigger is enough to inject her renewing awareness with urgency.

Helen stirs. Then, a hand is on her shoulder.

She jerks. One eye opens what it can, the other stays shut. She sees The Machine, its lights dead, and her soul sinks.

"Helen," says a voice. Urgent. Male.

She focuses on his face. His hair is so clean and neat.

He's frowning, reaching with his long finger to gently tilt her face.

David, she thinks.

Shit, David!

They made it back.

She tries to sit, but her vision breaks into silver-black pools. David holds her shoulder, shakes his head. Says something about getting help.

"No," she manages. *Danger.* But she can't make her tongue move enough to tell him about the soldier, the one who did this to her.

Instead, when she hears steps coming back, she tightens her grip on David's arm. *Run,* she thinks, thinks it so hard she almost believes David hears her. But he doesn't move.

They wait, braced in the silence.

Silence?

She waits for the next siren wail, but it doesn't come.

She notices other things then. The table is upright, the computer undisturbed. Even the wall carpet seems a different color ... a pale yellow, perhaps, rather than the grey of before.

The steps draw close. A figure appears in the doorway, and David tenses. But it's not the black-suited soldier. It's a woman in a hi-vis vest, and a red hard hat, her face tipped down over a screen. She looks up and into the lab in a routine way.

Her steps falter, then she rushes in. "Oh my—what happened here?"

"A little accident," David says, wary. Then a pause. "Mary?"

"Oh, Doctor Blakeney, isn't it? Mary Humphries. I'm the warden for this floor. I was checking through before curfew." She pulls out a phone. "I'll call an ambulance."

"Two," David says, smoothly. "We've another injured man. He'll need oxygen."

Mary's frown deepens as she makes the call. Helen's head is swimming again. Curfew? Leo?

When Mary is waiting on the line, Helen tries to fumble for the phone in her pocket. She can't make her fingers work, but David does it for her. Without her asking, he flips to the news pages, calls up a search bar. Puts in *HoG*.

Top results are for pigs, while the search engine asks if he meant 'fog'.

Helen finds her heart is crashing in her ribs, setting up a painful pulse in the ruin of her face. David enters *London curfew*.

Article headlines appear, *London establishes curfew after threats of drone infiltration*; *Curfew for Londoners' own protection: PM*; and *Curfew on trial after unexplained disappearances*.

"It hasn't happened," David said, his voice faint with wonder. "At least, not yet."

〈〈〉〉

Helen can't speak to David for another week. She has to go to surgery three times to fix metal plates in her face, and after each she's scanned so the surgeon can grunt with satisfaction at the alignment of the bones. The swelling takes five days to come down enough to talk. She has a lot of time to observe. Most of the things in the hospital look no different from the world she remembers, but a few things take her notice. The scanner they put her in seems sleeker than it should, and the monitors on the desks have a logo she doesn't recognize. And the wall sockets … she could swear they aren't the ones they used to have. They're smaller, more compact, American-style. But then again, she is half off her face on medication.

David comes to see her on day seven. She knows already, from the difference between his state and Leo's, that he doesn't remember anything about the transmission. The David that came out of The Machine is the one that went in, not the one that experienced the timefield. Unlike Leo, he's unscathed by what went on. He can't tell her anything about what happened. Just like he couldn't tell her about what happened the couple of transmissions before that. But he can tell her about things he's observed.

Like the maglev line that runs from St Pancras to Edinburgh.

"Maglev?" she asks, though it's more a gurgle than a question.

David nods. "Magnetic levitation trains. I mention it because that's the line we travelling during our first conversation. The Underground is different, too. They're not maglevs, but they're … something else. The technology isn't quite what we had before."

Leo remains in ICU. Aside from his wounds, his lungs have swollen from what assumed to be an explosion. He cannot yet breathe for himself.

Naturally, there have been a lot of questions from lab management.

Helen claims not to remember, the easiest out. David has told them it was a gas bottle explosion. And when they'd frowned and asked about *from where*, he'd said *inside The Machine*. This had seemed to satisfy the in-house occupational safety officer, who no doubt saw his own responsibilities being called into question. A full risk review of their whole laboratory would no doubt be in their future, even in what appeared to be a private firm who wanted to keep things private.

Helen ignored all this. At least there was a future, and

she was too busy trying to work out what had happened. Without the context of history, she couldn't interpret the day to day headlines. She and David had to go back further, fill in the big picture.

The world wars had still happened; they discovered this quickly. In fact, it appeared initially that little was different. Then, Helen sees a reference to electric tank units. She skips forward, searches for *Hiroshima*. She feels a chill, then, looking at the pictures, and the heading *Death Ray Hit – A City Vaporized*. Ten more articles just like it. They're not calling it the HoG, but that's what it is. Eighty years ago. Jesus.

There's a race to disarm after the war, then nuclear technologies come later, accelerated by the space program, so the Cold War still happens, just not in quite the same way. Vietnam still happens. Communism still claims Russia and China; they both have particle beam weapons, and America still doesn't want the world turning red. Everyone is still burning a heap of coal and oil, because the technology is cheaper and it doesn't have the distaste that electromagnetics come with after Hiroshima. Revolutions in a dozen places. Global warming becomes an issue in the late nineties this time, after the slump that follows eighties excess. Same, same …

Only, the rhetoric has a slightly different flavor. Governments are slow to do anything, but private industry is further ahead with alternative energies than Helen remembers. Commercial electric cars had come online in the nineties, and nuclear fission and other renewables are more common, helped by nuclear having less stigma. Then, she finds an article from just a year ago about the first fusion power station, called *Sol*. A flagship of technology, promising enormous output, but maligned for its hideous and impractical cost … and thrown into shade by the secrecy of the private company who made it.

Helen stops when she sees the name of that company: *Potts*, searching her memory for recognition. Family owned, no records to read, so no reports to shareholders. Just commercially available products. It's their logo she saw on those computer monitors at the hospital.

"That mean anything to you?" she asks David.

He frowns. "Potts … no …" he says, but he has that look about him, the same one she used to see on his face when he couldn't remember a transmission. As if somehow, whatever happened in the timefield was resonating with him across time and space.

Helen goes back to reading. Tensions are mounting in the developing Asian continent, with climate modification the new rage for changing weather patterns, to alleviate drought and flood. There's a summit to discuss protocols for using such technologies, a meeting that ended in failure. Britain was a key player in that summit; not everyone's happy about their interference. The USA is still isolationist, as is Russia and half of Eastern Europe. But the States hasn't fractured into civil unrest. And no one's drone-bombing each other.

At least, not yet.

There's lots of rumors. Of surveillance drones at night. Of brewing tensions that might lead to dark times. Of the need for a summit of world leaders. And sometimes, rumors about the Potts reactor, which they quietly promise will revolutionize the world.

Helen feels elation and dread in equal measure.

They changed it. They changed enough to steer history onto a new course, one that isn't ripping countries apart.

But would it be enough?

She thinks about The Machine, and wonders if she could use it again. If she should. She's going to be thinking about it for a long time.

《〉》

Leo learns later that his medically induced coma lasted three weeks and two days. He has a scar in the front of his neck from where they set a tube for him to breathe. He feels like an old man for the two weeks extra he stays in the hospital. He rattles with pills.

The world is different. Subtly, as if the weeks have been water wearing away the edges of what he used to know.

When they finally release him, it's David who takes him back to the laboratories in Blackfriars. He looks for checkpoints along the way, but there are none.

He finds Helen in the lab, in front of the computer.

"It worked," he says, in the husky voice that he owns now. "I can't believe it."

She looks up at him with eyes both amazed and conflicted. "It … changed some things," she says carefully. "I'm still working it out."

He sees the fear of power and the excitement of it banking fires inside her.

And so they sit there, going through it. Helen keeps working backwards from now, sifting the details of politics and economics over the last twenty years. It's Leo who goes back to the start, who wants to look at what happened in the aftermath of that disaster in the timefield, the place that still feels like reality while this normal-when remains a dream.

In the *Wikipedia* entry on Queen Victoria – of all the places – he finds a passing reference. *After Albert's death in 1861, Victoria plunged into deep mourning and avoided public appearances, with the exception of a period from 1876 to 1884, which coincided with the building of the Royal Laboratories in St Alberts, London. Many scholars believe the work of the project in memory of Albert temporarily rallied her spirits, and represented an egalitarian approach to public betterment that Albert would have championed. After the project was famously destroyed by fire, and Tesla left London for New York, Victoria returned to mourning. As a result of her seclusion, republicanism temporarily gained strength, but in the latter half of her reign her popularity recovered.*

Helen raises an eyebrow, inviting him to talk, but Leo can't yet bring himself to do that. He feels he has lived half a lifetime in that night. And he can't think of Araminta and William without a deep sadness.

"Tesla shows up in America around the right time," Helen says. "His patents are all public early, but he does little more in the rest of his life than go through the motions. He gains a reputation for being an eccentric recluse again. He dies before the end of the war, just as before."

"Yes," Leo says. It's almost like Tesla had been trying to undo all the progress he'd always advocated.

And yet, Hiroshima.

"I've been thinking about that," Helen says. "All the modern physics of the early twentieth century, all of that still had to happen, otherwise we couldn't be here at all."

By *we*, Leo knows that she means *The Machine*.

"That's why we still see the development of nuclear technology, and of weapons. Of course. You were right … we always try to weaponise anything with potential." Helen pauses then, and glances uneasily towards The Machine. She clears her throat. "So the universal functions couldn't have solved without that. But the world is … different when the technology deployed at the end of the war wasn't nuclear. People have seen the test detonations in the Pacific. They know they have power stations based on nuclear technology, and it was an element of the Cold War, but it doesn't seem to have that ... iconic feel that I remember."

Leo is silent for a long while. "You have a theory, don't you?"

"I think Tesla found a way to trickle certain advancements out into the world. But in a subtle way, so it was distributed. I just don't know quite how yet."

Leo grunts.

"Is it happening for you, too?" he asks, finally. "Are you starting to forget? Or are my neurons being screwed by all the drugs?"

"Not forget, but it's confused. As if the time before is a movie, something that happened only in a fiction. An overlay on my life, a story, but nothing more."

"I guess that's right."

"No." Helen says it quickly. "It's not a fiction. They both happened. They are the two sides of the loop we made. But not remembering is dangerous. That's why we have to document this, what we remember, while we remember it."

She taps the monitor. The report is already in the tens of pages. In the header is the notation, *Loop 1873–1884.*

Leo looks at his hands. "Are you going to use The Machine again?"

Helen keeps typing, finishing the sentence she has started. Then she pulls her hands back to her lap.

"I don't know," she says softly. "We did this because we were going to be wiped out. But I catch myself thinking that if this world leaders' summit goes badly, could we just use The Machine to change it?"

"The hammer-nail paradigm again."

Helen nods. "And what if other people in history in the same position as us had had this Machine? What if they had one in Hiroshima?"

"I think," Leo says slowly, "Everyone wants a do-over. They might have thought differently about how to do it, but we wouldn't know either way. It would have come out how it came out."

"That's the thing about the first time," Helen says. "You can treat it as an experiment. Every time after that, you're doing things with intent. It's not the same at all the second time. We are going to have to think about this. Talk about it. Think more. And above all, keep it to ourselves."

Leo looks down at his hands, maddened by the abstraction. "Those people in the slums of St Alberts … their lives were better because of Tesla's lab. What happened to them when it burned down? Did everything just end?"

Helen shakes her head. "I suspect we'll find mass migration. People don't get a taste of empowerment like that and let it go. They had means, many of them. It's going to take time to trace all of that. Even so, the effects on time must have been very small, small enough to be stable."

Leo thinks about that for the rest of the day. It's turning to early evening when he is exhausted and wanting to go home, but he sits before a terminal, fingers poised on the search he doesn't want to do.

Finally, he types in her name.

He has to search for her, so much so that he even thinks for two long minutes that she never made it out of the building at all. But then, he finds a single line in a biography of Lord Montague, saying simply that his daughter had inherited his fortune, and had, on account of her disabilities, been a socially retiring but careful investor for the remainder of her life. It takes him until midnight to gather up anything more about her, as if someone had been actively erasing details of her life. Finally, he finds an obscure masters thesis on underrated feminists of the late Victorian era. There he finds a single photograph of her at the opening of the new medical school for women in London. No smile, right in the back, that same intense stare. Definitely her.

Leo is consumed with a thick black grief looking at her face. She had wanted to escape her place in when and where. Had wanted to see *now*. Would she be impressed with it or not? He didn't know. He only knew that she would not want him to answer for her.

He almost misses the small footnote in one of the last chapters, where the thesis student made the observation that as well as her feminist causes, Araminta was suspected of investing substantial funds in the early years of *Potts*, a private engineering business with substantial income from electrical systems design and now a multi-national technology firm.

Leo frowns. Potts. He's heard that name, somewhere. Maybe in the timefield?

He is still thinking about it when Helen knocks on the door, and leans on the jamb. He can tell from the way she stands there that she has something significant to say, something that could change the world. Usually, such statements were hyperbole. Not so much with Helen.

"What?" he asks, warily.

"You remember I told you that The Machine uses Light Trajectory Theory? It sends information encoded in a photo beam on a specific relativistic pathway that leads into the timefield."

"Yes …"

"Well, that pathway is a loop in our own timeline now. Because we reconciled."

"So?"

Helen chews her lip. "You remember that paint fleck, on the mouse?"

Leo blinks. It seems a million years ago. "What about it?"

"I went and looked, and you were right. It never got any attention before … we were focused on other things. But it seems there's traces of the loop, identifiable traces, even of changed events. So, there might be a way to communicate around the loop. Theoretically."

"Theoretically."

"Yeah. I'm not sure yet, it's just in the maths. And I need to re-run the numbers. Half of me thinks I should put it in the drawer and never look at it again."

He leans back, thinking much the same thing. "Did anyone ever prove the Grotthuss mechanism?" he asks suddenly.

"Where did that come from?" Helen says.

"It's the theory of how water conducts electrical—"

"I know what it is," Helen says, because *of course she does.* "I mean, why are you asking?"

"Something I thought about in the timefield."

Helen waves a hand. "Yes, a few years back. They used heavy water and molecular photography. Did David mention it? It's relevant to neural conduction. You know, for his work on the artificial brain stuff."

Leo lets the information settle inside him. He's thinking about what he does now, with the things he knows, with what Helen might be getting herself into. "Has David told you about what happened in the timefield?"

"He doesn't remember."

Leo closes his eyes against the peculiar feeling of loss. David doesn't remember. Doesn't remember what he'd done with the other Machine. Or Araminta. Or William. Or Victoria and Brown. Or the building burning to the ground around them. David doesn't remember things written in his field notes, now forever lost. Doesn't remember being shot. Or dragged out of the Timefield with questionable deservedness. Leo may as well have gone there alone, for now he is the only witness. The only one who knows what traps had come out of the blank spaces in David's memory. And maybe that's the thing that makes him say it. That inescapable human part of him who doesn't want to be the sole witness to the whole experience. And doesn't want Helen to be either.

"You should keep asking him," Leo says. "But if you want, I'll help you re-run the numbers."

Chapter 49

When William finally pushed the manhole aside, he was desperate for a clean breath of air. London didn't disappoint; even the traditionally fuggy air smelled as fresh as a green field on a dewy morning. The crowd had doubled since he had gone back inside, but had retreated to a safer distance, watching the bonfire end of the Royal Laboratories in the unusually dark night.

No one was looking as William reached in to help Araminta. Then, having replaced the manhole and moved away, they too watched as the roof and tower collapsed with a shower of meteoric sparks.

"Not exactly the way I expected this night to end," Araminta said, heavily, over the grief-filled moans of the St Alberts crowd.

William glanced at her. She was pasty white and grimy, her eyes glazed, limping badly. But something about her wasn't finished.

"I need a carriage. There's still time to intercept Edison before they reach the end of the line." She began limping towards the road, holding up the light, then stopped. She turned back. "William. Thank you for taking my note. And for the passage out. I won't forget it."

William only managed to duck his head before she hobbled away and collared a hovering carriage. He would have liked to go with her. She had a magnetism he liked, reminded him of his mother who wished better things for him. Lost, he stuck his hands in his pockets, and drew out the money she had given him. The coins were heavy, gold sovereigns, joining three folded banknotes that Tesla had slipped him. More money than he'd have earned working in a year; possibly in a lifetime.

His eyes roamed the crowd. The Met had arrived now, and had established a line to keep the watchers back. Another crash from inside the building reverberated through the pavement. William flinched, wondering if Tesla even made it out.

And what of the two thieves Tesla had left with his friend at the townhouse? Should William follow Araminta's lead and tell a bobby about those men? Or maybe he should just slink back across the bridge and go home.

He found himself behind the crowd, up on the hill in a protected lee, the same place where Red had stood out of the wind just twelve hours earlier, thinking of petticoats and paycheques. From that vantage, William caught movement down a set of nearby stairs in the darkness.

Two figures, moving in the shadows of infrequent old-technology lanterns. Each familiar enough for William's attention to hold fast on them.

Was that …?

He stumbled towards the stairs. They were already too far away to be sure, but William could have sworn the shorter of the pair was the Queen, leaning on the arm of a much taller figure, his characteristic profile momentarily glinting in a light.

Tesla.

William trotted down one, two, four stairs. They were gone in a shadow, now. He could only be sure he had seen a short figure in a skirt, and the other in a suit. It made no sense that the Queen would walk with Tesla – the two of them didn't even like each other if the rumors were true, and they usually were.

The William of yesterday could have convinced himself that this situation was not special. But that had been before he'd watched a man killed before his eyes, before he'd met Araminta. Before he'd ridden the streets of London with Tesla himself, and run back into a burning building. He could not be more different than he'd been yesterday.

So, he finished with the stairway and ran for Tesla's electric carriage, to wait. If the inventor returned, William would find out for sure. If not, then he would go home and, with the money in his pocket, make a new kind of life.

〈〈〉〉

SOME TIME EARLIER – TESLA

Tesla had not expected to meet anyone during his exit of the Royal Laboratories, least of all the Queen of England lost at the bottom of his secret stairway.

"Mr. Tesla. This is most unexpected," she had said. A crash sounded somewhere overhead. "Quite the disaster," she added, but with a flinch and hysteria Tesla had never seen in her before.

Tesla had considered this diminutive woman, who had at times been an investor, a champion, and a thorn in his side.

"Ambitious plans have a tendency to run close to disaster," he said. "There is no safety to be found in innovation. It is a pursuit for the brave."

She had given him grim consideration in return. "Be that as it may, I advise not just standing here. Show the way out."

That is how Tesla came to be standing in a sewer pipe, with the Queen of the Realm, helping her up out of the manhole and through the inky black of the night without his lights.

He began to walk towards his electric carriage, but reconsidered as she spoke.

"I want to know what you are to do, now that my laboratory is destroyed," she said.

"You mean, now that your time machine to retrieve Albert is destroyed."

Victoria regarded him, the quilted muscle of her jaw evidence of surprise and chagrin.

"Your Majesty," Tesla apologized. "Electrical systems have no secrets from me. I have known for some time about the load your machine placed on my system. It was not a complex task to discover the source, and its purpose."

That flash in her eye was tempered by some inner decorum. "What was that you said about ambitious plans, Mr. Tesla?"

He tilted his head in acknowledgment. "Anything done publicly suffers the same problem. Or, within reach of enough ears. It brings out the opportunists."

Victoria made a grunt of a reply, as if her whole life had been a dance with such opportunists. They crossed the road away from the burning building, turning down towards Brick Lane, drawn by some shared truth not to part, just yet. And into a concealing darkness.

"So, what do you propose to do about it? You know your own future," she said.

"As do you," Tesla countered.

Victoria shook her head. "No. I never asked to know it."

Tesla was surprised. They turned a corner, finding the

shadow path. He spoke slowly the idea that has been forming in his mind since he was first confronted by the thugs in his townhouse. "I resolve to be more cautious. I will take my research into secrecy, and only I will know how much I have done, and when the world will have it."

"And what if there was significant incentive for you to develop your ideas for me, in secret?"

Tesla kept walking, but he felt a cold grip of fear about his heart. He knew he could never be shackled like that again, a servant of someone else's vision. He sensed the danger, here. Before the week was out, he planned to be on a boat to America, and to follow his first life's course as well as he could in public. But if he said as much to Victoria, he wondered if he would find himself detained, perhaps permanently. Araminta's note had implored him to go to Disraeli, to call on the resources at the Prime Minister's disposal to intercept the bandits. He knew it was time to honor her request, as insurance if nothing else. But he would not breathe a word to the Queen. Nor would he ever betray the Time Walker console device that William had given him. He knew nothing of how it really worked, but he had time to investigate it. Time to learn.

He said, "We should talk further, Your Majesty, when I am presentable again. My hair and suit, you see, are quite unfit for company."

He had learned his lesson. Anything that went beyond his first life, he would bury it somewhere deep and safe, until such time as he saw fit to release it into the chaos.

Epilogue

In the Baker Street townhouse, Checks spread his knees around the corner of the table and leaned closer. "But how can you move it there?" he asked, plucking the tiny wooden horse from the chess board.

"It's the rules," Clemens said patiently. "The knights move in an L-shape. The bishops on diagonals, and so on. It's the rules of the game."

"He's gonna have our heads," Yellow complained from the window.

"Might I ask how you settled on a career in thuggery?" Clemens asked. "It seems high risk. You'd have done better heading south out of the mines, and taking to the Mississippi. And no, the Queen cannot jump the line of pawns like that."

"You just did it with your 'orse."

"As I said, it's the rules of the game."

"The rules are stupid."

Clemens inclined his head. He was actually making headway with these men, especially Checks, who confessed a liking for the Arthurian tales.

"Look, think of it like this," Clemens said. "I have the gun, so I make the rules of right-now, but I'm disinclined to kill you because that would violate rules of someone more powerful than myself – such as the State, or God, if you prefer. Chess is like that. Someone else made the rules to allow the play to proceed in a reasonable and predictable fashion."

Yellow finally gave up on his reticence, and took two steps closer to peer at the board. Clemens let his hand rest casually on his hip, close to the railgun, lest the big man get any ideas. "Them's like two armies facing each other," Yellow said.

"Indeed," Clemens agreed. "Chess is a game not unlike war, with strategy and tactics, and carnage." He emphasized the point by taking Checks' much-maligned knight with a pawn.

"Hey, hang that a minute! How come it moves diagonal-like and that?"

"Rules of the game," Clemens repeated. Then, when Checks gave him a wounded look that said Clemens was making all of this up, "It is not romantic, and takes some time to learn. But master the rules, and you can begin to refine how you will act."

The phone rang on the main control panel and Clemens rose to answer it, subtly indicating, by taking the railgun with him, that he didn't yet trust either of these men. He was unsurprised to find Tesla on the other end of the line.

"The building is lost," Tesla said, rushing and dispensing with formalities. "The intruders are dead or gone. I am reconsidering my whole investment in this country, Samuel. I think you may have been right on a few counts."

"I see," Clemens said. "Are you coming back here?"

"Yes, but not yet. The less said the better. Will you wait?"

"I can't. I have an early appointment."

"Before you go back across the Atlantic, then?"

Clemens paused. Tesla was always fast, but the urgency in his voice now spoke of unprecedented possibilities. Clemens could no more refuse to be a part of it than cut off his own leg. "Of course. You know where to find me."

"Thank you, Clemens."

And he was gone. Clemens fingered the gun. Tesla had not mentioned anything about the current situation.

"Well, gentleman," he said, returning to the table where Checks was now attempting to relay the rules of chess to Yellow. "It appears your employment is at an end. The Royal Laboratories have burned to the ground. No one rescued, apparently."

Checks and Yellow exchanged a long look. "Bollocks."

"As I see it," Clemens went on, "You gentleman have two choices. I can walk you to the nearest sheriff's office and save us some time, or, we can discuss an alternative arrangement."

"Like what?" Yellow had his suspicion back on like a favorite coat.

"I'm soon to return to New York. I could use two strong fellows to manage my luggage and so on, and also to keep me away from the dice tables."

"We'll think about it," Checks said finally, after Clemens had put forward a proposed set of duties, none of which would involve thuggery, killing people, or dealing with explosives.

"Good. You should also think about your future. There's opportunities everywhere for enterprising men like yourselves," he added, searching Tesla's desk for a blank sheet of paper. "Now, feel free to keep playing. I have an idea for a novel and I must put it down."

❮❰❱❯

Araminta waited at the mouth of the new station, still in the same torn suit she'd been wearing for the last day. The buttons of her waistcoat were missing, her hair a mass of knots and tangles. Despite her appearance, Disraeli had admitted her into Downing Street three hours ago without question. Tesla, apparently, had been there before her.

There, she disclosed her own account of what had transpired in the Royal Laboratories, enough to invite action. Disraeli set recovery in motion, transporting Araminta in his own carriage to witness the operation. There, under duress, she allowed Disraeli's private physician to attend to her wounds. She spurned his further investigations as soon as she was happy. Araminta felt bruised inside and out, but purpose drove her forward. She would finish this tonight.

"I must say," Disraeli said now, peering into the dark hole where the soldiers had disappeared. "This was actually a good opportunity. After the loss in South Africa, we've been training this unit largely as an experiment in the commando system of the Boers. But we haven't had a chance to prove them in the field."

"It's more important that we stop the theft." She no longer felt a spark of interest in what he might have to say, and her thoughts kept returning to the conversation she'd had with Leo about war.

Disraeli inclined his head, and paused to cough into a handkerchief. He was grey and sickly looking tonight, more so than the last time Araminta had seen him. "Of course, my dear. I'm expecting reports from St Alberts, soon. I sent an investigator to assess the fire. What else can you tell me about these men?"

Araminta hesitated. "They are American," she said.

"Ah," Disraeli said, drawing himself up as one of the soldiers emerged from the tunnel and said, "We have them now, Sir."

Disraeli helped her from the carriage and gestured

down the tunnel. "After you, my dear."

"Would you mind very much remaining here?" Araminta asked. Then, when Disraeli made to protest, "After you misrepresented yourself to me as Tesla, which led me into the situation at the laboratories tonight, I rather think I have earned the right to make an end to this dealing myself."

Disraeli took a breath; Araminta did not allow him room to speak. "You may save whatever you are going to say. I had the chance to compare his handwriting, and when I spoke to him, it was clear he did not know me from our correspondence. You can be the only one who profited from the ruse."

Disraeli's apologies followed her as she stepped forward.

The tunnel was cold, and opened into a near-finished station, the terminus of this new Underground line. The soldiers had surrounded a rail-mounted cart. Edison, Green and Black stood with their hands raised. Glinting behind them in reflected lamp light was the hulk of the B-Machine. It was the first time she had seen it, and yet it seemed exactly as it should be.

"This is the end of the line," she told Edison. He took a breath to say something, and she cut him off. "There is nothing more to say. This Machine is being impounded. You will return to America if the government allows you, and you will never speak of this again."

"I propose an alternative arrangement," Edison said. "A lease of this equipment. So it can be put to proper use."

Araminta stepped back, her leg teetering on collapse. Proper use, she knew, would be to destroy the B-Machine as soon as she was able. At least, to destroy the microtorus, so that it could have no effects on the stability of the loop with Leo's time. But could she do it? She closed her eyes, making her intent.

"This is not a negotiation," she said, and gave the nod to the soldiers to finish their work.

She returned slowly down the tunnel to Disraeli, thinking about what she would say to him. But at the same time, she was thinking about her father's estate. Which would, sometime soon, be her estate. About the large cellar under the north wing, currently in disuse. She had David's thick notebook in her pocket, and a sheet of worn paper with its spiral calibration. And time. Lots of time.

Acknowledgements

Timefield is an odd story, born of an early love for Michael Crichton's technothrillers and a much later infatuation with Neal Stephenson's baroque-style novels that are clearly speculative but otherwise of indeterminate genre. Likewise, *Timefield* started as a steampunk idea that morphed into something else entirely, and those stories are always hard to put together, and to pull off. Which you, dear reader, are the only judge of.

For my part, though, I extend my thanks to the readers, writing partners, editors and supervisors (as the novel originates in my PhD thesis) who helped in the forming, writing, re-writing and production of *Timefield*: Rebekah Turner, Dion Turner, Kevin Stewart, Natalie Collie, Kim Wilkins, and Christine Wells.

I also hugely thank the spec fic and wider writing community (including editors, publishers and readers) who have supported my work over many years in all kinds of ways, especially: Kevin Gillespie, Talie Helene, Liz Grzyb, Kate Forsyth, Keith Stevenson and Simon Petrie.

A final thank you to you, the reader who got to this point. Your honest review is greatfully appreciated, and the only thing remaining I might ask for. It helps keep me in paper and pencils.

— Charlie, February 2021

Also by Charlie Nash

Waygate

A new far-flung future space opera novella of warring human factions, allegiances and tech. What waits beyond the waygate was never meant to be found...

In print and digital.

Men and Machines I: space operas and special ops

Four original science fiction stories, including the award shortlisted "Dellinger".

In print and digital.

Men and Machines II:
punks and postapocalypticans

Four original stories of cyberpunk, steampunk and post-apocalyptic inspired fiction, including the award shortlisted "Alchemy & Ice".

In print and digital.

All Your Dark Faces

Seven original fantasy stories with a dark twist, including the multi-award shortlisted slipstream experience "The Ghost of Hephaestus".

In print and digital.